MRAC
10/10

THE WHITE RAVEN

About the author

Robert Low has been a journalist and writer since the age of seventeen in places as diverse as Vietnam, Sarajevo, Romania and Kosovo until common sense and the concerns of his wife and daughter prevailed.

To satisfy his craving for action, he took up re-enactment, joining The Vikings. He now spends his summers fighting furiously in helmet and mail in shieldwalls all over Britain and winters training hard. He lives in Largs, Scotland where the Vikings were finally defeated and expelled from the UK.

This is the third novel in the Oathsworn series. He is currently working on his fourth novel, *The Prow Beast*, which continues the adventures of Orm and the Oathsworn.

Visit Robert Low's website www.robert-low.com for more.

D0063520

Also by Robert Low

The Whale Road
The Wolf Sea

ROBERT LOW

The White Raven

HARPER

HARPER

HarperCollins*Publishers*
77–85 Fulham Palace Road,
Hammersmith, London W6 8JB

www.harpercollins.co.uk

This paperback edition 2009
1

Copyright © Robert Low 2009

Map © John Gilkes 2009

Robert Low asserts the moral right to
be identified as the author of this work

A catalogue record for this book
is available from the British Library

ISBN-13: 978-0-00-728798-7

Printed by Clays Ltd, St Ives plc

This novel is entirely a work of fiction.
The names, characters and incidents portrayed in it,
while in some cases based on historical figures, are
the work of the author's imagination.

All rights reserved. No part of this publication may be
reproduced, stored in a retrieval system, or transmitted,
in any form or by any means, electronic, mechanical,
photocopying, recording or otherwise, without the prior
written permission of the publishers.

Mixed Sources
Product group from well-managed
forests and other controlled sources
www.fsc.org Cert no. SW-COC-1806
© 1996 Forest Stewardship Council
FSC

FSC is a non-profit international organisation established to promote the
responsible management of the world's forests. Products carrying the FSC
label are independently certified to assure consumers that they come
from forests that are managed to meet the social, economic and
ecological needs of present and future generations.

Find out more about HarperCollins and the environment at
www.harpercollins.co.uk/green

To my beautiful wife Kate, who navigates us through the stormiest of waters to let me write in peace.

NOVGOROD, Winter, 972 A.D.

On a crisp day with a grey sky and only a blinding white smear to show where the sun lurked, the prince's executioners cut a good pine pole slightly taller than the height of a man, thin at one end, thick at the other.

The thin end they sharpened and greased, then they took the legs of the face-down woman and roped them by the ankles, pulling them wide apart. A man took a saddle-cloth, placed it on her back then sat on it to keep her still, while another bound each of her wrists with leather thongs, then tied them to two stakes, also wide apart. She screamed blood on to her teeth.

'On this day, in the eighth year of the lordship of Prince Vladimir,' intoned the crier, 'this Metcherak woman was found guilty . . .' and so on and so on.

'Danica,' muttered Thordis, soft enough so only we heard it. 'Her name is Danica.'

Morning Star, it meant in the tongue of her Slav tribe. There would be no more morning stars for her. The stake was driven up into her while the executioners ignored her shrieks but made sure her white buttocks were decently covered as they hammered and pushed, to preserve her dignity from the droolers in the crowd. The white shift she wore was soon clinging provocatively to her all the same, soaked with her blood.

Impalement is not simple savagery; there is art to it and Vladimir's executioners knew their work.

The sharpened stake was pushed, slowly and with skill up the woman's body. It was, in a Loki joke, a healer's art they used, for they knew how to avoid all the serious soft organs, the lungs and the heart and liver, despite her jerks and screams. There were frequent stops for adjustment, brief panting instructions and advice, one expert to another, as obscenely intimate as if they were all lovers. They stopped only once, to scatter wood shavings on the bloody snow and prevent them slipping in the slush of it.

One slash with a knife helped the point of the stake out through the skin of the upper back on the right side of the spine, proving that the stake had missed her heart; the crowd roared and the dignified, well-dressed worthies of Novgorod's *veche* nodded their beards in approval as Danica was skewered like an ox on a spit. Still alive, as was proper.

They unroped her, then re-tied her legs together to the foot of the stake to avoid slippage when they raised it – gently, so as not to jolt the body – into a hole, which they packed with earth. It began to feather with new snow as the pole was then strutted with supports – and that was that, everything done according to the law and the rights of the *veche*.

Her bound feet offered no support and slowly, agonizingly, her own body-weight dragged her down the pole. It would take three days for the moaning, bleeding woman to die, while the snow turned crimson at her feet.

There was skill there and much to be admired in it as a statement of justice that made even the hardest balk at committing crimes in a city whose people called it Lord Novgorod the Great.

All the same, it was difficult to appreciate the full merit of this justice, since I was next in the queue – but I wondered if it was possible to find a price that would make the rulers of Novgorod keep that stake from my own puckering hole.

Would a burial mound with all the silver of the world be enough?

ONE

HESTRENG, Ostergotland, early autumn, 972AD

The day before we were due to bring the horses down, it rained. I stuck my head out the door and, from the way the wind drove it, hissing like snakes from the sea, I knew it would rain for days.

Inside, Thorgunna fed the fire, stirring a cauldron already on it. Elfin-faced and breasted like a fine ship, that was Thorgunna. Dark haired and, as Kvasir put it 'a prow-built woman', she had a way of arching an eyebrow and staring at you with eyes black as old sheep droppings that made most of us wither. Everyone had marvelled at Kvasir marrying her – as Finn said, drunk at the wedding: 'Too long at sea. What does the like of Kvasir Spittle want with a wife? Six months wintering with one of those and you will be begging to be back behind the prow beast.'

Beside her, Ingrid chopped kale, as blonde and slim as Thorgunna was not, her braids bobbing as she shot what she thought were sly looks for Botolf. She was already pupped by him and promised in public.

From Gunnarsgard, the next toft over, Thorgunna was sister to Thordis, who had married Tor Iron-Hand. The sisters had half-shares in Gunnarsgard – an unnatural way to treat a good steading, which should always go to the eldest – and their cousin, Ingrid, lived with them.

Tor had had a good life of it, some said, with three women under his roof. Those who knew better pointed out how that meant three times the trouble. He had wanted to marry Thorgunna as well and so gain the other half of the steading until Kvasir spoke up and brought her to Hestreng, with Ingrid in tow, not long after fetching up here with the rest of us.

'What does it look like out there?' Thorgunna asked me.

'The yard's a lake,' I reported, hunkering down by the fire. 'Throw something special in that pot – everyone will need cheering.'

She snorted. 'No doubt. And no work done for it on a day like this.'

Which was unfair, for there was always work, even indoors. There were two looms that had never been still for weeks as a brace of thrall women wove the panels of *wadmal* into a striped sail for the Elk. Everyone had sewing, or binding, or leather, or wood to work, even the children.

Still, they circled big Botolf in the pewter dark, demanding stories. There were three older ones, all boys and bairned on the thrall women by the previous owners and two new babes by my own Oathsworn – and one cuckoo from Jarl Brand. The hall rang with the sound of them as the men straggled in for their day meal, grey shapes in a grey day, blowing rain off their noses and shaking out cloaks.

I moved to the high seat, where I wouldn't be bothered, while the hall filled with chatter and the smell of wet wool. The Irisher thrall woman, Aoife, was trying to put her son's chubby arms in a wool tunic and he kept throwing it off again. In the end, she managed it, just as Thorgunna smacked her shoulder and told her to fetch mussels from the store. She left, throwing anxious glances as her boy – Cormac, she called him – crawled towards the deerhounds in the corner.

I sat, hunched in wool and brooding like a black dog, the

rune sword curving down from my hands to the earth floor while I stared at the hilt of it and the scratches on it. I had made them, with Short Eldgrim's help, as we staggered back from Attila's howe and the great hoard of silver hidden there; for all I was not good with runes, they were enough for me to find my way back to that secret place.

The deaths and the horror there had resolved me never to go back, yet I had made these marks, as if planning to do just that. Odin's hand, for sure.

I had thrashed and wriggled on the hook of that and found good reason and salted it with plunder to keep the Oathsworn from forcing me back to Atil's howe. Even so, I had always known I would have to lead Kvasir and the others to that cursed place – or give Kvasir the secret of it and let him go alone. I could not do that, either, for we were Oathsworn and my fear of breaking that vow was almost as great as facing the dark of the howe again.

That oath.

We swear to be brothers to each other, bone, blood and steel, on Gungnir, Odin's spear we swear, may he curse us to the Nine Realms and beyond if we break this faith, one to another.

It bound us in chains of god-fear, drove us coldwards and stormwards, goaded us to acts that skalds would sing of – and others best hidden under a stone in the night for the shame of it. Yet, when we stood with our backs to each other and facing all those who were not us, we knew each shoulder that rubbed our own belonged to a man who would die rather than step away from your side.

It lifted me from nithing boy to the high seat of my own hall – yet even the seat itself had not been my own, taken as spoil from the last gasp of fighting for Jarl Brand and the new king, Eirik. I lifted it from the hall of Ivar Weatherhat, whose headwear was reputed to raise storms and he should have waved it at us as we rowed into his bay, for by the time we sailed off on a calm sea, he was burned out and emptied of everything, even his chair.

After that raid, we had all sailed here. Hard men, raiding men, here to this hall which reeked of wet wool and dogs, loud with children and nagging women. I had spent all the time since trying to make those hard, raiding men fit in it and had thought I was succeeding, so much so that I had decided on a stone for us, to root us all here like trees.

There are only a handful of master rune-carvers in the whole world who can cut the warp and weft of a man's life into stone so perfectly that those who come after can read it for a thousand years. We want everyone to know how bravely we struggled, how passionately we loved. Anyone who can magic that up is given the best place at a bench in any hall.

The stone for the Oathsworn would be skeined with serpent runes, tip-tapped out with a tool delicate as a bird's beak by the runemaster Klepp Spaki, who says he learned from a man who learned from a man who learned from Varinn. The same Varinn who carved out the fame of his lost son and did it so well that the steading nearby was called Rauk – Stone – ever after.

The first time I ran my fingers down the snake-knot grooves of the one Klepp made for us they were fresh-cut, still gritted and uncoloured. I came to rune-reading late and never mastered the Odin-magic of its numbers, the secret of its form – or even where to start, unless it was pointed out to me.

You read with your fingers as much as your eyes. It is supposed to be difficult – after all, the very word means 'whisper' and Odin himself had to hang nine nights on the World Tree and stab himself with his own spear to uncover the mystery.

Klepp runed the Oathsworn stone with my life as part of it and I know that well enough, even as age and weather smooth the stone and line me. I could, for instance, find and trace the gallop of the horse called Hrafn, bought from a dealer called Bardi the Fat.

He was black that horse, with not one white hair on him and his name – Raven – sat on him easier than any rider ever would. He was not for riding. He was for fucking and fighting. He was for making dynasties and turning the Oathsworn from raiders to breeders of fine fighting horses on the pastures Jarl Brand of Oestergotland had given us in the land of the Svears and Geats, which was being crafted into Greater Sweden by Eirik Victorious.

Hrafn. I should have been warned by the very name of the beast, but I was trying too hard to live in peace on this prime land, trying too hard not to lead the Oathsworn back into the lands of the east chasing a cursed hoard of silver. So a horse called Raven was a good omen, I thought.

As was the name of our steading: Hestreng, Meadow of Stallions. Rolling gently along the edge of one of the better inlets, it was good land, with good hayfields and better grazing.

Yet it stood on the edge of Austrvegrfjord, the East Way Fjord. It was called that not because of where it lay, but because it was the waterway all the ships left to go raiding and trading eastwards into the Baltic.

The Oathsworn, for all they tried to ignore it, felt the whale road call of that fjord every waking day, stood on the shingle with the water lapping their boots and their hair blowing round their faces as they watched the sails vanish to where they wanted to go. They knew where all the silver of the world lay buried and no norther who went on the vik could ignore the bright call of that. Not even me.

I watched the women bustle round the fire, thought of the stone that would root itself and hoped I had settled them all to steading life – but all they were doing was waiting for the new *Elk* to be built.

I had that made clear to me one day when Kvasir and I went up to the valley where our horses pastured out their summer and he kept looking over his shoulder at the sea. Because he only had the one eye, he had to squirm round on the little mare he rode to stare back at the fringe of trees, all wind-bowed towards him as if they offered homage, and so I noticed it more.

You could not see the hayfields or grassland beyond, or the ridge beyond that, which offered shelter to fields and steading from the slate grey sea and the hissing wind. But you could taste the sea, the salt of it, rich on the tongue and when Kvasir faced front again and saw me looking, he tilted a wry head and rubbed under the patch at the old ruin of his dead eye.

'Well,' he gruffed. 'I like the sea.'

'You have a woman now,' I pointed out. 'Learn to like the land.'

'She will, I am thinking, perhaps have to learn to like the sea,' he growled and then scowled at my laugh . . . before he joined in. Thorgunna was not one who perhaps had to learn anything unless she wanted to.

We had ridden in broody silence after that, into that valley with the hills marching on either side, rising into thick green forests, shouldering them aside and offering their bare, grey heads to the sky and the snow. It was a green jewel, perfect summer pasture that never got too dry. The hills at the end of it sloped up into pine and fir; fog roofed the tall peaks.

There was a hut in this snake-slither of a valley, almost unseen save by a thread of smoke, where Kalk and his son, the horse-herders, lived all summer. As we came up, Kalk appeared, wearing what thralls always wore – a *kjafal*, which had a hood at the top, was open on the sides, had no sleeves and fastened between the legs with a loop and a bone toggle. It was all he ever wore, summer or winter, save for some battered ox-hide shoes when the snow was bad.

He greeted us both with a nod of his cropped head and waited, rubbing the grizzled tangle of his chin while we sat our ponies.

9

'Where is the boy?' I asked and he cleared his throat a little, thought to spit and remembered that this was his jarl. It was, I was thinking, hard for him to believe that such a youngster was his master and that came as little surprise to me; I needed no brass reflection or fancy-glass to know what I looked like.

Thin faced, crop-bearded, blue eyed, hair the colour of autumn bracken braided several times and fastened back, reaching down to shoulders that had too much muscle on them for a youth with barely twenty-one years on him.

These shoulders and a breadth of chest told tales of oar and sword work. Even without the telltale scars on the knuckles that spoke of shield and blade, you could see this youth was a hard man.

Rich, too and travelled, with a necklet of silver coins from Serkland, punched and threaded on a thong and finished off with a fine silver Odin charm – the three locked triangles of the *valknut*, which was a dangerous sign. Those who wore it had a tendency to end up dead at the whim of the One-Eyed God.

There was a fine sword and several good arm rings of silver, too. And the great braided rope of a silver torc, the rune-serpent mark of a jarl, the dragon-headed ends snarling at each other on the chest of a coloured tunic.

I knew well enough what I looked like, what that made Kalk think and took it as my due when he dropped his eyes and swallowed his spit and came up grinning and bobbing and eager to please.

Jarl Brand's return, complete with mailed men with hard eyes, had sent more than a few scurrying off his lands and the farms they left behind made fat prizes for chosen men like me. For the likes of Kalk and his son, the change made little difference – thralls were chattels, whoever sat in the high seat of the steading.

He told us it was time to bring the horses down from the

10

high pasture, that one had a split hoof and of how Tor Ironhand was still turning his own mares loose in the valley, which he considered his own.

We said we would be back the next day and then rode back to the hall, towing the limping colt behind us.

'Is this Tor's valley, do you think?' Kvasir asked eventually.

I shrugged. 'I hope not. Thorgunna says it belongs to her, as her share of the steading. I use it because I am your jarl and the pair of you live under my roof – but both you and she can tell me to get out of it if you choose. Why do you ask?'

Kvasir hawked and spat and shook his head. 'Seems as if you would know a thing like that. Owning a whole valley, like a pair of boots, or a seax.'

'What? Should the land roll over and ask you to tickle its grass belly when you ride over it? Offer you a grin of rocks and congratulate you for being its owner?'

Kvasir grunted moodily and we rode in silence again, slowly so that the lamed grey could limp comfortably. We did not speak again that day, though I felt the brooding of him on me like an itch I could not scratch.

The next day he moved to my side, squatting by the high seat as I watched Aoife's Cormac put his fat little arms round the neck of one of the deerhounds, which licked his face until he laughed. He was so pale-headed he might have been bairned on Aoife by the white-haired Jarl Brand himself, which we suspected, since he had been given that comfort as an honoured guest. No-one knew, least of all Aoife for, as she said, 'It was dark and he had mead.'

Which did not narrow the search much, as we all admitted when we tried to work out who the father was.

'What will you do about Thorkel?' Kvasir asked eventually and I shrugged, mainly because I didn't know. Thorkel was another problem I hoped would just go away.

He had arrived on Hoskuld's trading *knarr*, which carried

11

bolts of cloth and fine threads and needles that set all the women to yowling with delight. Stepping off the boat, pushing through the women, he had stared at me with his sea-grey eyes and grinned a rueful grin.

I had last seen his grin on a beach in that bit of Bretland the Scots called the Kingdom of Strathclyde. That was where he had stepped aside and let me into the Oathsworn without having to fight, having arranged it all beforehand. I had been fifteen and raw as a saddle-sore, but Einar the Black, who led us then, had gone along with the deception with good grace and jarl cunning.

Thorkel had gone to be with a woman in Dyfflin. Now he sat in my hall drinking ale and telling everyone how he had failed at farming, how the woman had died and how he had failed at selling leather and a few other things besides.

He sat in my hall, having heard that the story of the hoard of Atil silver was true, the tale he had scoffed at and the reason he had wanted to leave the Oathsworn in the first place.

'We should call you Lucky,' Finn grunted, hearing all this. Thorkel laughed, too hearty and trying to be polite, for what he wanted was back into the Oathsworn and a chance at the mound of treasure he had so easily dismissed.

'Ever since he came back,' Kvasir mused pitching straw chips into the pitfire, 'all our men have been leaning to the left a little more.'

I did not understand him and said so.

'As if they had axes or swords weighing their belts,' he answered flatly. He shifted sideways to allow a deerhound to put its chin on my knee and gaze mournfully up at me.

'Eventually, a man has to choose,' he went on. 'We came up the Rus rivers of Gardariki with Jarl Brand almost five years ago, Orm. Five.'

'We agreed to serve him every year,' I pointed out, feeling – as I always did when I fought this battle – that the earth was shifting under my feet. 'I am remembering that you, like the rest, enjoyed the pay from it.'

'Aye,' Kvasir admitted. 'The first year and the next were good for us, though we lost as much as we gained, for so it is with men such as we – it comes hard and goes easy. Those were the times we thought you had a plan to get us outfitted and so return to the Grass Sea to find Atil's silver tomb again. Then you took land from the jarl.'

'We had no ship of our own until we built one,' I protested, feeling my cheeks and the back of my neck start to prickle and flame at the lie of it. 'We need a . . .' The word 'home' leaped up in me, but I could not say it to these, whose home was the shifting sea.

'Anyway,' I ploughed on stubbornly, 'while there was red war we were welcome in any hov that esteemed Jarl Brand; when red war is done with, no-one cares for the likes of us. Why – there are probably not two halls along the whole coast-line here glad to see a boatload of hard men like us sail into their happy lives. Would you prefer sleeping in the snow? Eating sheep shite?'

'The third year of war was hard,' admitted Kvasir, 'and made a man think on it, so that we were glad, then, of a hall of our own.'

That third year of red war against the enemies of Jarl Brand had spilled a lot of blood, right enough, but I had not known the likes of Kvasir had thoughts such as he admitted to now. I gave him a sharp look, but he matched me, even with one eye less.

'Last year made it clear you were finding reasons not to go where we all thought you should,' he declared. 'And while we spent, you hoarded, which we all thought strange in a young jarl such as yourself.'

'Because you spent I hoarded,' I replied hotly. 'A jarl gives and armrings are expensive.'

'Aye, right enough,' replied Kvasir, 'and you are a byword

13

for the giving out, for sure. But this year, when Eirik became *rig-jarl* of all, you had to be made to start the *Elk* building and thought more of trade and horses.'

'A ship like the *Elk* costs money,' I bridled back at him. 'Good crewmen need purse-money and keep – or had you planned to go silver-hunting with what remains of the Oathsworn only? There are a dozen left in all the world and two of them are in Hedeby, one caring for the addled other. Hardly enough to crew a *knarr*, never mind go raiding.'

Kvasir rode out the storm of my scorn, then thumbed snot from his nose and shrugged. He took to looking at me with some sadness, I was thinking, which did not make my temper any cooler.

'You have tried to make those left into herders of neet and horses, with a hayfield to plough and a scatter of hens scratching at the door,' he growled.

'Shows what you know,' I snapped back, sulky as a child, digging the point of the sabre into the beaten earth at my feet and gouging out a hole. 'We coop our hens – had you not noticed?'

He wiped his fingers on his breeks.

'No. Nor want to, when it comes to it,' he replied levelly. 'I am thinking none of the others know much about hens, or hay, or horses either. They know ships, though – that's why all of them are cutting and hauling timber for Gizur every day, building the new *Fjord Elk*. That's why they stay – and I would not be concerned at gaining a crew, Orm; Thorkel, I am thinking, is only the first to arrive looking for a place at an oar. Even after five years the silver in that hoard is bright.'

'You have a wife,' I pointed out, desperate now, for he was right and I knew it. 'I was thinking you meant it when you hand-fasted to her – is she as easy to leave as the chickens?'

Kvasir made a wry face. 'As I said – she will have to learn to like the sea.'

I was astonished. Was he telling me he would take her with us, all the way to the lands of the Slavs and the wild empty of the Grass Sea?

'Just so,' he answered and that left me speechless and numbed. If he was so determined, then I had failed – the tap-tap of the adze and axes drifting faintly from the shore was almost a mockery. It was nearly done, this new *Fjord Elk*, the latest in a long line. When it was finished . . .

'When it is finished,' Kvasir said, as if reading my thoughts, 'you will have to decide, Orm. The oath keeps us patient – well, all but Finn – but it won't keep us that way forever. You will have to decide.'

I was spared the need to reply as the door was flung wide and Gizur trooped in with Onund Hnufa, followed by Finn and Runolf Harelip. Botolf and Ingrid had moved to each other, murmuring softly.

'If you plane the front strakes any thinner,' Gizur was saying to Onund, who was shipwrighting the *Elk*, 'it will leak like a sieve.'

The hunchbacked Onund climbed out of the great sealskin coat that made him look like a sea-monster and said nothing, for he was a tight-lipped Icelander at the best of times and especially when it came to explaining what he was doing with ship wood. He sat silently, his hump-shoulder towering over one ear like a mountain.

They all jostled, looking for places to hang cloaks so that they would not drip on someone else and yet be close enough to the fire to dry. The door banged open again, bringing in a blast of cold, wet air and Red Njal, stamping mud off his boots and suffering withering scorn for it from Thorgunna.

'The worst of wounds come from a woman's lips, as my granny used to say,' he growled, shouldering into her black look.

Ingrid unlocked herself from Botolf to slam it shut. Botolf, grinning, stumped to the fire and sat, while the children swarmed him, demanding stories and he protesting feebly, swamped by them.

'I would give in,' Red Njal said cheerfully. 'Little wolves can bring down the biggest bear, as my granny used to say.'

'Pretty scene,' growled a voice in my ear. Finn hunkered down at my elbow in the smoke-pearled dimness of the hall. 'As like what you see in a still fjord on a sunny day, eh, Orm? All that seems real, written on water.'

I glanced from him to Kvasir and back. Like twin prows on either side of my high seat, I thought blackly. Like ravens on my shoulders. I stared, unseeing, at the hilt of the sabre as I turned it in my fingers, the point cutting the hole at my feet even deeper.

Finn stroked the head of the blissful deerhound and kept looking at this pretty scene, so that I saw only part of his face, red-gleamed by the fire. His beard, I saw, threw back some silver lights in the tar-black of it; where his left ear should have been was only a puckered red scar. He had lost it in Serkland, on that gods-cursed mountain where we had fought our own, those who had broken their Oath and worse.

There were few left of those I had sailed off with from Bjornshafen six years ago. As I had said to Kvasir – hardly enough to crew a *knarr*.

'Keep looking,' I said sourly to Finn. 'Raise your hopes and eyes a little – written on water below, real enough above.'

'Real as dreams, Orm,' he said, waving a hand to the throng round the pitfire. 'You are over-young to be looking for a hearthfire and partitioning a hall. Anyway – I know how much you had and how much you have laid out and your purse is wind-thin now, I am thinking. This dream feeds on silver.'

'Perhaps – but this steading will make all our fortunes in the end if you let it. And the silver itch is not on me,' I answered, annoyed at this reference to my dwindling fortunes and to dividing my hall up into private places, rather than an open feasting space for raiding men.

He looked at me at last, his eyes all white in the dark of his face, refusing to be put aside. I saw that look and knew it well; Finn only had one way of wresting silver from the world and he measured it by looking down the length of a blade. In that he was not alone – truth was that I was the one out of step with the Oathsworn.

'But the sea itch is on you. I have seen you look out at it, same as the rest of us,' he answered and I was growing irritated by this now. The closer the new *Elk* got to being finished the worse it became and I did not want to think of the sea at all and said so.

'Afraid, Bear Slayer?' Finn said and there was more taunt in it than I think even he had intended. Or perhaps that was my own shame, for the name Bear Slayer had come to me falsely, for something I had not done. No-one knew that, though, save the white bear and a witch-woman called Freydis and they were both dead.

I was afraid, all the same. Afraid of the sea, of the tug of it, like an ebbing tide. There was a longing that came on me when I heard the break of waves on the shoreline, sharp and pulling as a drunk to an ale barrel. Once on the whale road again, I feared I would never come back. I told him so and he nodded, as if he had known that all along.

'That's the call of the prow beast. There's too much Gunnar Raudi in you for sitting here, scratching with hens,' he said. He was one of the two – the other was Kvasir – who knew I was not Orm Ruriksson, but Orm Gunnarsson. Gunnar. My true father, dead and cold these long years.

Finn's stare ground out my eyeballs, then he flicked it to the hilt of that rune blade as I turned it slowly.

'Strange how you can scratch into the hilt, yet that rune serpent spell is supposed to keep it and you safe from harm,' he murmured.

His voice was low and scathing, for he did not believe that my health and lack of wounds came from any runes on a sword and both he and Kvasir – the only ones I had shared this thought with – spent long hours trying to persuade me otherwise.

'The spell is on the blade,' I answered, having thought this through myself, long since. Hilts and trappings could be replaced; it was the blade itself that mattered in a sword.

'Aye, perhaps so, for it never gets sea-rot or dull-edged,' he admitted, then added a sharp little dismissive laugh. 'The truth of it is that the power of that blade is in the hand of the one who wields it.'

'If that was true,' I answered, 'then you and I would be worm food.'

There was a pause, while both of us remembered the dying and the heat and the struggle to get back this sword after it had been stolen. Remembered Short Eldgrim, who had lost the inside of his head and was looked after now by Cod-Biter who hirpled from side to side when he walked. Remembered Botolf losing a leg to the curve of this same sword whose hilt now rested under my palm, heavy with the secret of all the silver in the world. Remembered all those who had chased the mystery of Atil's silvered tomb and fallen on the road.

Then Finn shifted, rising to his feet.

'Just so,' he grunted heavily. 'Oarmates have died under wave and edge and fire from the waters of the North Sea to the sands of Serkland in order to be worthy of Odin's gift of all the silver of the world. I can hear the Oathsworn dead growl that they did not suffer all that to watch us sit here growing old and wondering about what might have been. I hear better with just the one ear than you do with both, it seems.'

There it was, that oath. 'Odin's gift is always a curse,' I answered dully, knowing he was right. Every feast brought the inevitable *bragafull* – the toasts drunk and wild promises made – followed later, when the drink had made us mournful, by the *minni*, the horns raised in remembrance. It grew harder, in the harsh, sober light, to ignore either of them.

This hov had double-thickness walls, was sunk deep into the soil, windproof and waterproof and sitting in it made you feel as solid and fixed as the runestone I planned to have carved. Yet a fierce wind was blowing us all away and I felt the scent of it in the air, with the wrack and flying salt spume that leaped the ridgeline and hunted round the roofs. It was the breath of the prow beast, snorting and fretting at anchor and wanting to be free.

We sat for a while in the swirling smoke, listening to the wind fingering the door and rapping to get in, while Botolf, more belly and less muscle on him these days, stretched out his carved timber foot to ease the stump and told stories to the children.

He told them of Geirrod the Giant and Thor's Journey to Utgard and the Theft of Idun's Apples and Otter's Ransom. This last was told deliberately, I thought, for it touched on the dragon Fafnir, Regin the Smith and a hoard of cursed silver, the very one sent to Attila, the one buried with him – the one we had found.

Into the silence that followed came Thorgunna and Ingrid, doling out bowls of stew and it was so good everyone forgot Otter's Ransom. She had taken me at my word and made good cheer in a cauldron; there was mutton, hare, duck, eel, prawns, mussels, barley, onions and root vegetables in that stew. I tasted kale and seaweeds and watercress and the lees of red wine.

'By Thor's balls, Thorgunna,' growled Red Njal, 'the sea is the test of a man as the cauldron is of a woman, as my granny once said. Jarl Brand doesn't eat as well as this.'

'He does,' Thorgunna answered, 'but he adds cinnamon to his, I have heard. And watch your tongue.'

'Cinnamon,' muttered Gizur. 'There's fancy for you. I cannot think that it would add much to the taste of this, all the same.'

'We had buckets of the stuff once,' Hauk Fast-Sailor said as I elbowed him aside to get a place on a bench nearer the fire. The high seat was my right, but too far from a good heat.

'Remember, Orm?' he said, nudging me so that stew slopped over my knuckles. 'On that island where we fought the Serkland pirates? We used the dead Dane for a battering ram on the door to their stronghold.'

'That was later,' Kvasir growled, wiping ale from his beard. 'The island where we got the cinnamon was where we found some of Starkad's men who had been taken prisoner and had their balls and tozzles cut off by the camel-humping Arabs. They had killed themselves in their shame. The last ran himself at his prison wall until his head broke open.'

'I have missed some moments, it seems,' Thorkel said into the silence that followed. I ignored him as much as I could, though I felt his eyes on me as I spooned my stew.

The smoke eddied, dragging itself to the eavesholes and out into the rain and wind while I listened to Red Njal and Harelip arguing about where other enemies and old oarmates had died. All gone, pale-faced fetches sailing my dreams as dark shapes on a charcoal sea.

Thorgunna came softly up behind me, dragged the hair back over my shoulders and began to tie it off.

'Don't get your hair in your food,' she said softly. 'And those stories are not ones for children.'

Finn clattered his bowl angrily to the ground and rose, while the deerhounds came in among us, licking platters and fingers and wolfing scraps. Cormac came with them, scrabbling and laughing.

'Perhaps we should set this one to routing out a stag or two before winter comes,' chuckled Botolf, sweeping the gurgling boy up. Aoife grinned and Ingrid fired arrows at her from her eyes.

Finn looked at them, then at me, then shook his head and banged out in a blast of rain-cold wind.

'Why does Finn have a face like a goat chewing a wasp?'

demanded Botolf as Ingrid glared at Aoife and hung on Botolf's big arm.

'He thinks we are living in a dream and going soft,' Kvasir said, wiping bread round his platter and tossing it into the snapping maw of a deerhound. He looked softly at his wife. 'Being chided for how we speak and needing our hair cut. He thinks we should be off on a hunt for silver.'

Botolf, who knew what he meant, grunted thoughtfully. Thorgunna, who simply thought it was warriors being restless, snorted.

'Go raiding then – though it is no pastime for honest men if you ask me. At least you will be putting in some effort for the food in your bowl. Seems to me Jarl Orm is overly tolerant of every lazy one of you.'

She scooped up bowls with meaningful noise and shot me one of her looks as she went. No-one spoke for a moment or two, for it is a well-known saying that there are only two ways of arguing with a woman and neither work.

There was moody silence after this.

'Play music instead,' I said to Botolf, 'in the event you find yourself attracted to the story of Otter again.'

Botolf, grinning ruefully, fetched his hand-drum and Hauk fished out his pipes and they tootled and banged away while the children danced and sang and even the thrall women joined in, sheathed in drab grey *wadmal* cloth, linen kerchiefs tied around brows and braids. For a while they stopped being chattels worn threadbare to the elbows – the power of drum and piping whistle has never ceased to amaze me.

A heathen thing that scene these days, thanks to the White Christ priests. The hand-drum is banned for being pagan and fine children all stained with bastardy, where no such mark was when Odin smiled on us and every child was as good as the next.

That day, while the wind wrecked itself against the hall and the rain battered in from the sea, it was as warming a

21

heartscene as any sailor could dream of on a rolling, wet deck – but somewhere, I was sure of it, Odin had persuaded the Norns to weave in blood scarlet for us.

The thought worried me like a dog on a rat's neck, made me get up and go out into a night smelling of rain and sea, to where the horses were stabled. They stirred and stamped, unused to being so prisoned, swirling up the warmth and sweet smell of hay and bedding. In the dark, the air was thick and suddenly crowded, as if a host of unseen people were there, circling me.

I felt them, the hidden dead of the Oathsworn, wondering what they had given their lives for and my belly contracted. I thought someone laughed and the dark seemed odd, somehow glowing.

It came from outside, in the sky, where faint strokes of green and red light danced in the north. I had seen this before, so it held no real terrors, but the mystery of the fox fires always raised my hackles.

'Others', too. Thorkel stepped out of the darkness and stood beside me.

'Troll fires,' he said, wonderingly. 'Some hold that the red in those fires marks battle, where the warriors fight in Valholl.'

'I had heard it marks where dragons fight and bodes ill,' I replied. 'Pest and war omens.'

'All it means,' said a voice, a blade cutting through the hushed reverence of our voices, 'is that winter comes early and it will freeze the flames in a fire.'

Turning, we saw Finn come up, swathed in a thick green cloak against the cold, his breath smoking into ours as he joined us.

'The sea will be cold when we sail,' he added and left that dangling there, like the lights flaring in the sky.

TWO

Odin started to turn my world to his bidding not long after, on a day when I was woken by Aoife rolling away from me, out of the closed box space which was my right and off to see to Cormac. It was cold in the hall, where everyone slept as close to the fire embers as they could get or were allowed. It was colder still after Aoife had left my side.

Thorgunna and Ingrid were up, the one barrelling towards me, the other coaxing flames back into the fire and kicking thralls awake to fetch wood and water. I groaned. It was too early for Thorgunna.

She stopped, hands on hips and looked down at me, one eyebrow crooked. 'You look like a sack of dirt.'

'Lord.'

'What?'

'You look like a sack of dirt, Lord. I am the jarl here.'

She snorted. 'It is an hour past *rismal* by the sun, which is scorching eyes out. Lord. And it is because you are jarl that I am here to give you a clean tunic and make sure your hair is combed. Lord. Men are here; they came with Hoskuld Trader, looking for you and Thorkel. They say they know Thorkel.'

I groaned louder still, for I had an idea who they were and

why they were here. Thorkel would have spread the word and here they came, the next ones wanting an oar on the finished *Elk*.

'Let Finn deal with it,' I attemped. 'I don't believe you about the sun, either.'

'Finn has already gone plank-hunting with Heg, as you ordered,' Thorgunna answered briskly, throwing a blue tunic at me. It smelled of summer flowers and clean salt air. 'But I will give you the part about the sun. It is there, though, somewhere in the rain clouds over the mountains.'

There was nothing else for it. I rolled out of bed, shivering and then had to splash water on myself before Thorgunna would let me into the clean tunic and warm breeks.

'If you had not rutted with that Aoife all night you would not stink so much,' she declared as I fastened my way into stiff shoes.

'Keep you awake, did we?' I growled back at her. 'I seem to remember you and Kvasir making so much noise when first you arrived in this hall that I thought to build you a place of your own, just so I could get to sleep.'

There was a hint of colour in her cheeks as she snorted her derision and turned me round to braid up my hair as though she was my mother, though I was younger only by a half-fist of years. When I turned back, she was smiling and it was not a smile you could resist.

I lost the grin stepping out into the muddy yard, where Thorkel and four men waited patiently, in the lee of the log store. They sat picking at a *rismal* – a rising meal – of bread and salt fish on a platter, fat wooden ale beakers in their hands. Thorgunna would not let them into a hall of sleepers, but had offered them fair hospitality, even so.

It was cold, a day when the last leaves whirled in russet eddies and the trees spitted a pearled sky. Thorkel nodded in friendly fashion, twisting his stained wool hat nervously in his hands, indicating the men.

24

'This is Finnlaith from Dyfflin, Ospak, Tjorvir and Throst Silfra. They are all wondering if you need good crewmen. As am I.'

I looked them over. Hard men, all of them. Finnlaith was clearly a half-Irisher, the other three were Svears and all had the rough-red knuckles you get from rubbing on the inside of a shield. I knew they had cuts on the backs of their other hands and calloused palms from sword and axe work, even though I could not see them. They had probably been fighting us only recently, but that was all over and a king over both Svears and Geats was being crowned in Uppsala this very year.

'Silfra,' I said to the one called Throst. 'Why do you need me, then?'

His by-name – Silver Owner – was a joke, he explained in his thick accent. He never owned any for long, for he enjoyed dice too much. He needed me, he added with a twisted smile, because he had heard from Thorkel and elsewhere that I had a mountain of it. Thorkel had the wit to shrug and look ashamed for a moment when I shot him a look.

'Find Kvasir inside,' I said. 'Thorkel will show you who he is. Do what Kvasir tells you and enjoy the hospitality of my hall. There is a ship being built which may need a crew and then again, it may not.'

Even as I said it I felt the heart of me sink like stone. The word was out, leaping from head to head like nits – Orm the White Bear Slayer, the Odin-favoured who held the secret of a mountain of silver, was preparing a ship. That attracted hard men, sword and axe men, from near and far, as Kvasir had pointed out.

That day was the beginning of it. Every day for the next few weeks they arrived, by land and sea, in ones and twos and little groups, all wanting a berth on the *Elk*. The hall filled with them and their noise and Thorgunna grew less inclined to smile and more inclined to bang kitchen stuff together and cuff thralls round the ears.

25

Then came the moment I had dreaded, when Gizur and Botolf came up, beaming, to announce that the carved prow-head had been placed and the *Fjord Elk* was finished.

I remembered the first of that name, the one I had been hauled up the side of at fifteen, plucked from a life at Bjornshafen into the maelstrom of sea-raiding, stripped from a life of field and sea into one of blade and shield. There was, it seemed to my sinking soul, no way back – and the hulk of all those steading dreams was wrecked beyond repair by my own heart-leap of joy at the sight of what Onund and Gizur had crafted. I had paid it scant attention before, not wanting to see it grow, not wanting to feel the power of the prow beast, dragging me from the land. Now the sight of it struck me like Thor's own hammer.

It was sleek and new, smelling of pine and tar and salt, rocking easily at the wharf we had built, while men flaked the new sail on the spar, a red and white striped expanse which had occupied two years of loom work. I had paid Hoskuld in silver and promises for that sail; this new *Elk* had sucked the last of what little fortune I had away.

There was carved scrollwork on the sides and on the steering board; the weathervane was silvered. The *meginhufr*, that extra thick plank fitted just beneath the waterline on both sides of the hull, was gilded and, even now, the thralls' hands were stained blue and yellow from the painting they had done. That also had cost me a fortune – lapis and copper for the blue, ochre and orpiment for the yellow and all mixed with expensive oil.

No wonder Hoskuld's grin was as wide as the one splitting Gizur's face – the trader could live idle for two seasons on what I had paid him for bits of this ship. The joy was on Gizur over what had been made, but it was rightly Onund's work, though the hunchback gave no more sign of content-ment than the odd grunt, like a scratching bear.

Thorgunna admitted it was a fine-looking ship, even if she

sniffed at what it cost and the uselessness of it compared with a new *knarr*, or some decent fishing craft. And the hours it took good men to build, when they should have been mucking out stables, or spreading seaweed on fields.

But no-one listened to her, for this was the *Fjord Elk*, with its antlered prow-beast and wave-sleekness.

Gizur looked at me pointedly. My heart scudded with the wind on the wave. The moment was here and I knew what was needed – a *blot* ceremony, with a pair of fighting horses, the victor's sacrifice and an oath-swearing. The old Oath that bound some of us still.

We swear to be brothers to each other, bone, blood and steel, on Gungnir, Odin's spear we swear, may he curse us to the Nine Realms and beyond if we break this faith, one to another.

A hard Oath, that. Once taken, it was for life, or until someone replaced you, which happened by agreement, or by challenge from a hopeful. I had not thought Odin done with us only that he dozed a little – but I should have known better; the One-Eyed All-Father never sleeps and when he does, one eye is always open.

So I sighed and said to them that it would be done, when I had decided – with Finn and Kvasir – just where we should raid.

In fact, I hoped the weather would change, from the watered-sun days which spat rain from a milk and iron sky to something harsher, with the wind lashing the pine forests like the breath of Thor and the sea rearing up, all froth and whipping mane. That would put a stop to the whole thing, at least for this season, I was hoping, for if Jarl Brand heard how men were raiding out of his lands – on top of neighbour-feuding – things would not go well with us in Hestreng.

I had forgotten that, while Thor hurls his Hammer from storm-clouds, Odin prefers his strike to come out of a calm sky.

We had one the day we took the *Fjord Elk* out to test it, a silver and pewter day, with the sea grey green and the gulls whirling. A good day to find out if it was a sweet sail, as Gizur pointed out, with more than enough wind to make oar-work almost an afterthought.

The men lugged their sea-chests up to bench them by a rowlock. The Irishers, only half Danes for the most part, were not shipmen of any note and craned their necks this way and that at the sight of shields and spears.

'Are we raiding, then?' demanded Ospak. Red Njal, lumbering past him to plooter into the shallows with his boots round his neck, gave a sharp bark of a laugh. Other old hands joined in, knowing no sensible man of our kind goes even as far as the privy without an edge on him somewhere.

'A smile blocks most cuts,' Red Njal shouted over his shoulder as he slung a shield up to the thwarts, 'but best to have a blade for those who scowl, as my granny used to say.'

The wind whipped my braids on either side of my face and the new, splendid sail bellied and strained above me. The prow beast went up a long wave and skidded down the other side and I heard Onund and Gizur cry out with the delight of it, while I stole a look at Finn, who was muttering and clutching his battered, broad-brimmed hat.

He caught me at it and scowled.

'There is a bag of winds in this hat, for sure,' he growled. 'I am thinking we should seek out old Ivar and have him tell the secret of it.'

Old Ivar, less his famous weather-hat and almost everything else he possessed, was fled to Gotland and unlikely to feel disposed to share any secrets with the likes of us, but I did not even have to voice that aloud to Finn. We stood for a while, he turning the hat this way and that and muttering runespells Klepp had taught him, me feeling the skin of my face stiffen and stretch with the salt in the air.

We ran with the wind until Gizur and Hauk decided they had found all the faults with *beitass* and *rakki* lines and all the other ship-stuff that bothered them, then we turned round into the wind, flaking the great striped sail back to the mast. Sighing, men took to their benches and started to pull back to the land.

Crew light as we were and running into an off-shore wind, the *Fjord Elk* danced on the water while men offered 'heyas' of admiration to Onund for making such a fine vessel. For his part, he hunched into his furs and watched the amount of water swilling down between the rowers' feet with a critical scowl.

I stood in the prow, glad not to be pulling on an oar. I stared out across the grey-green glass of stippled water to the dusted blue of the land, one foot on the thwart, one hand on a bracing line.

'It is the still and silent sea that drowns a man,' said a voice, like the doom of an unseen reef, right in my ear. I leaped, startled and stared into the apologetic face of Red Njal who had left his oar to piss.

'As my granny used to say,' he added, directing a hot stream over the side.

'Point that away, you thrallborn whelp,' roared Finnlaith from beneath him, 'for if you wet me it will be this silent sea that drowns you.'

'Thrallborn!' Red Njal spat back indignantly, half-turning towards Finnlaith as he spoke; men cursed him and he hastily pointed himself back to the sea, yelling his apologies and curses at Finnlaith for insulting him.

'Do not despise thralls,' Onund growled blackly at Red Njal. 'The best man I knew was a thrall, the reason I left Iceland.' The panting rowers lifted their heads like hounds on a spoor, for Onund rarely spoke of anything and never of why he had left Iceland. They kept their eyes on the man in front, all the same, to keep the rhythm of the rowing.

Onund went on, 'I was with Gisli, the one they call Soursop, from Geirthiofsfirth, in Thorsnes, who was declared outlaw there some years ago. He had a thrall called Thord Hareheart, for he was not a brave man, but a fast runner.'

There were chuckles between the pulling-grunts; a good by-name was as fine as good verse. Finn moved down the ranks, offering water from a skin, feeding it to men who kept pulling as they sucked it greedily.

'Outlawed or not, Gisli was not about to quit Thorsnes,' Onund told us. 'So men hunted him. He took his spear, formed from a blade-magic sword called Graysteel, which he had stolen and not returned, though it worked out badly for him – but that's another story.'

Men grinned as they pulled, for the winter seemed to promise some good Iceland tales round the fire. Finn left off with his watering and came closer to listen.

Onund grunted and went on. 'He also took Thord and as they were heading towards the steading, in the dark and cautious, he suddenly handed Thord his favourite blue cloak. For friendship he said, against the cold. Then they were attacked by three men and Thord ran, as he always did – but the attackers saw the cloak and thought it was Gisli.

'They hurled their spears and one went through Thord's back and out the other side. Then Gisli, who had spotted the men lying in wait for him, came out of hiding and killed them all, now that they had only seaxes.'

'Seems like a fair fight to me,' Finn growled and Onund shrugged, which was a fearsome sight.

'So others say,' he replied, 'but I thought it a mean trick on a helpless and faithful nithing, and one which brought no honour to Gisli, who was already lacking in that richness for many other reasons, not least his easy Christ-signing. So I left his boat unfinished and came here.'

'Others have signed to the White Christ,' Finn argued and

Onund, who knew well that Finn, among others of the Oathsworn, had done that once, nodded, considering.

'I know it. The Englisc and others west of Jutland are nearly all Christ-followers now and will not trade with those who are not,' he growled. 'For all that, it is no honourable thing to throw off your gods, even for a little time, just for silver.'

'To be without silver is better than to be without honour,' Red Njal agreed sombrely, tucking himself back into his breeks and moving back to his bench. Finn, mired in an argument he felt he was losing, glared at him.

'Before you mention her,' he snarled, 'let me just say that your old granny should have remembered the oldest saw of all – a tongue cut out seldom gossips.'

Red Njal pursed his lips with sorrow, shaking his head. 'There is only mingled friendship when a man can utter his whole mind to another,' he countered. 'You have my granny to thank for that and my forbearance.'

'Never trust the words of a woman,' Finn intoned, 'for their hearts were shaped on a wheel.'

'With his ears let him listen, with his eyes let him look – so a wise man spies out the way,' Red Njal spat back.

'Shut up, the pair of you,' shouted Kvasir, which brought a brief spasm of throaty chuckles.

It was there, basking in that glow of being on a fine, new ship with the only true family I knew and aware that I was enjoying it, that I felt the breath of Odin, a sharp chill that shuddered me, made me turn to where the antlered prow beast snarled.

The grey-green sea was the same and the gloomed blue of the land – but now there was a dark stain on part of it and the evil wink of a single red eye.

I stared, trying to make sense of it, until Finn shoved his spray-dusted beard inches from my cheek and did it for me.

'Smoke and fire,' he said. 'Hestreng.'

I was still grasping at the swirling leaves of my thoughts when he turned back to where the men bent and pulled.

'Row, fuck your mothers!' he roared. 'Our hall is burning.'

We hauled hard, creaming the *Fjord Elk* up and over the waves, pounding her into the shore, while those not rowing fixed helmets, checked thonging and studied the edge of blades for sharpness.

The panic in me was a spur that kept me pacing like a caged dog from mastfish to prow beast and back, until Kvasir smacked the flat of his blade on my helmet, hard enough to ring some sense into me.

He did not have to speak at all, but I met him eye to eye and nodded my thanks. His grin was hard-eyed and I remembered, with a start, about his wife, Thorgunna, as well as Botolf, Ingrid and Aoife and all the others. Like a fret of swirling wind, the thoughts circled in me. Who? Who would dare?

There was no answer to it. We had more enemies than friends, like all sea-raiders and the curse of it was that I made us vulnerable by giving those enemies a place to attack, a sure place where they knew we could be found.

Gizur howled at the rowers, who grunted and sweated and hauled until the last moment, then clattered in the oars while the keel drove hard and grinding up the shingle and men spilled out.

I scrambled to the thwarts and hurled on to the shells and pebbles, stumbled a few steps and saw men ahead, fired by fear of what they might have lost, churning up the stones and coarse sand towards Hestreng.

'Finn . . .' I yelled and he saw it and bellowed like a bull in heat, bringing most of them to a stop.

'Wait, you dirty swords,' Kvasir added at the top of his voice, as men swilled like foam. 'We go together. The Oathsworn. As a crew.'

They roared and clattered blades on shields at that, but the truth was that most of them had sworn no oath yet; even as they trotted after me, panting like hounds, I had to hope they would fight, if only to protect their own wee bits and pieces littering my hall.

It was clear, when we came up over the rise that sheltered Hestreng from the sea, that it was not my hall that burned, or any part of it – I felt a dizzying wave of relief, followed at once by an equal wash of guilt at those who had been unlucky.

'Gunnarsgard,' Kvasir said, squinting to the feathered smoke and the red stain beneath it. 'Tor's steading has gone up.'

No real friend to us, but a neighbour for all that and I was on the point of stepping out towards the place when Kvasir bulled off towards Hestreng's hall, dragging Finnlaith and others in his wake. Heading, of course, for his wife; shamed, I followed on.

I heard the clatter of iron on wood and the high, thin bell of steel on steel. By the time I had caught up with Kvasir and the knot of Oathsworn grunting their way round the privy to the yard beyond, I could hear individual panting and roars.

When I spilled into the yard, Finnlaith and Ospak were already screaming 'Ui Neill' and charging at a knot of men held at bay by the great, sweat-soaked figure of Botolf, timber foot firmly rooted in the lower slope of the dung heap and a great long axe circling and scything in his hands. Kvasir, ignoring all of them, charged on towards the hall.

A man, all dirty fleece and snarl, heaved a spear at me, which took me by surprise so that I barely got my shield in the way and had it torn from my finger-short grasp by the smack of it.

There was nothing in me but stoked anger, blood-red and driving. I did not even have my own blade out of the sheath, but placed one booted foot on the shield and wrenched the spear from the linden. Then I came at the man, who had a seax and the red-mawed look of a man who knew how to use it.

I remember using the butt of the spear in a half circle, catching the short blade of his seax and whirling it sideways, bringing the blade of the spear down in a cut that made him jerk his face away. It tore down his fleece and he gave a yelp, but it was all too late for him.

I drove the point into his belly, just below the breastbone and kept moving, so that he jerked like a gaffed fish and shrieked, his legs milling uselessly as I shoved him back and back and back until he hit the side of the brewhouse, where I impaled him on the sagging wattle wall.

Finn dragged me away from him, eventually. Later he told me I had crushed the man into the wall and looked to be bringing the whole brewhouse down, screaming for him to tell me who he was, who had dared attack the Oathsworn.

The rest of the crew came panting up and those arrived too late kicked the dead in their disappointment – and all the men were dead, I saw. Six of them.

Botolf, panting and red-faced, stumped towards me, grinning.

'Nithing whoresons,' he said and spat on the nearest. 'A *strandhogg*, I was thinking, come to steal chickens and horses. Thorgunna saw them in the meadow, rounding up mares with no great skill and knew them for what they were at once.'

Thorgunna . . . my head came up, ashamed and guilty at having forgotten her, but Botolf broadened his grin.

'A woman, that,' he said admiringly and, just then, Kvasir appeared, Thorgunna with him, Ingrid behind her. Following on came Aoife, with Cormac on her hip and the thralls, Drumba and Heg.

'They had barred the hall door,' Kvasir said.

'That was sound,' Finn offered, beaming and Thorgunna huffed and folded her arms under her ample breasts.

'That was only sense,' she spat back, 'when such friends as yours come to call.'

'No friends of mine,' Finn answered grimly and turned a body with his toe. 'Yet, mind you, this one looks familiar.'

'Parted at birth, I am sure,' Ingrid muttered bitterly and, for all they seemed more angry than afraid, I saw the fluster and tremble in them.

'My sister,' Thorgunna said flatly and I blinked at that, having forgotten that Thordis was at Gunnarsgard, wife to Tor.

'Finn – choose some good men,' I said swiftly, seeing the path clearly for the first time since the smoke had stained my world. 'Botolf – guard the women here. Kvasir – stay with your wife and command the men I leave.'

'Guard the women,' muttered Botolf moodily. 'Guard the women . . .'

'And your tongue,' Ingrid snapped and then, to her horror, burst into tears. Thorgunna gathered her up and turned away.

'They came looking for you,' she said to me suddenly. 'Yelled out your name, as if they knew you.'

'Shot arrows into Hrafn, all the same,' Botolf added grimly, 'when he came at them for stealing his mares. The beast is limping about like a hedgepig, if he is standing at all.'

Finn and I looked at each other and he looked down at the lolled body of the man he thought he knew.

'Old friends,' he grunted.

THREE

It was a shock seeing him at his ease beside Tor's hearthfire, feet up on a bench, picking the remains of one of my mares out of his teeth with a bone needle and grinning, for he knew he had caused me as much stir as if I had found a turd at the bottom of my soup bowl.

Klerkon. He had a good Svear name somewhere, but the dwarves guarded it as carefully as they protected the sound of cat's paws, the breath of a fish and all the other things the world had forgotten. Klerkon they called him, after his father, who had been a *klerkr*. In the Svear tongue, that simply meant someone who had learned Latin, though it was more often given to a Northman who had become a Christ priest.

'A surprise for you,' he said, chuckling out of his button-nosed, bright-eyed face, the curl of grey hair framing it like smoke.

He had a face like a statue I had seen once in the Great City, one long broken in pieces so that only the head remained. It had sly eyes, tiny horns and tight-curled hair and Brother John, who was with me at the time, said it was a little Greek god called Pan. He had had goat legs and played pipes and fucked anything that moved, said Brother John.

That Pan could have fathered this Klerkon, who shoved a

stool towards me and indicated I should sit, as if the hall was his own. In the shadows behind him, as I searched for Tor or Thordis, I saw shapes, the grinning faces fireglowed briefly and then gone, the gleam of metal. I knew the rasp of hard men's breathing well enough and the rich smell of my own livestock cooking reeked through the hall.

When I strode out for the smoke of Tor's steading, sick and furious, a dozen men followed. First we saw that only outbuildings burned – a byre and a bakehouse. Not long after, we found Flann, Tor's thrall and, guddling about for plunder in Flann's blood, a stranger with sea-rotted ringmail and tatters of wool and weave hung about him. He looked like something long dead risen from the grave and climbed slowly to his feet at the sight of us, wiping his palms down the front of his breeks.

'Are you Jarl Orm?' he asked in a voice thick with Finn accent.

'Who wants to know?' I countered and he shrugged.

'I am Stoor and serve someone who wishes you well,' he replied, sonorous as if he was a real herald. 'He bids you come to the hall ahead, in safety. I was left here to guide you.'

'Fuck you,' Finn growled and would have said more, about traps and stupidity had I not stilled him with one hand. I looked at him and he at me. Then I followed Stoor, alone.

It was a wolf den now, Tor's comfortable hov; the idea of it drove a dry spear into my throat and clenched my balls up into my belly.

'There is pleasure in renewing old friendships,' Klerkon went on easily. 'A pity about the misunderstanding earlier, but such things happen on a *strandhogg*. Men get excited chasing chickens, you know how it goes. No slight was intended and little harm done.'

His voice made it clear that what I had lost in the way of livestock was well offset by the death of six of his men. Then he called for ale, which Thordis brought. She did not look at me when she laid the wooden cup at my elbow, but her whole body was hugged tight to her and there was a straggled lock of dark hair escaped from one coiled braid, which she would never usually have allowed.

'Tor,' I said to her and she blinked once or twice. Klerkon gave a little laugh and men shifted out of the darkness, grating a bench into the light. Tor swayed on it, his face a bruise, his lips fat and raw as burst blood puddings. His feet, I saw, hung unnaturally sideways; hamstrung so that he would never walk again.

'I did not think you would object over-much to having an awkward neighbour put at a disadvantage,' Klerkon said. 'We needed some bread and cheese and the men needed to dip their beaks a little, so this place seemed good enough.'

'I am sorry for it,' I said to Tor and his single working eye flicked open.

'Your fault,' he managed to puff through his broken mouth. 'Your kind. Your friends. You brought them here.'

Men laughed at that. I stared at the bald patch on top of Tor's slumped head and felt sick. They were no friends to me, but he had it right – my fault, for sure. For bringing hard raiding men as neighbours to a peaceful *bondi* farmer. For thinking I could get away with it.

Not now, all the same, for Jarl Brand would see it, too. Once this mess was fixed, he would sigh and have to admit that he had no use for us now that the fighting was done. He would be sorrowful, but point out that he could not have swords such as us waving about on his lands, frightening decent folk, inviting bad cess on them.

Bad cess sat opposite, smiling his Pan-smile and sliding his platter across to me, the meat-grease cooling. I ignored it.

'Not hungry?' he asked and men chuckled. 'Pity – that was a tasty horse.'

'I hope you have silver left from other raids,' I managed to answer him. 'That meat you are enjoying will cost you.

38

Jarl Brand will scour every wavelet for you after this. So will I. It will take a fat blood-price to still our hands.'

He leaned back and waved a languid hand.

'A risk worth taking,' he answered, narrow-eyed. 'I am betting-sure that you can afford a horse and more besides. I hear you have a mountain of silver to draw on.'

Well, there it was. The circling rumours that had brought hard men flocking to join me had whispered in his ear and brought him. I knew Klerkon of old, had sailed with him on many a *strandhogg*, a supply raid, when we had both fought for Jarl Brand. Even among hard and vicious men like us, Klerkon was shunned as something sick.

'Now you know more, so you know something,' I answered. 'I did not take you for a man who followed bairn's tales.'

'Just so,' said Klerkon, watching me like a cat with a mouse, daring it to move. 'I am not. But just as priests parted us on bad terms, one brings us together, as friends. As partners.'

My left knee was twitching and I could not stop it. The air was thick with rank breath, meat smells and the acrid stink of men sweating fear and he saw me struggle with the bewilderment and curiousity his words had forged. I had crossed him once, over a pair of Christ priests he had captured and I had grown tired of his bloody attempts to shake their faith by having them hold red-hot iron and the like. Klerkon was twisted when it came to Christ priests and some folk who claimed they knew said it was because one had been his father and abandoned him as a boy.

'Priests?' I managed.

'Aye. You knew one, once, I understand. Tame Christ-dog of Brondolf Lambisson, who ruled Birka.'

'Birka is gone,' I harshed back at him. 'Lambisson and the priest with it.'

Klerkon nodded, still smiling the fixed smile that never reached those slitted, feral eyes.

'True, it was diminished the last time we paid a visit. Hardly

39

anything worth taking and the borg had been burned. But we burned it again anyway.'

He slid his feet off the stool and sat forward.

'Lambisson is alive, if not entirely well. The priest also and he is even less good to look on.'

He sat back while the wave of this crashed on me and his smile was a twist of evil.

'I know this because Lambisson paid me to bring the priest to him,' he said. 'In Aldeigjuborg, last year it was. I plucked the priest – Martin, his name is – from Gotland, where he was easy to find, since he was asking after Jarl Orm and the Oathsworn. Why is that, do you think?'

I knew, felt a rising sickness at what Klerkon might still have to reveal. Lambisson and the priest Martin had set us off on this cursed search for Atil's tomb years before, when I joined the Oathsworn under Einar the Black.

The priest had used Lambisson's resources to ferret out something for himself, the Holy Lance of the Christ-followers and used the Oathsworn to get it. Now I had it, snugged up in my sea-chest alongside the curved sabre it had made and Martin would walk across the flames of Muspell to seek me out and get that Christ stick back. What Lambisson wanted with Martin was less clear – revenge, perhaps.

Klerkon saw some of that chase its own tail across my face and his smile grew more twisted.

'Well,' he went on, his voice griming softly through my ears, 'perhaps this priest wanted his share of Atil's silver and so sought you out. The rumours say you found it, Bear Slayer.'

'If so, only I know how to reach it,' I said, feeling that pointing out that fact at this time might prevent him from growing white around his mouth and a red mist in his eyes.

This time there was no smile in the wrench that took his lips.

'Not the only one,' he said. 'Before the priest, Lambisson gave me another task – to fetch two from Hedeby. I knew they were Oathsworn. Only later did I find out that they knew the way to this treasure of Atil, but I had given them to Lambisson by then.'

Short Eldgrim and Cod-Biter. Their names thundered in my head and I was on my feet before I knew it; benches went over with a clatter.

Klerkon leaped to his feet, too, but held out his empty hands.

'Soft, soft – Lambisson wanted them hale and hearty,' he said. 'It was only recently that it came to me there might be more in this than wild tales for bairns or coal-eating fire-starers. It would seem I had the right of it – all the same, Brondolf Lambisson has a head start on us.'

'Us?' I managed to grim out, husky and crow-voiced.

'Together we can take him on,' Klerkon said, as if he soothed a snarling dog in a yard. 'He has gathered a wheen of men round him – too many for me, too many for you. Together . . .'

'Together is not a word that sits between you and me,' I told him, sick with thought of what might have been done to Short Eldgrim and Cod-Biter. Neither of them knew enough – Eldgrim, perhaps, who had helped me cut the runes into the hilt of the sword, but the inside of his head was as jumbled as a woman's sewing box.

'This is an invitation you would be wise not to turn down,' Klerkon replied and I could see the effort it took to keep his smile in place.

'There are frothing dogs I would rather walk with,' I said, which was true, though this was hardly the time or place to be telling it. Steel rasped. Someone smeared out an ugly laugh. Klerkon snapped the eye contact with me, straightened a little and sighed.

'Perhaps a trade partnership was too much to expect,' he said softly and the smile was already a fading memory. 'If we cannot join, then I have it more in the way of you telling me all you know and me sparing those you hold in regard.'

41

'You are crew light for a task like that,' I told him, seeing it for the truth – otherwise he would not have offered any deal. 'I do not think I will tell you anything today.'

'By the time I am done with you,' Klerkon said, whitening round the eyes and mouth, 'you will beg to tell me every little secret you hold.'

I hauled out my blade and the sound of his own echoed it. The sucking whispers of other blades being drawn in the darkness was the soft hiss of a snake slithering in on a fear-stunned mouse.

Then the door hurled open with a crash and daylight flared in, catching us so that we froze, as if caught fondling each other.

'Your watchmen are shite,' growled a familiar voice and Finn bulked out the light. 'So I have done you a favour.'

Something flew through the air and smacked wetly on the table, hitting the edge of the platter, which sprayed horse meat and half-congealed grease everywhere. The object bounced up, rolled and dropped neatly into Klerkon's lap.

He jerked back from it, so that it crunched to the floor. The eyes were the only recognizable things in the smashed, bloody ruin of a face. Stoor. Watery blood leaked from the raw mess where his neck had been parted from the rest of him. Somewhere a woman shrieked; Thordis, of course, one hand to her mouth and her hair awry.

'Thordis,' I said and held out one hand. She looked at me, then at Tor and I knew, with a lurch of sick fear, that she would not leave him – and that we could not carry a hamstrung man.

There was a moment where I thought to take her round the waist and cart her off – but it was an eyeblink only. If we failed, Klerkon would know she was sister to Kvasir's wife and would use that to lever the secret he wanted out of me. Finn knew it, too, knew that she was safer if Klerkon stayed ignorant. He laid a free, gentling hand on my forearm; it left bloody smears.

42

'Time to be going, I am thinking, Jarl Orm,' he said and I moved to the door as the light from it slid down the bright, gleaming blade he called The Godi – Priest. He pointed it at Klerkon and the snarlers behind him, a warning as we backed out of the hall and ran for the waiting comfort of our own armed men.

Even as we sprinted out in a spray of mud and feverish elation, howling at each other with the sheer relief of having cheated our way to safety, there was the bitter taste of it all in the back of my throat, thick and metalled.

The wolf packs were gathering for the feast of Atil's tomb. Short Eldgrim and Cod-Biter were prisoners of one, Thordis was prisoner of another.

I set men to watch and we held an *Althing* of it round the hearthfire as Thorgunna doled out the night-meal. No-one felt much like eating, though and our weapons were within hand's reach.

Botolf was all for taking all the newly sworn crew in an attack in the dark to finish it all. Kvasir spoke up for blocking Klerkon from leaving and sending to Jarl Brand for help. Thorgunna wanted to know what we were going to do about her sister. Ingrid wept.

Finn stayed silent until everyone else had talked themselves exhausted. He went out once – to check on the guards, I thought, which was sensible. When he returned, he sat in the shadows and said nothing.

Then he came and hunkered by the fire, while I slumped in the carved chair and tried to think up a way out.

Attacking was no answer – it would be a sore battle and one of the first things they would do would be to kill their prisoners, who would be hand-bound only and able to run if not watched.

Running to Jarl Brand might help, but no matter how gold-browed my words were to him, all the same, it came out as

43

too many sea-raiders running around his lands, frightening folk with their swords and I did not think he would take kindly to me having kept the secret of Atil's tomb from him all these years. Worse, I had barefaced lied to him about the tale being true.

There was a deep sick feeling in me that I might, after all, have to trade with Klerkon.

'We should beware the night,' Botolf declared. 'Klerkon is a fox for cunning and he has that Kveldulf with him, too.'

Kveldulf – Night Wolf – was a man rumoured to be other than a man when the moon came up. Finn grunted and picked some choice morsels out of the pot and Botolf tilted his head questioningly, just as Ingrid told him to pull his wooden foot back from the fire, for it was charring.

'You do not agree, Finn Horsehead?' Botolf said mildly, though he was annoyed, both at his own foot-carelessness and Finn's casual dismissal of his plan.

Finn, wiping gravy from his beard, chewed and shook his head.

'You have all gone soft and forgotten about what we truly are,' he said, harsh as crow-song, his face blooded by the fire. 'What would we do in Klerkon's sea boots?'

There was silence. Botolf looked at Kvasir, who looked at me, cocking his head like a bird, the way he had taken to doing recently. The certainty of it struck us all, so that we almost leaped up at the same time. Thralls squeaked; Thorgunna, alarmed, demanded to know what was happening, grabbing up the long roasting fork.

'It has already happened,' Finn declared as we headed for the door. 'I went outside to see for myself.'

'And said nothing?' I roared, sick with the surety that, even knowing, I could have done nothing. Kvasir ducked out the door and Thorgunna shushed the squealing thralls and demanded to know what was happening. Cormac bawled, red-faced.

44

Kvasir came back in, the rain-scented night swirling in with him, rank with woodsmoke. He nodded to me.

'What is happening?' demanded Thorgunna with a roar. 'Are we attacked?'

We were not, nor would we be. Klerkon had done what any sensible sea-raider would do, given that his enterprise had not woven itself as tight as he would have liked. He had made the best of matters.

As Kvasir explained it, soothing and soft and patting to Thorgunna, I opened the door and stepped out to where the wind soughed, driving a mist of cloud over the moon, heavy with smell of wet earth and rain. But that could not hide the sharp tang of smoke and the horizon glowed where Tor's steading burned.

In the smeared-silver dawn, I rode over with Kvasir, Finn and Thorgunna to where the raven feathers of smoke stained the sky, but there was nothing left of Gunnarsgard other than charred timbers. Flann's body was where it had been and crows flapped heavily off it as we came up, but they had taken Stoor, body and head both. There was only one other corpse and that was a shrivelled horror perched on a bench in the black ruin of the hov.

Thorgunna slithered off the back of her pony, her dress caught up between her legs and looped over her belt in front for riding, so that it looked as if she wore fat breeks. Her strong calves flexed as she stumped to where the hall smoked damply and stood, legs slightly apart, rocking backwards and forwards for a long moment, staring at the grisly mess.

'Tor,' she said eventually and I nodded. It made sense – Klerkon dealt in profit and had killed the useless, hamstrung Tor, then taken his thralls and his woman and everything he could, down to the very chickens.

Thorgunna bent, picked something up, turned and walked back, looking up at where I sat on the pony.

She placed one hand on my knee and I felt it tremble like

45

a nested bird. In her dirt-calloused palm was a snapped thong and a bone slice threaded on it. Tor Owns Me, said the runes on it; one of the tokens Tor tied on the neck of his thralls in case any thought of running. Klerkon had herded them to *Dragon Wings* and a new market – and not just the thralls.

He had taken what profit he could and gone off to brood and chew his nails on what to do next to prise the secret of treasure from me and it was clear he did not yet know Thordis could be used for it. If he found out . . .

'We will go after my sister,' Thorgunna said. I looked at Kvasir, who peered at me sideways and nodded. I looked at Thorgunna; it was clear this was not a question.

So I nodded.

'Heya,' said Finn and I could have sworn there was joy in his voice.

FOUR

The sea was the colour of wet slate, the spray coming off the tops of the chop like the manes of white horses. Somewhere, at that almost invisible point where the grey-black of sky and sea smeared, lay the land of the Vods and Ests.

Two days. Three days. Who knows? A day's sail from a shipmaster is how far a good ship takes to travel some thirty ship-miles – but it could take you two sunrises to do it. Gizur kept saying we were three days from the Vod coast, looking for a range of mountain peaks like the teeth of a dog, but we never seemed to get closer.

Everyone was boat-clenched, which is what happens when the weather closes in. You sink deeper inside, like a bear in winter, sucking into the cave of yourself where you hunch up and endure.

The sail was racked midway down on the mast, we were driving east and a little south with a good wind and the oars were stowed inboard, so most of us had nothing to do but huddle in our sealskin sleeping bags. Everyone was busy, in silence, trying to keep dry and warm, while the lines hummed and the rain slashed in.

Thorgunna and the thrall women and the deerhounds huddled beside me under the little awning which was my right as jarl. Not that it gave much more than the illusion of shelter, but there was the warmth of shared bodies and the added, strange enjoyment of them being women.

I had done Botolf little favour appointing him steward in my absence – though Ingrid took the store keys from Thorgunna with a triumphant smile, which made Kvasir's wife scowl. It was bad enough what Thorgunna was leaving behind – her chest of heavy oak with its massive iron lock, filled with fine-wrought wool and bedlinen stitched by her grandmother's hands – without handing over her status in my hall to another woman who was not my first-wife. Not even my wife.

I then had to promise to get those keys back for her when we returned.

'Stay quiet, do nothing,' I advised Botolf, who was unhappy at being left behind and thought it more to do with his missing leg than anything else. I needed a level head and a brave heart, for Tor had friends in the region and there was no telling who they would blame or what they might do. Ingrid would supply the first and Botolf the second.

'I plan to deal with Klerkon, get Thorgunna's sister back, then go to Gardariki lands and find Short Eldgrim and Cod-Biter,' I explained. He nodded as if he understood, but the truth was there was as much clever in Botolf as in a bull's behind. Now and then, though, he surprised me.

'Jarl Brand will have much to say on this and none of it good,' he declared. 'You should find a way of telling him how matters stand, before he takes it into his head to make you outlaw.'

Then he grinned at my astonishment.

'You should sell Hestreng to me for an acorn, or a chicken,' he added. 'Then I can sell it back when you return. That way . . .'

'That way,' I finished for him, 'Jarl Brand would spit blood at me selling that which I only hold from his hand.'

He stared for a moment, then astonished me further.

'If you want Hestreng and the love of Jarl Brand,' he

grunted, 'then you will have to put a rare weight in the pan to counter what he is thinking – that you lied to him about Atil's treasure and are running about frightening decent farming folk with your sea-raider ways.'

His eyes went flat, like a sea where the wind has died to nothing.

'It comes to me that you will need to travel all the way to Atil's tomb and take all the silver you can,' he added, his voice bitter-bleak because he knew he would not be part of that. Then he forced a smile and stuck out his hand.

'I expect my share, all the same,' he ended and, mazed at all this, I clasped him, wrist to wrist, more sure now that I had left matters in Hestreng in good hands. Then I stole the smile from him.

I told him we would be taking Drumba and Heg and three thrall women as well, because we had Thorgunna with us. This was a hard dunt for Botolf; two thralls had died in the winter before and losing five more was bad enough without also waving goodbye to Thorgunna, who was a pillar of Hestreng. I did not want her with us, but Kvasir did and Thorgunna was determined to chase after her sister, so there it was. I pointed this out patiently to a scowling Botolf.

'We are oar-short on the *Elk*,' I added, 'but at least all those hard men with big bellies will be going with me, so you won't have the expense of feeding them.'

There were twenty fighting men, bench-light for a *drakkar* like the *Fjord Elk*, which properly needed two watches of thirty oarsmen apiece – we barely had enough to sail her, as Gizur pointed out at the oath-swearing.

Hrafn provided the blood for it, as expensive and sad a *blot* offering as Odin would ever have. We found him, flanks heaving for breath, streaming blood and sweat, lying in the meadow shot full of arrows, as Botolf had said. Now his head reared accusingly on a shame-pole of carved runes, streaming out bad cess at Klerkon's steading on Svartey, the Black Island, hidden miles beyond the grey mist and sea. Unlike us, Klerkon had no hall, but this was a winter-place he used and it was likely he was heading there.

'We will pick up more men,' I told Gizur and the new Oathsworn, more firmly than I believed. It was more than likely we would – but not from the land of the Livs and Vods and Ests. We would get no decent ship men until we reached Aldeigjuburg, which the Slavs call Staraja Ladoga and so would be raiding the steading of Klerkon with about half the men he had.

Finn pointed this out, too, when everyone was huddled in the hall out of the sleet, fishing chunks of Hrafn out of the pot, blowing on their fingers and trying to forget the hard oath they had just sworn.

'Well,' I said to him, uneasy and angry because he was right, 'you were the one who wanted to go raiding. You were the one never still-tongued about Atil's silver hoard, so that men would come to Hestreng and force me back to the tomb. Pity you did not think that the likes of Klerkon would hear you, too.'

Which was unfair, for he had saved my life in Tor's hov, but all of this had smashed whatever shackles bound me to the land and the thought that Finn had had a hand in it nagged me. There was more cunning in it than he had ever shown before, so I could not be sure – but I was watching men eat my prize stallion and so was in no mood for him at that moment. He saw it and had the sense to go away.

Kvasir came to me while men shouted and fought good-naturedly in the ale-feast that followed the oath-swearing. He hunkered down at my knee as I sat, glowering and spider-black over the fun raging up and down the hall, and took his time about speaking, as if he had to pay for the words in hacksilver and was thin in the purse.

'You were hard with Finn, I hear,' he said eventually, not looking at me.

'Is he aggrieved of it?' I asked moodily.

'No,' answered Kvasir cheerfully, 'for he knows you have other things to think on. Like me, he believes the sea air will clear your head.'

Well, Finn had the right of that, at least, though I did not know it myself at the time – or even when I was in the joy of it.

But when it happened, Finn came and stood with me in the prow, while the wind lashed our cheeks with our own braids and sluiced us with manes of foam.

The spray fanned up as the *Elk* planed and sliced down the great heave of wave, moving and groaning beneath us like the great beast of the forest itself. Those waves we swept over would not be stopped save by the skerries and the cliffs we had left behind. Only the whales and us dared to match skill and strength with those waves – but only the whales had no fear.

I was filled with the cold and storm, threw back my head, face pebbled with the salt dash of the waves and roared out the sheer delight of being in that moment. When I turned, Finn was roaring and grinning with me, while Thorgunna and the thralls watched us, sour and disapproving, hunched with misery and the deerhounds under a dripping awning that flapped like a mad bird's wing.

'You look a sight,' Finn said, blowing rain off his nose. Which was hard to take from a man wearing a hat whose broad brim had melted down his head in the rain and was kept on his head by a length of tablet-woven braid fastened under his chin.

I said so and he peeled the sodden thing off looking at the ruin of it.

'Ivar's weather hat,' he declared, ruefully. 'There must be a cunning trick to it, for I cannot get it to work.'

'Keep trying,' urged Klepp Spaki, peering miserably out from under his cloak, 'for if you can get the sea to stop heaving my innards up and down, I would be grateful.'

Others nearby chuckled and I wondered, once again, about

the wisdom of bringing Klepp along at all. He had turned up at the hall with the rest of some hopefuls and I had taken him for just another looking for an oar on the *Elk*, though he did not look like the usual cut of hard men. When he had announced he was Klepp Spaki, I groaned, for I had forgotten I had put the word out for a rune-carver and now I had no time – nor silver – for his service.

However, he had looked delighted at the news we were off on a raid and said he would do the stone for free if he could take the oath and come with us, for he had never done such a thing and did not feel himself a true man of the vik.

Now he sat under his drenched cloak, hoiking up his guts into the bilges, feeling exactly like a true man of the vik and no doubt wishing he was back in the best place by the fire, which was his due as a runemaster of note. It was a joke on his name, this journey – Spaki meant Wise.

Later, I woke suddenly, jerking out of some dream that spumed away from me as my eyes opened. The deck was wet, but no water washed over the planks and the air was thick with chill, grey and misted with haar that jewelled everyone's beards and hair. Breath smoked.

Thorgunna squatted on the bucket, only her hem-sodden skirts providing some privacy and I saw the thrall women passing out dried fish and wet bread to those on the oars, who were steaming as they pulled, eyes fixed to the lead oar for the timing. No thumping drums here, like they did on Roman ships; we were raiders and never wanted to let folk know we were coming up on them.

Gizur rolled up, blinking pearls from his eyelashes and grinning, the squat mis-shape of Onund hunched in behind him like some tame dancing bear.

'Rain, wind, sleet, haar, flat calm – we have had every season in a few hours,' he said. 'But the *Elk* is sound. No more than cupful has shipped through the planks.'

'More than can be said for my breeks,' grumbled Hauk,

picking his way down the deck. Gizur laughed, clapping Onund on his good shoulder so that the water spurted up from the wool. Onund grunted and lumbered, swaying alarmingly, to examine the bilges and ballast stones.

Gizur glanced over at the water. He could read it like a good hunter does a trail and I watched him pitch a wood chip over the side and study it, judging speed as it slid away down the side of the boat. Two hours later, the haar-mist smoked off the black water and Lambi Ketilsson, whom we called Pai for his peacock ways, stood up in the prow, yelling and pointing.

Black peaks like dog's teeth. Gizur beamed; everyone cheered.

'Now comes the hard part,' Finn reminded everyone loudly and that stuck a sharp blade in the laughter.

Not long after, it started to snow.

The dawn was silver milk over Svartey, the Black Island. We were huddled in a stand of wet-claw trees above Klerkon's camp, where the smoke wisped freshly and figures moved, sluggish as grazing sheep and just woken.

I watched two thralls stumble to the fringe of trees and squat; another fetched wood. The camp stretched and farted itself into a new day and we had been there an hour at least and had seen no-one who could fairly be called a man, only women and thralls. I had seen that Klerkon had built himself a wattle hall, while other ramshackle buildings clustered round it, all easily abandoned come Spring.

I looked across at Finn, who grinned over the great Roman nail he had clenched sideways in his teeth to stop himself howling out like a wolf, which is what he did when he was going to fight. Slaver dripped and his eyes were wild.

We had talked this through while the *Fjord Elk* slid through grey, snow-drifting mist on black water slick and sluggish as gruel.

'It wants to be ice, that water,' grunted Onund and Gizur

shushed him, for he was leaning out, head cocked and listening for the sound of shoals, of water breaking on skerries. Now and then he would screech out a short, shrill whistle and listen for it echoing back off stone cliffs. The oars dipped, slow and wary.

'We should talk to Klerkon,' I argued with Finn. 'If we can get Thordis back with no blood shed, all the better.'

Finn grunted. 'We should hit them hard and fast, for he will have more men than us and we must come on them like Mjollnir. If we talk, we give up that and they will laugh in our faces and carve us up.'

'Klerkon may just kill Thordis even if we do strike like Thor's Hammer,' Kvasir pointed out and I waved a hand to quiet his voice for, though we sat with our heads touching, it was not a large boat and Thorgunna was not far away.

'No,' said Finn. 'I am thinking he will keep her to bargain with if it goes badly for him. He wants the secret of Atil's treasure, so she is worth more to him alive.'

It was more likely to go badly with us, for if we could have taken Klerkon surely, I would have done it at Gunnarsgard. Neither of us had had enough men for certain victory then – but, in his own place, Klerkon probably had more. I did not say this, for it was no help; we had not sailed all this way to gather shells on Klerkon's beach.

There was a flurry of movement, some hissed commands and then, with a crunch and a lurch, the *Elk* slid an oak keel scar up the shingle beach of Svartey, the Black Island of Klerkon.

The thralls and women stayed behind, for they were useless in a fight. Gizur and Onund stayed, too, for they were too valuable to the ship to be risked. The rest of us hauled out weapons, checked shield straps, slithered into mail if it was there to be worn.

In the dim before dawn they were grim and glittering with hoar, bearded, tangle-haired under their helmets and grinning the savage grin of wolves on a kill. Hauk Fast Sailor had a bow, which he preferred. So did Finnlaith, who was a hunter of skill and I had marked that. The rest had good blades, axe or spear. Few swords. All the blades were dull with sheep grease against the sea-rot.

They were hard men, wild men, rough-dressed and tattered, but their battle gear and blades were cared for as women care for bairns and no matter what they had done before, they had put the words in their own mouths and were bound to each other now, blade-brothers of the Oathsworn.

I reminded them of this at the same time as telling them to leave off the loot and women until we were sure all the fighters were dead. They growled and grunted in the dark, teeth and eyes gleaming.

Then Finn stepped up, a battle leader as was Kvasir. But Kvasir said little at these moments and had seemed even more preoccupied than usual. I took it to be because he had Thorgunna with him; a woman is always a worry.

'It is as Jarl Orm says,' Finn growled. 'Obey him. Obey me and Kvasir Spittle here, too, for we are his right and left hands. You are no strangers to red war, so I will not give you the usual talk, of Hewers of Men and Feeders of Eagles.'

He paused, hauled out his long Roman nail and grinned.

'Just remember – this is Jarl Orm, who slew the White Bear. Jarl Orm, who has stood in the tomb of Atil, Lord of the Huns and has seen more silver in a glance than any of you will see in a thousand lifetimes. Jarl Orm, who has fought with the Romans against the Serklanders. Jarl Orm, who is called friend by the Emperor of the Great City.'

I winced at all this, only some of which was true – but Finn's audience would have howled and set up a din of shield-clanging if we had not been looking for stealth.

As we moved off, I saw Thorkel grin at me and raise his axe in salute and I realized that a lot of those things had been done by me right enough. I was now in my twenty-first year in the world, no longer the boy Thorkel had let into the Oathsworn on a shingle beach like this one, on a night much like this one, six years ago. I touched the dragon-ended silver torc round my neck, that great curve that snarled at itself and marked me as a man men followed.

No-one challenged us as we watched and waited above Klerkon's holding, looking to count hard men and seeing none. The trees dripped. A bird fluttered in, was shocked and whirred out again, cackling. I did not like this and said so.

'We had better move fast,' said Kvasir, his mouth fish-breath close to my face. 'Sooner or later we will give ourselves away and the lighter it gets . . .'

The sky was all silver, dulling to lead beyond the huddle of wattle huts. I half-rose and hauled out my sword – not the sabre this time, but a good, solid weapon given to me by King Eirik himself, with little silver inserts hammered into the cross-guard and a fat silver oathing ring in the pommel. I had a shield, but it was mostly for show, since I only had two fingers and a thumb on that hand to grip it with and any sound blow would wrench it away.

Grunting, red-faced, teeth grinding on his nail, Finn slid down through the trees, letting the rest of us follow. He had The Godi, his big sword, in one hand and carried no shield. The free hand was for that nail.

Then, just as he was seen by the two thralls squatting to shit, he ripped the nail from his mouth, threw back his head and let out a howl that raised the hairs on my arms.

The Oathsworn wolfed down on the camp, skilled and savage and sliding together like ship planks. The first thralls, gawping in terror and surprise with their *kjafal* flapping round their knees, vanished in a red flurry of blows and it was clear, from the start, that there were no warriors here.

Well, there was, but not much of one. He barrelled out of a doorway with only his breeks on, mouth red and wet and screaming in his mad-bearded face and a great shieldbreaker sword swinging.

Finn and Kvasir, like two wolves on a kill, swung right

and left and, while Mad Beard was turning his shaggy head, deciding which one to go for first, Finn darted in with his Roman nail and Kvasir snarled from the other side with his axe, though he missed by a foot with his first swing. It did not matter much, though, for there were two of them and only one defender.

When they broke apart, panting, tongues lolling like dogs, I saw that the man they had been hacking to bloody pats of flesh was Amundi, who was called Brawl. We had all shared ale and laughed round the same fire three summers before.

'So much for him, then,' growled Finn, giving the ruined thing a kick. He shot Kvasir a hard look and added accusingly, 'You need more practice with that axe.'

I had done nothing much in the fight save snarl and wave a menacing blade at a couple of thralls armed with snatched-up wood axes, who thought better of it and dropped them, whimpering. Now I watched these hard men, the new Oathsworn, do what they did best, standing back and weighing them up, for this was a new crew to me for the most part. It was also an old crew, let loose like a pack of hunting dogs too-long kennelled.

Hlenni Brimill and Red Njal and Hauk Fast-Sailor were old Oathsworn, yet they raved through that place, mad with the lust of it, so that the terror in faces only made them worse. Others, too, showed that they were no strangers to raiding and, for all that I had done this before, this time seemed too bloody and harsh, full of screaming women, dying bairns and revenge.

I saw Klepp Spaki, bent over with hands on his thighs, retching up at the sight of Brawl's bloody mess. Now he knew the truth of the bold runes he carved for brave raiders who would never come home.

I saw Thorkel and Finnlaith laughing and slithering in the mud trying to round up a couple of pigs, which was foolish. We wanted no livestock on this raid – we had provision enough for where we were going.

It was the others who brought red war and ruin to that place. Women and thralls died there, right away or later, after they had been used. Weans died, too.

In the dim, blue-smoked hall, men overturned benches, flung aside hangings, cursed and slapped thralls, looking for loot. When they saw me, they fell silent and went still. Ospak, Tjorvir and Throst Silfra, like three bairns caught in the larder with stolen apples, dropped their thieving when they saw me. It was a half-naked, weeping thrall woman they had stripped between them – but they only dropped her because I had told them to leave the women until we were sure all the fighting men were dead.

Finn lost himself in it – him most of all. Like a drunk kept from ale, he dived headfirst into the barrel and tried to drown himself, losing his sense so much that I had to save him from the boy who was trying to avenge his mother. Since Finn had killed her before he flung her down on a dead ox in the yard and started humping her, it was futile, but I had to kill the boy anyway, for he had a seax at Finn's exposed back.

A few kept their heads. Runolf Harelip spilled into the red light of the *rann-sack* in the hall, dragging a struggling thrall-boy with him, cuffing the child round the head, hard enough to throw him at my feet and almost into the hearthfire. I looked down as the boy looked up and a jolt went through me, as if I had been slapped.

A sensible man crops the hair of a thrall – it keeps the nits down and reminds them of their place – but this boy had been shaved and badly, so that hair stuck in odd dirty-straw tufts between scabs. He wore an iron collar with a ring on it and I knew there would be runes that told how he was the property of Klerkon.

None of the other thralls, I noted, had as much as a thong and bone slice, for Klerkon's steading was an island with no place for a thrall to run – but this one had tried. More than once, I suspected, for Klerkon to collar him; Harelip had noted that, too, and thought it strange enough to bring him to me rather than kill him.

'Chained up outside the privy,' Harelip grunted, confirming my thoughts. Fastened like a mad dog, dumped near filth for more punishment.

The boy continued to stare at me. Like a cat, that stare, out of the muck and bruises of his face. Unwavering and strange – then I saw, with a shock, that he had one eye blue-green and one yellow-brown and that was what was strangest in that gaze.

'Klerkon is not here,' offered Ospak, stepping away from the weeping woman, though not without a brief look of regret. Light speared through the badly-daubed walls of the rough hall, dappling the stamped-earth of the floor.

'That much I had worked out,' I answered, glad of the excuse to break away from the boy's eyes and angry at being made so twitched by him. I stepped towards what was Klerkon's private space in the hall, throwing back the curtain of it.

Furs, purest white fox. A cloak with bright-green trim. The frame of a proper box-bed, planked over and thick with good pelts. No chest. No money. No Thordis.

'I am a Northman,' the boy said. A West Norse tongue, stumbling through the Slav he had been forced to speak, stiff with the old misuse of defiant silences.

I turned back into those eyes. He stood, chin up and challenging and, for a moment, reminded me of the Goat Boy as he had been when we found him on Cyprus. About the same age as the Goat Boy was then, I noted. Of course, we had stopped calling him the Goat Boy when he had grown into resenting it – Jon Asanes he was now, being schooled by a trader I knew in Holmgard, which the Slavs call Novgorod.

'I am from Norway and a prince,' the boy added. Throst Silfra gave a loud laugh and those strange eyes swung on him, eagle fierce. I saw Throst quail in an eyeblink, then recover as quickly, also angered at having been so disconcerted by a thrall boy. He moved, lip curled.

'Stay,' I warned and, for a moment, he glowered at me, then lowered his hand and stepped back.

'I AM a prince,' the boy insisted.

'Aye, just so,' thundered Finn, ducking into the middle of all this. 'Wipe the muck off every thrall and they will swear they were pure gold in their own country.'

'A prince of where?' I asked.

The boy stirred uncomfortably. 'Somewhere,' he said, hesitantly. Then, more firmly: 'But my mother was a Princess. She died. So did my *fostri*. Klerkon killed them both.'

'There isn't so much as a bead in this place,' Finn growled, ignoring the boy. 'Klerkon did not return here with his loot, so he must have sailed straight to Aldeigjuborg.'

'The storerooms are full,' Kvasir added, coming in to the hall. 'Winter feed. Honey in pots, seal and deer hides, fox pelts, feathers for pillows, sacks of acorns . . .'

'Feathers,' sneered Finn. 'Fucking acorns . . .'

'Take it, load it,' I said and Kvasir nodded. 'When you have everything, burn this place to the ground. Leave the thralls – they take up too much room and they are not what we came for.'

Kvasir ducked out of the hall, bawling for people to help him; Red Njal came in and glanced at me, then looked away. His knees and hands were clotted with gore where he had knelt to plunder a woman and the bairns he had killed; I had stepped in on him and being watched had shamed him away from the small bodies.

'Is it wise to burn it?' Finn asked.

'Wise?'

'You know Klerkon,' Finn offered. 'Unless we finish him, he will have his revenge. He has already torched Gunnarsgard and half of it was mine – he may decide to kill all the thralls and Thordis with them, out of fury.'

He was right and this was reason enough, as Finn often pointed out, for not owning anything you could not stuff into a sea chest. Yet, outside, I could hear what we had brought to this place, in the screams and the harsh laughter. Humping a dead woman on the flank of a dead ox in the yard was the least of it. I said that, too and we glared at each other.

'Fear the reckoning of those you have wronged,' Red Njal said mournfully and I shot him a savage glance; he, above all, had much to fear, for I suspected the bairns whose blood he had been paddling about in were Klerkon's own.

He saw my look and stiffened, then shrugged.

'The shame you cannot lift you had better let lie, as my granny used to say,' he muttered darkly.

'Happy woman who never saw you guddling in the blood of bairns for what you could steal,' I spat at him and he winced away from it. It was unfair, for others had done worse and none of us were snow-pure.

'I know where Klerkon's gold is,' the boy said. 'I will tell you if you do not fire the steading.'

'If I tickle you with a hot blade you will tell us anyway,' Throst Silfra growled, but the boy's double-coloured eyes never left mine.

'I would have thought you would warm yourself at such a fire,' I said, flicking the iron collar. He flinched.

'The thralls you leave will die without shelter,' he replied. 'It is enough that you take their food. They are not able to run, are not to blame and some are my friends here.'

'Other princes?' chuckled Finn scornfully.

The boy grinned. 'No. But some have been kinder than kings. The free folk here are another matter and I have my own thoughts on that.'

Was he the age he looked? Nine, I had reckoned – but he spoke like someone ten times as old.

'So it is agreed,' I said. 'Show us Klerkon's secret.'

'Lend me your axe,' demanded the boy and Kvasir, after a

moment's narrow-eyed pause, handed it over. The boy weighed it with little bounces of his thin arm, then stepped to the boxbed and swung it, hard. Chips flew.

He swung it again and part of the frame cracked. A coin flew out and smacked on the beaten earth of the floor. Kvasir picked it up, turned it over, bit it. 'Gold, by Odin's arse,' he said. 'A Serkland *dinar* in gold, no less.'

The boy swung again and more chips flew.

'Here, give me that – you need more muscle,' said Runolf Harelip with a grin. The boy handed him the axe and stepped back. Harelip split the bed in two blows and Kvasir, Tjorvir, Throst and the others scrambled to gather the coins that spilled from the hollow frame.

In the end, they filled a sack the size of a the thrall boy's head, all gold coins, most of them Serkland *dinar* with their squiggly markings, each worth, I reckoned it up in my head, about twenty silver *dirham* each. It was as great a loss for Klerkon as it was a gain for us.

The boy stood, unsmiling and straight. I saw that the iron collar was rubbing his skin raw and looked at Kvasir, who had also seen it.

'Ref Steinsson has tools,' he said, 'that can strike that off.'

'Just so,' I said, then turned to the boy, feeling that heart-leap as our eyes met. 'Do you have a name, then, or will we simply call you Prince?'

'Olaf,' said the boy with a frown. 'But Klerkon called me *Craccoben*.'

There was silence. The name squatted in the hall like a raven in a tree. It was a name you gave to a full-cunning man, rich in Odin's rune magic and one who, like him, could sit at the feet of hanged men to hear the whispered secrets of the dead.

Not a name you took or gave lightly and I wondered what had made Klerkon hand it out to this thrall boy.

Crowbone.

FIVE

We came up the coast, running before a freezing wind until we had found the narrow mouth of the river we sought and had to drop sail or risk running aground.

We all groaned, for we would have to row upriver now and crew light at that. It was a heavy, lumbering beast of a ship when there were not even enough men on benches for one oar shift, never mind two.

I sweated with the others, which at least took my mind off the boy, who had been cooed over by Thorgunna the minute she had set eyes on him. Ref had deftly struck off the iron collar and Thorgunna had at once started to wash and salve the sores it had made on his neck – not to mention the ones on his head, which showed where he had been shaved by ungentle hands. Old, white scars showed that such a razoring had not been his first and she tutted and crooned at him.

Finn, grinning and happy now that he was raiding and getting money out of it rather than feathers and acorns, gave Kvasir a nudge where he sat, in front of Finn and pulling hard to the stroke.

'You have been hung up like old breeks, Spittle,' he chuckled, nodding to where Thorgunna was wrapping the boy in a warm cloak and patting him. I wondered if she would croon quite so softly when she found out the whole story of what he had done, what he had urged hard men to do back there in Svartey.

The wind hissed, the skin of the river crinkled and the thrall women huddled, blowing into chapped, cupped hands, but none of that was as cold as the dead we rowed away from.

'It seems,' Kvasir agreed, grunting the words out between pulls, 'that I brought back a treasure greater than my share of those *dinar* coins, which I plan to make into a necklace for her.'

'She's broody as an old hen. You will have to bairn that one and soon,' agreed Finn, which left Kvasir silent and moody.

There was a flash behind my eyes of the fat limbs and round little belly, fish-white and so small it made Thorkel's blood-smeared hand look massive. The bud-mouth and wide, outraged blue eyes crinkling in bawls in a red face while, somewhere off to the right and pinioned, the mother screamed.

Crowbone had glared at her with savage triumph, then looked back to Thorkel and nodded; Thorkel hurled the bairn against a stone and the bawling ended in a wet slap and the mother's even louder screams. And I watched, doing nothing, saying less.

What had she done to Crowbone? He would not say, save that she was one of Randr Sterki's women, so the bairn was his and hers. Most probably she had been less than kind to him – perhaps even the one who shaved him so cruelly. There was no point in trying to stop the shrieking, bloody mess he had fermented, so that the mother's death soon after was almost a mercy.

Aye, he was a strange one, that boy. Afterwards, men could scarce look each other in the eye for what they had done, though they were no strangers to hard raiding and red war. Yet there had been something slimed about what he had driven them to do that left even these ashamed.

If it was not unmanly *seidr* he had unleashed, it was a close cousin and further proof of his powers came when we ran up to the river mouth, slashing through the ice-grue water, Gizur looking this way and that, cupping the sides of his eyes with his cold-split red hands, looking for the signs that would tell us where land lay in the mist.

Then the boy had stood up and pointed. 'That way,' he said.

There were chuckles and a few good-natured jibes at Gizur. Then Pai, the lookout, shouted out that there was smoke.

'No,' said the boy, certain as sunrise. 'It is not smoke. Those are birds.'

So it was, a great wheeling mass of them. Terns, said the boy, before even sharp-eyed Pai could spot whether they were terns or gannet.

'How do you know that?' demanded Hauk Fast-Sailor.

'You can hear them,' said the boy. 'They are calling each other to the feast, shouting with delight. Herring are there, too, if you want to fish.'

He was right – terns were diving and feeding furiously and it was easy to follow them to where Gizur picked up the marks for steering to the mouth of the Neva and into Lake Ladoga, where we turned south on the Volkhov river.

By that time, of course, the men were silent and grim around a boy who could hear birds and knew what they said and was called Crowbone. He reminded me of Sighvat and when I mentioned it, Finn and Kvasir agreed.

'Perhaps he is Sighvat's son,' Finn offered and we fell silent, remembering our old oarmate and his talk of what birds and bees did. Remembering, too, him lying in the dusty street of a filthy Serkland village with the gaping red smile of his cut throat attracting the flies.

By the time the dark rushed us on our first day's pull upriver to Aldeigjuborg, we were still too far away to risk going on, so headed to the bank. Cookfires were lit and the awning stretched on deck, so that we ate ashore and slept aboard.

Kvasir, Finn and I, sitting together as usual, talked about the boy and wondered. Kvasir said Thorgunna was good at finding things out and would listen while she and the boy talked.

All of us agreed, half-laughing at ourselves, that little Prince Olaf was a strange child. Finn half-joked that it was just as well we had kept to our bargain and left the thralls alive, for he looked like a dangerous child to cross.

I did not think it a laughing moment, for we had killed all the freeborn there, wives and weans – even the dogs – of Klerkon and his crew. That little nine-year-old boy had taken his revenge on everyone who had done him wrong, so that he was red-dyed to the elbows with his hate, even if others had done the slaughter.

Thorgunna bustled up not long after, looking for the same strange child and fretting about him being alone in the dark on an unknown shore, so we all had to turn out and look for him.

He turned up after an hour, sauntering out of the shadows so silently that Thorkel nearly burned his own hair off jumping with fright with a torch in his hand.

'Where were you?' demanded Thorgunna and those two-coloured eyes, both reddening in the torch glow, turned on her.

'Listening to the owls talk about the hunting,' he said.

'Was it good for them?' chuckled Finn and the boy shook his head, serious as a stone pillar.

'Too cold,' he said and walked to the fire, leaving us trailing in his wake, stunned and thoughtful.

'Here,' said Thorgunna sharply, thrusting something at him. 'Play this and stay by the fire. It will keep you out of mischief.'

It was a tafl board and some polished stones for it in a bag. Men chuckled, but the boy took the wooden board politely enough and laid it beside him.

'It is too dark to play,' he said, 'but I know a story about a tafl board, which I will tell.'

Men blinked and rubbed their beards. This was new – a boy of nine was going to tell all of us full-grown a story; Kvasir laughed out loud at the delight of it.

The boy cleared his throat and began, in a strong, clear, piping little voice. And all those hard axe men leaned forward to listen.

'Once a man in a steading in Vestfold carved a beautiful tafl board for his son,' the boy began. 'He made it from oak, which is Thor wood. When he was finished he showed his son how to play games upon it. The boy was very glad to have such a beautiful thing and in the morning, when he went out with the sheep up to the tree-bare hills where they grazed, he took his tafl board along, for he could always get stones as counters for it.'

The boy paused and the men leaned forward further. He had them now, better than any skop. I marvelled at the *seidr* spell he wove round the fire, even as I was wary of it. How did he know this story? It was certain Klerkon never tucked him in at night with such tales and his foster-father had died when he was young. Maybe his mother had, before she turned her head to the wall.

'Everywhere he went he carried his board under his arm,' the boy went on. 'Then, one day, he met some men from the next village up, making charcoal around a small fire. "Where in this country of yours can a man get wood?" the charcoal burners asked. "Why, here is wood," the boy said. And he gave them the fine tafl board, which they put into the fire. As it went up in flames, the boy began to cry. "Do not make such fash," the charcoal burners said, and they gave him a fine new seax in place of the game board.'

'That was a good trade,' growled Red Njal from out of the shadows. 'A boy will get more use from a good seax than a tafl board. That and the forest is the best teacher for a boy, as my granny used to say.'

They shushed him and Olaf shifted to be more comfortable.

'The boy took the knife and went away with his sheep,' he went on. 'As he wandered he came to a place where a man was digging a big stone out of his field, so that he could

67

plough it. "The ground is hard," the man said. "Lend me your seax to dig with." The boy gave the man the seax, but the man dug so vigorously with it that it broke. "Ah, what has become of my knife?" the boy wailed. "Quiet yourself," the man said. "Take this spear in its place." And he gave the boy a beautiful spear, trimmed with silver and copper.'

A few chuckled, seeing where the story was going and others asked where a farmer who could not afford a decent shovel got a silver-trimmed spear – but they were quickly silenced by the others.

'The boy went away with his sheep and his spear,' little Olaf continued. 'He met a party of hunters. When they saw him one of them said: "Lend me your spear, so that we may kill the deer we are trailing." So the boy did.'

'Piss poor hunters,' muttered Kvasir, 'without a spear between them.'

Thorgunna glared her worst glare at him.

'Oho,' chuckled Finn. 'There's a look to sink ships. This is why you should not take a wife out on the vik.'

Kvasir scowled. Olaf waited patiently, until they subsided, then cleared his throat again. In the dark, his one pale eye caught the fire and flashed like pearl.

'The boy gave them the spear and the hunters went out and killed the deer. But in the hunt the shaft of the spear was splintered. "See what you've done with my spear!" the boy cried. "Don't fuss about it," the hunter said. "Here is a horse for you in place of your spear."

'The hunter gave him a horse with fine leather trappings and he started back toward the village. On the way he came to where some farmers were keeping crows off their rye, running at them and waving sheets. This made the horse frightened and it ran away.'

'This sounds like the story of my life,' growled Thorkel from across the fire and everyone laughed, for they had heard of his lack of luck.

Finn bellowed at them to shut up and listen. 'For I want to hear this. This sheep-herding boy seems much like a trader I know.'

There were some chuckles at my expense, then the story went on.

'The horse had gone for good,' Olaf said. 'But the farmers told the boy not to worry. They gave the boy an old wood axe and he took it and went on towards his home. He came to a woodcutter who said: "Lend me your large axe for this tree. Mine is too small." So the boy did and the woodcutter chopped with it and broke it.'

'He should have quit and gone home when he had the horse,' shouted someone.

Olaf smiled. 'Perhaps so, for the woodcutter gave him the limb of a tree, which he then had to load on his back and carry. When he came near the village a woman said: "Where did you find the wood? I need it for my fire."

'The boy gave it to her, and she put it in the fire. As it went up in flames he said: "Now where is my wood?" The woman looked around, then gave him a fine tafl board, which he took home with the sheep.

'As he entered his house his mother smiled with satisfaction and said: "What is better than a tafl board to keep a small boy out of trouble?"'

The roars and leg slapping went on a long time, especially when Olaf, with a courtly little bow, handed the tafl board and bag of counters back to Thorgunna, who took it, beaming with as much delight as if she was mother to this princeling.

Into the middle of this, his breath smoking with cold and reeking of porridge and fish as he leaned closer to my ear, Kvasir hissed: 'That boy is not nine years old.'

I stepped off a *strug*, one of those blocky riverboats the Slavs love so much, on to the wooden wharf of Novgorod, which we call Holmgard. I had been here before, so it felt almost like a home.

We had taken the *strug* from Aldeigjuborg, since it had been a hard enough task to work the *Elk* along the river to that place, never mind to Novgorod. My lungs had burned in the cold with the effort and, for days afterwards, my shoulders felt as if someone had shoved a red-hot bar from one side to the other. I was, I admitted ruefully to myself, no longer used to pulling on an oar.

The weather did not help. Gizur, when the *Elk* had edged painfully into the mouth of the river on which Aldeigjuborg stood, heaved the slop bucket over the side and hauled it in. He looked briefly, then shoved it at me. Ice rolled.

'I did not need that to tell me how cold it is,' I said, blowing on my hands. He nodded and emptied the water, then set the bucket in its place with red-blue hands, already studded with sores. Everyone had them, split from the cold and the rowing. Noses were scarlet; breath smoked and the air was sharp enough to sting your throat.

'Too early for such ice,' Gizur growled. 'By a month at least. The river is freezing and this close to the sea, too. The sea will freeze for a good way out this winter, mark me.'

That thought had floated with us all the way to the berth, bringing little cheer. No sooner had we lashed ourselves to the land than Finn and Kvasir, swathed in cloaks and wrapped to the ears in *wadmal* and hats, came up and nodded in the direction of another *drakkar*, snugged up to the bank and with it's mast off, the sail tented up across the deck, which spoke of an over-wintering. Klerkon's ship, *Dragon Wings*. Two men all wild hair and silver arm rings watchfully tended a box-brazier of charcoals on the mid-ballast stones.

'Small crew only,' Kvasir reported after a brief open-handed saunter in their direction. They had seen us and were guarded after events in Gunnarsgard, though it was not a sensible thing to start swinging swords in someone else's realm. What would happen when they learned what we had done on Svartey was another matter entirely.

'Klerkon has gone south to Konugard,' he added, cocking his head in that bird way he had these days.

'He will have taken his captives,' Finn said, almost cheerfully. 'They will sell better in that place.'

I scowled at him, while Kvasir said nothing. I knew why Finn was so joyous – he was out on the raid and expected to winter in Novgorod and then head off in the spring to find the mountain of silver he thought we had left alone too long.

I was hoping that it would be a long winter and that, at the end of it, Sviatoslav, Prince of the Rus, would renew his mad fight against the Great City and make it too dangerous to travel south of Konugard, which the locals called Kiev. I was hoping those events had trapped Lambisson with Short Eldgrim and Cod-Biter.

I also knew I was Odin-cursed with this mountain of silver. It was like being in a thorn patch – the harder you struggled, the worse you were caught. Sooner or later, I was thinking day after day, I would have to go back to Atil's howe and every time the thought came to me it was like swallowing a stone.

But first there was Thordis to get back and Eldgrim and Cod-Biter to rescue.

We stayed long enough in Aldeigjuborg to find that Lambisson, if he had been there at all, was long gone. We stayed a little longer, to stand by the Oathsworn Stone which Einar had raised to those we had lost getting this far on the original journey down to seek Atil's treasure.

Six years since and now the survivors of that time stood round it, a mere handful and a half – Hauk, Gizur, Finn, Kvasir, Hlenni Brimill, Runolf Harelip, Red Njal and me. Thorkel stood with us, for he had known Pinleg and Skapti Halftroll and the others the stone remembered but he had not been with us at the time. Crippled Cod-Biter and the addled

Short Eldgrim were two more and we remembered on their behalf.

'Someone has been,' Kvasir noted, nodding at the garland of withered oak leaves fluttering on the stone's crown.

Not for a long time. Yet the names were there and, though the paint had faded, the grooves were etched deep on the stone and the story was there still. We made our prayers and small offerings and left.

Finn thought the garland might have been left by Pinleg's woman, who had stayed in the town with her son and daughter. When we went to where they had been, those who had known them told us they had left for the south long since. I remembered, then, that Pinleg's wife had been a Slav, his children half-Norse *Rus*.

Only the stone was left, where the wind traced the grooves of all their names.

The *Elk* stayed in Aldeigjuborg with everybody on it save me, Finn, Kvasir and Thorgunna – and Crowbone, who trembled and scowled and stared at *Dragon Wings* and the men he saw there. I did not want him starting trouble and hoped Gizur had enough men to keep the *Elk* safe, but it would be a dangerous time, even berthed as far from *Dragon Wings* as we could get and both sides leashed by what would happen if we started in to killing each other in Sviatoslav's kingdom.

I had thought of taking the *Elk* down to Novgorod but was glad I had not as we were poled along the cold river, through the dripping fir and pine forests where people still struggled to work the hacked-out clearings using their strange little three-toothed ploughs. The Volkhov seemed even more swirling and treacherous with currents than I remembered from sailing it with Einar.

It seemed all marsh and fish to me this time, an ugly place when the trees were stripped to claws. Further south was where the good black steppe earth was, the stuff the Slavs call *chernoziom* and so rich you need plough it just the once and, after letting it fallow for a few years, harvest wheat a number of times without tillage.

'Aye, poor land, this,' decided Red Njal. 'And what are they doing boiling water in those huge pans?'

'Salt,' grunted Kvasir. 'There is water here from springs and it is salt as the sea.'

'Not a bad trick at all,' noted Ospak. 'Selling people boiled sea water.'

It was his first visit and everything was new.

'Just so,' chuckled Finn. 'So you see we are richer aboard the *Elk* even than Kvasir Spittle here, for we are always floating in the stuff.'

Everyone laughed, while Kvasir ignored them, punching careful holes in his share of the gold *dinar* coins, making his necklace for Thorgunna. For her part, she still sat fussing over Crowbone, who now had a tow fuzz under the healing scabs. It was also clear that we could hardly treat him as a thrall, no matter what he was, so I went to him as we climbed aboard the *strug*.

'Prince you may be, or you may not,' I said, while a knowing Thorgunna beamed, 'but free you can be, for sure.'

I held out my hand. He blinked those marvellous eyes at me, then grinned and took my wrist in his own small grip.

Later, when we were sliding between the green banks, poled by chanting Krivichi rivermen, Kvasir came to me with what he and Thorgunna had coaxed from this little Prince.

'He says,' Kvasir told me, speaking low, 'that he was with his mother and staying with his grandfather and his foster-father, whom he knew as Old Thorolf. He was hunted by men, that much he knows, for his mother warned him always of it. They were hiding in this place, which he cannot remember the name of, for he was three when they fled it, heading, he says, for Novgorod. He has an uncle here, or so his mother told him, but does not know his name. They were coming to this uncle when they ran out of luck.'

I thought on it, rolling it over and over like a new coin in my head while Kvasir looked at me, his one good eye dulled as a dying fish in the growing twilight.

'Klerkon took him? Or bought him from someone else?'

Kvasir frowned, getting the story straight.

'Took him. Killed the foster-father right off. The boy remembers him doing it, saying Thorolf was too old and pitching him into the sea to drown.'

'The mother?'

Kvasir shrugged. 'I think she died later. He knows more but either will not or cannot say more. Only that she died on Svartey.'

Probably under Klerkon, I thought moodily.

'Anything else?'

Kvasir shrugged. 'He knows the names of his mother, father and grandfather, but he will not say them. I think his mother made him swear it. Which is not a surprise if men are hunting you – a closed mouth keeps you hidden.'

There was something here half-buried. I felt like someone who finds a ring in the dirt and knows if he gives it a hard enough tug it will unearth the whole glorious oathing-sword whose hilt it is attached to.

We were silent again, then Kvasir shook his head, bemused.

'We are in a saga here,' he declared. 'A hunted prince, captured by raiders. Sold to slavery and rescued by the Bear Slayer and the Oathsworn – if that boy doesn't end up a great man, then I am no reader of the Norn's weave.'

'Read less of his Norn-weave and more of our own,' I answered. 'Let's hope there is not a thread in it that winds his greatness round our doom.'

That thought occupied both of us all the way to where the *strug* tied up to the wharf at Novgorod. Then the Norns showed us what they had weaved so far and Odin's laughter was louder still.

SIX

The great walled fortress of Novgorod, with its central keep – the Slavs call them *kreml* and *detinets* – was a formidable affair even in those early days, before it was rebuilt in stone. All sharpened wood and earthworks, it glowered above the town like a stern father.

Inside, it was then and is now, as snug as a turf-roofed Iceland hall, with fine hangings and sable furs and such – but it also has a stinking pit prison, all filth and sweating rock walls and meant for the likes of the ragged-arse Krivichi, Goliads and Slovenes, not decent Norse like us.

The *druzhina* guards didn't see it that way at all when they pitched us in, jeering and pointing out that no-one climbed out who was not destined either to be nailed upside down or staked.

We were all there – me, Finn, Kvasir, Jon Asanes, Thorgunna, Thordis, two thrall women who gabbled in some strange tribe tongue and Olaf who, for all his defiant chin, was trembling, both at what might happen and at the fact he had killed his first man.

In the dark, chill and crushing as a tomb, our ragged breathing was all that told me anyone was there at all and yet it seemed to me that there were shapes, blacker shadows in the dark, shifting and moving. I felt them, as I had felt them the night of the fox-fires back in the stables in Hestreng; the restless dead, come to look and leach the last warmth of life from someone about to join them. Aye, and gloat, too, perhaps.

The day started well enough, when we had made our way over the great split-log walkways, greasy with soft mirr and age, to the Gotland quarter where the Norse trading houses sat. I was seeking Jon Asanes, known to us as The Goat Boy.

Eventually we found Tvorimir, into whose care we had handed The Goat Boy to be taught how to trade, deal with sharp men and read and write birch-bark accounts. Tvorimir, it was generally agreed, was the best for this, since he was nicknamed Soroka – Magpie – for his attraction to anything even vaguely sheened.

His house, of the better sort called an *izba*, was like a steading hall dropped into a town, arranged on three sides around a courtyard, with stables, storage for hay and grain and one of the bath houses they liked so much. Instead of a pitfire, it had a clay oven in one corner, which was a fine thing.

He looked less like a magpie than a fat fussing hen, a man built, as Kvasir noted, in a pile of circles, from the ones which made his fat legs, to the one that made his belly and the little red one framed with a puff of white hair that made his head.

After we had been hugged and backslapped, been given bread and salt and ale from the cellar, he puffed himself to a wooden bench near the big clay oven and shook his head at the mention of Jon Asanes.

'Quick and clever that one,' he told me. 'Works well, too – when he can be fastened to it. Has taken to writing, but not for accounts.'

He paused, shut one eye and laid a finger along his nose. 'Love verse,' he said and laughed, an alarming effect of wheeze and wobble. He rolled his eyes heavenward and intoned: 'What fire in my heart and my body and my soul for you and your body and your person, let it set fire to your heart and your body and your soul for me and for my body and for my person.'

'Tyr's bones,' breathed Finn, half admiring, half disgusted.

'We have arrived just in time, it seems,' Kvasir declared.

'You should write such for me,' declared Thorgunna, nudging Kvasir, who looked shocked at the very idea, then grinned.

'Happily, I am unable to read or write, save a bit of rune here and there. And now that I am down to one eye, I will not risk straining it on such.'

'Then whisper me such things instead,' countered Thorgunna, while Tvorimir closed one eye reflectively and said nothing. He was well-travelled was Magpie, but he was more Slav than Swede and, like all of them, knew women had their place. As all Slavs will tell you, a chicken is not a bird, as a woman is not a person – but they do not say it around a prow-built woman from the vik.

'Where is Jon Asanes?' I asked and Tvorimir arranged his blackened teeth into a smile.

'At the Yuriev Monastery,' he declared and did his wobble and wheeze laugh again at our faces.

'It used to be a salt-maker's yard,' he added, 'until some Bulgar monks arrived from a place called Ohrid with their White Christ and Greek ways. The young Prince Vladimir is interested in such things. It is useful, for they owe me and I can get the boy taught to write Latin and Greek.'

It made good sense, for Jon Asanes was a Christ-follower from the island of Cyprus, where his mother still lived – if she still lived – and of the Greek style, too. He had done us a service on Cyprus and we had brought him away with us but, for all we had become his family, the gods of Asgard had made no headway in him.

'He spends all his time with the Greeks there – priests and

lay brothers, mainly, as well as merchants from the Great City,' Tvorimir continued. 'He learns a deal, but it has to be said that he prefers their ways to ours. He is pestering me to send him to the Great City, which he insists on calling Constantinople and tells me I am a barbarian for saying it is Miklagard, or even just the Great City.'

'Ach – young Pai is just the same,' Thorgunna offered. 'Young men coming to manhood are always fretting with opinions on this and that.'

Which was true enough and seemed an end of the matter. I should have paid it more attention, but had more to think about, so we sat and talked, of Jon's health – good, considering he was olive-skinned and practically a Serklander, none of whom cared for the ice and snow – and trade and Sviatoslav's mad war with the Great City that made it impossible.

Tvorimir asked if we wanted to use his bath house, at which Kvasir choked on his ale and Finn gave the Slav merchant a look to strip the gilding off his house's fancy carvings. We were good Norsemen and, unlike the filth of the Franks and Saxlanders and Livs and Ests, were not against washing most weeks – though, in winter, you tend to be sensible about such things.

Rus bathing was another matter altogether. I have seen these people at their baths, which they heat fiercely, then go into naked and pour some sort of oil over themselves, then beat themselves with young twigs until they stagger out, half dead.

After that, they pour cold water over themselves. They do this every day, without being forced, in order to bathe and not as any strange personal torment. Even the Greek-Romans of the Great City are not as vicious at getting clean.

Instead, we idled round the clay oven, picking salt out of the elegantly-carved little throne of a salt holder, sprinkling it on good bread and drinking. We talked of people we knew and what fish were plentiful in the Ilmen and, because it led to it from there, argued about how many rivers flowed into that lake – fifty-two, we counted in the end, though only one, the Volkhov, flowed out and down to Kiev.

It was pleasant talk and easily turned to the trade in slaves and who was doing it and whether they had any new ones.

Frowning, Tvorimir said: 'Late in the year for it. The Ilmen is freezing early and soon you will not get a boat out the mouth of the Volkhov south. If your slaves are from the north, you will be looking to go south. The only dealer still in Novgorod who is still planning to go south is Takoub.'

Finn grunted and we all shifted a little. Takoub we knew well, because he was the one who had bought our oarmates as slaves some years before, when we had thought them snugged up in Novgorod while Einar led the rest of us in search of Atil's secret tomb and the silver in it.

We had annoyed Sviatoslav doing it and he had seized our men and sold them to Takoub, who had sold them to an emir in Serkland. Those of us left after Einar had died had the unpleasant task of going after them, among other matters and it had been on that journey we had found the Goat Boy.

We were still in the memory of it when the lad himself arrived, blasting in the cold air and a smile that warmed us all. He glowed and beamed and was wrapped in bearhugs by Kvasir and buried in Finn's beard, both at the same time, until all three broke apart, faces twisted.

'Fauugh, you stink.'

'Is that perfume, boy?'

They looked at each other and all of us burst out laughing. Of course Jon Asanes would be clean, washed and perfumed, for he was Greek and had been three years away from the honest sweaty wool and fish smell of us from the north. So far away it wrinkled his nose now, even as Finn wrinkled his nose at the sweet-smelling boy.

All the same, we clasped forearms as old friends and I felt

the leap of my heart at that – him, too, I fancied, from the look in his eyes. He had grown from the skinny boy with only a dozen years on him and his tangled black curls were combed and oiled and fell to the shoulders of the white shirt he wore over sea-green breeks.

'Is that a beard?' demanded Finn and Jon Asanes, laughing and blushing, batted the gnarled and filthy hand which was trying to feel his chin. Little Olaf watched it all with interest, saying nothing.

'Either you flew,' Jon said, looping a leg over a bench as if it were a horse and pouring ale, 'or my message to you is still sailing.'

'What message?' grunted Kvasir, then was nudged by Thorgunna into making introductions. Jon Asanes had been told of Kvasir's marriage, but this was his first meeting with Thorgunna and everyone could see she was dazzled by him. It was hard not to be for, with a youth's summers on him, The Goat Boy now had a breadth of chest and a slender waist and a bright and even smile that was always echoed in his dark eyes.

Then Olaf stepped up, having to look up to Jon Asanes, who now had some height on him, too. Jon was, I realized as I watched him and Olaf study each other, about the same age now as I was when we had met on Cyprus and called him Goat Boy. Yet, with less than a handful of years between us, I felt old enough to be the Goat Boy's grandfather.

'You smell nice,' said Olaf. 'Not like a man, though. Like a flower.'

Jon Asanes astounded me and showed how much he had learned about dealing with traders, for he didn't bristle at this, as I expected from someone of his age. Instead, he grinned.

'You smell like fish dung,' he countered. 'And your eyes cannot make up their minds on colour.'

They stared for a moment longer, then Olaf laughed with genuine delight and you could see the pair of them were friends already.

'The message?' I asked and Jon Asanes smiled a last smile at little Olaf and turned to me, a storm gathering on his brow.

'I sent it awhiles since, by a Gotland trader,' he said and looked sideways at me. 'An old friend is arrived,' he added. 'He is staying with Christ-followers in the German quarter. I say friend, but I doubt if it is true.'

He paused and looked at me, then the others.

'I did not tell Tvorimir,' he added, 'since it was a matter best kept between few, I was thinking.'

I felt the chill then and it was nothing to do with draughts from the door. Magpie caught my eye and slapped a grin on his red face.

'I will go if you like,' he said, but I shook my head; I trusted Tvorimir – well, as much as I trusted any trader – and, besides, we had few friends in this part of the world. Instead, I turned to Jon Asanes and asked, though I already knew the answer.

'Who?'

'Martin, the monk, with news for you, he says.'

'Odin's eye,' growled Finn. 'That name again, like a strange turd in your privy. I thought he had died.'

'Not yet,' Jon answered with a grin, 'though he looks much like a corpse.'

'I had thought to have seen the last of him in Serkland,' Kvasir admitted. Thorgunna, who had heard some of this, kept quiet and Magpie, who was bemused by all of it, looked from one to the other, demanding explanations.

'What does he want?' I asked and, again, I already knew the answer – his holy spear, which I had in my sea chest, wrapped in sealskin. Jon Asanes confirmed it.

'In exchange,' he went on, 'he says he will give you news worth the value of it to you.'

'I doubt that,' muttered Finn, 'for he was ever as slippery as a fresh-caught herring.'

They tossed the tale of it between them for Magpie's benefit – how Martin, the German monk, had stumbled on the secret of Attila's treasure and been forced to reveal it by Einar, so putting all the Oathsworn on the hard road to that cursed hoard.

Martin, though, had only ever wanted one thing – the holy spear he swore was the one the Old Romans had thrust into the side of his Christ and whose iron point had been used in forging two sabres for Attila. They had been buried with him – and I had brought one of them out of the tomb.

I sat and listened to them chewing on it, though I already knew Martin and I would have to meet. I had no use for his Christ icon and had simply picked it up from the body of the man who had stolen it – but never throw away anything that might be of use, my old foster-mother Halldis had dinned into me.

'You know where Martin is?' I asked into the middle of their conversation, killing it. Jon Asanes nodded.

'Where is best to meet?' I asked. It would be better in a public place, this first one, for Martin was a man easy to dislike and somehow sparked me to anger like no other. I had almost killed him once and there were times since I wished I had.

Jon nodded, knowing all this. 'The Perun likeness,' he said. 'Everyone uses it as a landmark and it is in the marketplace.'

I knew it well – you could not miss the great oak pillar on its mound of concentric circles, the top carved in the shape of a powerful warrior carrying an axe and with a head of silver and moustaches of gold. Perun, the Slav god of storms, who was as like Thor as to be his brother. I nodded.

We laid out the tale of what had happened to us thus far and Jon sucked it in as if it was no more than air, nodding and silent. At the end of it, he blew out his cheeks, stuffed bread in his mouth and rose from the bench.

'We will start with Martin, then,' he said simply and slammed out, dragging a warm cloak in his wake.

'Bloody boy goes everywhere at a run,' complained Magpie.

'He will learn when he gets to our age,' grunted Kvasir, 'the truth of the old bull.'

We chuckled, while Thorgunna scowled. Magpie was too Slav to have heard this tale, so Finn took great delight in telling him, because it outraged Thorgunna that he did.

'Let us not run down and hump one of the heifers,' Finn finished, in his role of the old bull advising his eager son. 'Let us walk gently down and hump them all.'

So we laughed and argued the rest of that morning, in the warm of Magpie's *izba*, until Jon Asanes returned and said, simply: 'Nones'.

I told them it was Latin for the way Christ-priests from the west judge the day – late afternoon, by which time it would growing dark.

'We will keep a sharper eye open then,' Finn said cheerfully, 'in case he has found people stupid enough to try and take what he wants.'

I thought it unlikely, for he knew I wouldn't bring the holy spear with me. Better for Finn to go with Kvasir and Thorgunna, who were taking Olaf to buy him new clothes.

'You might need someone to help you string Martin up,' Finn growled moodily, 'while you use the Truth Knife on him to get what he knows. He is no stranger to it, after all.'

I shook my head, while the flash of memory, like lightning on a darkened sea, flared up the scene – Martin, swinging like a trussed goose from the mast of Einar's *Elk*, spraying blood and green snot as Einar hacked off the monk's little finger and threw it over the side. Einar's magic Truth Knife, which, he told victims, knew when someone lied and would cut off a piece every time they did. It was now sheathed in the small of my back and I had used it once or twice myself. Most did not keep their secrets beyond two fingers.

Shrugging at my folly, Finn strode off after Thorgunna, Kvasir and Olaf, leaving me with Jon Asanes, who rolled his eyes towards the sky.

'I have not seen Finn for some years,' he said. 'He seems even wilder than he was before.'

'As you say,' I countered, 'you have not seen him for some years. You have just forgotten how he is.'

Even though I knew it was a lie.

We were silent, pushing through the throng on the wooden walkways of the city while the sky pewtered and the rain spat itself to sleet.

'You seem . . . older,' Jon Asanes said eventually, as we stopped to watch an army of carters manhandle a huge brass bell, almost as big as a small house, destined for the *kreml* over the Volkhov Bridge. They love their bells, do the Slavs of Novgorod and Kiev and ring them on every ceremonial they can think of.

I said nothing. We crossed behind the sweating, shouting men, to where the great statue of Perun, offerings littering his feet, towered over the marketplace.

'I know what it is,' Jon said suddenly, stopping me to look into my face.

'What?'

'Why you seem older,' he said and grinned. 'You do not smile now,' he added.

I gave him one to make him a liar; but he shook his head and forked two fingers at his eyes.

'You can do it with your mouth,' he said, 'but not here.'

He was right and I scowled at him for being so, while being proud of him at the same time. I never had a chance to say anything more on it, for I saw a figure who made my belly curl.

He walked with a staff, wore a ragged brown robe which ended at his knees, yet trailed strips in the mud and flapped uneven dags wetly round his shins. Under it, he wore heavy woollen breeks, which might have been blue once. He had shoes, new and heavy – a gift, probably, from his German Christ worshippers – and leg-bindings filthy enough to have come from a corpse-winding.

It was his eyes that told me who it was and they were all that could be seen in the thicket of his face. His beard was long and matted into his hair, which hung below his shoulders – but his eyes, on either side of a nose like a curved dagger, were still the dark ones I remembered, though the calculating look had gone from them, burned away by his obsession. Now they looked like the eyes of a pole-sitter, one of those crazed hermits who go out into the wilderness and perch in high places.

Martin.

When I had first seen the little monk, in Birka years before, he wore a similar brown robe, but clean and neat and tied with a pale rope. He slippered over polished floors in soft shoes, though he wore sensible heavy wool socks against the cold. His face then was sharp, smooth, clean-shaven enough to reflect lantern-light, his brown hair cut the same length all round, shaved carefully in the middle.

His God was not treating him lightly.

'Orm,' he rasped, the all too familiar voice making my insides turn over. He leaned on his staff, both hands clasping it. I saw his nails were short, broken and black-rimmed, saw the maimed stump of his little finger. When he tried a smile, I wished he had not, for all it revealed was the mess of his mouth, smashed somewhere on his journey and the teeth left to blacken and rot.

'Martin,' I answered.

'You have grown and prospered,' he said.

'You have not.'

'I am rich in God.'

'If that is all you have to exchange for your holy stick, we can end this now.'

He leaned further forward, so tense his beard seemed to curl. Everything quivered, even his voice. 'You have it?'

'I have it. I took it from Sigurd Heppni in Serkland. He no longer had need of it, since Finn had cut his life away. A bad joke on Sigurd, to be called Heppni.'

He did not smile, though I knew he had enough Norse to understand that '*heppni*' meant 'lucky'.

'I must have it,' was all he said, those dark eyes glittering.

Jon shifted slightly, anxious to join in with a few choice insults, but aware that I would be annoyed if he did. Around us, the marketplace of Novgorod heaved with life, buying and selling, shifting with furs and green clay pots and amber and offerings laid at the feet of Perun – yet it seemed that there was a circle round us three and, inside it, we were unseen, unapproached.

When I did not answer, Martin blinked like a lizard and grinned his rotting grin. 'I see you have a heathen sign on you, as always. Odin's sign. Swear on it that you will give me what I seek when I tell you what I know.'

'No great bargain for me there. I have no wish to know how to feed a multitude with a loaf and a herring, even if I believed you knew the trick of it. Mind you, if you know the way to turn water into wine . . .'

That harsh voice interrupted me. 'Judge for yourself. My secret concerns an old enemy and a tomb packed with silver.' And then he said simply, 'Brondolf Lambisson is the old enemy.'

When the dig of that did not make me flinch as he had hoped he narrowed his eyes.

'Brondolf went back to Birka,' I said, as casually as I could, as if the man meant nothing to me now.

Martin saw it and nodded.

'Ja, Birka. Where else would he go? He sat there, watching the place die round him and desperate for something to save it. He failed; Birka is a town of empty doorways and crumbling timbers. Brondolf went to Hedeby, following the trade. When he found two Oathsworn he knew there, he must have thought the hand of God was in it – if he hadn't been a Hell-damned pagan.'

'So? What did he hope to gain?' I snarled, knowing full well.

'The secret of Atil's tomb, of course.'

'Cod-Biter couldn't find his arse with both hands and Short Eldgrim is . . .'

'Eldgrim,' repeated Martin, as if tasting the name. 'The little one with the scars on his face, ja?' He had become more German these days.

'He is addled,' I said and Martin agreed with a nod.

'Which is why Lambisson came to me,' he answered. 'He thought I owed him a debt, thought that I might know a way into Eldgrim's head. He had some of it from Cod-Biter, enough to let him know that this Eldgrim knew more.'

Now the gaff of it took me under the chin and made me jerk and Martin saw it. Aye, Eldgrim knew some of it. Me, who could speak Latin and Greek, had no better knowledge of runes than a bairn. Who else could I have asked to help carve the secret on that sword hilt but the man who, of all the Oathsworn left on the steppe then, made the least mistakes with runes?

A sore dunt in a fight in Serkland had left him addled. I wished I was sure his mind was washed clean of the secret, but his thought-cage was a strange place now, where he could sometimes recall old events as if they had happened the day before and yet forget everything that happened an hour ago.

'You could not help Lambisson,' I said flatly to the monk, more hopeful than sure.

Martin grinned his rotted grin. 'He persuaded me to do my best. He smashed all the teeth in my mouth and gave me healthy bowls of tough meat, which I could only suck. Until I managed to free something from Eldgrim's mouth, nothing would pass my own that I could eat.'

There was clever and vicious in it, but it was only another little Truth Knife when all said and done. I said as much and he glanced at the stump of his finger, remembering. It was a nasty lash from me, born of fear for Eldgrim and Cod-Biter and should not have been done, for he had an answer to it and more.

'I am alive. I ate.'

I was silent, the words penned up in me and my mouth locked.

'And Short Eldgrim?' I managed after a struggle.

Martin twisted his face in what was now the parody of a sneer. 'Alive. He and I raked through his mind and came up with just enough, when added to what Cod-Biter was persuaded to recall. But Lambisson took them both when he went to Sarkel.'

That name made me twitch and Martin's black grin grew even wider. Not for the first time I wished I had killed him when I had had the chance.

'And he let you go?' I managed scornfully, as if that fact made his tale no more than a confection for children.

'No,' he answered simply. 'He needed me, too. I took myself away at the first chance.'

Aye, he would have done that. Martin had many skills, but his greatest was the ability to vanish.

'He has had a month or more,' Martin said. 'He has hired men, as hard as the Oathsworn – Krivichians and even Khazars, I hear. He has taken your friends and gone after Atil's hoard, but there is a limit to how much Eldgrim can be made to remember. It may take Brondolf some time. He may not find it at all.'

Then he stiffened and one eye twitched.

'Christ's bones,' he said and I turned to where he looked.

Jon's hand on my forearm gripped tighter and I thought it was for what had been said, but when I looked, he was staring across the market square – to where Klerkon knelt at the feet of Perun, offering coins and trinkets.

Martin's stare was raddled with hate for Klerkon and as I strode past him towards Klerkon I wondered what he had been subjected to by his captor, only seeing, at the last moment, the little man with him, his high cheekboned face turning towards me, a grin revealing more gap than tooth – Takoub.

He held a length of chain and attached to it were three women, one of them Thordis. On the far side, coming up at a brisk pace, was Finn and, behind him, Kvasir and Thorgunna.

Klerkon straightened, bowed once to the great oak pillar and turned to see me. He blinked at me, turned and shot a glance round at Finn, then grinned.

'*A fronte praeciptium, a tergo lupi,*' he declared.

'That had better be translated as "here you are lads, sorry I stole them", or you will feel my blade up your arse, Klerkon,' snarled Finn.

'A cliff in front, wolves behind,' I informed Finn. 'Klerkon is caught and wondering how to wriggle out of it.'

Klerkon raised an eyebrow, stretched a languid hand – slowly, to show it was empty and going nowhere to be filled.

'It would not be a clever thing, I am thinking, to start something in the market square of Lord Novgorod the Great,' he smiled. 'Especially since Takoub here has just bought three slaves. Legally.'

'They are not slaves,' growled Finn, then scrubbed his face in confusion, for two of them were, in fact, thralls from Tor's steading. Only Thordis was freeborn. I saw her, face set like bad dough but with eyes hard and determined, knowing I would not let this happen. There was also the heart-leap in me at the knowledge that he had not known who Thordis was, or else he would never have sold her.

'*Beati possidentes,*' smiled Klerkon. Finn's mouth twisted and even if he had understood about possession and the law, it wouldn't have mattered. I raised a hand and he stopped in mid stride.

'Greek boys and – well, well, the very Christ priest I came to find,' noted Klerkon, glancing over my shoulder to where Martin scowled and crouched like a rat looking for a hole.

'I was thinking you might come to find him and shut his mouth – not that you would be so quick over it, all the same.'

'You should not have come to Hestreng,' I told him. He spread his hands.

'Just a wee *strandhogg*. A dip of the beak. No hard feelings – you hardly lost a thing from it and had a rival neighbour removed. *Hodie mihi, cras tibi.*'

I felt Finn tremble on the unseen leash. One more drawl of Latin and there would be blood spilled, which I did not want. Klerkon was right; this was a city ruled by the *veche*, a council who treated their city as if it were alive, who settled disputes between them with mass brawls on the Volkhov Bridge and who staked people who offended the peace.

I was almost dizzy with relief, all the same; Klerkon had not known the true value of Thordis as a lever against me and had sold her as a simple slave. He had come looking for Martin, to see what he could force the priest to tell him – I saw that priest, hunched and rat-crouched, looking to sidle away to the shadows.

Today me, tomorrow you, Klerkon had said and he was right. Except that I had already collected my tomorrow.

'I will buy them,' I said to Takoub and Klerkon smiled, knowing the price that the robbing little slave dealer would set. He relished me handing over the gold, even if the stone of my face denied him the pleasure of seeing me suffer.

I was not suffering; the gold was Klerkon's own and a ludicrous amount of it vanished inside Takoub's disgusting silks, then he unlocked the chains and the three women were free. Thordis moved to me briefly, tucked herself under my arm and I felt her tremble under my grip though her dirt-smeared face, so like her sister's, had no tear-streaks. She looked up into my eyes and nodded, just the once.

Then, from across the square, I heard Thorgunna shout: 'Thordis!' The sisters met, embracing, while Kvasir came up to stand near Finn. The two dull-eyed thrall women stood, heads down, like waiting cattle. Klerkon looked from the embracing sisters to me and back again, the truth settling on him slowly, like sifting snow.

He gathered himself well, though the white lines puckered round his cat's-arse mouth for a moment.

'Ah well,' he said, with a forced smile. 'I missed the prize, it seems and so there is a touching scene to end the day. Almost worth the cost, eh, Orm?'

He parried well, did Klerkon. No rant or rave about losing the chance to force me to reveal what I knew, just a swift coming about on a new tack. I knew what it was, too – Martin the priest. Klerkon was looking over my shoulder to keep him in sight.

Finn, of course, could not resist the moment.

'No cost to Orm, you arse,' he savaged out. Klerkon turned, a lopsided, sardonic smile on his Pan face. Finn grinned back.

'You need a new bed,' he said and Klerkon stiffened, jerked his head back to me, then back to Finn. The smile transformed to a feral snarl when he realized what had happened; Takoub shrank back – from experience, I was thinking.

I was also cursing Finn, for I knew where Klerkon would go, what he would do. I was only hoping that we could get back to the *Elk* and away back to Botolf before Klerkon managed to rout out his crew, sort out his half-dismantled ship and sail home. Then he would go to Hestreng for revenge.

Finn saw it, too, almost as soon as the words were out, and knew where his solution lay.

'Finn – no!'

To his credit, the blade was half out of the sheath and he still managed to slam it back, even when Klerkon sneered at him and turned contemptuously away. I was so rushed with relief, so blinded by it, that I did not see the little shape move across the square.

He took four quick steps, a skip and a hop. He gave a sharp little shout on the hop, just loud enough for Klerkon to turn and see what was about to happen to him –there was hatred and fear in equal measure on his face as Olaf Crowbone, the little monster, came at him, free of chains, free of the Black Island, dressed in new finery and armed with a brand-new little axe.

Like a salmon, Crowbone popped up into Klerkon's astounded gaze and buried his brand-new axe, with as good a stroke as I have ever seen, in the front of his hated captor's skull.

SEVEN

'Little turd,' grunted Finn as we were led to the pit.

He had started speaking against Olaf almost as soon as we had been dragged to the pit prison from the yelling chaos of Novgorod's marketplace where the body of Klerkon lay in a spreading pool of blood like some long-nosed beast. People screamed.

'This is what comes of giving thralls a weapon,' Finn had growled, a scowl twisting his face into worse shadows in the faint light from the hole far above.

'I am not a thrall,' Olaf piped back. 'Jarl Orm said so. And I am a prince, besides.'

'The generosity of Jarl Orm is great, I am thinking,' countered Finn, 'but not as great as his bad judgement in that matter.'

'Leave the boy,' said Thorgunna from the dark, at which Finn hawked meaningfully and spat, careless of where it landed in the dark.

'I will speak as I please,' he growled.

'You are a fool, Finn Horsehead,' rasped the voice of Martin.

It was the first thing the monk had said that was not a whining protest about how he had nothing at all to do with us. For once he spoke the truth and the fact that he was caught with us, despite his innocence let Finn gloat so much he did not even mind being called a fool.

'Your Christ-god seems to have got himself entangled with the Norns' weave,' chuckled Finn and Martin turned, his eyes the only thing that showed in the dark.

'The Lord will not be mocked,' he said in that file-rasp voice of his. Finn's laugh was just as harsh.

'He mocks you, priest. Every time you get near that holy stick of yours, he snatches it away again.'

Martin's mouth flecked foam at the corners and he waved furious hands, as if to bat Finn's words away.

'You do not yet see the advantage in taking Christ,' he mushed. 'What can your goat-chariot god do for you now? Or your one-eyed All-Father, patron of devils? They give you nothing and you will die unblessed. I, meanwhile, need only repent and confess my sins and Christ will give me life eternal. No-one lives the way you want to live these days, as I am sure Orm has told you.'

I did not want this monk standing beside me as if I was his horn-partner at a feast and said so. I also added that I did not think it much of a bargain which says you have to die first to be saved.

'Better than what your gods offer,' Martin spat back. 'They save you from death only to go to this feasting hall – for what? So you can fight for them at the end of the world and die a second time?'

'Every man comes to die,' piped up that little voice from the dark. 'That is the price of life and what the Norns weave – all that remains is to meet it well.'

It was so well spoken that even scowling Finn could not bring himself to sneer at Olaf.

Martin snorted. 'That shows how weak the old way is – if there is no choice, a man is a worthless slave of fate, which you pagans call the Norns. Christ has freed us from that.'

'You have no claim on freedom,' Olaf said, quick as the

94

dart of a bird's tongue. 'You Christ-followers are forever telling everyone how they should behave.'

'That is not such a bad thing in your case,' Finn growled. 'It might have stayed your hand from hitting Klerkon with that axe. Little turd – who do you think you are? Egil Skallagrimsson?'

Kvasir chuckled at that, for the tale of the six-year-old Egil smacking an older boy with an axe in a fight had been the talk of Iceland at the time and was so well known to us now that Egil was a fame-rich man.

The words tinkled from Olaf like ice into the darkness.

> *'My mouth strains*
> *To move the tongue,*
> *To weigh and wing,*
> *The choicer word;*
> *Not easy to breathe*
> *Odin's inspiration*
> *In my heart's hinterland.*
> *Little hope there.'*

This left us stunned, for most of us knew this was a verse of Egil Skallagrimsson's lament to his dead son. Kvasir muttered a sibilant 'heya' and even Finn offered a grudging growl of approval.

I remembered Kvasir's fish-breath whisper in my ear. That boy is not nine years old.

'At least that stopped your mouth for a while, Horsehead,' Martin rasped into the quiet dim. The faint light from the hole above resolved his darker shape against the charcoal.

'Orm should have killed you when he had the chance,' answered Finn bitterly, hugging himself against the damp chill of the rough carved walls. 'I may yet step in and claim the right of it,' he added viciously.

'There was once a good Norseman from the viks,' said

Olaf, high and sharp as a flighted arrow into the middle of this, 'who went out to chop wood.'

Kvasir laughed aloud and Thorgunna, sensing a story might calm things, urged Olaf to go on.

'This Norseman,' the boy went on, 'we shall call . . . Finn.'

You could almost hear Finn's scowl squeak as it wrenched his face.

'So off went Finn to fetch firewood. The trees nearby had been cut away, so he walked until he came to a large oak tree at the edge of the river. His eyes lighted up with pleasure, for it was a tree that would make many fires in his house.

'He climbed up into its branches and sat upon the largest and most comfortable of them. Then he began to chop upon the very limb on which he was sitting. While he worked, a Christ priest from a nearby village came along. He looked up into the tree and saw Finn there. Finn was wary, for he had heard Christ priests had great magic.'

'Was this Christ priest called Martin, by any chance?' demanded Kvasir and Olaf, his voice a smile in the dark, agreed that this was just so.

'So Martin the priest asked Finn what he was doing,' Olaf went on. 'And Finn told him he was chopping wood for the fire. What else could it be? "That is a poor way to chop wood," says Martin. "It is the only way to chop wood," Finn said. "You take your axe and you chop."'

'True enough,' interrupted Finn with a grunt and everyone shushed him.

'So Martin then told Finn it would be better to chop the tree down first, for if Finn sat there on the same branch he was cutting off he was going to fall down and be killed. But Finn told him to go and fuck goats.'

Thorgunna gave a squeal of outrage, while Kvasir and Jon Asanes laughed out loud, for this was as like Finn as to have been his fetch, even down to the voice and that was a feat coming from the throat of little Olaf.

'Martin shook his head at the stupidity of Finn and went away,' Olaf went on. 'Finn chopped and chopped, thinking about the stupidity of Martin, though still a little worried about whether the priest was off somewhere unseen, cursing him.

'Suddenly, without warning, the branch broke off and Finn fell to the ground. He lay on the ground with the branch under his arse, and as he lay there he thought about what Martin had said and the more he thought on it, the more he was convinced that the priest had the second sight. "He said that the branch would break and I would fall and be killed," Finn reasoned. "The branch really did break, the way he said it would. He is a priest and so knew what he was talking about – so that must mean that I am dead." And so he lay there as if dead.'

Kvasir was beating his thighs and shaking his head with the joy of it. He and Jon Asanes were holding each other up, while Finn harrumphed in the dark and each grunt he gave only made it worse.

'So, thinking he was dead, Finn did not try to get up at all, but just lay there without moving,' Olaf went on. 'After a while some of his friends – let's call them Kvasir Spittle and Jon – came along and found him. They shook him and talked to him and rubbed his head, but he did not move or speak, because he had decided he was dead. They picked him up and set him on his feet, but he fell down again, because whoever heard of a dead man standing up?'

Even Finn was grinning in the dark now, for I saw a flash of his face as he turned into the milk-light from the grille they had closed on us.

'So Kvasir and Jon Asanes also decided that he was dead and they picked him up to carry him back to the steading. "Do not leave my good axe," Finn said as they started off, so one went back and picked it up, all the while talking about the misfortune of their friend to end up dead in such a way.

'When they came to a fork in the path they stopped. Kvasir Spittle said they should go along the river, while Jon thought they should go over the hill. They argued hotly about it, still holding their friend on their shoulders like a corpse. Finally, Finn sat up impatiently and pointed to the hill trail. "That's the best way. It's the way I came," he said. Then he lay down and closed his eyes. His friends stopped arguing and carried him over the hill trail, still lamenting the accident. They came over the hill and into the steading, just as Finn had said.

'As they passed the forge, the smith came out to see what had happened and Kvasir and Jon put Finn on the ground to look at him. "We found him lying dead under an oak tree," Kvasir explained. "A branch fell on him and killed him."

'Finn opened one eye and said: "That's not the way it happened. I was sitting on the branch and it broke." Then he closed his eye again.'

By which time we were all laughing and the guards blotted out the light to peer down, clearly bewildered by a sound they had never heard from the depths of the prison pit before.

'The smith shook his head sadly,' Olaf continued, 'and Kvasir and Jon picked Finn up again and carried him to his house – but when they arrived there was no-one at home. So they put him on the ground and began to argue about what they should do. Everything was very confused. While they argued a dog wandered in and licked Finn's face. "Take him away!" yelled Finn. "Is there no respect for the dead?"'

At which point I thought Kvasir and Jon Asanes and Thorgunna would collapse and die on the spot, for they were wheezing and tear-blind now.

'So they drove the dog out of the house and began to argue again,' Olaf continued, relentless and unsmiling. 'At last, since nothing seemed to be happening, Finn sat up and said angrily: "Send for my wife! She's probably gossiping outside." Then he lay down again and closed his eyes, while his friends sent for his wife.

'In a little while she came running to the house, crying in grief, with the other women of the village behind her. Many villagers crowded into the house until it was full and Kvasir Spittle told once more how they had found him. "A branch from an oak tree fell on him and killed him," he said.

'At which Finn roared with anger. "I was sitting on the branch and it broke!" he yelled. "How many times do I have to say this?"

'At which his wife, more sensible a woman than he deserved, pointed out that, if he was dead, he could not speak. "Just so – but as you see, he is dead," the others replied. "For so he insists."

'His sensible wife quietly pointed out that perhaps he was not dead after all. Finn sat up and said angrily: "Martin the monk said I would surely fall and be killed. I fell. He was right. He always speaks only the truth, he tells us. Therefore, I must be dead." His sensible wife pointed out that the priest had not seen Finn after he fell, only before. "Argue, argue, argue!" Finn said, getting up from the ground in disgust. "Will there be no end to it?"

'And he picked up his axe and went out of the house. "Where are you going?" his wife asked. "To get some wood for the fire," says Finn, disappearing down the hill.

'At which everyone marvelled at so good a man, thinking only of his wife's comfort and him dead like that.'

Finn clapped a hand on Olaf's shoulder, while the hoots and howls and my own chuckles floated up to the bewildered guards.

'By Odin's hairy arse, boy, you tell a good tale,' he said, 'though I wish you were as clever at working out when to use an axe.'

Martin said nothing at all, sliding into the dark where he could hug his scowls to himself – but the laughter raised us out of the pit, for the guards reported that there were mad people making merry in the prison and that got Crowbone and myself hauled up and out and stuck in front of little Prince Vladimir.

He was a boy, scarcely older than Olaf and ruler of this city since the age of four. When the *veche*, the council of the city, had decreed to Vladimir's father, Sviatoslav, Grand Prince of Kiev, that if he did not send them one of his sons to rule over them, they would pick their own, he had been sent there. But the *veche* had decreed that Prince Vladimir could not live inside Lord Novgorod the Great, only outside it, in the fortress on the hill, such was its power.

Vladimir's two iron pillars were with him, his uncle Dobrynya on his right, and Sigurd, the head of young Vladimir's *druzhina*, on the prince's left.

Of that pair, it had to be said that Sigurd was the one who made you blink, for he was called Axebitten for good reason and what the axe had bitten was his nose, legacy of a fight where he forgot to draw back all the way in good time. Now he wore a silver one in its place, strapped on with a silk ribbon that tied at the back of his head and was almost covered by his greying beard and hair, so that it seemed nothing at all held on that marvellous nose.

Nor did you mention it if you valued keeping your own; losing a nose was punishment in most vik for thieving and so was a dread mark for a man who loved his dignity and valued his honour highly, as Sigurd did.

But it was little Vladimir, in blue breeks and a simple white linen shirt belted at the waist, who was the one who mattered, for all he only had a dozen years on him. He was capless, his hair shaved from his head save for two plaited braids hanging from his temples in the Khazar style, like his father, Sviatoslav.

'I am told we have met before,' he said in his light, high voice, frowning at me.

We had, when Einar was jarl of the Oathsworn and Vladimir, all of six then, had stopped to watch us when we were part of his father's army bound for the Khazar city of Sarkel to siege it.

I told him this and he nodded. 'I remember Einar. I have heard how he betrayed my brother Jaropolk and vanished into the steppe in search of some treasure. I hear he died there.'

'True, great prince,' I said, feeling the slow slide of sweat down my back. 'The years have flowed like the Dnepr under all that.'

'Rare is it to have laughter from my prisons,' he answered, after a short pause to make it seem as if he considered his words carefully. He played the prince well at twelve.

'Rare it is,' I countered, sweating more and desperate, for I knew our lives rode on how gold-browed my words were now, 'to have a tale to laugh at.'

'I told it,' interrupted Olaf and I cursed the little rat. 'Would you like to hear it?'

I closed my eyes with the horror of it, while Vladmir, back-footed by this surprise stroke, wanted to turn and look to his Uncle Dobrynya, but had enough prince in him to resist it. That and boyish curiousity made him command Olaf to tell it.

'There was once a good Slav from Lord Novgorod the Great,' Olaf began, while my belly flipped over and my mouth dried so much my tongue almost choked me.

'We shall call him Vladimir.'

And he told the whole tale, only it wasn't a priest, it was an uncle called Dobrynya and, at every new stanza of it, I felt the wolf-hot breath of the Valkyrie wash closer and closer.

Then, at the end of it, while Vladimir hid his grins behind his hand, I saw Dobrynya smiling through his salted-black spade of a beard and felt a moment of light. A chance. There was a chance. Then I saw Sigurd, who was frowning above his silver nose and that was enough to drive my hopes deeper than the pit prison.

101

'What name do you have, boy?' demanded Sigurd so harshly that both Vladimir and Dobrynya looked at him in surprise.

'Olaf, lord.'

'And your father's name?'

I closed my eyes, for Olaf would never reveal that. The silence stretched.

'Was it Tryggve, by any chance?' growled Sigurd and I blinked as Olaf jerked.

'And your mother was called Astrid,' he said, softer now and again Olaf jerked again like a speared whale. Then the truth of it smacked me like snow from a roof – Sigurd. Olaf's lost uncle.

'You know this boy, Sigurd Axebitten?' asked Dobrynya and the *druzhina* captain nodded, smiling at long last – not that it was a better sight than a frown with that silver nose.

'I believe he is my nephew, who was being sent to me for safety after his father was slain. Some raiders kidnapped him and his mother and *fostri* – that was six years ago and I have heard nothing until now.'

'We freed him,' I interrupted hurriedly. 'Klerkon it was – the man little Olaf here killed. He had been mistreated, chained up, beaten, his mother was cruelly . . .'

I tailed off, realizing the whole story, the final tug of that ring, unearthing the whole glorious sword of it.

Olaf, son of Tryggve. I knew of a Tryggve whose son would be a prince, whose mother was a princess called Astrid, daughter of Eirik Bjodaskalle from Obrestad in Rogaland.

King Tryggve Olafsson, of Viken and Vingulmark, grandson of Harald Fairhair of Norway. Not a king really, but enough of a mighty jarl – a *rig-jarl* – to call himself so in the north of Norway, until he had fallen under the blades of the sons of Eirik Bloodaxe, driven on by their mother, Gunnhild.

Aye, there was a woman. Gunnhild, the fearsome witch who could nurse night-wolves with the bile that she held in her breast. Who could chew grindstones to powder when she gnashed her teeth on a matter. She had searched out what she called 'the brat' all over Norway, determined to end the line and make her sons safe. Everyone thought she had done so since the boy and his mother and foster-father Lousebeard – properly known as Thorolf, I now remembered – had simply gone from every view and, in the end, from every lip and mind.

Now here was the truth of it, standing in this pine-smelling hall, frowning uncertainly up at the man with a silver nose who claimed to be his uncle.

I looked at the boy, pulled up as tall as he could, his chin jutting. A knife slipped between his ribs at any point would have been worth more than his own weight in gold to Gunnhild. Half the men who crewed the Elk would have done it in an eyeblink – the other half would have hoisted him on their shoulders and gone off to claim him king.

'Then we cannot kill him, surely,' Vladimir said in a shocked voice. 'Not a prince of the Norways, a nephew of Sigurd Axebitten.'

Dobrynya said nothing, though he looked at Sigurd, then at us, then at Olaf. I almost hoiked my guts up there and then, for you could see it written on his face, like a birch-bark account.

No, they couldn't stick a stake up little Olaf's arse – but the *veche* would want their blood price for the killing of Klerkon.

So Vladimir started with one of the thrall women, to see if the *veche* would be satisfied with that.

They took us all out to witness their sharp judgement on the thrall woman, Danica.

While his skilled men worked with their stake, I looked up to where little Prince Vladimir stood. Today he was a fine-looking prince, in brocaded breeks and silk shirt, his dark-blue coat hemmed in red and with gold at the cuffs, wearing an over-robe of the same colour decorated with

103

gold and fastened with a ruby clasp. Topping all this was a sable cap crowned with silver and the great crushing weight of an eagle-headed gold torc screaming on his chest. His two pillars were with him. And nestling under the embrace of Sigurd's comforting hand on his shoulder was Olaf, who had found his lost uncle.

At the end of it, both Dobrynya and Sigurd inclined their heads to the beards of the *veche*, the horsehair plume on Dobrynya's helmet stirring in the snow-thick wind. This one slave woman was clearly not enough: the *veche* shook their heads to a man. They wanted us all in a neat line, turning the snow to red slush.

Martin waved his hand in front of his chest in that Christsign they use to ward off evil and even Finn and Kvasir looked stone grim when the guards prodded us back to the pit. The other thrall woman was dissolving into snot and tears and had to be carried by Thordis and Thorgunna.

Finn gave a bitter laugh, the only laugh left of the ones which had floated us out of the pit prison to this moment. 'Little turd,' he muttered, glancing bitterly back at Crowbone, safe beside his new uncle.

In the dark of the pit I still heard laughter and knew who it was, though I did not know what he had to laugh at. It had seemed to me as if Odin was steering me, like a wind-driven *knarr*, back to Atil's mountain of silver – yet making sure we would never reach it. Even for him, this was a twisted knot of planning.

'I will not die a nithing death on a stake like that,' Finn growled and Kvasir agreed. In the fetid dark they started on a plan to break free and fight until they were killed, with decent weapons in their fists. The women said nothing and Martin muttered prayers.

'Are you with us, Jon Asanes?' asked Kvasir and I heard the trembling answer.

'Yes – but I am not much of a fighter.'

'Orm?' growled Finn. I said nothing and wished he would stop yapping; there was something strange, a sound . . .

'Odin's bones, boy, you are our jarl. Will you lead us?'

It was laughter, pealing and rolling like distant chimes. Odin . . .

'Perhaps his bowels have turned to water,' growled Finn and Kvasir snarled at him to watch his tongue, but he was uncertain and added that it might be that my thought-cage had warped a little.

'Bells,' I said, recognizing the sound. 'Bells.'

It was. Chimes, rich and deep, tumbling like water down a cliff face.

I could not see their faces in the dark, but I could feel them look one to the other and back to me. Bells in Novgorod meant something momentous and there was a stirring in me, a hackle-raise that let me know Odin had passed close by.

As the dawn emptied thick silver light down the shaft of the pit – our last dawn in this world, I was thinking – Finn shouted up to the guards, asking what had happened.

'The great Prince is dead,' answered the guard, his voice stunned and hushed by the tragedy of it.

'Vladimir?' demanded Kvasir.

Finn hugged himself and shook his head with awe. 'I asked Odin for it,' he said, an awed voice in the dark. 'I called on him in the dark and he has answered me.'

'Ha!' snorted Martin with disgust.

'What did you call for?' demanded Kvasir angrily. 'Revenge? And what did you offer?'

Finn said nothing and yet spoke loudly.

I knew differently, all the same – there were too many bells for Vladimir to be dead and I felt the Odin-moment of it. Sviatoslav, his father, was the one who was dead – I learned later how he had been ambushed by his own Pechenegs, bribed by the Great City he had challenged and failed to beat. The ruler of all the Rus, gone at the hands of a hairy-arsed steppe warrior with a bow and an arrow you get by the dozen for a copper coin. His skull would end up set in silver as a drinking cup for a Pecheneg chief.

But in the pit, knowing only that Vladimir's father was dead, I felt the power of Odin and bowed my head to him.

With Sviatoslav gone, Vladimir was in trouble. He was the youngest of the three brothers and the one least considered, being born of a woman most thought little more than a thrall. Of the other two, Oleg was stupid and strong while the eldest, Jaropolk, was shrewd, cowardly and vicious.

They would fight, these brothers, sooner rather than later and the bells for Sviatoslav could be a knell for the least of his sons – unless that son had some clout in his fists.

Like a hoard of silver.

Now I had no way of avoiding a return to Atil's howe; Odin had strapped me to the prow beast of his ship and blew a wind that would not be avoided.

Finn and Kvasir were bewildered by the laughter that spilled out of the pit. It even sounded crazed to my own ear and me it was doing it.

EIGHT

When the starling fell from the roof beams, stone dead with cold, Olaf Crowbone stirred it with his toe and said it was the last one we would see this year, for they had all gone into hiding save for this one, who was clearly killed of stupidity.

'Hiding?' demanded Thorgunna, swathed in wool and fur so that only her eyes showed. 'Hiding from what?'

'The white raven,' Crowbone answered, his cheeks rosed in his pale face. A few of those within earshot looked uneasily at the boy and Thordis made a warding sign. Sunken-eyed, she was, from all she had suffered and Finn, standing close to her, moved closer still.

'You should not speak of such things,' Kvasir said, looking up from where he worried a piece of leather into a new strap for his helmet. Crowbone shrugged and pulled the white-furred cloak tighter round him, for snow had blown in under the door of the hall and spread across the floor. A pool of mead was frozen in an amber lump, stuck through with the floor-straw – even the spiders were dead and the nets they curled in trembled in the snell wind, thin and sharply cold as the edge of a shaving knife.

Onund Hnufa gave the grunt that led any speech he made.

'I don't need that bird to tell me it will be a bad winter,' he growled. 'The green wine is icing a month early.'

Jon Asanes leaned over, his breath smoking warmly in my ear. 'White raven?' he asked in a whisper.

I told him of the white raven, which the dwarves held in keeping with all the other secret things of the world – the sound of a cat's paw, the hairs of a maiden's beard, the roots of a mountain, the dreams of a bear, the breath of a fish, the spittle of a bird. All the things that should not be heard or seen, yet had to be kept somewhere.

The dwarves hid them and only revealed them once, when they used some to make Gleipnir, the chain that bound the devouring wolf, Fenris. He was tricked into being tied with it only because the god Tyr placed his hand in the beast's mouth as security that the gods would untie the wolf afterwards. Tyr lost it as a result, but his sacrifice allowed the world-eating wolf to be secured.

The only thing the dwarves made sure they did not use in making Gleipnir was a feather from the white raven, Odin's third pet.

Sometimes old One Eye sends that bird into the world, as he sends the other two, Thought and Memory – but the white one does not come back to whisper secrets in the god's ear. It flies over the world shaking out feathers as snow to make the worst winters; a warning that, one day, it will make Fimbulwinter, the great freeze that heralds Ragna Rok.

'So Crowbone is telling us the end of the world is here?' demanded Jon.

Finn gave a sharp bark of laughter. 'Little Crowbone is telling us that the birds think so,' he corrected. 'Since birds have thought-cages so tiny they can only keep a few in them, I am not concerned about what birds think.'

'Not all bird thoughts are of songs,' Crowbone said and that brought an echo of Sighvat, long dead in Serkland. I remembered Sighvat, hunkered down on the steppe, looking

108

at the battered silver plate ripped out of the earth as we dug into Atil's tomb. It was the first sign that treasure was there at all, a blackened piece of a plate with pictures round the edges, which Sighvat said were the dreams of birds.

'I never heard of a white raven,' growled Gyrth and Finn told him this was because he was an ignorant outlander. Gyrth gave him a scowl – he was named Gyrth Albrechtsohn and was as big as Botolf, with a belly bigger than Skapti's had been, but solid as a barrel. When he had strolled up like some huge bear to join us in Kiev and claiming to be a Dane, Finn had laughed.

'Gyrth is an Englisc name,' he had chuckled, 'and your da was a Saxlander, which is plain to see. I don't see any Dane there.'

'My ma was,' Gyrth had rumbled back, frowning.

'Perhaps she had a horse, too,' Finn grinned, 'or a fast faering, to have got round so many men. You may not have any Dane in you, but she had, I am sure of it.'

Men laughed and Gyrth blinked and frowned.

'You are Finn,' he said slowly, 'who fears nothing. If you talk of my ma any longer, you will fear me, for I will fall on you.'

Finn held up placatory hands and admitted that having such a rock fall on him would be a fearful experience, right enough. Then he clasped Gyrth by the wrist.

'So Steinnbrodir it will be then – welcome aboard.'

And Gyrth, grinning lopsidely at his new by-name – Boulder Brother – lumbered into our midst like an amiable bear, one Finn was never done baiting, as now.

'An ignorant outlander,' Finn repeated. 'Whose marvellously-travelled ma was too occupied to tell him such tales.'

'I saw a white crow once,' Gyrth admitted, frowning. 'All its black brothers stabbed it with their beaks and chased it off.'

'None is found so good that some fault attends him, or so

ill that he is not of use for something, as my granny used to say,' Red Njal offered him.

'Never heard of a white raven,' Gyrth persisted stubbornly.

'But the green wine is icing,' Jon pointed out, shaking me back from where I still hunkered with Sighvat on the steppe, into the wither of Finn's frown. The iced wine was a sign you could not ignore.

Made from young wheat, the brew was filtered through seven layers of charcoal and seven of clean, fine river sand and the resulting liquid was as clear as tears and casked in oak, which was Perun's wood. It was then left outside most houses all winter and people passing tried to guess when such a casking would grow the first ice crystals.

They were removed at once, for ice is water and the more you removed, the more powerful – and green – the drink that was left. The colder the weather, the more ice formed on the green wine, the more you removed and the stronger it got.

It had to be cold for ice to start forming on the green wine at all and that was a bad sign this early, as was the snow and the clear, cold air that promised more of the same. This year would produce some of the strongest green wine and only those who had drunk too much of it would head out on to the steppe now.

I had pointed this out to young Vladimir after we had been hauled out of the pit the morning Sviatoslav's death was announced in Novgorod and after I had told him of the hoard and how the Oathsworn were a benefit to him.

'If what you say is true,' he answered in his strong, high voice, 'then this man Lambisson from Birka is already out on the steppe and every day we leave him, the closer he comes to my silver hoard.'

And he looked at me with his clear blue eyes on either side of a frown.

His silver hoard. Dobrynya saw the sick look on my face and offered only a throaty grunt of a laugh from the other side of the table, where I had spent an hour explaining why we should not be staked like Danica, the thrall woman.

'By the time we have done with the rites for your father, the meetings with your brother's representatives and preparing for such an expedition,' Dobrynya then said gently to his young prince, 'it may well be so late in the year as to be better waiting for the thaw.'

Vladimir shook his head angrily. 'Uncle, my brothers may not wait.'

He had the right of it there, sure enough and all that Dobrynya had spoken of was simply time wasted for Vladimir, so that he was fretted like a dog's jaw with impatience.

It took two days of tough talking with the *veche* and a deal of promises here and there to get them to accept the thrall woman as their only victim. It was finally managed with some cunning from Dobrynya, who told the *veche* that young Vladimir would not sully the memory of his father with the blood of common criminals. That one they bowed to.

So we were released, but kept in the fortress, supposedly for our own protection, for the next five days. On the sixth day, as Vladimir and all Novgorod prepared to enter into the rituals to mourn the loss of Sviatoslav, Jaropolk's hounds appeared at the gates.

Sveinald and his son Lyut they knew them as here, the father a grizzled old Dane who had served Sviatoslav as a general and who had brought back the remnants of the army after his master's death. Now he advised Vladimir's elder brother Jaropolk, as Dobrynya advised Vladimir.

Jaropolk, though eldest of the three Rus princes, was barely into his teens and easily swayed. Sveinald and Lyut had always been an arrogant pair and now that they held their young prince in thrall they acted as if they ruled Kiev and not he.

They had arrived as Jaropolk's representatives, to honour the funeral rites for Sviatoslav – at least, on the front of it. In reality, they were here to find out what Vladimir would do and had brought at least a hundred men, seasoned *druzhina* warriors with their armour and big red shields marked with a yellow *algiz* rune, which had been the symbol of Rurik when he had founded Kiev. Shield, it meant, and alertness, too – but now the Kiev Slavs called it 'a golden trident' from the shape, which was like one of those three-tined forks.

It took four days to send Sviatoslav to the halls of his gods, four days of wailing and bowing and kneeling and bloody sacrifice round Perun's pole, where horse heads were stuck on stakes and young Vladimir exhausted himself, the gore dripping off his elbows. But everyone agreed he had done well for a boy of twelve.

At night he had no rest, having to preside over the feasts in the *kreml* hall, where his men and the *druzhina* of old Sveinald snarled at each other, barely leashed. Here, the high table was a tafl game of words as Sveinald tried to find out if Vladimir was going to acknowledge Jaropolk as Prince of all the Rus or resist him and young Vladimir and his uncle tried not to say one thing or the other. Oleg, the third brother, I noted, was not considered at all.

The rest of the Oathsworn had turned up by this time, summoned south from Aldeigjuborg and having brought the *Elk* with them. Gizur insisted on this despite the sweat and labour on a river already porridge thick during the day and iced over every night, for he did not want it left almost untended near *Dragon Wings*.

'Klerkon's crew is divided,' he reported. '*Dragon Wing*s is too laid up for winter to sail and the way out to the Baltic is frozen solid anyway. Half of them are swearing revenge on us, led by Randr Sterki. The other half is leaving, in twos and threes. Most of those are hoping to take service with Vladimir, so they are coming here. They wanted to sail down with us, for they knew we were crew light, but I thought it best to let them find their own way.'

I had all this to chew over – and Finn, scowling-angry

because, he said, I had handed away the secret of Atil's tomb, without even a guarantee that we would get anything out of it. We had our lives, I pointed out to him and he grudgingly admitted that to be true, though it did nothing for his mood and it was a foolish man who crossed Finn at times like this.

There is always a fool when you don't need one. Lyut had been elbowing and snarling among his own *druzhina* on the last feast night. You could see that they were used to it, deferring to him because he was Sveinald's boy and had power over them as a result.

So, flushed and strutting, he made a mistake when Finn slid on to an ale bench to talk to someone he knew slightly.

'You are in my place,' he snarled and Finn looked up in surprise.

'Perhaps, though I do not see your name on it. I will not be here long – look, there is a place here and another over there.'

'Move,' Lyut answered, 'when your betters order it.'

Finn turned. There was silence now from those closest, a silence that spread slowly out, like the ripples from a dipped oar.

'Betters?' he said, raising an eyebrow.

'In fact,' Lyut said, sneering, 'so much better you should kiss my foot and acknowledge it.'

He put his foot up on the same bench Finn sat on. No-one spoke. Sveinald, grinning over his ale horn, looked at Dobrynya, then at Vladimir. It was a challenge, pure and simple and all the ruffs were up now. I did not dare speak; no-one did. The silence began to hurt.

Then Finn grinned, a loose, wicked grin. He inclined his head, as if in acceptance and Lyut smirked. Finn handed his ale horn to his neighbour, then placed both his hands on Lyut's ankle and raised the foot to his lips.

I was stunned. Most of us were. I saw Kvasir half rise in outrage – then there was a yelp from Lyut, for Finn had kept

113

on going, straightening with Lyut's foot in his hands, forcing the man to hop like a mad bird to keep his balance.

With a final, dismissive gesture, Finn threw the foot in the air and Lyut went over with a yell and a crash.

'Kiss my arse, boy,' Finn said, dusting his hands. The hall erupted with hoots and bellows and catcalls and it was clear that half of Sveinald's men were drunk enough to be pleased to see Lyut sprawled in the sick and spilled drink.

Finn was no fool. A man with no clever in him at all would have turned back to his ale horn and the backslaps and appreciative howls of laughter and Lyut, coming off the floor in a scrabbling rush, whipping the seax from his boot, would have had him in the liver and lights.

Instead, Lyut found his knife hand slapping into the iron grip of Finn's left. When he swung a wild fist with the other, he found it shackled in Finn's right. Then Finn grinned his wolf grin and butted Lyut, so that the snarling boy's handsome beak of a nose splayed and blood flew.

Lyut fell backwards, over an ale bench and into the hearth-fire. It took no more than an eyeblink or two to realize he was not getting up on his own, but his hair was on fire by then. Those nearest dragged him out and beat out the flames.

Now Sveinald's men were roaring and growling with anger, for this was another matter entirely. Sveinald himself kept his seat, his knuckles white on the fancy gilt-rimmed horn.

Sigurd, his silver nose gleaming, moved a little closer to his charges, the young prince and his now-constant companion, little Crowbone. On that one's face I saw no fear, only a studied interest, as if he had found a new kind of bird.

Finn turned, his face streaked with Lyut's blood, the seax held in one hand. He glared round them all and the roaring subsided.

'I am Finn Bardisson from Skani, called Horsehead,' he said softly. 'Is there anyone else wants their foot kissing?'

Silence.

Behind him, Lyut whimpered and men were carrying him away, to where the women would balm his toasted face with goose fat.

'Sit down Finn Bardisson from Skani, called Horsearse,' Gyrth Steinnbrodir called out into the silence. 'You have taught the boy how to dance on one foot and not to sit so close to the fire and now I want to get back to my drinking.'

There was a chuckle or two, then the hall noise washed back in like a tide on the turn and Finn shunked Lyut's seax into the ale bench and took his horn back, raising it in toast to Gyrth. I raised my own to him and he acknowledged it, while I felt Sveinald staring, could hear him ask through clenched teeth who this Finn Bardisson was and who this Jarl Orm.

I was swelled with the pride of it, that my name was on lips all over the hall and aware also, with a sick, sinking feeling, that we had done neither ourselves nor little Vladimir any favours.

Then, in the cold light of morning as everyone sorted themselved out for the day, the bird fell from the rafters and little Crowbone, his face whalebone-pale, cheeks flushed from the cold, started in to speaking about white ravens.

He was wearing a fine tunic the colour of a robin's egg, wool breeks, fur-trimmed Slav boots and a white wool cloak trimmed with a swathe of sable fur that came up round his ears and met the rough curls of a fine goat-wool cap.

He peered at the dead starling, while the great elkhound with him sniffed it and warily watched our own deerhounds. That huge white-grey beast, as like a wolf as a brother, only added to the unease surrounding Crowbone, for it had eyes of different colours, exactly like his.

When he had first appeared with it, the warding signs made a flutter like bird wings and Klepp Spaki had been busy since, carving protection runes on bits of bone. Only Thorgunna, on whom *seidr* magic was wasted, was unafraid.

115

'My, you look like a little prince now, right enough,' she said, beaming – then broke off to cuff the Scots thrall woman for dropping her pin case and spilling the bone needles out of it.

All Olaf's finery – even the white, wolf-ruffed elkhound – was gifted from Prince Vladimir. It was, as Kvasir had already pointed out quietly, just as well I hadn't decided to sell Crowbone as a thrall, since it seemed the little turd had charmed the ruler of Novgorod and had gone from slave to prince in one hare-leap. Things, he added, could be much worse.

'How much worse can it already be?' grunted Finn, red-eyed from the night before and just as sullen in the chill daylight. 'The world is lining up to rob us.'

'If you would rather have a stake up your arse,' I snapped back at him, stung by his scowling, 'I can probably arrange it.'

One of the deerhounds laid its great bony head on my knee and sighed mournfully into the mood of the hall. The other snarled at the too-close elkhound, whose ruff stiffened.

'Bleikr,' chided Olaf. 'Stop that.'

Bleikr – White Fair, it meant to us, though most tongues could translate it no better than Pale. Whatever his name, the dog paid Olaf no heed, but was wise enough not to take on both deerhounds. None of the dogs wanted a fight, but the elkhound's ruff stuck out like hedgehog spines and the rough brindle hair on the deerhounds' back was clenched and dark. We watched warily, not eager to get between them.

Then Thorgunna gave a little grunt of annoyance at our holding back and moved in fearlessly, cuffing right and left. The dogs scattered, yelping.

'Bleikr,' she said, tucking a stray wisp of hair back under her braids, while warriors did not dare look at each other for the shame of it. 'There is nice. Now you have a new dog – and kin, too, I hear. Your mother's father in Bjodaskalle and her sisters, too. Not forgetting your Uncle Sigurd here.'

Crowbone nodded, though it was clear that Bleikr was deeper in his heart than these folk, who were only names to him. Even Sigurd. It came to me then that little Crowbone was a boy alone and, after all that had happened to him, might well be for all his life.

Finn looked at the white dog and grunted cynically. Olaf frowned.

'You do not like the name?' he asked. Then he pointed to the deerhound who had slunk back to Finn's knee.

'What is this one called, then?' he challenged.

'Dog,' Finn said flatly. Olaf, thinking he was being made fun of, scowled and pointed to the other deerhound.

'And this?'

'The other dog,' Finn answered, then cocked himself to the side and farted.

Kvasir chuckled as Olaf started to get his own hackles up.

'There is a wise rule we use,' he said, clapping the boy on one shoulder, 'and it is this – never give a name to something you might have to eat.'

Olaf was taken aback at that and looked down at his new pride and joy, now trying to lick its own balls. 'Eat Bleikr?'

'Well – not that one's tongue, perhaps,' Kvasir said and folk laughed.

'Aye,' growled Gyrth, surfacing from under a pile of cloaks and pelts, where he had been trying to keep warm and sleep. 'If we go to find that cursed hoard in this weather, we will end up eating worse than that before we are done. Helmet straps will taste good, mark me.'

'Do you no harm,' Finn answered and Gyrth patted his belly and smiled.

I was aware of the winter steppe, the Great White, brooded on it all the rest of that long day while the men in the hall surfaced, stretching and farting and shivering into the breath-smoking chill, dousing their heads and breaking ice in the bowls and buckets to do it, roaring and blowing.

Thorgunna and Thordis, who had wisely avoided the affair and the risk of being up-ended and tupped by drunks – and the obvious reactions of Kvasir and everyone else to that – were the freshest faces in that hall and made sure their healthy cheerfulness set everyone else's teeth grinding. They and the thralls bustled in, stirring the hearthfire to life, hanging pots, rattling skillets.

Eventually, chewing feast left-overs and picking their molars, most of the men all wandered off to sort out their lives – Sveinald's men were heading home and I heard that Lyut was having to be litter-carried. That he was alive at all was good luck, I was thinking.

My own crew were staying, of course, and getting as ready as they could for a trip into the open steppe in winter. Most of them were unworried by what I had done – they still thought they would get a share as they had been promised, and few looked beyond that. Some counted the involvement of Vladimir as jarl-cleverness by me, since it would mean more protection and better supplies for such a dangerous trip.

Outside the keep, in the crushed snow of the *kreml*, there was now noise and purpose and carts with sledge-runners, the wheels slung on the sides like shields on a *drakkar*, just in case they were needed. There were strong little horses for pulling and others for riding and supplies being loaded and men sorting out gear and weapons.

Vladimir had expected me to point to his carefully-drawn vellum chart and mark it with the location of Atil's cursed tomb, but when it came to it, there was just a dot that read 'Biela Viezha', which was the Slav name for Sarkel, and acres of grey-white skin. Nor was I daft enough in the head to lay out the X of it, for him then not to need me at all.

No-one but me knew exactly where the tomb lay and the path of it was scratched on the hilt of my rune-bladed sabre. Short Eldgrim had a rough idea of it, for he had helped me with the runes I made, but even he did not know all the steps. Neither did I unless we got to Sarkel, the first landmark.

They saw it, of course, Vladimir and big Uncle Dobrynya. They looked from one to the other as I glanced scornfully at the vellum.

'I can take you,' I said, hoping my sweat was not visible in the dim light of that private room. 'There is no landmark on this chart.'

Silence, in which I was sure I heard men greasing a stake. Then Dobrynya rolled up the chart with brisk movements as he said: 'Of course you will.'

Now I wondered. The steppe in winter was as grey-white an emptiness as Vladimir's vellum chart and a sick chill washed me; I was loading a lot of lives and hope on those few runes I had scratched out.

Ostensibly, the Oathsworn were free to come and go – yet all had been brought into Vladimir's own hall, even Martin the monk. Dobrynya had insisted: everyone who knew anything of the matter was to be kept where they could be seen. Now Martin was thrashing around like a fish in a keep-net.

He scurried up to me in the cold light of the morning, as Olaf chucked and snapped his fingers at the unresponsive elkhound, finally following it as it wandered off.

'Which pup is taking which for a walk?' demanded Finnlaith and others laughed, though they did so when they were sure little Olaf Crowbone could not hear and none of them was ashamed of being afraid of a nine-year-old boy.

'Speaking of dogs,' growled Hauk Fast-Sailor and nodded towards the hurrying figure of the monk. I sighed; the deer-hound sighed. Neither of us wanted to be bothered with this.

'You must speak to the prince,' Martin declared, his eyes wild and black from under his tangled hair and matted beard. 'I will not go on this cursed fool's errand.'

'Must I?'

'I will not go.'

I leaned slightly towards him, thinking – yet again – that I should have killed him when I had had the chance.

'Vladimir has decreed it. I do not want to go and yet I must,' I answered, more weary than patient. 'If I cannot get out of it, what makes you think I can make him leave you behind?'

'Christ will provide,' intoned Finn, in what he fondly believed was a mock of the Christ-priests. Martin savaged him with a glare, then folded his arms and stuck his chin out until his beard bristled.

'I will not go.'

'Then stay and sit on a sharp stick,' Kvasir said with a shrug, raising his head slightly from repairing the strap. 'You mistake us for folk who worry about you.'

'This is no matter of mine,' Martin insisted. His ruined mouth made white foam at the corners. 'I want no share in this silver foolishness.'

'Good,' grunted Finn morosely, 'then we'll take your share. If any of us get a share at all, that is.'

He shot me a knowing look but, to my surprise, it was Martin who managed to knock him off his perch.

'Why do you want it, this silver?' he snapped.

Finn blinked owlishly, for it was clearly a stupid question, which he said, then added: 'A hoard of silver? Why would you not want it?'

'For what it can buy?' countered Martin. 'The fine food, the best drink and the most beautiful of women. And so you have them all – what then, Finn Horsehead?'

'A magnificent sword,' commented Pai wistfully. 'Fine furs for a cloak.'

'Ships,' Jon Asanes threw in, grinning.

Martin nodded, but Finn was frowning.

'Until you have them all and more,' the monk said, flecks spilling from his ruined mouth. 'Then what? More of it until you puke and your prick drops off? What is the use of a magnificent sword if you never use it for raiding, eh Finn? Yet what is the point of raiding if you already have all you can want and more?'

'Ha,' said Red Njal, waving one hand dismissively. 'You are a Christ-priest, so what do you know of such things? You want riches, too – that spear is your hoard. Deceit sleeps with greed, as my granny used to say.'

Martin's glance was sour, then he turned it back on Finn.

'I know it is no good thing for folk such as you to end your days bent-backed and stumbling with age, drooling on a bench and wondering if you have hidden your coin well enough to fool all the women who laugh because you can do nothing with them now, while your sons conspire and cannot wait for you to die.'

That straw-death vision silenced everyone and I was surprised to see something slither across Finn's face that I had never seen before.

Fear.

Into that long, painful silence, Jon Asanes offered: 'You will still have to go, I am thinking.'

'I will not go,' Martin said stiffly.

'Say that once more, you streak of piss and I will make it come true – you will stay here forever,' growled Red Njal. 'Put to the sword those that disagree, said my granny and she had the right of it there, for sure.'

'I am, at one and same moment,' chuckled Gyrth, 'both sorrowed and glad that I never met this granny of yours.'

'You will go,' I answered Martin, staring back into the black coals of his eyes. 'I have a stick that you will follow.'

He blinked, hesitated. His face twitched, but a new hook was in and deeper than any. 'You promised me the Holy Spear for what I told you,' he snapped, hoarse with anger, trembling with it, so that his fingers shook and clenched.

'Things change. I don't care if you end up spitted, but

121

Vladimir thinks you belong to me and so I am responsible. You will put no-one at risk. Obey me and you will get your little stick at the end.'

'Disobey,' added Runolf Harelip with a twisted smile, 'and you get a little stick IN your end.'

Martin sucked in breath as if it pained him, while everyone else laughed.

'Am I to believe this promise above the last?'

'I swear it, as Odin is my witness.'

He sneered out a black grin. 'You swore that before, on your pagan amulet in the square in Novgorod. You swore to give me Christ's Holy Lance in return for the news I brought you. Is this new oath any better than that one?'

My head jerked at that – who was he to dare accuse the jarl of the Oathsworn that he did not hold to any oaths? I leaned over and opened my sea chest, drew out a cloak, the runed sabre and the wrapped bundle that he wanted. He was fixed by the sight of it and his tongue darted like a snake's. I almost waved it back and forth to see if he would follow it with his eyes.

'I promised you your silly spear and so you will have it. I did not say when.'

I dropped it in the tall, narrow sea chest and slammed the lid, so that he jumped with the bang of it. His eyes were poison pools, but I held the stare, for I hated him enough in return.

'If you run,' I said. 'We will bear the hurt of it and Vladimir and his uncle will hunt you down with all the power they have. So will Oleg. So will Jaropolk. All of them will want what you know and all of them will stake you out rather than have you tell the others.'

'But I know nothing,' Martin declared angrily. 'I was not part of your silver-greed, as you know. Tell them.'

'You think they would believe me? Anyway – you know what Eldgrim and Cod-Biter remembered. It is not as good as what I know, but it is good enough for Vladimir to keep you close. You know too much, monk – even Lambisson will want you dead now. Little Vlad only keeps you alive now because you are a holy man and he fears the curse of your White Christ if he has you killed.'

He blinked once or twice. Then his shoulders slumped as the weight of what he knew to be true crushed him. The safest place was with us, even if it meant coming into the steppe snows of the Great White. More than all that, he would follow the spear, snuffling for it like a dog after a bitch in heat.

'Anyway,' said Gyrth, wandering into the middle of this tense moment to peer hopefully in the pot and hunker by the fire, 'it is worse than that for you, monk. The White Christ followers are never staked here.'

Surprised, we all looked at him and he became aware of the eyes, stopped searching for more food and grew flustered at our stares.

'I had it from a Jew trader,' he explained. 'They hang those condemned who are Christ followers upside down. Like their god on the tree, only the other way up.'

Martin's eye twitched, for it was a terrible thing, it seemed, for Christ men to be hung – crucified, they called it – upside down. It was also a hard and long way to die.

'Our little Christ priest is used to that,' Finn sneered. 'He has been hung upside down before.'

Those who remembered Martin from the first time we had met him – slung from the mast of our ship, spraying tears and piss on to the planks together with everything he thought we might want to know – chuckled.

'He can do it standing on his head,' agreed Kvasir sombrely and the hoots and thigh-slaps chased after the flapping hem of Martin's robe as he strode from the hall.

'He will run,' Kvasir said, tilting his head to peer closely at his strap work.

'Not without his little stick,' Finn declared.

They took odds on it but I knew he would run only when he had the spear cradled in his arms and was sure of being able to run to somewhere safe; out on the winter steppe, I was thinking, the only safe place was with us.

Finn and others, meanwhile, muttered with their heads touching about how, when the time came, we might have to fight the *druzhina* of Vladimir to get their silver hoard. I let them; it was as lunatic as trying to throw a loop around the moon, but it kept them from becoming too morose. All the same, when the time came, I was thinking, I would have to come up with some gold-browed plan or they would be looking upward and shaking out hopeful rope.

Later, as I sat with Jon Asanes composing a careful letter to Jarl Brand, I paused to watch the bustle in the courtyard, dictating as Jon scratched in his best hand.

'Now there's the thing of it,' declared Jon, following my gaze as I rubbed one of Thorgunna's salves into the ankle that always gave me trouble in cold weather. 'Old Sveinald there is no fool and could not miss such preparation as this, yet he rides off without a backward glance at all these carts and loading and such. Is he burning too much at what happened to his boy to wonder what we are doing?'

'It is his boy who is burning,' I pointed out, 'and will, I am thinking, for a long while yet.'

'Yet one more trouble to add to the heap,' answered Jon and his voice was so wormwood bitter that I turned to look at him. By then, however, he was hidden behind his hair, hunched over, scratching away at the vellum with his tongue between his teeth.

Jon was smart, even when he sulked. Our going to seek out Atil's silver was the worst secret never kept; the markets were alive with it and men arrived every day to clamour to join Vladimir's *druzhina*, or the Oathsworn.

Sveinald knew of it, for all his indifference. That meant Jaropolk, whom I had last seen as a spotty youth, knew of

124

it. So would Oleg, the second of Vladimir's brothers and even allowing for the fact that there were stones more clever than him, he would know the importance of it, even if someone had to spell the words of it for him.

It was, I was thinking, as if Odin – a Volsung himself, I remembered – had bent and twisted and heated and forged this treasure hoard into an ever-increasing curse, dragging more and more people into it, beating it white-hot and ever-larger. But for what?

The wet feathers of the white raven drifted, light and cold on my upturned face, making me blink as they fastened on my lashes. Perhaps Crowbone had the right of it after all – perhaps this was Fimbulwinter, the heralding freeze at the end of the world.

Then, on the day the white raven stuck its head under a wing and roosted, permitting a blue sky and a red sun, we left Novgorod and went out on to the wolf sea.

NINE

The Oathsworn were lined up in a parody of the prince's *druzhina* but only half-mocking. Anything the dour folk of Novgorod could do, good men from the vik could do better they had decided.

Vladimir rode out to look his own men over. He was all gleaming with gold and silver, wearing a little sabre and perched like an acorn on a too-large black horse – so I had to wear my own finery and that cursed sabre and stride out to look the Oathsworn over.

The good people of Novgorod cheered and the carts creaked and the horses and ponies stamped in the cold, dropping cairns of steaming dung on to the freshly-swept oak walkways. I felt, at that moment, closer to being a jarl than I had ever felt.

They did not look too bad, the Oathsworn, for all that they had drunk through most of the money they had won from raiding Klerkon and rattled every whore in the city until her teeth loosened. Some had even thought to squander money on sensible gear fit for a winter steppe.

There was Kvasir, wearing a new coat padded and sewn like a quilt and stuffed with cotton. We called it *aketon*, which was as close as any norther could get to mouthing *al-qutn*, the Serkland word for cotton.

We knew the benefits of having padding under mail, but three wool tunics were usually enough, until we had found the soldiers of the Great City wearing these Turk garments. Not only did they keep off arrows but dulled a hard dunt that might otherwise break your ribs – and kept you warm in weather like this, too.

On the other hand, there was Lambi Pai, the Peacock, barely old enough to grow a wisp of beard and shivering in his new, fat silk breeks striped in red and white, with a silly hat fringed with long-haired goat. Which was still not as silly as the one Finn wore, which was Ivar's weather hat with a strip of wadmal tied round it and over his ears – but at least Finn's would keep him warm.

They were all grinning back at me, stamping feet and blowing out smoke-breath and stuffing their fingers inside cloaks and tunics to keep them warm; Klepp Spaki, Onund Hnufa, Finnlaith the Irisher, Bjaelfi – whom we called Laeknir, Healer, because he had some skills there – Gyrth, wrapped in sensible furs so that he looked like a dancing bear and all the others. Well – all grinning save Jon Asanes, who looked sour as turned milk and stared blankly back at me.

I saw Gizur and Red Njal and nodded acknowledgment of Hauk Fast Sailor's wave. Beyond them all, wrapped up like bundles in the carts, Thorgunna and Thordis watched me, while the deerhounds alone seemed immune to the chill on a day of blue skies and a blood sun with no heat left in it.

I wanted to tell them it was foolishness, of how many had already died on this quest, but I knew they had heard all that already from those who had survived the first time. It did not matter now – the silver hook was sunk deep and Odin reeled us all in. Bone, blood and steel – that oath would haul us all out on to the cold-wasted steppe.

So we trooped out through the gate, a long, winding column of sledge-carts and horses, men and boys, thralls and women and one reluctant Christ priest.

The little princes rode together, surrounded by the hulking shapes of Sigurd and Dobrynya and picked men of the *druzhina* in full mail and helmets and lances with forked pennants fluttering, forcing the thralls and drovers to scamper or be ridden over. I saw that a lot of the drovers were Klerkon's crewmen, reduced to hiring on as paid labour and lured to this demeaning thrall-work by the gleam of distant silver.

I vowed to watch them, in case any were holding grudges for Klerkon's death – though I did not think the man attracted such loyalty, I remembered what we had done on Svartey.

I forgot my vow, of course, a week later, when the winter steppe closed its icy jaws and gnawed even reasoning out of us.

There was snow, night and day and yet again, then it eased but only to give the snell wind a chance to catch up. Then it snowed again, small-flaked and dry, piling round the camp in high circles where the fires kept it at bay.

It fell, fine as flour from a quern, from a lead-dulled sky, sifted like smoke along the land, stinging the face and piling up, all the time piling up so that, finally, you could not get your feet above it and had to plough through it. Yet, when I turned, once, to get the sting out of my face and free my lashes from ice, there was not a mark; all smoothed and smothered, the snow left not even the voice of it to show where we had been.

The Great White, Tien called it and he should know, being a Bulgar from the Itil River, which Slavs call Volga. Vladimir had brought him, along with some Khazars as guides and his name, he told us with a grin, meant nothing. It was a good joke for it was true – *tien* was the name of a small coin, a trifle in the language of his tribe, the Eksel.

'I will trade you my fine name,' moaned Pai when he heard this, 'for your hat and coat.'

Tien laughed with fine, strong teeth. He wore a cone-shaped fur hat with flaps right down over his ears, a long sable coat belted at the waist with a sash and long fur boots, all of which were eyed enviously. In the sash, though, Tien had a curved dagger in a sheath and his hand was never far from it – particularly when the Khazars were close.

Sviatoslav had broken the power of the Khazars before he died and the tribes of the Bulgars, once dominated by the Khazars, were now free – nothing marked this more than Tien, who had gone back to the old ways of the Eksel, even to calculating the seasons and the years. It was a deliberate heathen insult to the Khazar Jews.

'This is the Time Of Small Frosts, in the second year of the Hedgepig,' he told us on the last night of our first week in the steppe, the oval of his face flickered by firelight. The camp was so sunk that no-one wanted to go far from it for private business, for you could not see it a hundred steps away, save for blue smoke in the last hour of evening – at night, even the red glow vanished.

'Small frosts?' grunted Gyrth. 'Any larger and Finn's other ear will drop off.'

Finn, who did not like mention of his missing ear, scowled and there were chuckles at Gyrth getting the better of him for once – but not many and not for long. The cold seeped into bones, even round the fire, so that your face and toes were warm but your back was numbed. It sucked away even the desire to laugh.

Tien shrugged. 'It has been colder,' he said and looked across to where the Khazars sat, stolidly listening and saying nothing.

He graciously accepted a refill from Kvasir's horn – green wine, I knew, cold as a whore's heart and which burned satisfyingly in your belly – and smacked his lips. Finn gave a sharp grunt of annoyance as Kvasir's shivering spilled some while pouring, for he loved that green wine and there was precious little of it with us.

'There was a time,' Tien went on, 'when we fought the

Khazars, even as we were part of the Khazar nation and even when no-one else dared.'

The Khazars stayed quiet, though their eyes were chips of blue ice in the firelight. Red haired and blue eyed were the Khazar Jews, while the little Eksel Bulgar was dark as an underground dwarf – which he may well have been, as Jon pointed out, for he knew more than any other Greek about the Old Norse.

'Alas,' said Tien, 'we were forced to flee, for I was a boy then and, clearly if I had been a full fighting man, we would have won. We went north and more north still and winter came.'

He swallowed and we waited. He smacked his lips and grinned, his eyes drink-bright in the firelight. 'That was when the green wine poured like honey, thick and slow,' he said, almost dreamily, 'so cold it was. When trees exploded with a crack and shot blue fire when they fell. When first I saw the whisper of stars.'

'What?' we demanded.

'The whisper of stars,' he repeated and blew out his breath in a long stream of vanishing grey. 'When you speak, the very breath in your body turns the words to ice and they fall to the ground with the sound of a whisper,' he explained.

There was silence, then a snort from Avraham, one of the Khazars, a big man with a bigger scowl and the haughtiness of a man who thought well of himself.

'Your stories are like your name, little man,' he said. 'But, as you say, you fled there having been beaten by us, so perhaps grief and shame clouded your boyish memories.'

'Once Kiev paid you scat, of a sword and a squirrel skin for every home,' Tien answered smartly, 'but Kiev came and destroyed you, which is clearly the will of Senmerv, Mother Goddess. Nothing will cloud my memory of Itil burning.'

Avraham half-raised himself, but was stopped by the smaller one, Morut. 'Bolgary, too, if I remember,' he said softly and

130

Tien acknowledged, with a slight nod, that Sviatoslav had torched his people's capital city as well.

Avraham waved a deprecating hand and added: 'Which is what comes from worshipping a woman. The maker of heaven and earth must, of his nature, be male, otherwise the creator would be female. Which is absurd since, all over the world we know, the female is subject to the male. How, then, can it be different in heaven?'

There was a derisive snort from the other side of the fire and some, recognizing Thorgunna, chuckled.

'*Oior pata*,' said Tien and both the Khazar Jews stiffened.

'We do not speak of them,' Avraham replied flatly.

'What is it?' demanded Jon Asanes curiously. 'Is it the name of a Jewish goddess?'

Avraham grunted and glared back at Jon, with little courtesy. 'If I thought you genuinely sought the truth, I would enlighten you,' he declared. 'Yet, afterwards, you will still worship those evil, heathen spirits of the North, unconvinced.'

'I am a Christian,' Jon answered indignantly, but Avraham curled a lip.

'Only the Jews, the Chosen People of God, have been granted the true insight into the nature of the creator,' he said stiffly.

'That did not help you much against Sviatoslav and the gods of the Slavs,' growled Finn and the Khazar scowled.

'We are the people of exile,' he commented bitterly. 'The world lines up to scatter us every time we gain a country of our own, paying scat to no man. They envy us for being the Chosen of God.'

'More likely they wanted to be rid of paying scat of their own,' I offered him back. 'The Romans, for one, will help one people one day and another against you the next.'

'They are Christian,' Avraham noted with a scowl, shooting a glance at Jon. 'They hate us.'

'What does he mean?' Finn wanted to know and Jon shrugged.

131

'The Jews killed Jesus,' he answered. 'Everyone knows that.'

'Truly?' enthused Finn, turning to Avraham. 'You killed this White Christ? You are the torturers of the Tortured God?'

'No,' replied Avraham, defiantly sullen. 'The Romans did, but now they follow the Christ ways and blame us for it.'

Finn sat back, his delight at what he had learned tempered. He shook his head, sorrowful and bemused.

'Even dead this white-livered Christ certainly knows how to cause trouble in an empty room,' he declared and Jon shot him an angry look.

'Still – it was no Christ-follower who warred on the Khazar and Bulgar,' I offered and there was silence at that as folk remembered Sviatoslav, great Prince of Kiev.

'*Idu na vy*,' said Tien sadly and everyone fell silent. *Idu na vy* – I am coming against you – was what Sviatoslav had sent as his last message to those he planned to conquer. Now he, too, was gone and the steppe was unleashed. Avraham scowled at the memory.

'Will they fight each other?' Jon asked softly and I shrugged. Tien said nothing for a moment, while we all watched with interest – it was nothing to us if they snarled at each other like dungheap dogs.

'We will see how cold it gets,' the little Bulgar said at last in his halting, thick-accented Norse. 'I can read the signs. If we stay this far north in the Great White you will see the green wine turn to syrup.'

'Well,' grunted Gyrth, looking like a mangy bear woken too early from winter-sleep, 'we had better drink it all then before such a tragedy happens.'

Finn toasted him, then thrust his drinking horn at Thordis, who looked at him steadily, then accepted it and drank.

'Move closer,' Finn ordered her, 'and find warmth.'

'That's an old trick,' Thordis replied flatly.

'No trick,' said Finn. 'You are cold. I am cold. I owe you heat, at least, as *weregild*.'

Her eyes widened, for it was the first time that such had been mentioned, though the fact of it had hung between us all like a blade – her husband had died because raiders came looking for the Oathsworn, after all, yet the same Oathsworn had risked their lives to rescue her from slavery. It would take a lot of waggling grey beards to law-speak that one out at a *Ting*.

Thorgunna nudged her sister pointedly and she moved up the fire a way and into the lee of Finn's body. He grunted, satisfied.

'Well,' declared Kvasir, beaming round, 'here we all are, warm and fed and heading for riches. Life could be worse.'

'As the swallow said,' answered a familiar, lilting voice from the darkness. Olaf stepped in, the elkhound padding after him to the fire, while all the eyes watched him and only Thorgunna's were warm.

'What swallow?' demanded Jon and Crowbone, so pale his lips and cheeks were blood-red, gathered the great swathe of fur-trimmed white wool round him and sat down at Thorgunna's feet, while she dreamily took off his white wool cap and began to comb his lengthening yellow hair.

'There was a swallow who ignored winter,' Olaf said and everyone grunted and shifted to be more comfortable, for though he unnerved them, they liked his stories.

'Let's call it Kvasir,' he added and people chuckled. Kvasir raised his wooden cup across the fire to the little prince.

'So Kvasir-Swallow dipped and swooped and enjoyed himself all summer and well into the russet days, when all his friends and brothers and sisters told him they were leaving to be warm elsewhere, before the snows came.

'But Kvasir-Swallow was having too much fun and ignored them, so they left without him. And he continued to swoop and dip, though it grew colder and he caught less to eat with his swooping.

'Then, one day, it was so cold he knew he had made a mistake. "I must fly hard and fast and catch up with my brothers and sisters and friends," he said to himself. So he did, but it was too late. Blizzards came and howled down on him, flinging him this way and that and far, far off course . . .'

'Sounds like every journey in the *Elk*,' growled Klepp Spaki, who had discovered he hated the sea. People shushed him and Olaf went on.

'Half freezing, he flew on and on, then the snowstorms blew harder than ever until his wings froze entire and he tumbled, beak over tail, down from the sky.'

He paused, for he had a feel for such things – he was never nine, that boy.

'What happened?' demanded an impatient Jon, leaning forward.

'He died, of course,' growled Finn, which brought some belly laughs, for that was an old tale-telling trick.

Olaf, grinning, said: 'He would have – but he fell into the biggest, fattest, freshest heap of dung just shat by a grain-fed milk cow in the farm that lay under his flight. The heat of it thawed him. In fact, it made him realize what a narrow escape he had just had, so he fluttered about and sang loudly about how lucky he was – at which point the farm dog heard it, came out, sniffed and ate him in one gulp.'

There was silence and into it, looking round the stunned faces, Olaf smiled.

'So it is clear,' he said slowly. 'If you end up in the shite and are warm, happy and safe – keep your beak shut and stay quiet, for worse will happen.'

We laughed long at that one, for it was a fine tale, well told and made us forget the keen edge of winter for those moments. Though, as Kvasir said when he had stopped laughing, it was no good omen to hear your name spoken in such a way. Olaf merely smiled, as if he knew more he was not saying and moved quietly to me when we were alone.

'There are men to be watched,' he said, unblinking serious. 'Klerkon's old crew – especially the one called Kveldulf.'

134

I knew Crowbone had some reason for hating this Kveldulf but, even so, his warnings made sense – the men from the *Dragon Wings* kept to their own fires and, more often than not, Martin sat with them. This had suited me, since his company was not one I cared for, but now Crowbone's warning made me uneasy.

Yet, I was thinking, what could they do? Out in this cold, we lived or died by what we did together; no-one would survive long alone.

This was proved the next morning, when we found two good horses dead from that cold, solid as stones, their eyes open and frosted and their hides too hard even to flay off them for the leather.

We trudged on, slithering and sliding across frozen grass, the snow blown into drifts and frozen-crusted on top, cloud soft beneath. One day followed the next and more horses died, all the ones too fine for the steppe and mostly ridden by the *druzhina* warriors. Then it was the turn of people to suffer.

Four of the hunter-scouts Vladimir had hired – all Klerkon's men – came to Bjaelfi Healer after being out on the steppe on their own, showing him their blackened toes and one the tip of his nose.

Onund Hnufa knew what it was at once and told them. 'The cold rots the flesh. When it turns black it is dead and such will spread. The only cure is to have it lopped off and quick.'

The least hurt was the big, strong, dangerous Kveldulf, who submitted to having the ends of three toes nipped. Two of the others, however, died of the cure the next day, for Bjaelfi had to take a foot from one of them and most of all the toes from another. Before he died, the toeless one revealed that he had seen the smoke of fires, no more than a day's journey to the west – for a man with two good legs, he added mournfully.

The last one, with most of his nose removed – and part of the tip of an ear – told us nothing at all, but moaned and wept about his plight.

Onund was hard on him. 'You should have spent more on fur and less on fucking,' he growled. 'At least you had the sense of a pair of good wool socks. Those others had bare feet in their boots.'

'You should have spent Orm's money wisely,' Gyrth added, stamping his warmly-booted feet. The others of Klerkon's crew looked grimly and pointedly at one another and I marked it – though the village we came on next day was such a welcome sight that it made me forget. Again.

The Rus called them *goradichtches* and I thought it was the name of the place at first, but it turned out only to be their name for villages. In summer, it would have been a pretty place, snuggled up to the banks of a river, which flowed quietly and dreamily between two rows of gently sloping hills, clumped with lush, tall willows. Now the trees were skeletal and the river marked only as a glittering ribbon between the faint snow-blown squares of fields and meadows.

On the far side of the river was a vast flat plain that glittered, studded with the tufted spears that told us this was marsh in summer. In the distance, a faint haze of blue hinted at ground higher than the rolling steppe.

There were no fences, only rows of willows to mark boundaries around this place and the snow piled deep at the base of a sea of those trees, which sheltered the fields. In summer, they would be orchards, fields of hemp and sunflowers, grain and, in the fringes of the marsh, thick-growing sedge. Now they were just clumps of stiffened tawny grass across which the snow blew.

The village was an earthwork circle with a huddle of houses, hunched low to the ground to fool the winter snow and the summer heat. The gaps between the houses were lined with tall willows that seemed to have been planted there on purpose, but the big Khazar said they were willow fence poles which had taken root, for this was the rich lands of the south, where you could stick a stripped pole in the ground and it would sprout.

A high tower dripped with ice and held a bell and there was a brewhouse and a brace of forges, for these Polianians were noted for sword-making and made most of their trade in blades. The place had been well fortified against the Khazars when they were a power and now there were new and uncertain dangers with the death of the Great Prince of Kiev.

As we rode up, the bell rang out and the place seethed. Women shrieked and children burst into tears because their mothers were crying and their fathers were shouting.

Sigurd rode forward and called out to them, which was not, perhaps, the cleverest move with his silver nose. Where it touched his face, the cold had turned the flesh as purple as an emperor's robe and if it had been me I would have kept the gates shut on him, for he looked blue-black as a dead man.

But they were Polianians and knew of Sigurd Axebitten, so eventually, the gates opened and we rode in – though the wailing had not stopped and the headman, his face as blank as the white steppe, stood with his hat in his hands as we slid misery through his gates.

He was old, lean and tall, with a pale, worn-out face, a long greyish moustache and eyes sorrowed as a whipped dog. Deep furrows scarred his cheeks and forehead, his rough hands and the wrinkled back of his neck. The skin on his fingers and palms was cracked and creased as if burned by fire. There were thralls who looked better than he did.

Kovach he called himself and Malkyiv he called the place – Little Fortress, I worked it out as, though I could have been wrong – and he had a right to look sorrowful, for a Prince had arrived with too many men and even more animals and that was worse than steppe raiders. Those he could have fought, at least, before they burst in to demand the winter stores.

Our men were quartered under every roof, elbowing for floor space, shoving aside livestock and considering themselves lucky to be in such warmth. The Oathsworn had two storehouses – conspicuously empty – and piled in, dumping gear and setting fires while the stolid-faced locals came and offered what service they could.

As they did so, I stumped across to the headman's own hut, where the prince had naturally taken himself and as many of his retinue as could be crammed in.

'Four days from Kiev,' Dobrynya said softly, pointing to the chart as he and Vladimir and Sigurd and myself huddled together at one end of the hut to plan what to do next. Which, as Vladimir would have it, was simple enough and he laid it out for us, pointing at the chart with his little bone-handled dagger – we go on, swiftly.

'We should stay here,' Sigurd argued, which was sense. Getting this far had taken three times as long as it would have in summer, floating downriver to Kiev. But, of course, we could not go to Kiev; even four days east was too close to Vladimir's smart brother, Jaropolk and the two men I least wanted to meet – Sveinald and his face-ruined son.

'We will gather what fodder and supplies we can take from here,' the little prince said in his piping voice, 'and head to the Don. Tomorrow, or the day after, but no later than that.'

'What of the villagers, my prince?' Dobrynya said and Vladimir frowned, knowing that to take what they had would condemn them.

'Pay them,' said Olaf and he and Vladimir looked at each other and nodded. Vladimir then turned and stared straight back into his uncle's eyes until Dobrynya lowered his and nodded. Everyone knew full well what he had ordered; the villagers could hardly eat hacksilver.

The headman, Kovach, knew it, too. He came into the

presence of the little prince, greasy fur cap in hand and head lowered as was proper. For all his deference, he was like the willow, bending in the wind yet rooted and immovable. There was food and it was hidden and he would not tell where it was, nor would searching do much good, for there were too many floors to be dug up, too many roof-spaces.

'Do you know who this is, old one?' demanded Dobrynya sternly, pointing to the whey-faced, tight-lipped Vladimir, but Kovach had endured shrieking winter and broiling summer and red war, so the likes of Dobrynya and a pouting boy was not going to cow him. Even Sigurd's silver nose only made him blink his rheumy pale-blue eyes.

'I thought it was my prince,' he answered levelly, 'the young Jaropolk, come in answer to my pleas, but I see this boy is too young.'

'This is his brother, Vladimir, prince of Novgorod,' Sigurd growled. The headman nodded and the ploughed furrows on his forehead grew deeper.

'Is that the right of it? Well, well . . . but if you did not come in answer to my pleas, it puzzles me why you are on the steppe at this time of year.'

'No matter of yours,' Dobrynya snapped. 'All you need to know is that we are here and you must tell us what we want to know.'

'Ah well,' answered Kovach, 'as to that, I am thinking that the prince of Novgorod, fine boy though he may be, is asking for what belongs to his brother. I am wondering if his brother knows.'

I chuckled, for there was a fox look in those pale eyes, which then flicked to me, interested. Little Vladimir flushed and his lips tightened.

'It is not your place to think,' he snapped, though his voice broke on it, robbing it of much of its sting.

This was pointless. Kovach was not about to break, even if I strung him, his daughter and all his relatives up by the heels and carved away the lies from them with the Truth Knife nestled in the small of my back. This was a stone of a man, like all his sort and there was much to be admired in how he could endure.

Beside – these were not Vladimir's lands and he could not do as he liked without raising the ire of his brother, Prince Jaropolk.

'What pleas?' I asked and heads turned. Kovach raised his eyebrows as he looked at me questioningly, mild as milk. Oh, he would have been a terror in Miklagard's marbled halls of intrigue, that old *bondi*.

'Orm,' I told him, as pleasantly as I could, for it does no harm to start politely, offering names and smiles.

'A Norse,' said Kovach, rasping a gnarled hand across his stubble. 'I know some of that tongue. Your name is . . . serpent?'

'Wyrm,' I said lightly, then leaned forward. 'It would be better to speak, old one. We are hungry as serpents and you know what hungry serpents are like.'

He blinked and nodded, then smiled, more gap than grin.

'My pleas,' he said and, remembering I had asked, I nodded. Dobrynya cleared his throat pointedly, but we ignored him.

'*Vodoniye*,' he said and there was a hiss of breath from Dobrynya and Sigurd. Little Vladimir went pale. I had no idea what he meant and said so.

'Creatures,' muttered Dobrynya. 'They feast on the souls of the drowned.'

'Child's tales,' added Sigurd, but he did not sound convinced.

'They live in the high ground in the middle of the swamp,' Kovach went on, his voice flat and level and bitter as wormwood. 'There are forty-eight families in this village and all of them have suffered.'

'Suffered how?' demanded Dobrynya.

'They come, these *vodoniye*, to steal our women and make them into *rusalka*. For years, once, perhaps twice every year.

140

They came in the autumn this year and took another. My grand-daughter.'

He fell silent and I felt a chill in this warm, stove-heated hut that had nothing to do with winter draughts.

'Yet you have done nothing,' piped Vladimir and Kovach cocked one spider-legged eyebrow in his direction.

'We sent men into the swamp at first,' he said. 'Six died the first time and we did it again and lost four and they were all good forgemen. We did not send any more, for we need men to make blades and work fields and can fight most things, but not this. So we built up our defences instead and each year we send to Kiev for help and each year it never comes.'

'Your defences are not good, old man, if they keep stealing from you,' I said.

'Magic, one supposes,' Kovach said matter-of-factly, though his eyes were cunning slits. 'They come at night and from the marshes. I saw one, once – scaled like a serpent, running through the streets in the moonlight, making no sound. Now you have come. Perhaps Perun has sent us a warrior called Wyrm to bring an end to these Scaled Ones, who are clearly hatched from a serpent's egg. The god has, after all, sent this cold, which has frozen the impassable marsh; I cannot remember the marsh ever having frozen.'

From the looks on the faces of those who knew him, I guessed it was the most that old Kovach had said in one place at any time and the silence after it was longer and more still as a result. It was broken only by the sudden pop of a log bursting in the fire; sparks flared and flames dyed everyone red.

'So – if we end this menace, you will share your hidden food, is that it, cunning old man?' growled Sigurd. He greeted the nod of reply with a sharp snort of disapproval.

'Hung from your stringy thumbs,' he added, 'you will tell us soon enough.'

'Hung from thumbs,' Dobrynya said into the silence that

followed, 'any one of your charges would tell us. Do you want us to do that? I can bring, say, the mother of your grand-daughter.'

Kovach blinked and his head went down; when all was said and done, he was a poor man, with no say in the storms that lashed him – but there had been so many storms in his life they had honed him; he had less fear than Finn, I was thinking.

Dobrynya and I exchanged glances, all the same. Dealing harshly with these nithing farmers and smiths was a privilege that belonged to Vladimir's brother and abusing them could provoke the very conflict Novgorod did not want.

'A small trek across some frozen marsh,' Dobrynya said finally, shrugging and and looking at me. 'Little enough.'

'Then let him take it,' growled Finn bitterly when I shared this out in the place the Oathsworn had been bundled into and proudly called a hall. 'What the fuck is a voy-ded-oy, or the other thing?'

'*Vodoniye*,' answered Crowbone brightly. 'Water *draugr*. It is said they take young girls and make them into *rusalka*, spirits of the marshes and water's edge. These *rusalka* are beautiful, pale-skinned and with long green hair that is always damp – if their hair ever dries out, they die, and thus they always carry combs with them, combs which can cause floods when pulled through their tresses. They are said to be able to turn into waterbirds and have webbed feet . . .'

He tailed off when he realized we were all staring at him.

'I know a tale about them,' he added, defiantly.

'Then keep it behind your teeth,' rasped Finn, furious with frustration. 'This old fuck of a headman has a thought-cage twisted by the cold. Does he seriously believe all this?'

'If he is touched,' Thorgunna declared, 'then others are, too – there is a woman and her man mourning for the loss of a daughter in this very house.'

She was Kovach's own daughter, who stood with wooden

spoons in each hand, stirring life back into some old ale as she told us – between sobs – of seeing a shadow in their house, hearing a muffled scream. Her round face was chap-cheeked, brown eyes red-rimmed and mournful; I did not tell her how things could have been worse for her, strung up by the thumbs and questioned by Sigurd and Dobrynya. She sounded scared enough, all the same and her tears were real.

Her husband claimed to have tackled the creature with a hand-scythe and I looked him over as he dragged out the tale of it. He had a broad, flat face, where the cheeks and nose stuck like galls on an oak and the wind had ploughed out wrinkles in it until tree bark looked softer. His hair was braided and had never been cut, only burned, so that the ends were crumbled.

He did not look like a man easily cowed and had arms hard with work-muscle, skin-marked roughly with the outline of a horse.

'Scaled like a chicken's leg,' he confirmed, but his eyes kept shifting and I wondered why.

The creature had run off with their daughter, fourteen summers old and corn-hair pretty, according to her ma and others I spoke to. There were other stories, some of daughters stolen, others of livestock taken and, because they were who they were, it seemed the grief-loss was equal to these people. Yet there was something rank as *lutefiske* about the affair.

Later, in the lumpen, shifting shadows, surrounded by murmur and the laughter of those with full bellies and warm feet, I sat and breathed in the smell of ale and unwashed bodies, while a small girl, one eye blind-white as a boiled egg, played fox-and-hens with the men and made them laugh when she won with considerable skill.

Huddled in a corner, faces murked by the uneasy glow of the fire, me and Finn, Kvasir and some others talked round this matter we had clearly been tasked with, quiet as the smoke which swirled round a sooted kettle.

None of us liked the idea of scaled creatures who could scamper silently over a deadly marsh, cross a stream, then a palisade and evade all the guards, both in and out, laden with struggling women or bawling calves.

By the time our tongues hurt, it came down to the same as it had been at the start; we would have to go to this place in the marsh and see for ourselves.

'We will find only some ragged-arse outlaws,' Kvasir declared. 'Mark me. Runaways, living badly out on the steppe and stealing what they need – including a decent hump.'

'Invisible outlaws I do not need either,' I growled back and that left them, like me, chewing on whether Kovach and the villagers were being entirely truthful.

In the end, Red Njal broke his silence, heaving himself up and sighing.

'Well, there is no way but to do it,' he growled. 'Steady and careful. The sun rises little by little, but it crosses all the world in a day, as my granny told me.'

'I wish it was your granny who was going and not me,' Finn grunted back.

In the morning, it had been decided that myself, Kvasir and Finn would go, with Sigurd and a dozen of his men, all suitably mailed and armed, as well as Morut and Avraham. Jon Asanes was sulky, because I had said he could not come with us for, as he admitted himself, he was no great fighter.

'Olaf is going,' he pouted back bitterly. Crowbone was going because his Uncle Sigurd was going and I had no say in that, but it did not help Jon's sulk. Crowbone teased him about wanting the princely gift of a smile from Vladimir, which made Jon flush to his ears and stamp off.

Blowing and stamping, we came out to our horses. We all had horses, which Finn looked at dubiously, for he hated riding; it did not help to see me easy in the saddle and smiling down into his scowl.

'Take care,' Thorgunna said to Kvasir, tugging his cloak

tighter round his neck. 'There are bannocks and cheese and the last of our meat in a bag on the saddle horn. Oh, and a skin of ale is hooked there. I don't expect you home before dark, so wrap warm this night.'

'Don't fuss, woman,' he said, though it was lightly done. Finn heaved himself up into the saddle, black-browed at all this. He aimed a storm-scowl at Crowbone and rumbled: 'We are not having that silly dog.'

Crowbone agreed with a nod, for I had already made it plain that the elkhound was staying behind. He was tied up and yowling as we left through the main gate, circling round to the opaque ribbon of the river, watched by cold-pinched, anxious faces and one of the village curs, who had routed out a bird frozen in the eaves of a house and fallen to the rutted path.

The river was iced and drifted with powdered snow, so we crossed it where there would have been a shallow ford and never as much as cracked it. In a moment we were into the tussocked, snow-scoured marsh and the palisade of the village shrank to a line behind us as we moved away from it, towards the faint scar at the edge of the sky.

The marsh glistened and, when it was full thawed, would be a formidable place of bog and sink holes – impassable, as Crowbone pointed out, if you did not know the secret way of it, as these creatures surely did.

'Outlaws,' Kvasir corrected, rubbing his weeping eye and we hugged that hope to us with our cloaks as we slithered through the stiff-spiked sedges, towards the scab of rock that grew even darker as we came up on it.

The sun hovered like a blood-drop on the edge of the world and our shadows grew eldritch, thin and long in front of us, while that black rock seemed more ominous with every mile. There was something about it that lined the heart with chill.

Trees sprouted, grew stark claws and thickened in clumps as we came up on the dark-cragged gall on the steppe, which was choked with them. In summer, it would be a mass of green and the rock would be softer and more rounded – but now it looked as if Jormundgand, the world dragon, had brushed a coil through the crust of the earth and left a single scale behind.

'A real outlaw lair,' Kvasir remarked, chewing on some thick bran bread and spitting out little pieces of grit.

Closer still, we heard strange sounds, like bells would make if they were made of water. The hairs on my neck were up and we all put hands on weapons and went slower, peering this way and that through the scatter of bare, twisted trees; Finn climbed off the horse, for he would not fight on it and had been complaining about his sore buttocks for so long now that I knew more about his arse than his own breeks.

Morut found the source of the sounds soon after; in one taloned tree hung the whitened skull of a cow, with other bones dangled from it, fastened by tail hair. In the wind, they turned and chimed against each other and the big, bold, bearded men of the *druzhina* shifted uneasily and made warding signs until Sigurd snarled at them to stop being women.

'Outlaw signs,' Finn growled sarcastically. Kvasir said nothing, but glanced back to where the sun trembled on the edge of the world. His look was enough; the idea of being in this place when it got dark was turning my bowels to gruel.

There was no choice, all the same and at least we had wood for a fire – though it was not only the chill that made us bank it high. We perched round it warily, under a millstone moon and a blaze of stars, so many, when the clouds flitted clear of them, that they made a man hunch his neck into his shoulders, as if ducking under a low arch.

'There was once a band of men,' Crowbone said, staring into the fire, 'up in the Finnmark, who thought they would hunt out troll treasure.'

I wished he would not tell one of his tales; they had a nasty way of stinging you. I said as much and he merely blinked

146

his two-coloured eyes and hunched himself under his now dirty white cloak.

'Let the boy speak,' growled one of the Slavs, a big slab-faced scowl of a man called Gesilo. His comrades in the *druzhina* nicknamed him *Bezdrug*, which meant 'friendless' and you could see why.

'You will not like it,' Avraham growled back, but Gesilo only grunted. Crowbone cleared his throat.

'There were three of them and they knew the rock trolls in that part of the world were always gathering gold and silver to them and they thought it would be a fine thing to get some of it. One – we shall call him Gesilo – said that it would be easy, for rock trolls became boulders in daylight and only came alive at night. It would be a little matter only to rob them when they were stone and be gone by nightfall.'

'A smart plan,' agreed Gesilo. 'This man has a good name, for it is a plan I would have come up with myself.'

He nudged his neighbours, who did not laugh.

'The three friends travelled high up into the Dovrefell,' Crowbone went on. 'They saw many a boulder like a stone-fixed troll, but none with any sign of treasure and it was growing harder and harder to find a night-camp where there were no such stones at all.

'The other two were wanting to go home after a few nights of this, but Gesilo pointed to a great hill, a lump of rock that stood high above the Fell and was shrouded with trees like the claws of birds. He was sure there would be troll treasure there.'

The listeners shifted and it was not hard to see why, since Crowbone had just described the very place we sat under. I wanted to tell the little cow's hole to clip his teeth to his lips, but I could not do it. Like a man in a longship heading off the edge of the world, I could not turn the steerboard one way or the other for wanting to see what lay through the mirr of falling water.

'The three friends took all day to travel to the place,' Crowbone went on in his bone-chiming little voice. 'It was growing dark when they came up on it, a great hump of black rock thick with bare-branched trees and surrounded by crops of rocks and boulders, many of which could easily be sun-fastened trolls. The other two said that there would be trouble, for there was no shelter and as soon as it grew dark the trolls would come out, stamping and angry.

'But Gesilo started up the steep sides of the rock, shouting out that there was a cave half-way up and it was too small for any of these boulder-sized perhaps-trolls to get in if they did come alive.

'That settled it; the other two followed on and soon reached the cave, which was as Gesilo described. It was too dark to see how far back it went, though it narrowed considerably, so could not be a bear den. It was just tall enough for them to sit in and light a fire, which they did. Darkness fell, but everyone was cheerful, because they seemed safe and had a big roaring fire going.'

Kvasir threw a stick on our own, which caused the sparks and flames to flare up and some of the listeners to shift. Grinning, rueful and half-ashamed, they sank down as Crowbone tugged his dirty-white cloak round him and went on.

'Eventually, they ran out of wood and drew lots to see who would brave the dark and fetch some time. One – we shall call him Orm – drew the shortest twig and reluctantly left the safety and fireglow for the dark of the hill.'

'Now there's the lie of it, right there,' grunted Kvasir. 'For I cannot remember Orm ever having fetched wood. Or water. Or . . .'

'I am the jarl, you dog turd,' I gave back, looking for a bit of flyting to put an end to this Olaf-saga – but Crowbone's tales were like the magic salt-mill that tainted the seas; once started, there was no stopping.

'Orm went out,' Crowbone continued. 'The trees seemed

to reach for him like claws, so he resolved to gather what fallen wood he could, as swiftly as he could and return to the cave, which was now a welcome glow above and behind him.

'Then he heard a noise. A grinding-grim sort of a noise. When he turned, there was a rock troll, tall as a house, made up of stones in the shape of a man, like a well-made dyke. When it spoke, it had a voice like a turning quern and demanded to know what Orm was doing in this place and why he had annoyed his old grandfather.

'Orm, puzzled, decided it would be a bad idea to speak of treasure, so he answered that he was collecting sticks for a fire and surely there was no harm in that and how could gathering a few sticks annoy this large troll's grandfather?

'The large stone troll raised his large stone fists and it was clear he was going to smash Orm into the ground. Orm, unable to get away and facing his doom, demanded again to know how gathering sticks for a fire should have annoyed the troll's old grandfather.

'There was screaming and the light of the fire went out above Orm's head, then the screaming of his friends was cut off. The big stone fists were raised to smash Orm to pulp and the big stone head smiled like a cleft in a cliff.

'"You should not have lit your fire in his mouth," answered the troll.'

There was silence and those with the great dark rock behind them hunched down a little, as if feeling breath on the back of their necks. Everyone was now remembering how much like the top of a head it had looked, sticking up through the glistening marsh, thin-furred with trees like the nap on a thrall's skull.

Avraham chuckled at Gesilo's stricken face. 'I said you would not like it.'

Gesilo – and the rest of them – liked it even less the next morning, when the light crept up and turned the trees into shadowed hands. It slid, honey slow, like the milk mist that

149

tendriled the scarred slopes of that dark place, looping in chilled coils round our knees. No-one was happy.

The rock was no higher than a few hundred paces, but in that flat, white nothing, seemed big as a mountain, cut and slashed as if one of Crowbone's trolls had taken a frenzied flint axe to it. It made us all move quiet and speak soft.

Crowbone stood, wrapped in his white cloak as usual, head cocked to one side as if listening, while men moved around like wraiths, upset if a horse stamped too loudly or snorted. Naturally, someone had to ask him.

'What do you hear?'

Crowbone turned his coloured eyes on the speaker, a vast-bearded giant called Rulav, who was standing at the head of his big horse.

'Nothing,' he said. 'Not a sound.'

Which was only the truth, but the way he said it made us all suddenly discover the utter silence of the place. No wind sighed, no bird fluttered or sang. Men made warding signs and muttered.

'White-livered bunch,' growled Sigurd blackly, though he saved some dark looks to shoot at his nephew. Morut laughed and slithered on to his shaggy steppe pony. He moved out into the mists, faded, then vanished and the shaggy-bearded giants in their long, leather-backed ring-coats watched him go and wished for his courage.

I laid a hand on Crowbone's shoulder as we sorted ourselves out.

'Time you learned the value of such a silence as you have found here,' I said to him and he nodded, now as pale and afraid as any nine-year-old.

The *druzhina* were more unhappy than ever, once they discovered that they had to leave their horses behind and go on foot towards this dark rock. Finn and I and Kvasir, on the other hand, were pleased and, when we shrugged into our light ring-mail coats, caught the envious stare of the big Slavs, encumbered with their own weighty garments, split to the crotch for riding and dangling heavily down to their ankles.

We waited; Morut ghosted back to us, wiping the pearls of mirr from his dripping face where the freezing mist had melted.

'There is a pool, the ice fresh cracked, not far ahead and just where the steep slopes begin,' he said. 'It is where they get water, for sure – recently, too. A trail leads up into the rocks.'

'Any green-haired beauties there?' demanded Finn scornfully. 'Combing their tresses, perhaps?'

Morut chuckled while the big Slavs sucked in the reference to slope and rocks. Not the words the great, trudging, dripbearded warriors wanted to hear, but Sigurd adjusted his silver nose and whistled scorn down it at them. They shipped shields on their backs, took the peace-strings off their swords and stumbled on, those mailed coats flapping at their feet. Those left to guard the horses were no happier, a few men on their own and looking right and left.

The pool was just as Morut had described – opaque, stippled ice with black in the middle where it had been chopped to the water. If there was a trail away from it, all the same, I could not see it – but it was hardly necessary. A boy raced away from it, bounding like a hare, leather bucket flapping in one hand, pointing the way up the slope as clearly as a blazed sign.

With a whoop and a roar the *druzhina* lumbered after him, despite Sigurd's furious bellows and Finn stopped, blew drops off the straggle of his moustache and shook his head.

'Can bulls catch a hare like that? My bet is on the boy.'

He won, but only just. The boy half-turned on the run to look at the roarers who waddled after him – and went straight into a tree, flying backwards on to his arse, the bucket bouncing back down the slope. One of the Slavs gave it a kick in passing and a triumphant bellow.

The boy was caught, for sure – he was up and reeling, but

the breath had been driven out of him and you could see his little chest heave. Dark, wild hair, I saw and skins over ragged wool and scraps of fur. Barefoot. Doomed.

The first one to him was Gesilo, reaching out one hand to grab him, the other heavy with a big, straight blade.

'Take him alive,' roared Sigurd, but who knows what Gesilo might have done. Not that he had a chance; his horny, broken fingernails barely brushed the boy's skin-covered shoulders and something broke from the snow-splattered rocks nearby with a throaty roar and a spear that drove straight into the Slav's face.

He howled and went over backwards with his jaw flapping loose and blood flying. A hand grabbed the boy and shoved him further up the slope. I say a hand, but it was more of a claw. What stood in front of the boy, spread-legged and spear-armed and snarling protectively, brought all the roaring Slavs to a skittering stop. Everybody gawped.

It was the shape of a man, but the face was warped, as if the bones had been squeezed and the skin tightened, so that it looked like a wide-mouthed frog. The eyes bulged, hair patched in a parody of a beard and straggled in wisps across the skull and it was naked, save for a skin wrapped round the loins.

And scaled. Every visible inch of it. Scaled as a chicken leg, just as we had been told, from thick-nailed feet to that wisp-haired skull. The hands that gripped the spear – a well-made weapon, I saw – were yellow-horned with nails long as talons.

There was silence, save for the scrabble of the boy vanishing up the trail into the rocks of the slope and the harsh panting of the Scaled Troll standing guard as he did so. Then Finn gave a rheum-thick growl, hefted The Godi and charged, howling out Odin's name and elbowing aside the startled, rooted Slavs.

Cursing that *valknut*-sign he wore, I went after him and, a step behind me on my shieldless side, was Kvasir.

As Finn came up, the Scaled Troll braced, stepped back, reversed the spear and dropped low, scything it in a tripping

152

arc. A lesser man would have been ankle-felled, but Finn leaped up and over it and the Scaled Troll was open for a downward cut – except that Finn's foot slipped on the iced rocks and he fell flat on his face.

With a howl, the Scaled Troll stepped back, spun the spear back to the point and stabbed. I got my shield there a second before; the spear thunked into it, wrenched it out of my grip and spun it down the slope like a wheel.

Kvasir, an eyeblink later, brought his wave-sword glittering down on the Troll's neck where it joined his left shoulder, carving deep so that blood and collarbone flew up. He – it – died with a howl and a series of skin-crawling mews, slushing blood in streams down the rocks while Finn and I hauled each other up, wrist to wrist.

'Good stroke,' Finn grunted, blowing blood from where his nose had battered the stones. Then half his face twisted in a grin at Kvasir. 'Outlaws,' he added. 'My arse.'

Kvasir did not grin. He stood and stared at what he had killed, while the scaled heels drummed and an arm twitched once or twice. The *druzhina* Slavs came up, cautious as cats and touching amulets and little magic bags.

Later, when we had recovered our courage, we examined the Scaled Troll more closely and discovered that it was a man after all, though barely old enough to be called one. The scales were like callouses all over the creature, flowed together, thick as fingernails, though here and there, the creases seemed cracked and red-raw.

'A disease, perhaps,' Sigurd said, using his sword to unravel the skin loincloth. 'Look – he has a prick like a man and that isn't scaled.'

'Yet,' growled Finn, unimpressed. 'It is a youngling.'

Sigurd, whistling through his silver nose, plunged his sword into the snow to wipe it clean and even then stared at it as if wondering whether to keep it or not.

There were other parts of the dead boy that were free of

scale – a hip, a patch behind one knee, most of a buttock – and the skin here was as normal as any slain man's, turning blue-white with death and cold.

'The other boy was not like this one,' Morut pointed out, looking up the slope to where the wild-haired little boy had run.

'That you could see,' Kvasir pointed out.

'This one protected him, died for him,' Avraham pointed out. 'Hardly the act of a monster.'

Finn spat. 'Wolves will fight for the pack,' he answered. 'Does that make them men?'

It made these creatures monsters to the Slavs, were-wyrms, or scaled trolls or worse. That and the threat of some strange disease made them grumble and mutter among themselves and, in the end, Sigurd came across to me and admitted, furious with the shame of it, that they believed these scaled creatures to be offspring of Chernobog, black god of death. It would be difficult, he thought, to get his men to go on.

'How difficult?' I demanded, angry myself and not anxious to unhook him from his shame easily. He glared back at me, the skin white round his silver nose, which was answer enough.

'Then we will go on without you,' I said, hoping it sounded bold enough for a Norseman and wishing I was Slav right then. Finn added a 'heya' of approval; his bad foot-luck had annoyed him and he was anxious to prove, to himself and Odin, that these scaled Grendels were no match for him and The Godi.

'I will go, if you will have me,' said Morut and I nodded at once, for his tracking skills would be good to have.

'And I,' added Avraham, 'for I have never seen the like of this before on my steppe and would know more of it.'

'Your steppe . . .' scoffed Morut.

'As much mine as yours,' Avraham snarled back defiantly. They fell into the familiar chaffer of it, as comforting to them as a pitfire and thick-walled hov is to a man from the north.

Crowbone wanted to go too, which was brave of him, but Sigurd told him – more abruptly than he had done in previous times – to stow his tongue in the chest of his head and stay where he was. Crowbone, cowed for once, obeyed without comment.

We left them milling round the drinking pool, gathering sticks to make a fire and not at all eager to even be there. They would not go near the stiffening body of the creature, though they hauled Gesilo off to where they could bury him.

'I said he would not care for Crowbone's tale and I was right,' Avraham noted with grim amusement, though the smile died on his face when he saw the scowls of the rest of the *druzhina*. He hurried to catch up with Morut, tracking ahead.

An hour later, the sun was up over the edge of the world, but not this rock. In the lee of it, the mist clung, cold as the white raven's eye, threading between the gnarled trees and patched thick as eiderdown here and there.

It was from one of these duck-feather mists that we were attacked. Morut led the way, following signs only he could read, from fresh-turned stone to barely visible broken twig. At a bend between rocks, he knelt to study the ground and a spear hissed over his shoulder, skittering across the frozen earth and almost across my toes.

'Form!' I yelled out of habit and, out of habit, Kvasir and Finn slid to me, shields up. From the rocks bounded three figures, much as before, though one carried a shield and another wore clothing and had a skin cap and no sign of scale.

Morut, caught on the knee, rolled sideways and scrabbled away. Avraham, with a yelp, sprang forward and took a blow meant for the little tracker – from a shovel. The shaft smacking Avraham's armoured forearm hard enough to make him grunt; he struck back and the scaled creature shrieked, carved under the ribs.

The one with the fur cap came louping at me, a great curved pick held above his head and relying on speed and power to crash through my shield. His mouth was red and open in a russet-bearded face and his eyes were wild.

Just at the moment he reached me, was about to bring his pick down, I stepped sideways, away from Kvasir and the man ploughed between us; it was moot which of our blades killed him, but both carved steaks off him and he fell, skidding on his face along the rocks.

The last, more powerful than the others, had hurled his spear and had no other weapons. He bounded forward and hurled himself, shrieking and snarling, at Finn, who took this rush on his shield and went over backwards, the creature clawing and biting the edge of it, his scaled, eye-bulged frog-face foaming with spittle and inches from Finn's own.

They fell backwards, in a clatter like someone beating iron on an anvil, broke and rolled. The creature came up, cat fast and spitting, while Finn was slower in his mail. Two powerful blows smacked him, one on the shield and the other under his ribs, so that he grunted. I saw mail rings flying and started in to help – but Kvasir laid a hand across my chest, as if to say that it was Finn's fight. A *valknut* fight.

It was then that a shape flew from the top of a head-height rock and crashed into Kvasir, so that he went over with a sharp yelp and a crash. I whirled and struck, fast as an adder's tongue and, in that same instant, tried to stop the blade.

It would not be halted, ripped through the ragged wool and the thin flesh and the small, knobbed backbone of the wild-haired boy, whose screeches of hate and fear turned to a great wailing whimper and then to nothing as he hit the ground, cut almost in half.

The scaled creature fighting Finn saw the boy dying in a scream of blood and drumming heels and wailed, high and anguished. Finn, grunting and winded, hurled his shield and the troll batted it away – but Finn was across the distance between them and The Godi swung, changed direction and hissed right into the path the creature took to avoid the feint.

The blade cut half-way through the thing's body, just above the hip and it fell away with a screech and writhed, scrabbling like a crab. Finn finished it with two more blows and then leaned on the hilt of his sword, holding one side and panting.

We straightened ourselves out and took stock. Finn's mail was torn – torn, by the gods, and only with the taloned claws of the creature, which was now twitching in a congealing pool of black blood. His *aketon* padding leaked wisps of cotton and the linen tunic beneath was shredded almost to the skin, which was marked with a solid red thump, though unbroken. The edge of his shield was shredded and three deep scores ran down the triangles of the *valknut* symbol.

We looked at what he had killed; powerful, muscled, hair like tree-moss on an old branch and a faded yellow – but human, for all that. He was big and clearly the leader – perhaps father, from his attitude to the dead boy – and might have been a fine, tall man save that he was scaled, frog-faced and wet-lipped as a slug; like the others, the creases of him were raw.

The scaled man Avraham had killed was already stiff, the one Kvasir and I had chopped was cold and looked normal, a dark young Slav with no visible sign of scales. No-one wanted to touch him, so we did not find out what lurked beneath his clothing.

Then there was the wild-haired boy, a fine black-haired boy no older than Crowbone, his face dirty and scraped raw where he had fallen on rocks, his teeth bloody and smashed. Not that he would have felt any of that pain after my stroke had all but ripped his backbone out; he lay, shapeless as an empty wineskin.

I felt the bile in my throat and spat it out; these were, apart from the one Finn had killed, no warriors. Clearly not invisible. For certain-sure they could not cross a marsh, a palisade, evade guards and all the rest without magic and if they had

157

any, they would have used it here. I said as much, the words spilling bitterly off my lips.

'Aye,' agreed Kvasir, rubbing the breath-ice off his beard. 'Something smells like bad cod here.'

Morut took the offered wrist and was heaved back to his feet by Avraham. They exchanged silent glances that said everything about what had just happened and grinned at each other.

'Mizpah,' Morut said, which I learned later was a prayer about their God watching out for each of them when they were absent from one another.

'While we are at it,' replied Avraham, wiping the blood off his sabre, 'I thank you, Lord of Israel, for not making me a slave, a Gentile, a woman – or one of these creatures. *Hakadosh baruch hu.*'

Grinning still, Morut moved cautiously forward and we followed, stepping as though the ground could open. We had gone no more than a few hundred yards before Morut said: 'There is a hov.'

It was a good hov in a little curve of clearing in the rocks, well built and much like what the Finns call a *gamma*, though they make them of turf. This one, thirty foot long and bowed at the ends like a boat from the weight of its own roof, was dry-stane, the spaces caulked with mosses and mud and the whole of it to the roof came up only to my shoulders. There was one way in, a low doorway, the wooden door stout and barred.

Finn smacked it with the hilt of The Godi. Someone – something – wailed.

'Well, they are home,' he grinned, wolvish as a pack on a hunt. 'Though they are mean with their hospitality.'

He leaned on the door with one shoulder, bounced against it to test, then drew back, took a breath and crashed forward. The door splintered. He kicked it with one foot and it burst inward. There were louder wails and whimpers.

He made to duck inside, but I laid my blade across the entrance, stopping him, though it took all I had in me to do it.

'This is why I do not fetch wood,' I said and he grinned and offered me a go-before-me bow.

Inside, it had been dug out down to the rock and there was headroom to spare. I ducked through the dark door, blade up, shield up. The floor was stone rather than the hard-packed earth of a hov in the vik, the light dim and woodsmoked and I was blinking, ready for anything.

Anything but the soft, gentle, pleading voice that said: 'Spare us.'

I made out four of them, all women. One was old, roughened by hard work and use, hands twisting in her ragged clothing. A younger woman was propped up in a box bed alcove, her quiet weeping drifting through the mirk. Another young one was still blonde and pretty under the filth, then I saw she had bold eyes and forearms as muscled as my own. These arms she was holding protectively round her stomach.

The fourth was a young girl crouched by the near-dead embers of the pitfire, naked. She was frog-faced, bulbous-eyed, scaled and afraid. 'Spare us,' she said in thick east Norse.

The older woman started to weep and the blonde came forward, hands outstretched and it came to me that these ones were, perhaps, some of those supposedly taken from the village. I had a moment of panic, remembering the tales of *rusalka* – but these were not the exquisite, green-haired temptresses with magic combs that Crowbone had described.

'Are you from the village?' I asked and the one coming towards me stopped, more at the tone of my voice than my speech. I didn't speak her Polianian tongue.

'Malkyiv,' I said, recalling the name. The woman nodded her corn-coloured head and her head drooped a little. She sighed.

'Spare us,' said the scaled girl, still crouching by the dead pitfire. One tiny robin-egg breast, I noticed was half-white and ruby-tipped. It was clearly all the Norse she knew and I wondered how she even knew that.

The others crowded in; the women wailed. I had Avraham and Morut take the two older ones out, while the scaled girl scuttled into a corner. The one in the boxbed, obviously younger, did not move, only cried as if her heart would break.

'Come,' I said, as gentle as I would to a nervous foal and holding out one hand.

'My baby,' she said – I did not understand the words, but the gesture and the pain in her was enough There was a crib next to her and something moved and mewed, a cat sound, strange and disturbing. I peered in.

It was a new-born changeling horror. Sickly pale, the face was tightened and stretched into the same frog shape as the others, but the eyes in its head bulged out, blind, red and wet as raw liver. The lips were fat, slug-wet strips of weeping sores and the skin seemed like hard plates, with every crease a stripe of vicious redness, so that the little pale body was a mosaic of pain. It mewed.

I fell back from it and the woman – the mother, I realized – wailed and thrashed her head in despair, for she wanted to pick it up and comfort it but it was clear that her very touch was agony to this mite.

Finn and Kvasir saw it and backed away, swallowing.

'Take the woman,' I said to Kvasir, my voice harsh and echoing under my helm. He hesitated, then bundled her out of the bed, carried her, thrashing weakly and shrieking about her baby, out of the hov. The others scuttled after, all save the scaled girl, who tried to make herself smaller in a corner.

I looked at Finn and he at me.

'Spare us,' said the scaled girl.

We never spoke of it after, Finn and I, neither to each other nor to any of those who later demanded the saga-tale of how

160

Orm and his two companions had taken on a nest of were-dragons and cut those beasts down.

All the long way back to the *druzhina*, with the smoke from the burning hov curling like a wolf tail over the dark rock, while the questions rang and the women wept and wailed, we said nothing other than that the task was done.

Sigurd rubbed his silver nose and tugged his beard with frustration. Crowbone stared at the rescued women with interest, but, like everyone else, did not see why they wailed, since they had been freed from monsters. I knew. I saw the anguish at the loss of their menfolk and a newborn babe and the scaled girl who begged for mercy.

In the end, Sigurd and the others gave up asking and the only sound the rest of that way back to the village was our ragged breathing and the women weeping and the ring of hooves on the ice of the marsh.

I did not know what they were, those creatures, or what had made them – but snakes will protect their young, I reasoned, so it is better to kill them when you see them, rather than wait for them to bite you.

Yet they had fought as a family, those afflicted and those not, and had done it brave as Baldurs; the bile rose in me every time I thought of the wild-haired boy and the red-eyed babe – and especially the girl who pleaded.

We came back to the village and were swept into the joy of the people there, now freed from fear of the creatures. The rescued women, no tears left and silent as tombs, sat like stones in this stream of triumph and said nothing.

I also said nothing to Kovach, just stared into his pale eyes and held out my hand so that he could see what I had discovered. To anyone else, it would be a stone, no more. But he knew and took it from me and, as I walked away, I felt his eyes on my back like arrows.

Shovels and picks and a spoil heap, that's what I had found. Behind the hov, a narrow cleft, dug out and shored up and, nearby, a neat, hidden heap of good iron ore which these . . . creatures . . . had traded to the sword-forgers of Malkyiv.

In the end, the price, perhaps, became too high – from good livestock, to spare women to keep the little marsh clan going, despite whatever god had inflicted fish-skin on them.

Then there was the grand-daughter, with forearms muscled from forge work. In the north, we did not have women at the forge, but we were no strangers to it and some fine blades were crafted by women.

Once Kovach had to part with his skilled grand-daughter to get the all-important iron-ore, that was the end of it for the miners in the marsh. Kovach had, indeed, sent men – but it was to wipe out the marsh-miners and take over. Nor did it surprise me that the marsh and the miners had done for them all.

Well, we had done for the little marsh clan and brought Kovach's grand-daughter back, blonde and weeping; the cunning old man wept his thanks to the gods, then told the villagers to bring out the hidden supplies and declared a cele-bratory feast.

Now they had what they needed, Kovach and his village; they would get the rescued women to guide them back through the marsh and work the ore for themselves, which they had gained at no loss.

I wished them well of it, though I thought they would never be free of what they had done – nor would I. I would have it in my dreams forever, while Kovach's own doom lay under that blonde head he caressed; once, she caught my eye and the misery in it was plain, as was the plea. I had seen her, protecting her belly with those muscled forearms as I came stumbling into the hov, all metal and edge.

I did not know what she would give birth to – and neither did she – but I suspected Kovach would not be caressing her this time next year, blade-working skill or no.

I told some of it to Vladimir and Dobrynya, quietly, while

162

Sigurd and Crowbone listened and it was clear they were there to make sure I told it true. I left out what we had burned and what might still appear with the spring.

In the end, little Vladimir nodded, smiling and generous as a prince should be. 'Good work, Orm Bear Slayer. Skalds will sing of this for a long time and the saga of it will be told round fires for ages yet to come. Eh, Olaf?'

'I will tell it myself,' agreed Crowbone, 'especially since I am in it.'

They smiled, bright little suns to each other. Vladimir and Olaf were the coming men and showing all the signs of being rulers you did not want to be anywhere near when they grew into the full of their lives.

I left them, avoiding the mad joy gracing the village. The night was washed with moonglow so that the land glittered blue-white; I tried to get enough clean, cold air in me to wash away the sickness I felt. I watched from the shadows as Crowbone went off, whistling vainly for Bleikr.

Cooking smells drifted, meat rich and mouth watering. Somewhere, Thorgunna would be seasoning what was in our pot, the others clashing cups and ale horns, grease-faced and grinning and making verses on the bravery of Orm Bear Slayer, Finn Horsehead and Kvasir Spittle. The number of creatures would grow in the telling, the hero-work swell and all of it, like the bear that had given me my name, was a lie.

I knew, though, that Finn and Kvasir would be quiet in a corner, saying nothing, thinking – like me – of the well-built hov, now ashes and smoulder and what we had burned in it and at the cold-hearted people who had engineered it.

A dog barked, then howled, a sound I did not like much. Someone called my name and I trudged down to where I thought it came from, near the frozen river, thinking one of my men had spotted wolf and wanting to be sure the pack was not lured by desperate hunger into going after our horses. I wanted to lose my thoughts in simple tasks. In the distance behind me, music suddenly squealed out, a tendril lure that made me half turn.

I stumbled and went down on one knee, came up cursing and wet. The obstacle was almost invisible against the drifted snow, but it was a dog. A white elkhound. And my hands and knees were too wet just for snow.

Just as I saw the blood, I saw the shapes and started to turn. The blow was a hard dunt, a star-whirler that knocked me flat but not out. For all that, I could only see the raging fire of the pain and the sickness that rose up, so that someone cursed as I bokked it up on his shoes.

I thought of Short Eldgrim and panicked at the idea of waking with my mind smoothed out like a sea after a storm, empty and blue and featureless.

'Struggle and you will get another one,' snarled a voice I did not know.

'Enough,' snapped another. 'Sack him up and bring him with the boy. Fast now . . .'

That voice I knew, even as my head flared and roared and darkness fell with the grain sack they bundled over my face to keep me from shouting.

Martin.

TEN

Someone took the sack off when the day came up and they thought themselves far enough away. I blinked into the glare until my watering eyes made out the shape of Olaf, sitting next to me in one of the sledge-carts, bundled in his white fur cloak. There was blood on it.

The air was full of shimmering ice particles despite a blue sky. The snow squeaked, the horses' breath froze and we slid, in a panic of haste, across a sea that surged and swelled in pearl-white waves.

'Are you well, Jarl Orm?' he asked, peering at me this way and that from under his fur hat, his face pinched and pale with cold. 'You took a hard dunt.'

I felt it. Anyone who boasts of being knocked spinning by a crack to the head, then springs up the next minute to take his enemy by surprise is a toad-puffed liar. I did not want to move my head at all for the first hour after I had woken, for it made my belly heave. The lurch and sway of the sledge-wagon was barely tolerable.

The light hurt and I shut my eyes, but I heard everything; voices I did not know, Geats or Svears from their accents. Martin, that cursed monk, with his rasping Saxlander bite urging them to move. And a Slav accent that sounded familiar, though I could not put a face to it.

Eventually, I managed to open my eyes again – the tears had frozen them shut and for a brief moment of panic I thought I had been blinded. Wrapped to the eyebrows in his fur-trimmed cloak and goat-wool hat, Olaf huddled in the lee of horse-fodder and food bundles, watching me. There were little icicles on the strands of his hat and one from his nose that he did not want to remove, I knew, because he would have to unwrap himself.

I leaned over and wiped it away and he smiled, shivering. 'I thought you would die,' he said and, at the moment, he was a nine-year-old boy. I managed a grin, though it felt as if my face was a mask and cracked when I did it. I felt clumps frozen in my beard and moustache.

'I look better than you – is that your blood?'

He shook his head. 'Bleikr,' he said miserably.

The cold bit, but I was sweating by the time I had managed to sit up and look out of the sledge-cart to find we were slithering and fish-tailing through chest-high pale yellow grass, with the exhausted ponies stumbling in the snow. Up ahead, a man bulked by clothing was leading the little horses which pulled the cart. Turning carefully, I saw other figures, counting them without thinking. Seven in all.

'Ha – now you are up, you can get out and walk,' yelled a voice and I turned to see a black-bearded face, rimed with ice, glaring at me. He was bundled in a cloak and another was swaddled round his head, but he was red-faced and sweating with the effort of staggering after the cart. That was bad for him, I saw with some satisfaction.

'Leave him where he is,' rasped the familiar voice of Martin, stepping forward from behind him. 'Safer where we can see him, Tyrfing.'

Then he moved away before I could find words to curse him.

I remembered the black-bearded one now; the German Tyrfing who had been one of Klerkon's men. I saw a couple of others I recognized from that crew – then blinked as two faces I knew well lumbered up to put shoulders to the back of the sledge-cart and help the stumbling horses. They kept their heads down, to avoid looking me in the eye.

Drumba and Heg, my own thralls – wearing warm furs and cloaks that were clearly stolen and with axes and knives in their belts. Drumba's had been the Slav voice I had failed to recognize.

Slavs – I cursed myself for a fool. I had only gone and brought these thralls back to their homeland without even considering that they would bolt for it first chance they got. Odin's arse, they could even be a fart-length away from the home they had not seen in a decade or more. But who ever considers what thralls think?

'Vladimir will track you down,' I said to the tops of their wool-hatted heads. 'You should have thought this out to the end.'

Heg looked up, chin thrust out defiantly. 'Better this than dying on some mad chase for a hoard of silver,' he growled. 'What would we get from that?'

Nothing at all, being thralls. What had they been promised for this, I wondered? So I asked and Drumba gave the sledge-cart a final heave and stood, flapping his cracked, worn hands against the cold.

'Enough,' he said to the gap opening between us. 'A stake for the future and a chance to be free.'

'You will never be free,' I shouted to the gap between us, sounding more sure than I felt, 'and the only stake you will get will be rammed up your arse.'

The pony ahead wheeled round at that and came alongside at a shambling half-trot, scattering snow fine as flour. The rider peeled back the cloak that covered his face, all but the eyes, which had been circled with great dark rings of

167

charcoal, a steppe tribe trick against the glare from the Great White.

'Yell away, young Orm,' he said with a chuckle. 'No-one can hear you who cares much.'

Thorkel. He grinned at me and I almost hurled myself at him from the cart – but even the surge of anger in me made my head hurt and I swallowed it back.

'This is the worst luck you have had,' I said to him. 'Which is a feat, considering your life to this point. The Norns hate you, Thorkel, for sure; they are unpicking the threads of your life.'

He scowled a little at that, then shrugged. 'No. I am thinking this is where my luck changes. We will sell you and the boy to Jaropolk, which is surer money and safer, too, than chasing down this hoard across a frozen steppe.'

So that was it. Martin's idea, clearly – though what did the monk gain?

Thorkel shrugged when I asked. 'Away with his holy stick and no part of your quest,' he said, looking over to where Martin trudged, two bundles wrapped and slung on his back, wild hair flying. He had to be freezing in his tattered robes and big leather shoes, but gave no sign of it other than the hand that grasped his staff, which was blue-white.

'You believe this? After all you know of that monk?'

Thorkel frowned, then brightened. 'We will know soon enough, when we reach Kiev.'

'You will never reach Kiev.'

He chuckled then and reined the weary pony round. 'Well, it will be a hard run, right enough,' he admitted, 'for Vladimir will want you back, since you know the way to Atil's hoard, while Sigurd Axebitten cares what happens to Crowbone. But we will beat them and what will they do when Sveinald has you?'

I wanted to spit a clever answer back at him, viper-venomed and fast, but my tongue stuck to the roof of my mouth at what he had said.

It was true enough. They had a head start and even if little Vladimir, all bright-eyed with silver greed, flogged horses to death he would not get to us in time. Olaf saw all that flicker across my face and hunched deeper into his cloak as the wind hissed and rattled the frozen grass.

The Oathsworn would keep coming, though, relentless and grim and driven. I pointed that out to Thorkel while reminding him that he had broken his oath. He frowned, for he remembered the words of it now and I twisted the knife of that in him.

'May he curse us to the Nine Realms and beyond if we break this faith, one to another.'

He winced and looked over to where Martin trudged and I knew the monk had persuaded him that embracing the White Christ would save him from Odin. It came to him that Christ would need to have considerable powers to save him from the wrath of the Oathsworn.

The power of that oath suddenly washed me; before, I had always been the one forced to action by it, hag-ridden to risk myself to rescue the stupid I had shackled myself to. This was the way of things, I had thought. Now I was the one depending on the oath and for the first time in my life I felt the sun-warm glow of it, the exultant certainty that I was not alone.

He saw me smile knowingly from the ice tangle of my beard and, scowling, tugged the pony round and forced it back to the head of the column.

There was silence for a long time after that, while the short day died and the steppe reeled away, featureless save for some wolf tracks, which excited everyone. But you could see a long way and nothing moved, not even the chill blue air.

Then, as the sun died at the end of the short day, squeezed into a great orange-red pillar by the cold so that it seemed to hold the sky up from the edge of the world, we stumbled up to a stand of birch trees, bloodied in the dying light.

We stopped then, for here was wood for fires, though it was almost too frozen to be cut never mind burn. Thorkel had stuffed the tops of grass inside his tunic, which kept him warm during the march and thawed out to provide tinder, so he made a fire, careful and slow, as if he was rubbing a fainted maiden's hand to bring her back to life.

There was heat and food, after a fashion, but the cold seeped through for all that and the horses whimpered and scraped hungrily at the ground, for there was little food for them.

'They will die soon,' muttered Heg and Drumba shushed him.

'We will make it to Kiev,' rasped Martin, hunched by the fire. Thorkel and the others, the melted ice glistening like pearls in their hair and beards, spooned gruel or stared at the flames, enduring.

'There was once a rich man,' said Crowbone softly, 'who lived in Kiev long ago, do not ask me when.'

'Enough,' warned Martin and crossed himself. 'Your stories are spawned by the Devil himself, for how could a boy like you know so many and so well?'

'I like them,' argued Heg and Thorkel grunted.

'Who cares what you like?' he said. 'You mistake yourself for a man.'

'He is a man, as am I,' growled Drumba. 'You mistake us for the thralls we were.'

'So all dogs fight,' Crowbone said with a sad sigh and a shake of his head. 'Once it was not so.'

'You call me a dog, you brat?' rumbled Tyrfing.

'If it yaps like one,' Crowbone said and I was wishing he would keep quiet, for my head would not take another good thumping.

'I will yap you, boy,' grunted Tyrfing and made to rise.

'Enough of all this,' snarled Martin. 'Leave the boy – have you understood nothing? We need him and Orm alive.'

'Of course, all Christ priests are like cats,' little Olaf said and heads came up.

'Why cats?' demanded Thorkel, pushing more wood near the flames to thaw it out enough to feed the fire.

'There was once a rich man,' Crowbone said, 'who lived in Kiev long ago, do not ask me when.'

No-one spoke when Olaf stopped and he looked up from the fire and into all their faces.

'This man,' he went on, 'lived in a fine *izba*. High walls hid it from view. He had no family and his only company was a cat and a pack of dogs. He never went out to work. He did not even go out to buy food. No-one ever visited him. Naturally, everyone was very curious – especially the thieves.

'One night, a thief sneaked into a neighbour's courtyard and peeked over the walls. He saw a wonderful place, of bath-houses and granaries and a forge. In the centre was a house fancy enough for the emperor of the Great City.

'The curious thief climbed over the wall and crept into the house, which was filled with fine furniture and rich hangings – a real jarl's hov. In a high seat of gold-studded wood sat the old man, richly dressed, wearing gold rings on his arms and round his neck.

'There were feasting benches and a great table carved from a single piece of shining wood and the old man sat in his high seat, with the cat and all the dogs opposite, like they were his guests at a feast – but there were neither plates of food on the table nor any thralls to cook and serve.'

'I know how that feels,' grunted a man from behind Thorkel.

'I know now how it feels to be the missing thrall,' answered Heg with a chuckle.

'Shut your bungholes,' growled Tyrfing. 'This at least takes my mind off the cold.' He gave a harsh look at Martin, who wisely clamped his ruined gums.

Crowbone smiled and went on with his story and I wondered why, for there was no reason to raise the spirits of this band.

'The old man smiled at the dogs and asked: "What do you want to eat tonight?" The dogs gave a bark and the old man nodded and drew out a Christ amulet from a small box, one of those fat crosses with the dead god nailed to it and said: "As you like it, as I like it, I would like some rich stew."

'A big golden bowl of fine lamb stew popped into the air above the table and landed with a clank in front of the dogs. The smell was delicious and they happily began to slurp down their food.'

'You turd,' growled Thorkel, 'I see your plan now – you are trying to kill us with longing for what we do not have.'

'Pagan imp,' growled Martin angrily. 'The holy cross is not some Devil's magic-maker.'

'The old man asked his cat – let us call it Martin,' declared Olaf, ignoring them both. Martin scowled but said nothing.

'The cat merely licked its paws, so the old man wished on the amulet and a big steaming carp appeared. With a disgusted look at the dogs, the cat began to eat daintily.

'Then the old man wished up his dinner on the amulet and the platters with it, all gold, crusted with jewels and a huge drinking horn banded with silver for him to drink his fine wine.'

'Blaspheming imp,' spat Martin. 'Enough – God will not be mocked.'

'Shut your hole,' snarled Tyrfing, shivering now, his inner layer of clothes having been soaked with sweat, now freezing. 'I like the sound of such a drinking horn and what it might contain.'

'At the end of this feast,' Olaf went on, 'the old rich man yawned and wished the dirty plates all away, then he and his pets slept – though it was the cat who ended up in the rich man's bed, covered with furs and fine linen. The dogs tried to crowd in, but Martin the cat yowled until the rich man scattered them off, leaving him and the cat alone in the huge comfortable bed.

172

'The thief waited patiently until the old man and his pets had begun to snore. Then he sneaked in and stole the amulet. The next morning, the old man woke and found his amulet missing. He hid his face in his hands and wept. "I am ruined. Ruined! And I am too old to go looking for the thief."'

'Sounds like Thorkel,' I said and he curled his lip at me. Olaf laid a hand on my arm and I wisely obeyed and kept quiet.

'Then the rich man felt something wet on the backs of his hands and he looked up to see that it was his cat and all the dogs licking him. He put his hands on the dogs' heads, one by one. "Will you be my strong legs and go and find him?" They howled and yelped.

'The old man looked at Martin the cat. "Will you be my clever mind and get the amulet?" And the cat licked his hand.

'So the loyal pets left. They looked all over the land, from Aldeigjuborg to the Great City, from the lands of the Livs and Ests to the wild steppe of the Khazar Jews and beyond, even to where silk comes from. They lived by their skills and their wits. The dogs sniffed around in alleys for things that people threw out. Sometimes, they had to fight the other beggars for it, but the pack was strong and always won – and always shared what they had with the cat.

'The cat learned how to leap up through kitchen windows and steal food. Often Martin would eat most of it inside the house and only bring the leftovers to the dogs.

'Eventually, the animals heard of a rich man who had appeared out of nowhere, who lived on the other side of the mighty Dnepr. "You dogs are strong enough to bear me," the cat said. "One must carry me."

'The strongest of them agreed. "But do not dig in your claws," he warned and crouched. The cat leaped on his back and the dog slipped into the river, the pack following. The water was so cold and swift that the dog soon grew tired.

'"I cannot do it," the dog groaned, leaking blood, for the

cat had not spared its claws. "Then another must," the cat urged. "Think of home. Think of hot meals and soft furs and linen."

'So the next dog took the cat and went on until he was too tired and the next after that. Eventually, in this way, the cat reached the other bank and the dogs climbed out exhausted. "Now for the amulet," the cat said, not tired at all and sped up the hill without waiting for the slow, wet, weary dogs.

'By now Martin the cat was an expert at sneaking into houses and crept silently into this fine one, hiding behind a richly-decorated seat. The thief strode by in a robe of silk embroidered with gold. Around his neck hung the Christ amulet on a golden chain – but he was not as careless as the rich old man. Two guards accompanied him at all times.

'Going outside, the cat just stopped the dogs from blundering inside. "We will have to use both your strength and my wits to get the amulet," explained Martin.

'"Anything for the old man," the loyal dogs promised.

'They waited until the thief went for a walk in his garden. The dogs suddenly darted out from bushes, bowling over the startled guards and leaping on the thief.

'"Stop them," the thief shouted frantically. The two guards could not use their swords because they might hurt their employer. Instead, they tried to pull the dogs away. A huge fight raged.

'Into this, the cat shot, a small streak of fur. Perching on the rich man's chest, Martin pressed both front paws against the Christ cross. When the thief reached for it, the cat bit his hand so he snatched it back. Silently, the cat wished, "As you like it, as I like it, I would like to be back home with the amulet."

'As the cat began to fade from sight, the dogs barked anxiously. "Wait for us, wait for us," they howled – but the cat vanished from sight and, next moment, was back in the old man's hov. The old man lay in a ragged robe on a pile

174

of straw. He had sold everything to pay his debts. Through the window, the cat could see that the garden itself had fallen into ruin.

'"Thank the White Christ, you have come back," the old man said. "I was near death here. Now give me my cross."

'Instead, the cat picked up the Christ amulet in her mouth and ran off with it, leaving the old man cursing. He never saw Martin the cat ever again. Months later, as he lay dying, he heard barking at his door and, suddenly, a handful of mangy, limping hounds burst in, tired, and dusty, all torn ears and scratches.

'"Too late," the old man said. "The cat's run off and hidden the amulet." Then he turned his face to the wall and died.

'The dogs slunk away, howling and arguing with each other and began to look for the cat, but Martin was long gone. So from that day to this, dogs have fought each other and only stop to chase every cat they see, hoping it is Martin with the amulet. They have distrusted all cats ever since – and men, if they are wise, should do the same, for not all those who carry the cross are good Christ-believers.'

In the silence that followed, the hissing wind was loud and mine was the only chuckle. Then men started half-up, afraid, as something flitted silently overhead.

'Only a hunting owl,' Martin snapped, then rounded on Thorkel, Tyrfing and the others and savaged them for their twitchiness.

'This is what comes from listening to that damned boy,' he thundered and they hunched their heads deeper into their shoulders, as much to endure him as the cold and the long night. Then he looked sideways at Olaf and made the sign of the cross.

'If you have such a Christ amulet,' growled Tyrfing, trembling with cold, 'now would be a good time to use it, priest.'

Martin only shook his head at such foolishness. The silence was brooding.

'A good tale,' I whispered to Crowbone when I could. 'It did not miss the mark, I am thinking.'

He turned to me, eyes round and serious. 'The owl tells me to watch out tomorrow,' he said. 'Things will happen and we must be ready for them.'

He turned back to stare at the flames and I felt the racing creep of my flesh that always told me when the Other was close, when the membrane between the worlds was thinnest.

He may have been earlier in the day, but he was not nine now, that little Crowbone.

Tyrfing was dead next morning, sitting by the black scar of the iced-over fire, wrapped in his cloak and ghost-white with rime. His face was a faded blue, his eyes fastened shut with lashes fine as silver wires.

'He will be the lucky one,' Olaf piped up and the remaining men scowled; Heg even reached out as if to cuff the boy, but freedom sat too new on him to behave like that.

Martin, a dark scar himself in that place of frosted ground and frozen white birch trees, slapped men to get them to move and they did, slowly, as if underwater. Thorkel, too, added his curses and cuffs and they staggered into a world like the inside of the frost-giant Ymir's skull, a huge curve of iced sky and snow plain that seemed to have no beginning and no end and was turning pewter-dark by the minute.

The last pony, trembling and head-bowed with misery, was fetched from where it had been tethered and Martin told us to get back in the cart.

'They should be made to work,' Drumba argued, scowling. 'That one pony will scarce pull the load. Get them out and pushing.'

Martin gave in and we climbed out, stiff with cold and me with my head aching still, each step a stab of pain in it. The wind hissed snow in my face and the pearl sky slid towards darkness.

'Whatever happens,' Olaf said, looking up into my face, 'do not worry. Yesterday, I saw a magpie in a tree over there and a raven joined it and they sat together for a while, watching us. Then the raven chased the magpie off.'

Raven – magpie? I heard it, as if from a long way off. The boy was mad for birds. Or just mad.

He saw my look and smiled, his lips blush-red against the pallor of his pinched face. 'The magpie is Hel's bird, made like her face – half ruin, half beauty. The raven belongs to Odin and the message is clear . . . Odin will prevent Hel from claiming us this day.'

'Not a straw death, at least,' I managed through my clattering teeth.

'If the Norns weave it,' Olaf answered, 'no death at all.'

Thorkel was trying to back the pony into the traces, had it halfway hooked up when someone yelled, shrill and high as a woman.

Drumba half-turned and the arrow took him high on the shoulder when it should have pinned him between the shoulderblades. Thorkel, fighting to hold the pony, took one there, a deep shunk of sound that staggered him – but he stayed upright and only seemed angrier.

The horsemen spilled around us like ghosts, the white cloths that had draped them and their horses flailing like winding sheets. Those cloths had hidden them from sight, the snow had hidden them from sound and now, breaking right and left round the little copse of trees, they galloped in a spray of white flakes and arrows.

Heg fled, screaming, vanishing into flurries of snow. Another arrow thudded into Thorkel, in his chest this time and he staggered back with the force of it and lost his grip on the pony, which reared and fought in terror.

They were silent, these horsemen. Silent and agile as cats, climbing up and ducking under, whirling almost completely round to keep the arrows coming while they rode round and round, flailing their horses into stumbling runs, the snow like gruel under their ponies' hooves.

Thorkel, snarling now, dragged out a sword – the frozen-stiff fur he wore was as good as armour against the arrows and he whirled one way, then another, spiked with them, like a mad hedgepig. Drumba choked off his last yelping cry when another arrow skewered his chest and punched a little way out of his back in a flick of time. He went down in a swirl of moans and red-dyed snow.

The wind was howling, I realized. Crowbone tugged my cloak and I saw him hunkered at my feet, but the pony and the wind and the screams of men turned him into a gawping fish, his mouth opening and closing soundlessly to me.

A figure lurched into me, bounced off and started to move away, half-turning to fling me away with a curse from a black-toothed, ruined mouth.

I grabbed out, caught something and heard him yell. Pain slammed into my shins and made me howl and something arced up and sideways into the snow – a great, hard-ridged leather shoe. Then something snapped and I fell backwards, clutching what I had grabbed, knowing Martin had just escaped.

The pony was mad with fear now, plunging and bucking. The cart tilted, went on one side, then over again, the sledge-runners in the air. The traces snapped and the pony staggered off.

Crowbone, on his knees, started to dig, while I lay there, head muzzed and pounding, waves of sick pain flowing up my leg from the kick on the shin.

Now I saw how dark it had become, how most of the shrieking was the wind and that the horse warriors were vague shapes in the seething snow and barely moving. I managed to get to my knees just as one of the horse-warriors lumbered out of the swirl, bow cased and a curved sword in one hand.

I heard a series of shrill screams as the sword went up and

came down, threw up the bundle I had and heard the edge whack on it, the blow almost jerking it from my hand and flinging me flat again. The rider gave a howl of triumph, fought the horse round, leaning out to be able to hit me.

Then Thorkel snarled out of the white mist of snow, the sword swinging, smacking the rider out of the saddle. Roaring and hacking, Thorkel flurried more blows on the fallen shape, half of them bouncing off because he was wild with fear and anger and using the flat as much as the edge.

'In here, Jarl Orm,' shouted Crowbone, tugging my leg. 'In here.'

He had dug out the snow at the edge of the cart, like the sunken door to an Iceland toft and, even as I moved, Thorkel spotted it and lumbered towards me, a hedgepig bristled with arrows that seeemed to have done him no harm at all.

Then, as ever with Thorkel, his luck ran out. He was three steps from me when the last arrow whirred out of the snow-storm, fired blind by riders already making off for shelter. It took him in the left eye, seemed just to appear there and came out above his right ear in a great gout of dark blood and bone shards. He was whirled by the force of it and fell away with a last, despairing shriek on the bad cess of his life.

I scrabbled furiously, while the dawn turned to midnight and was half-hauled by little Olaf into the shelter of the cart. In the dark, panting and sobbing with pain, I lay for a long time, while the snow-wind hissed through the cracks in the planks and the cart shook and trembled with the power of it.

We did not speak for a while. I fell asleep, or lost my senses more like, for when I awoke, it was clear Crowbone had been busy and had adjusted his eyes to the gloom under here. The wind howled, the snow flurried in the cracks, but not so much now, which meant it was piling up on that side.

Crowbone had stacked three bundles at the door he had clawed out, to stop the wind. As my eyes adjusted, I saw one of the sacks was split and rye spilled out.

'Well,' I managed, 'we have grain and snow for water. If we had a fire we could make flatbread.'

'If we had meat and gravy we could make a feast,' he answered, then grinned. 'But we have some old bread and even some strips of dried meat, so we will not starve. Do these storms last a long time, Jarl Orm?'

I shrugged, which could have meant anything. I did not know, but thought it best not to admit that – for all his resource, little Olaf was still but nine years old and his voice quavered when he asked.

I chewed and scooped snow to drink, plastered more on my aching leg and wished I could see how bad it was. That turd Martin had kicked me – but he had lost his shoe doing it. He was out there, surely dead by now. I hoped he had frozen slowly, starting with his bare foot that he had used to take the skin off my shin.

I remembered the bundle now and dragged it over. The sword cut I had parried had slashed the ties and the *wadmal* cloth hung in tatters, so I peeled it off. I half-expected to see Martin's Holy Spear, but it was my rune-marked sabre and I realized that the monk had stolen it as part of the package to sell to Sveinald – me and the rune blade, the secret of the silver hoard.

Then I had to wonder at the Odin-marvel of getting it back.

'That's the one you took from Atil's howe,' Crowbone said, peering at it. I turned it over in my hand, seeing the beautifully carved hilt and the runed scratches on it, how the blade gleamed even in this poor light, how it looked rainbow-slick as if oiled, the serpent of forged runes curling down the blade.

'Is it magical?' he asked and reached out one finger to touch it. He stopped a knuckle-length away and drew his hand back. He looked at me. I wrapped the weapon up and it seemed even darker with it covered.

We sat for a while longer as the storm swooped and swirled, savaging us through the knotholes in planks and rocking the

180

upturned cart. Snow sifted in. My head hurt and little Olaf's teeth clattered loudly.

'Get closer if you are cold,' I said. There was silence but he did not move. Then he cleared his throat.

'I pissed myself,' he chattered, his piping voice thick with the shame of his battle fear.

'Never mind,' I grunted at him. 'It will be the last piss you ever take if you do not get closer, for it will freeze you to the marrow.'

I felt him creep to me then, huddling in the lee of my arm, where we leached warmth from each other and trembled with cold in the fetid dark – but, in the confined space, with the cart wrapped in snow, it grew warm enough for the rime to melt and freeze into new and stranger shapes on the inside of the cart.

He smelled faintly of piss and the shame came off him in waves, as like heat as made no difference to me.

I watched the rime-shapes, slipping into sleep, knowing it and fighting it, for there is not a man from the north who does not know the cold that droops your eyes towards death.

I was in the prow of the Elk as it curved and flexed over a great swell of cold sea, the spray flying. When I turned I saw old faces – the closest to me was Kalf, who had vanished over the side on my first-ever run to Birka, slapped overboard in a careless moment by sodden sails and gone in an eyeblink. He grinned at me and waved and I knew I must be dead and heading for Aegir's kingdom – though how I had ended up in that underwater hall when I had died on land was a puzzle.

I turned back to stare beyond the prow for a clue to it, but the spume stung like an angry byke of bees, then a creature flew up in my face, a squid, or a jellyfish, straight on to my face, sucking and squelching . . .

'Leave off him. Good boy, well done – leave him, you hole.'

Light blinded me, white and flickering with shapes. Something whuffed and panted and rasped my face with hot wetness.

'Get off.'

The deerhound yelped as Finn whacked it, then his great grinning face loomed over me and he chuckled.

'He deserves a few kisses, all the same, Bear Slayer, since his nose has found you where nothing else could. Good trick, that cart business.'

ELEVEN

I was lucky, as Bjaelfi pointed out back in the shelter of the village, while he poked and prodded the back of my skull. There was a bruise between neck and shoulder the colour of Bifrost, the rainbow bridge to Valholl, while my shin was scraped raw, but no bones were broken.

I saw Kvasir look at me and shake his head with wry mirth. He knew I believed the sabre had powers to heal its owner and kept pointing out that nothing had happened to me that could not be put down to youth, strength and Odin-luck.

I looked back at him and nodded, adding: 'Bone, blood and steel.'

He acknowledged my thanks for the rescue with a dismissive flap of one hand, then tossed me an object, which I caught awkwardly. It was Martin's thick-ridged shoe.

'We unearthed it from the snow, just outside the entrance you dug under the cart,' he said. 'Near where we found Thorkel.'

I weighed the oxhide shoe, bouncing it in my hand and realizing how lucky I had been, for such a kick with one of these could have snapped my leg like a twig. I said so and Kvasir rubbed his good eye and shrugged.

'Its owner perhaps had a hand in that good luck – or a

foot,' he answered with a grim chuckle and nodded at the shoe when I looked at him with bewilderment.

'Helshoon,' he said and I blanched and carefully put the thing down, seeing now what it was. A Hel shoe, crafted for one wearing and one wearing only – on the feet of a man whose lack of mercy would take him to Hel's hall along a last road studded with thorns and across a river sharp with iron. With such thick-soled shoes he could avoid the pain of being sliced to shreds, an unwarranted kindness from those who had howed him up.

'Aye,' growled Finn, coming up in time to catch this. 'Somewhere on the road to Hel, a hard-hearted man is cursing that monk for robbing his grave.'

It would not have bothered Martin much, unearthing the dead he considered heathen to steal what he needed. Still, it marked how far Martin had sunk from the neat, fastidious Christ priest who had once argued gods with Illugi Godi in the polished hall of Birka's fortress.

'The boy?' I asked and Finn grinned.

'Piss-wet and a little cold. You saved his life.'

'He saved mine,' I answered. 'The trick with the cart was his.'

Finn raised both eyebrows and looked at me, which was enough speech on the matter, for he knew what I must be feeling, owing weregild to that boy for my life.

What was I feeling, then? As if I had slithered into a mire. Sooner or later, little Crowbone would claim his due from me and it would not be cheap nor simple. There was worse to worry about now, all the same.

'And the other . . . body?' I asked, hoping against hope that it had somehow changed from what had been unearthed alongside Thorkel's corpse.

'Still a woman, Trader,' grunted Finnlaith and we all turned to stare at the cloth-wrapped bundle, stiff with cold, that we had brought back from where Thorkel had killed it. Her. For a dizzying moment I heard her scream, saw the whirl of snow and the mad-mouthed frenzy of Thorkel, howling his hate and his blade on her before he died.

'*Oior-pata*,' Tien had whispered when Ospak had cleared the snow from the woman's face. The little Bulgar had hunched into himself after that and would say nothing more. It was Avraham, the big red-haired Khazar, who had finally told us it was an old Skythian word meaning 'man-haters'.

She was hacked bloody by Thorkel's mad rage, but enough was there to see the fine decorated clothing, the tattoos on her face made stark with her blood-drained pallor, the marks of old scars blue white on her cheeks, the hair gathered in braids and tied back, the way a fighting man does.

Young, too – but no thrall, nor a maid you would want to flirt with, as Jon Asanes pointed out when he and Silfra loaded her on the cart. She had a single boar's tooth on a leather loop round her neck and I did not doubt that she had killed it herself. Her palms, at the base of the frozen fingers, were callous hard and her thumbs muscled and ridged with hard flesh, the draw-ring still fitted to one.

'Sword and steppe bow,' Finn pointed out. 'She is bow-legged, too – see. She spent more years on a horse than on her feet and those hands did not get like that making soup or skelping bairns.'

But it was her head that bothered us all. Strange, stretched, sloping, it only accentuated the deep scars on either cheeks, too straight to be accidental. Men made signs against the evil eye; whispers of Nifelheim rose up like fumes from a swamp.

'Dwarves?' scoffed Gyrth. 'Underground smiths? When did they become spear-headed women from the Great White who ride and fight like men?'

It was Jon Asanes who knew it, even as the big Khazar, Avraham, muttered on and on about the Jewish sacred writings forbidding dealings with such unclean spirits.

'Herodotus,' Jon said, bright with the light that had sparked up in his head.

'Who?' growled Finn, trying to back the spare horse they had brought into the shafts of the cart, now turned back upright.

'A Greek. He wrote of women like these back in the old days of Greek heroes. *Amazonoi* they were called – warrior women of the Skyth tribes. Herakles, the strongest man in the world, fought them once, long ago. I read it in a book in the monastery in Novgorod.'

The fact that he had seen a book and even read it impressed most to silence for a moment and they stared, seeing the Greek youth in a new light.

'They live still,' said Morut, the small, dark Khazar. 'They are part of one of the tribes of the Yass . . .'

'There is *cherem* on even the mention of this,' thundered Avraham but Morut, though he flushed a little, merely shrugged.

'No matter of mine, *cherem*,' he said and Avraham stormed angrily off.

'What is this *cherem*?' Gyrth asked.

'A sort of decree,' Morut answered, 'that says you are no longer a follower of the Torah.'

The Torah was their name for their sacred sagas. Breaking such a decree would mean Morut was no longer a Jew and I had met enough of such people – Khazars and Rhadanites both – in Birka to know that was the worst of punishments for them.

The dark little Khazar shrugged again. 'I am a trapper and a hunter,' he said. 'Avraham is of the warrior caste, so he must be a Jew and embraced it properly, even to getting his foreskin cut as a boy. I did also – but now half my family are in the south and have probably become Mussulmen. I may go there too, so may become one myself, though it means forsaking green wine and ale, which is a hard thing.'

Finn ranted and argued firmly on the foolishness of a religion which stopped you drinking, not to mention one which

186

put a blade anywhere near your pizzle. I was storing away the knowledge that not all Khazars were Jews. Warriors and other high born were, but I found out later not even all of them. There were Khazars in the guard *hird* of the Great City who were baptized Christ-men.

More importantly, here was the strangeness I had come across before and was bewildered by. How could you put on and remove a belief in the gods, as if it were no more than a clean cloak?

Back in the village, I had more to worry about than that. After my head had been looked at, I met with Vladimir, Sigurd and Dobrynya in a quiet place, where we were joined by Crowbone. He and Vladimir went off into one corner, the latter clear in his delight that Olaf was safe.

'Bone, blood and steel,' I offered dryly as the other two offered their congratulations on my safe return. 'That old oath of ours even brought my sword out, too.'

Sigurd stiffened, for he knew I implied that he had only come after Crowbone, while Vladimir worried only about the sabre and how I could read a path from it to 'his' treasure. Only the Oathsworn had come after me alone, driven by the oath and the unveiling of that fact still left me dazed and shivering at the power in it – a power I had scorned and kicked against almost all my life, it seemed.

Crowbone, on the other hand, smiled a knowing twist on to his face.

'Right enough,' he said flatly, which could have meant anything, but Sigurd looked as if he would argue the point, then swallowed, admitting it even as the truth made him avoid my eyes.

Then Vladimir clasped Crowbone by both wrists and they stared into each other's faces, like long-lost brothers and I felt a doubt about Vladimir wanting only the silver secret and the sword that guided me.

I wondered, with a sudden sick lurch, if that boy was

working some subtle *seidr* on the young prince. Even as I said the words: 'He is only nine' to myself, I could not rid myself of the suspicion. And now I owed him my life.

'They were almost too late,' Dobrynya went on in his bass rumble. 'Tien says the *buran* came on more fierce and swift than any he has ever seen.'

The *buran*, I had found out, was the name for these winter ice storms. Kvasir said that the rescue party had only survived it because Tien had insisted they pack his *yurt*, those little round steppe huts which seemed just a puzzle of saplings and acres of *felt*. Finn agreed, saying admiringly that the *yurt* was as stout as an Iceland steading.

'Not just the *buran* was a danger,' growled Sigurd.

'Yes,' I agreed. 'There is the woman.'

Dobrynya tugged his beard into a two-tined fork and scowled. 'Tien says it is likely they were all women, all the ones who attacked. He says they are believers in the old ways, the old Hun ways, including some strange practices that stretch the heads of chosen children.'

We were all silent with wonder and the thrill of disgust over that one, while Vladimir and Crowbone grew loud in their private corner, laughing over Crowbone's account of events. I gave odds on it including nothing about pissing himself.

'These warrior women now belong to the Yass,' Dobrynya went on, 'though that tribe have little control over these women now. The Khazars ruled the Yass tribes and kept these Man-Haters from riding while they were a power, but now that we have broken the Khazars, it seems we have unleashed a horror on to the steppe.'

'Why do they ride?' demanded Sigurd, frowning.

'To stop us,' I said before Dobrynya could speak. I was sure of it, as sure as if someone had skeined the runes of it for me to read. 'To stop us reaching Atil's howe.'

Dobrynya looked up through the grizzle of his eyebrows and grunted.

'So Tien believes. He says the ancestors of these women were favourites of this Atil when he was a great chief of all the steppe tribes. Chosen, Tien says, because they amused him with their fierceness. In turn, they were his most loyal warriors, because it lifted them out of their womanly place.'

'How did you not know of this?' Sigurd demanded of me. 'Did they not try to prevent you the first time you reached this tomb?'

They had not and that was because they did not dare ride while the Khazars ruled. After all, these warrior women were the smallest part of one tribe of the Yass and the Khazars were a mighty empire at the time.

I mentioned this – but kept other thoughts to myself. Like how they knew where the howe was. Later, Tien said he thought it likely that such knowledge was passed on to a chosen few. I said nothing and had my own thought on who had led them to the place; the last sight of Hild, black-eyed with hate as she hacked at me inside Atil's tomb, rose up from the grue of my memories, like a corpse from silt.

'We have broken the steppe apart and now that Sviatoslav is also dead, there is no strong hand to stop these madwomen,' Dobrynya said.

Sigurd carefully adjusted the press of his silver nose against the flesh of his face, for scowling made it hurt and he was doing a lot of that.

'So we have a few women on horses who want to fight us as well as this Lambisson person ahead of us,' he growled. 'My lads are a match for all of them.'

'Tien will go no further without a sword in his back,' Dobrynya pointed out and Sigurd whistled down his silver nose, which was what passed for a snort of derision from him.

'We should stake the little turd for that – but what of it? We have other guides.'

It was Tien's fear that mattered and I said so as Dobrynya

nodded agreement. These Man-Haters may have been no more than a handful of good steppe light horse, but it was their strangeness, the sheer Other of having women shrieking down on you with bow and sword, that counted. Especially ones with stretched heads and blue marks all across their faces.

The *skjaldmeyjar* – shield-maidens – were no strangers to us, but they were from the Old Time, when Thor and Odin walked the earth. Visma was one and Vebjorg another and there were more, who had led a considerable number of heroes during old King Bjarni's day if the fire-tales were true, and so must have been hard women.

But that was then and this was now. While we admired a good woman who could take up weapons to defend what was hers, no man nowadays liked the idea of a woman who gave up hearth and homefire to stand in a shieldwall.

So the rumours would spread; Tien's fear would spread. Men's bowels would turn to water by degrees and the magic of these women would grow at every conversation round a mean fire in the cold night.

'We cannot turn back because of . . . women!' Sigurd exploded and Dobrynya hushed him to silence, his eyes moving from him to me, grim and sharp as a nail to the palm.

'The Prince would not agree to that, certainly,' he said bitterly, glancing at me. 'You knew the power of this hoard, eh, Jarl Orm. You have seen it at work before on the hearts of men.'

I nodded, which was all that was required. The sickness of it was plain to see, slathering little Vladimir like an invisible slick of poison, feeding him dreams of salvation and greatness.

'Then we go on,' growled Dobrynya. 'For we have no choice and none of the gods seem to be listening to my pleas.'

We all knew that, had seen the charred remains of his quiet sacrifices to Perun Thunderer, Svarog Heaven-Walker, Stribog of the winds and even Yarilo, the Shining One, who was not

190

much more than a great prick on legs. None of those Slav fakers were a match for All-Father Odin, who gave the whispered mystery of magic to the world and none answered Dobrynya's begging to have little Vladimir come to his senses.

'Ah well,' muttered Sigurd, 'a sandpiper isn't big, but it is still a bird, as they say in Lord Novgorod the Great.'

'Have you an old granny, by some chance?' I demanded. 'If so, it may be that Red Njal is another long-lost relation.'

The boys heard this and stopped talking to look back at us briefly, before bursting into laughter at the scowl on Sigurd.

It was scowl-dark, too, in the storehouse the Oathsworn were using as a hov. It was thick with fug and heat from a newly-dug pitfire but the faces round it, glowing in the red-dim light, were drawn and long. They made an effort to be pleased to see me – Onund Hnufa even smiled – but Pai was sick and the weight of a dying lay on them and smothered all joy.

Pai was in a shadowed corner, the wheezing rasp of his breathing ripping through the bellies of all those in the storehouse we now called our hall. Bjaelfi hovered nearby, while Jon Asanes sat at the boy's head, pressing cooling cloths to his brow.

Naked and gleaming, slick with sweat, every breath from Pai was a sucking wheeze. Thordis kept trying to wrap him, for it was chilled this far from the fire, but Pai would throw the covers off, thrashing droplets of sweat everywhere. I looked at Thordis, whose stare was blank and yet said everything. Bjaelfi moved away, back to the fire where a pot bubbled.

'How is the boy?' demanded Gizur and Bjaelfi hunkered down to stir the pot.

'Not good,' he admitted.

'He is choleric,' declared Jon firmly. 'I read it in one of the monk's books in Kiev. Fevers mean you are choleric.'

'Just so,' muttered Bjaelfi. 'I am sure you know best, Jon Asanes.'

Stung, Jon scowled back at him. 'What cures are you giving him? We would all like to know.'

Bjaelfi spooned some of the liquid from the pot into a wooden bowl and straightened with a grunt. He gave his beard a smooth and Jon a level stare.

'Sharing such wisdom would be like pouring mead into a full horn with you, boy,' he said finally. 'Much of it would be wasted.'

Men chuckled and Jon flushed. Wearily, Bjaelfi turned to move back to where Pai lay and almost collided with me.

'Jarl Orm . . .'

'Bjaelfi. How bad is he?'

The little healer shook his towsled head mournfully. 'He will die. The cold has taken his lungs. I have seen it before and have used what I know – honey, lime flowers and birch juice, plus a good Frey prayer I know. Some recover – I thought he might, being young. But he is weak in the chest. Always coughing is Pai.'

I watched the little man move back to Pai's side, then found Kvasir at my elbow, his face strange in the darkness because his patch and the charcoal he smeared round the other eye against the day's white glare melded into one and made him look like a blind man, eyes bound in a rag.

'Two of the *druzhina* will die this night also,' he told me quietly. 'One with the same thing as this, the other bleeding from the backside. He spent too long squatting to have a shit and it froze in him, they say. He burst something inside straining, which is no way for a warrior to die.'

Thorgunna appeared, holding a bowl of something savoury and a hunk of dark bread. She smiled and nodded. 'Hard times, Trader,' she said. 'I wish I was back at Hestreng, for sure. I have a feather-filled blanket there I am missing now. That Ingrid will be cosied under it with Botolf.'

She said it wistfully, with no hint of bitterness, using the sometime-name, Trader, that folk called me in happier times.

I touched her arm in sympathy, knowing how she felt, sick with the knowledge of what we would have to face before she got back to her feather-filled blankets. She went back, chivvying the two Scots thrall women, Hekja and Skirla, into some work.

Later, when Bjaelfi indicated that it was time, I moved to where Pai lay, panting and rolling with sweat, his hair plastered to a face as white as the snow outside. Finn was there, with Thorgunna and Thordis busy with cloths and soothing on one side, more to keep them from weeping than any help for Pai.

Jon Asanes, pale and red-eyed, was on the other, his hand soft on Pai's wrist. I remembered that they had been of an age and had been friends from the moment they had met in Kiev, had laughed and drunk together, as youths will. I remembered because I was not so much older and yet it seemed there were stones younger than me; I could never be part of their joy, envied them as they tested their strength and walked, arms draped round each other's necks.

'Heya,' I said softly to Pai. 'Here you are, then, lolling about with women dancing round you. I might have known.'

He managed a smile, struggling so much to breathe that he could not speak. His eyes were wild, though, fretted and white.

'I . . . have done . . . nothing,' he managed and Finn shook his head.

'The gods need no reason to inflict what they do,' he growled, bitterly.

'No. I mean . . . I have . . . not lived . . . enough. I wanted . . . to be known. My name . . .'

He stopped, exhausted and I heard Finn grunt as if hit, the muscle in his jaw shifting his beard. Olaf stepped into the space between us and Pai managed a faint grin while his chest heaved.

'Story,' he said. 'A funny . . . one. Keep . . . it . . . short, mind. I have . . . places to go.'

Olaf, his jaw so clenched I wondered if he could speak at all, nodded. They had been friends of a sort, I remembered – Pai admiring Olaf for his abilities, envying him for his status and Olaf, always amused by the glorious clothes that gave the youth his nickname, Pai, the Peacock. And, strangely, Olaf envied Pai, wanted to be that age himself, just that bit older than now and a young hawk in the wind.

'There was an outlaw who had outstayed the time allotted for him to safely quit the land,' Olaf began in a voice so low only those close to him could hear it. 'We shall call him . . . Pai. He drank too much in a feasting hov and fell asleep, then dreamed a dream that the other guests had decided to kill him, since he was now fair game. Four came at him from every side. One held a spear, to stab his eyes from his head. One had an axe to smash his fingers to pulp and chop his legs. One had a sword of considerable size, planning to ram it down his throat and the last had a knife, to cut off his tozzle and stick it in his ear.'

Pai gasped out a laugh, started to cough and could not stop for a long time. As he grew quieter, Olaf cleared his throat.

'Pai woke with a scream to find that he had, indeed, been snoring in a feasting hall, but not a friendly one – he was surrounded by enemies. One had a spear and the grin of an eye-remover. One had an axe that had clearly smashed fingers before. One had a sword of considerable size – but there was no fourth man with a knife.

'Pai looked everywhere, but there was definitely no fourth man. "Thank you, Odin," he gasped, settling back on his bench as the men closed in, "it was only a terrible dream."'

Pai chuckled and coughed and jerked and his chest heaved for a few moments longer, then stopped. Thorgunna, after a pause, wet her cheek and placed it close to his mouth, then shook her head and closed his eyes. Jon Asanes bent his head and wailed.

Finn let out his breath in a long sigh. 'Fair fame,' he grunted, to no-one it seemed to me. 'That was what he wanted. In the end, that is all there is.'

'A good tale,' I said to Olaf. 'You gave him what he wanted and not every man can do that for a dying friend. You have a gift.'

Crowbone, his different-coloured eyes glittering bright, shook his head, made so white in the light that he looked like a little old man.

'Sometimes,' he whispered, 'it is an affliction.'

There was talk of treating our dead in the old way, for we were all sure the people of the village would dig up the bodies and strip them of their finery. Vladimir refused, since that would have involved demolishing a building for the timbers to burn him.

'You have stripped them of winter feed, so that they will have to slaughter what livestock they have left,' growled Sigurd, annoyed that his men might not lie peacefully under the snow for long. 'They will be eating their belts and lacing thongs by Spring – what does one building mean now?'

Vladimir folded his arms and glared back at his *druzhina* captain. 'They are still my brother's people – but I will rule them one day. I want them to fear me – but not hate me.'

Sigurd could not see the sense of it, that was clear – I was having trouble working out this princely way of ruling myself – but Jon Asanes made Vladimir smile and nod.

'The Prince is a shepherd to his people,' he observed. 'A shepherd fleeces his flock. He does not butcher them.'

I left them weaving words round it, feeling like a man walking on greased ice. I knew what Jon and Vladimir and little Olaf did was the future of the world, the way jarls and princes and kings did things these days and in the ones to come. I also knew I did not have one clear idea of how to do it myself and that Jon Asanes was more fitting to be a jarl of this new age than I was.

But not a jarl of the Oathsworn. Not them, stamping their feet against the cold as they stood in sullen clumps round the dark scars of new-mounded graves, hacked out with sweat and axes from a reluctant earth. These were men of the old ways.

I took the chance to braid them back to one with a few choice words on breaking oaths and what it had cost. No-one needed much telling; all those who had run off with Martin and Thorkel had died and Finn made it glaringly clear that anyone else who tried the same would not live to feel Odin's wrath.

We spent the morning sorting gear and finding new ways to wrap against the cold. Then we untied the tether ropes, bashing the stakes out of the frozen ground, chipped ice out of the horse's hooves with a seax and lurched off south, into the steppe.

I twisted in the saddle once, to stare back at the settlement. On the earthwork walls I saw a figure and, though I could not clearly make it out, I knew it was Tien and felt his eyes on me long after he had vanished from sight.

The steppe spread out like a sea, like frozen waves. The sky was so big, the clouds in it rushing, whipped into strange shapes and sliding fast, like driven woodsmoke.

'Only the wind saves us,' Gyrth noted gloomily which, since it made life colder still, brought grunts and growls of disagreement.

'Snow has a plan,' Gyrth went on between gasps, his breath smoking and freezing his beard to spines. 'It wants to cloak the world in white, purest white, like a bleached linen sheet – but the wind says no. We will have some more here than there, says the wind. Get it off that roof and on that tree, says the wind. The snow hates the wind but cannot stop it from blowing. Which is why, when it is a windless day in winter, you can hear the snow sigh, for it knows the wind will come and make a mess of all its work.'

Which was nearly good enough to laugh some warm into us, but not quite. Our fingers and toes ached and we bound them in *wadmal* and layered grass between, the fuzzed tops of the yellow steppe grass, which was the best barrier against the cold. It kept toes from turning black, but made our feet so fat they would not fit in the stirrups.

One day merged into the next, shadows of life. Horses died, one after the other and the men on them now staggered and stumbled on foot. One or two of the *druzhina* threw their armour away because the long skirts and the weight of it made walking twice as hard. The Oathsworn, used to walking, jeered at them – then Sigurd killed one of the *druzhina* as a warning and that ended all laughter and armour-throwing.

So we listened to the snow sigh.

Sixteen more men died in as many days, mostly the *druzhina*, though two of the Oathsworn had to be left, too stiff even to be laid out flat, arms broken so as to fold them on their breasts. Klepp Spaki, blowing on his fingers, tapped out the runes of their names on small squares of bone – Halli was one and the other was Throst Silfra. Both just lay down, patiently waiting for the sweet relief from the hunger and cold, the gentle frozen sleep as the white raven folded them in huge wings.

Throst's closest oarmates, Tjorvir, Finnlaith and Ospak, threw some hacksilver into the shallow grave, then Finnlaith came to me, his wide face reddened with cold and buried in a tangled mass of cold-stiffened beard. His eyes were iced blue.

'It seems to us three that Throst also knew of Thorkel's treachery,' he said, which was flat-out bold enough to make me blink. These were words for an *Althing*, where convention kept the speaker from being killed.

'It is no surprise to us, then, that Odin took his luck,' he went on levelly. 'If more of those who came with Thorkel die, we want you to know, Jarl Orm, that it will be the wish of another god and not Odin's curse on an oath-breaker.'

197

Then he nodded and stumped off, leaving it clear to me that, if I could trust no others, I could depend on those three at my back.

It was, I noted wryly to myself, good to know. There were fewer now who could truly be depended on, even among the Oathsworn. Bone, blood and steel were all brittle in the cold and even the binding fear of the wrath of Odin was cracking. They had taken enough and all of us, hugging our shivers to ourselves, wondered whether we would do the same as Throst, this day or the next, just lie down and let our heart stop and think ourselves winners of that bargain. Some, I knew, wondered whether to let matters get that far.

Then there was the sabre and the runes on it. I took to wearing it, wrapped in the bundle Martin had made of it, looped over my shoulder like a bow. Folk thought it was so it was handy for me to study the hilt, but the truth was that I just wanted it to look that way.

The truth was that the runes were useless, for we were coming down from the north and would have to reach Sarkel and track back to find Atil's howe. It was a truth I did not want men who were dying to know.

We stuck Klepp's runed squares on dead men's tongues, in the hope that we would be able to identify them on the way back, for the wolves would dig them up from the shallow scrapings we rolled them into. There were a few who wondered if that was a waste of time and Klepp's talents, sure we would never be back in the warm lap of summer to howe their bones up properly.

The wind won and the land changed, from glaring white to patched brown and then to limitless miles of dun-coloured earth, frozen solid and dusted with snow, thick in drifts here and there. Leafless trees, squatting in sullen clumps, brushed their skeletal fingers across an icicle sky and the wind rattled the frozen stalks of yellow grass like chattering teeth.

'The whole world is ice,' whimpered Jon Asanes that night,

198

shivering close to anyone he could find – as we all did – and the dung fires. Anyone close scooped it up as the horses dropped it, sticking it inside their clothes to leach the warmth and stop it freezing too hard to burn later. But the fodder was running out; horses were eating less and shitting less. Those that were not dying.

'This is nothing,' answered Onund Hnufa. 'I have hunted whales up where the ice forms mountains. I am an expert on ice.'

'Aye,' agreed Gizur, as if he had done the same, though he only wished he had.

'It is a world of ice, up there in Bjarmaland,' Onund went on, in a bass rumble like a mating seal. 'Sea ice forms in autumn and early winter, out of the milk sea, which is thick with grit ground out of the land by the moving ice.

'Fast ice is what we call ice that is anchored to land; it breaks up with tides in spring. Floes are large and flat bits of ice, like those tiles they make pictures with in the churches you spoke of, Trader. They are broken up by wind and wave and moved with the same.

'Pack ice is formed from floes that herd like sheep and are crushed against each other. There is pack ice a hand's breadth thick and more, yet which bends on waves, fitted to them like cloth.

'Ice grows old, too, like people. You need to see that if you plan on taking a ship near it. Young ice is clear, a hand-width thick and brittle as stale bread – you can carve through that easily enough. First-year ice is as thick as a man is long and at two years it is thicker still, stands higher in the water, has small puddles and bare patches and is the colour of Olaf's left eye. You sail far round that stuff if you are smart.'

Olaf smiled and winked his blue-green eye to let everyone see what Onund meant. He had wandered over from Vladimir's fire, attracted by the savoury smells from ours and offered a story for a bowl of what we had. He gulped and chewed it down even as it burned his lips.

'Good,' he said and then made the mistake of asking what it was.

'Does it matter?' Finn demanded with a grin, but the boy's pinched face was unsmiling when he replied.

'You have never been a thrall Finn Horsehead,' he said, serious as plague. 'It is never necessary to know what it is you are eating; it is, I have found, vital to know what it was.'

Grinning, Gyrth tossed him the frozen, bloodied paw of a deerhound. 'That's Other Dog,' he said, rheum-throated with the cold. 'Dog we ate yesterday.'

'The oldest ice is thicker than two men, one standing on the other's shoulders. It is sometimes as blue as the sky,' Onund continued, in a voice heavy with *heimthra*, the longing for things that have been and are now lost, perhaps forever.

'Enough ice talk,' muttered Kvasir. 'I am cold enough already.'

They called for Olaf's story while I was marvelling at old humpbacked Onund, a man who had walked on a mountain of ice and saw that it had puddles and bare patches and was coloured blue-green. Even the Great White did not bother him.

In the morning, after an hour of travel, the Khazar scouts came back, flogging their bone-thin horses into staggering runs towards us. They spoke urgently with Vladimir, who was perched on his horse like the white raven itself.

Later, warily, we came up on what the scouts had found; the remains of a couple of *wadmal* and *felt* tents, a litter of snow-dusted debris; a saddle, brassware, a wooden bowl, a sword stuck in the earth and abandoned to rust, the hub of a wheel with a couple of spokes left in it. There were dead horses, thin steppe ponies sprawled on their sides, their legs stuck out straight like carved wooden toys that had fallen over.

200

And there were sharpened stakes, each with a head screaming frozen pain at us from rimed faces.

'Anyone you know?' asked Dobrynya, moving his horse to my side. There was no-one we recognized, though Gyrth hefted the sword and said: 'This is a good north-made weapon, Jarl Orm.'

'Lambisson's men,' Finn said, squinting at the signs of it. 'This one has braids like Botolf – see. That's the way the Svears and Slavs do them. It was said Lambisson had many Baltic Slavs with him.'

'Horsemen took them by surprise, scattered them,' added Avraham, pointing out the signs of it. 'Probably they were in the rear of the column. Hard to say when this happened or where the rest of them went – the ground is too frozen. They were not after plunder, else that sword would not have been left.'

'A day ago,' Morut said, hunching himself into his furs. 'Two, perhaps. The wolves have already been at these heads and the wounds are still raw, so were done when the flesh was unfrozen, which would be only a matter of hours, but there is no snow in the eye-sockets. There are three hoof-prints showing the attackers went south. I could track them.'

'Do so,' ordered Dobrynya, then turned to Sigurd and me, while Avraham scowled at Morut for his cleverness.

'Whoever attacked them may still be close,' Dobrynya said. 'We will close up and keep watch.'

The Man Hater women, I wanted to say, but decided not to. I did not worry as much as he over it – those steppe ponies were proof that the women warriors were in as bad a condition as ourselves and, besides, Short Eldgrim and Cod-Biter were so close now I could touch them if I shut my eyes and reached.

I shared this, quietly, with the rest of the Oathsworn, adding that the warrior-women might all be dead. I was thinking it would bring some cheer to the flames of the night's fire as we kicked snow off the earth to let it breathe a little smoke and ash.

'After all,' I declared brightly, 'if the *buran* didn't kill them, then the trek to here would. They would have had less fodder for those ponies and I am thinking most of them are on foot, if they live at all.'

'And a woman on foot,' Gyrth Steinnbrodir beamed, ignoring the scowls from Thorgunna and her sister, 'is an opportunity.'

Finn laughed, but you should never tempt the Norns. The next day, we stumbled over all our enemies at once.

TWELVE

We came upon a *balka*, one of those dried-out riverbeds that scar the steppe, but our eyes were fixed on the smoke. Wisps of it, scarring a milk-blue sky, marking a settlement and that meant warmth, shelter and food you did not have to carry under your armpit to be able to chew.

Avraham was out in front, on foot since he had woken to find his horse dead of cold and too frozen to be of use. He cursed the animal; if it had died during the day, when it could be seen, things would have been different.

Those nearest watched for such a moment, when all four legs buckled. Sometimes they would not even wait for a horse to die properly before they were on it, hacking out the warm meat and drinking the blood, flaying the hide off it before it froze. Even if the rider was one of the armoured *druzhina* he scrambled out of the way and quick, for people with knives – especially the likes of Thorgunna and Thordis – did not always see or care what they cut in their haste.

Morut was off tracking the Man-Haters and our only scout was now on foot, which is why we did not get enough warning. Not that it would have made much difference to us, with our minds dulled and what spark remained fixed on the smoke.

The riders whooped up and over the lip of the *balka* and

whirred down on us like a flock of birds. I saw Skirla take an arrow and go down, shrieking, while the stunned *druzhina* guards were still trying to gather up reins and sort out weapons. Avraham knew better than to try to run and hunkered under his shield as they galloped past him and on to us.

They were women on horseback. They were the Man-Haters and that paralysed everyone as much as the cold and the surprise.

Howling, a strange wolf-yipping series of yowls, they cut daringly through the middle of us on their bony, half-staggering little steppe ponies. I hauled out my sword, cursed the fact that I had long ago packed my shield in a cart as being too much burden; a man without a sword is still a warrior, but one with no shield is just a target.

A *druzhina* warrior went backwards off his horse, which panicked and bolted, though it was too weak to run far. The arrow that skewered him through the middle of his face came from a shrieking Valkyrie, braids flying, tattoos writhing in the snarl of her long-skulled face as she kicked and turned her shaggy pony towards me, fishing another shaft out.

She was, I was sure, one who could nick the eye out of a gnat at four hundred paces from the back of a full galloping horse and I was a dead man.

Gyrth swept past me, his swathe of cloaks and *wadmal* wrappings flapping like some huge bird as he lumbered. He paused, swept up the fallen man's big shield and took the woman's arrow in it – the one aimed at me. The shunk of it hitting was a clap of thunder.

Then he ran at the horse. Straight at it, shield up and roaring, the boss smacking the animal on the left shoulder, the rim clattering it in the teeth as he bellowed and shoved.

The horse went over in a screaming flail of limbs and the woman, fast and agile, leaped free, rolled and came up, spitting and snarling like a cat. She whipped round to face Gyrth, who was rolling about like a loose barrel and trying to avoid the animal's wildly flying hooves.

She went for him, but Finn was already there. She screamed and hacked and he brought the big heavy sword up, so that her little curved sabre spanged off it with a shower of sparks.

As Gyrth clambered heavily to his feet and the horse kicked itself back upright, snorting and rolling-eyed, Finn cut down, a chopping stroke that she met with the edge of her blade. It rang like a bell, even as it turned his stroke, but the shock of it ran back up her arm to her numbed fingers, tearing the sword from her grasp.

She howled then, all slaver and frustrated anger and even as I closed in on her I saw no fear in her at all. Then another shape loomed, sliding through the confusion and spraying snow, a dazzle to the eyes.

It was a golden horse. Not yellow. Metallic and sheened as if moulded from a single block of polished brass, it pranced between the warrior woman and us, made more splendid by the shaggy steppe ponies it moved through.

I gawped; the woman hurled herself up and back on to her own plunging steppe pony, while the big, gold-gleaming horse danced majestically between us, blowing twin streams out of its scarlet-edged nose. The rider was a silhouette above me, hair black and flying like snakes. I gawped. Something shone in an upraised hand and came down like a scythe of light; Finn yelled a warning.

I put up the big sword, felt the kick of it as it took the blow, heard the high ting of it shattering. The gold horse, high-stepping and snorting, swung sideways and its huge rump slammed into me, into the hand I put up feebly to stop it.

I went over backwards, arse over shoulders, a whirl of sky and snow with my only thought being that it had been warm. The gold horse had been warm and damp to the touch.

When I had sorted myself out, the golden horse was gone.

The women were gone. Only the moans and shouts they had caused were left.

'Odin's arse, Orm,' Finn yelled, scrambling to my side. 'I thought you were dead then, for sure.'

I got up, slowly. Finn looked at the splintered remains of my sword. He whistled admiringly.

'Some blow to have broken that good blade,' he muttered and I looked at it, the hilt in my hand. It did not seem to belong to me, neither the jagged stump of sword nor even the hand.

'You are bleeding,' Gyrth said, coming up on my left and I looked, bewildered, at the watery smear of blood soaking my mittened palm.

'Not mine,' I remembered, as it rushed in like a mad tide on the turn. 'The horse. The gold horse . . .'

'Aye,' gasped Jon Asanes, dashing up. 'Did you see that beast? Gleaming as a gold *dirham*, right enough. Like an amulet on a thong.'

'He saw it, right enough,' replied Gyrth, heaving for breath and chuckling with the exultation that always comes when you find yourself alive at the end of a fight. 'He almost had his head up its arse.'

We laughed, whooping and gasping, skeins of drool freezing the edges of our mouths. I stopped before they did, for I had remembered the rider, with her black hair like snakes writhing. And the sword, that scything sabre of light. My belly churned and I asked Finn if he had seen her.

He nodded, then held up one finger. 'Do not say it, young Orm. Do not. It was just a woman on a fancy horse, no more. Hild is dead. Long dead. Do not bring her back to life. Not now.'

'So this was just a woman?' I demanded, my fear swelling the anger in me. 'With a rune-sword like my own, that can shatter good northern steel?'

'Fuck you, Orm,' Finn said, furiously rubbing his face and

beard with one hand, a sign that he was truly confused and angry. 'Fuck your mother, too. It is not Hild. Hild is DEAD, Bear Slayer. Years since. You saw her die in Atil's tomb.'

I said nothing, sick with a confusion of fear and possibility, my thoughts of gulls that shrieked and swooped and would not stay still to be looked at.

'That was a horse,' Avraham declared, appearing into the middle of this, all unknowing and uncaring. 'A heavenly horse, no less. I never thought to see one.'

'A what?' demanded Ospak. Behind him, keening started as Hekja found the body of Skirla. They had been thralled together almost as babes, that pair and had been with Thorgunna and Thordis for as long.

'A heavenly horse, from far to the east,' Avraham said, jerking me away from the wailing women. 'They are sheened like metal when they sweat, yellow as brass and are so highly prized they are worth their weight in gold. Those steppe heathens say they sometimes sweat blood, too, which is the mark of what passes for their heaven.'

'Sweat blood,' repeated Jon Asanes wonderingly. I looked at the blood-soaked palm of my mittened hand, where it had smacked off that huge brass rump. Finn stumped off, making soft growls at Thordis and Thorgunna, as close as he came to a soothing noise, for the loss of Skirla.

'Just so,' agreed Avraham, then turned to me.

'Dobrynya wants you. It seems we have another problem today.'

The other problem stood on the village earthwork and grinned cheerily down at us from under the tangle of his yellow hair. One hand rested quietly on the frost-glittering points of the rampart timbers and the other twirled a great long axe on its butt, so that the head flashed in the weak red sun of the dying day as he spoke out of a twisted smile.

> '*He hath need of fire, who now is come,*
> *Numbed with cold to the knee;*
> *Food and clothing the wanderer craves*
> *Who has fared o'er the rimy fell.*'

Which let me know, from his accent, that he was more Slav than Norse and more learned than most – though one of the wise Sayings of the High One was scarcely gold-browed verse-making.

'No,' he added to Vladimir as I came up with Finn and the others, 'I do not think I am inclined to let you in, for all that you have done me the service of chasing off those madwomen. There is room enough only for me and my men.'

'Then there must be more than a few with you,' Dobrynya answered smoothly. 'Perhaps if you told us how many were in there, we could count out a suitable number that would not steal the food or shelter from you.'

'It is of no consequence how strong we are here, Uncle Dobrynya,' chuckled the man, thumbing his cold-reddened nose, 'since we are not letting any of you in. You should know that we are strong enough, all the same.'

'Do you know who I am?' demanded Vladimir indignantly and the man chuckled again.

'You are the young prince Vladimir. Your father is dead and you are now so far from Lord Novgorod the Great that you are in more danger here than I am and from your own brothers, too. You should have listened to your Uncle Dobrynya, boy, for I am sure he has advised you to go home.'

Vladimir flushed and fumed, for that was a solid hit to the mark. Dobrynya, seeing the boy fighting his horse, made anxious by nervous jerking, reached out a hand and touched his shoulder.

'We should talk this out later,' he said.

Vladimir rounded like a snake. 'Do NOT touch me. Ever.'

Dobrynya paused, then inclined his head in a bow. The

man on the ramparts laughed out loud and everyone, myself included, was annoyed that the prince had behaved like a charcoal-eating nithing. Dobrynya stayed smooth and cool as a still pond.

'As you say, my prince,' he said to Vladimir, 'but this great fool has made it clear that he prefers to be staked rather than deal with us pleasantly. Let us not disappoint him.'

Still furious, Vladimir half-reined his horse round, then paused and stared up at the man.

'You know me,' he piped, fury making his voice all the more shrill. 'Tell me your name also, that I might have it marked on the stake I have driven up your arse for this.'

'Farolf,' the man said, not smiling now. 'I know you – but I know the one with you better. Orm Bear Slayer, I am thinking.'

I jerked at the sound of my name and the by-name that went with it, the one that men used like a sneer, just before they challenged you. He grinned down at me and inclined his head in a mocking bow.

'I have heard much of you from Lambisson,' Farolf said. 'I heard more from that little scar-faced man he has, the one with his wits addled.'

'Then you know more than you did before,' I replied. 'Do you also know where Brondolf Lambisson is?'

'Gone from here,' replied Farolf cheerfully. 'Him and his little empty head. Dead, probably – those ball-cutting women have gone after him and left some here to see if we would be stupid enough to walk out and ask them to slaughter us.'

'Now those Man-Haters are gone,' I answered carefully, 'and we are here instead. It would be wise to lower a knee to the prince and the bar from the gate. We are not women and we will not wait for you to come out.'

'No,' he replied seriously. 'I was thinking that. You and the prince seek the same thing Lambisson seeks. You are a power, even though you look a little . . . diminished. For all that, I cannot see you getting in this gate.'

'You have left Lambisson,' I said, seeing it clearly. He nodded and smiled and it was his smiling that made me uneasy, for he was sure of himself, polished as a well-used handle. The others listened, swinging eyes from me to him and back, as if it was *holmgang* fight.

'Did you betray him, or he you? Not that it matters – you now go your own way,' I went on, half musing to myself, working the weft of it in my head as I spoke. 'Yet you will not join us, which means you have plans of your own. If you seek the silver, then you seek Atil's howe . . .'

It came to me then, in a rush and sick lurch of my belly. He knew where he had to go, or thought he did. The only way he could know for sure was if someone had told him. Short Eldgrim had gone with Lambisson, which left . . .

He saw my face and laughed, then made a signal. Men, all leather and snarls, brought Thorstein Cod-Biter forward and he hung in their grip like a sack, raising his face at the last. Face was what it had been once. Now it was a bruise with eyes in it.

'Heya, Orm,' he said through puffed and bloody lips. 'What kept you?'

Before I could say anything, Farolf jerked his chin at his men and they dragged Thorstein away and non-too gently at that – I heard the thumps of him being clattered down the rampart steps.

'Now go away,' Farolf said, 'or else I will hang him upside down from the ramparts and cut his throat.'

I said nothing, conscious of Vladimir's tense, white face, his uncle, Sigurd and all the rest. Farolf had no doubt thought it a good ploy and if it had just been the Oathsworn it might have been a problem, but Cod-Biter meant nothing to anyone else, alive or dead and little Vladimir would not offer the smell from his shit for his safe return. He wanted revenge and stakes and if he had not been mounted he would have stamped his little booted foot and screamed.

Farolf, of course, wanted us to assume he had forced Thorstein to tell all he knew and so could carry out his threat to kill his hostage – but Cod-Biter had nothing true to tell him; he did not know the way to the howe, though a man will babble any lie under blade, blow or hot iron.

I turned away, for there was nothing left to say. Or so I thought – but Finn had something and he stepped forward, just as Farolf turned to leave.

> 'The unwise man thinks all to know,
> While he sits in a sheltered nook;
> But he knows but one thing,
> What he shall answer,
> If men put him to proof.'

It was another verse from the same place Farolf had found his, so apt an answer and so astounding coming from Finn that I could not say anything. Nor was I alone in this; the gold-browed cleverness of it settled on us slow and gentle and warming as broth in the belly, so that the fire of it took time to seep in. When it did, men hoomed and cheered and rattled weapons on shields.

But all we had done was made Farolf scowl. To do more, as Dobrynya and Sigurd pointed out, would take the Oathsworn.

'My lads fight from horseback,' Sigurd declared, as we hunched round a miserable fire that failed to prevent the ice forming on our moustaches. 'I can get them on foot, but they will not be good at it and their ring-coats are too long.'

'They have bows,' said Dobrynya. 'They can keep heads down while others get over the walls, but it is as Sigurd says – they are horsed fighters.'

Not even much of that, I was thinking moodily, remembering them reacting to the Man-Hater's attack. What the Oathsworn had to do would not be easy; the village defences had been built to keep out the marauding Khazars and Pechenegs and consisted of an earthwork topped with a palisade of rough-hewn timbers. It was taller than two men, so we would need ladders to get over it and that would take wood we did not have. The only trees for a good walk in any direction were some scrawny birches huddled in a copse.

'We could break up a cart,' offered Sigurd and Vladimir, only a red nose in a heap of fur-trimmed cloak squeaked out in his annoyed little voice, 'No more carts. How will we haul away the treasure if we break them all up?'

There was a moody silence and then Dobrynya cleared his throat. 'So, we cannot go over the walls. Nor can we go through the gate, which will take a ram we do not have and cannot get.'

If it was not for Cod-Biter we could go away, I was thinking, while the silent little Olaf, Vladimir's constant shadow, poked the fire with a stick and sent sparks whirling up. From the walls, as if to mock us, we heard someone stamping to keep out the cold.

'We will burn it,' declared Vladimir. 'The gate. We will set it on fire.'

'With what?' I countered. 'Those timbers are iced solid. They will not burn without oil. Do we have oil?'

'Then you work out a way,' Vladimir shrilled angrily. 'You won't, though, for you don't want to, since as soon as you do . . .'

He clipped the rest off, realizing what he was about to say and buried his face right into the furs to hide his shame.

As soon as we attacked, Cod-Biter would die. It was possible, if Farolf saw all was up for him. If we were quick, all the same . . .

I got up, stiff with cold, and dragged the ice burrs off my beard, then walked away, conscious of their eyes on me. The darkness beyond the fire took me in even colder arms and hurried me towards the one the Oathsworn had lit, in the lee of a wagon and under a *wadmal* canopy. Behind, I heard the level rumble of Dobrynya, no doubt gently chiding his prince and telling him how much he needed Orm and the Oathsworn

Fuck them, I thought, sullen as a storm sky, for I could see no way out of this mess and wondered – not for the first time – what game Odin played now.

'So?' challenged Finn. 'What does the princeling want us to do?'

I told them and Kvasir grunted. Thorgunna said what I had been thinking, that we should just go away and I expected a sharp growl from Finn, was surprised when he stared into the flames and said nothing.

'Can we do that?' demanded Ospak. 'Surely we would be ridden down by those big Slav turds of the *druzhina* if we just took off?'

'A good long-handled axe will see that lot off,' muttered Gyrth, who had just such a weapon.

'A sword drenched in blood easily finds its mark,' agreed Red Njal, 'as my granny used to say.'

'The hacked-off foot cannot scurry far,' Hlenni Brimill countered, grinning and Red Njal frowned, considering the matter.

'The lame man runs when he has to,' he said eventually. Men groaned, but Tjorvir spat in the fire and scowled at them both.

'I came for silver. Bad enough we have to split it so many ways without running away empty-handed after all we have been through. As my own granny would say if she was here.'

Voices grunted assent, unseen in the dark.

'Are we so to split this great treasure?' Thorgunna's voice was light enough as she stepped into the firelight, but the eyes she laid on me were firm and black.

'Why else are we here, then?' demanded Ospak.

'To keep the stake from certain people's arses,' Hauk Fast-Sailor grunted. 'Namely our own.'

213

'Aye, but,' Ospak began and Gizur cut him off.

'But no buts,' he said. 'It is Vladimir's treasure now, sold to save us from what that little axe murderer Olaf Crowbone got us into, make no mistake on it.'

'Odin's arse it is,' spat Gyrth. 'It is our treasure.'

'Our treasure,' mimicked Finn suddenly. 'Our treasure? You are come late to that feast, Steinbrodir.'

'Aye, well,' Gyrth said uneasily. Then, more indignantly, he added: 'I am Oathsworn now, just as you. My arse is freezing here, just as yours is.'

'Did it burn in Serkland?' grunted Hauk Fast-Sailor. 'Did you fight under the walls of Sarkel the first time we came here in search of this hoard?'

'I am here now,' returned Gyrth steadily. 'And others like me. Without us, you would still be clucking at hens in Oestergotland, Hauk Fast-Sailor.'

'We should not quarrel over this,' Red Njal said and Hauk rounded on him.

'What? No granny-wisdom about arguing over all the riches of the world, Njal?'

Red Njal shrugged and favoured Hauk with a face as dour as a gathering storm. 'Brawl with a pig and you come away with its stink,' he said.

There were some chuckles and grunts of agreement at this, while others started in to arguing one way or the other and Hauk, blinking furiously at Red Njal, was clearly working up to serious anger. I silenced them all, surprised that I was the only one, it seemed, who could see the truth of it.

'It is not our treasure. Or Vladimir's. Or even Atil's. It is Odin's – and he gifts it to those he thinks most fitting.'

I stared at them all, one by one while their eyes slithered icily away.

'Bone, blood and steel,' I added pointedly. 'Cod-Biter is in there. We will not run off and leave our own to die.'

There was silence at that, sullen and dark, for the truth of

214

it bit as deep as the cold. Eventually, Finn stirred, blinked and poked sluggish embers out of the fire.

'Aye, well, first we have to get to over those walls. One step, then the other, as my old granny used to say.'

'You never had an old granny,' accused Red Njal.

'I did,' answered Finn. 'And a cunning woman she was. Knew about when folk would die by watching birds and that if you dreamed a dream three times in a row it would come true.'

'Sounds like Olaf Crowbone,' muttered Kvasir. 'Perhaps you are also his uncle. If you are, you have my sympathies.'

'Did this full-cunning mother's mother of yours have a way of leaping walls or walking through doors?' I demanded, which clamped their jaws shut as if they had been stitched.

'Well?' I demanded, feeling the eyes resting on me, dragging the weight of the jarl torc until I swore it dug into the flesh of my neck. 'We need to get over those walls or through the gate, so if anyone has some clever in him, now is the time to hoik it out for us all to share.'

They ran through the ram and ladders and I explained why that would not do. Jon Asanes came up with the idea of an upturned cart with men under it, running at the gate as a ram, which was not bad at all. We gave that one up because we could not be sure the cart would be strong enough, or the men to carry it, for that matter.

Eventually, Kvasir stretched and yawned. 'If we cannot go over the walls and through the gate, then we will have to go over the gate.'

There was a pause; those who had not heard it properly asked their neighbours what Kvasir had said. When they were told, they were no wiser than any the rest of us, so he laid it out and it became clear that, while we had been talking, he had been thinking.

When he was finished, we all chewed on it, looking for flaws in it until we realized that Kvasir had seen more with his one eye than all of us with our two.

'Can you do that?' Dobrynya asked, when I walked back to his fire to tell him what the Oathsworn would do when morning came.

'We will do it,' I answered, 'for we are the Oathsworn.'

I was glad they could not see my clenched belly and curled-up balls and discover how firmly I believed this.

Dobrynya glanced at Sigurd, then over at the sleeping Vladimir, little Olaf huddled beside him, and nodded wearily. I hunkered down beside him and we stared at the fire for a while, while the pair of them raked around for the delicate words to find out what the prince's pillars needed to know – if I had been so offended by this boy prince that I would leave or, worse, seek revenge.

I had no reason to do it, but saved them the trouble of speaking.

'In return for the lives he held in his hand,' I said to the fire, 'I agreed to hold up the prince's breaking sky. True, no oath was spoken on it – as you know, we oath only to each other, in the eye of Odin – but I am still shouldering the burden.'

There was silence while the fire found ice in its food and spat irritably. Then Dobrynya cleared his throat.

'He is young, but growing well,' he said. 'There will come a time when you will welcome the friendship of such a prince. The death of his father has flung him into this too early and unprepared.'

I nodded. The friendship of a prince would be welcome if I survived the winter – or if he did. I said as much and Sigurd grinned, which pinched the flesh white around his silver nose.

'The one thing I have learned,' he growled, 'is that some are born to greatness. He is one. Little Olaf there is another. They will survive.'

Even if everyone else has to die, I was thinking, while his little Olaf smiled and showed teeth bloody with firelight, as though he had just lifted his head from a fresh kill. Yet, for all his cub fierceness and his strange *seidr* magic, he was afraid most of the time. Afraid and alone, for all his Uncle Sigurd and his distant, unknown relatives, for Crowbone would always be fastened to Klerkon's privy, waiting in vain for them to rescue him.

Near him, Vladimir stirred and moaned, now only a boy in his sleep and one who could not ever have his father say all the things a father should, nor say all the things a son should.

I knew how they both felt, which was why I held up their sky.

That night, I dreamed of Hild, the woman who had led us originally to Atil's howe and had gone mad there – or been possessed by the fetch of Atil's dead bride who had, legend said, killed him and been fastened alive to his throne in that tomb.

I saw Hild as I had last seen her, hair flying like black snakes, the sabre she had, twin of my own, whirling like a skein of light as she slid away, back into that dark place, screaming curses at me while the flood-water rose round her.

I did not care what Finn believed. I knew Hild, or something like the *fetch* of her, was out on the steppe, leading Atil's own oathsworn against us.

In the dim light of morning most of us were too numbed to wake, sliding instead into a bleary-eyed awareness of a tiny, white, dreich world, unable to work out whether a night, a morning or a whole day had just gone by.

The strongest kicked the rest of us awake. That was Thorgunna, walking as if her legs had turned to timbers, but still capable of forcing me up, to make me do the jarl-task of forcing everyone else to their feet.

Cracking the skin of rime that had formed on me, clothes and beards and hair, I stumbled around looking for whitened mounds that had been men the night before, thumping them, growling – ranting, even, until the ice and snow cracked and heaved apart.

Slowly, the Oathsworn grunted themselves into the day; the whole camp did, sluggish and reluctant as a thawing river. Two were dead – none of mine, thank the gods – and those were stacked like driftwood, for there was no way even to uncurl them from their last frozen huddle let alone strip them of valuables, armour and weapons.

Ref Steinsson, rummaging in his sea-chest for anything that would give him warmth, showed us what had happened to the bits of poor tin he kept to make repairs on pots – we stared dully at how the cold had crumbled the slivers to a grey powder.

Fires were lit. I choked down some oats soaked in warmed meltwater – the horses had the same – and we armed for the day. By the time the sun was a red half-orb on the lip of the world, we were ready, a band of pinch-faced, sunken-eyed thrall-born, beards dripping with melting ice, faces beaded with melt-water from hair crammed under helmets and heating up, only to refreeze on our faces. We did not look capable of walking to the gate never mind storming it.

Worse than them were the Chosen, of whom I was one. We had taken off byrnies and layers of clothing, down to almost no more than a tunic, a helmet, breeks and boots. The cold no longer seeped, it chewed on us as we stamped and shivered – if it had not been for the battle-fire burning in us, we would already be blue and dying.

Dobrynya rode forward with little Vladimir, now in his silvered mail and plumed helmet, every inch a half-sized warrior. Sigurd led sixty horsemen – the last war horses still capable of being ridden by armoured men – in a long sweep to the far gate, a move designed to drag defenders away from this one. Olaf was with him and gave a cheerful wave.

The rest of the *druzhina*, on foot and with bows uncased,

218

were lined up and waiting behind the Oathsworn, beyond bowshot range of the defenders. From behind the gate came the sound of hammering; the defenders at work. I worried, then, that they were nailing the bar to the gate, which would make things hard for us.

'A good morning to die,' declared Vladimir sternly, which was something his father had no doubt been fond of saying. I said nothing, for such a statement was far short of a battle speech designed to get our ice-limbed men moving. Beside, unclenching my jaw only made my teeth chatter.

'Time to begin,' declared Dobrynya.

'Just so,' said Vladimir and hefted his little spear. Then the two of them set their shields, kicked their horses and ran straight at the gate.

Say what you like about Vladimir – and many did as he grew into his power – but he had courage. The idea was Dobrynya's, to test how many archers the defenders had and, I learned later, he had wanted to do it alone. A swift gallop, the throw of a spear into the gate – the traditional way to announce the start of a siege with no quarter – then another swift gallop back to safety.

Vladimir added himself to the plan and showed his deep-thinking even then, for the men were as impressed by this display as they had been depressed by his loss of face in front of Farolf the day before.

He thundered his way up to the walls, hurled his little spear over and then yelled, his voice cracked with youth and excitement: 'Idu na vy!'

The *druzhina* bawled out their approval. *Idu na vy* – I am coming against you, his father's war-cry to his enemies. Vladimir's followers were so roaring with what had been done that it leaped to the Oathsworn and the blood surged up in them, too, so that they beat on their shields and howled like wolves. Steam rose.

Only a few desultory arrows flew at the pair of riders as

they galloped back and slithered to a stop, the horses panting already, unfit and malnourished.

'Well,' said Dobrynya, his eyes glittering with excitement and amusement. 'We have done our part, Jarl Orm.'

I turned, the belly-clenching fear of what had to come next filling me. The Oathsworn were ready and I fought for something clever to say – then Odin, as ever, stepped in and made the dog bark inside the village.

All our heads turned. A dog, alive and uneaten. That meant they had food to spare and, even if it was stinking fare, that dog was good eating and belonged to us. I said so and it was enough. Heads went back and howls went up, so that the hackles on everyone else's neck went stiff – the Oathsworn had scented blood.

We trotted forward, shields up. The *druzhina* bowmen moved forward and fired in staggered volleys; shafts whirred, thunked into timbers. I looked to my left, to where Finn snarled, then to my right, where Ospak loped. Six men raced ahead, three of them with shields.

The gate was a double-door affair set in a frame of timber ramparts. There was no earthwork here, obviously, so two timber squares had been erected on the earthwork on either side of the gate – but the actual palisade was made from the same length of timbers as all the rest. Which meant it was feet shorter with no earthwork to stand on and there was no rampart above the gate, only a solid balk of timber; a man on horseback would have to duck to get through the opened doors.

Six men crashed into the timbers of the gate. The tower defenders bobbed up to shoot them and ducked hastily back down as arrows drummed into the wood near their heads. The three pairs unshipped a shield, grasped it between them and looked back at us.

'Bone, blood and steel,' Finn growled, grinning and savage as a mad dog and Ospak howled up at the sky, his neck cording. Our axes clashed, three as one, our breath smoked together and I found I was sweating-warm, though I could not feel my feet. Then we sprinted, a bearded axe in either hand, running, it seemed to me, on the stumps of our ankles.

We were the lightest – well, save for Finn and I wanted at least one mad fighting man for what we did. Ospak was small and I was no beefy oarsman, so we leaped on the shields and were hurled upwards with ease by those picked for the ox-hump rowing muscle across their shoulders.

I flopped over the top of the palisade, scrabbling on the age-smoothed points of the timbers, then swung my legs and dropped. Ospak, even lighter than me, practically vaulted over; Finn hooked one bearded axe in the top timbers and hauled himself up and over. Already, three more steam-smoked Chosen were hurling themselves at the shieldmen.

I landed with a crash and on my bad ankle. Ospak sprawled beside me and was up in a moment, snarling and roaring. He hurled one axe up and to his right, felling an archer. Then he waited for the rush of armed men.

Finn landed like a cat and did not wait for anything. Roaring, he hurled himself at the nearest men, both axes already blurring in his big fists.

'Get the gate, Orm!'

I got up, half-turned – a body hurled down, fell over cursing and rolled upright. Tjorvir. A second landed nearby, was getting up and an arrow took him in the foot. Howling, pinned to the frozen ground by it, Snorri Littli had to reach down and try to tug it free. Tjorvir cursed his way to the right-hand tower ladder, hurling one axe upwards and snarling at the men above as he forged up to them.

I turned all the way to the gate – and stopped. The bar was there, right enough but there was a man on it. His right hand was nailed to the bar and his left was nailed to the gate on the other side. Thorstein Cod-Biter hung between the double doors, dripping blood and looking at me from the

221

bruised ruin of his face. Farolf's last vicious joke and the hammering I had heard earlier.

'Get the gate!' screamed Finn as Runolf Harelip, crashing over the palisade, scrambled to his side to fight off the knots of defenders, armed with spears and shields and axes. Someone else cursed and slavered on top of the gate timbers and did not jump but I was only vaguely aware of him.

Cod-Biter's eyes met mine, blue and glittering as a summer sea. He grinned from a bloody mouth and I thought he winked, but one eye was already lost in blood and bruises, so I might have been mistaken.

All of that seemed to last a week but, looking back on it now, was no longer than the time it took me to draw breath, hold it and swing one axe at his right hand. It severed it at the wrist, slantwise and too high, so that half the forearm went with it, for I was a bad axeman and it was my left hand, with only a three-fingered grip.

My right-hand axe hooked under the bar and I found myself roaring into the effort of lifting it. I thought it was easy at the time; it came up and out of the sockets as if greased and the gates swung wide and inwards, dragging Cod-Biter, still nailed to the right-hand timbers, the remains of his forearm and hand nailed to the other side. Thor gave me his strength and the muscles on my arm ached for weeks afterwards – even Finn was admiring, for the beam took two men to lift.

I felt nothing at the time. I was busy trying to gently prise Cod-Biter off the timbers of the gate, while supporting his weight to stop the nail tearing through his remaining palm.

I was vaguely aware of men piling through the opened gate, shrieking and howling, cutting, stabbing and cursing but I took no part in it and killed no-one. Even when the man fell from the top of the gate with a crack and a thump I hardly looked up until he started to writhe and scream, high and shrill like a hurt horse. By then I had worked the nail out

222

and Cod-Biter was bleeding so badly that I concentrated on tying cords round his arms and forgot the screamer.

'I will take him now, Jarl Orm,' said a familiar voice and made me look up from the pool of bloody slush I knelt in, blinking at the opaque orb of a face. Slowly, it became Thorgunna, who smiled a sad, blue-pinched smile and knelt. The fighting was over.

'I will take him,' she said and I nodded and stumbled up, feeling Cod-Biter's blood start to congeal and freeze on my knees.

'A rare fight,' said a voice and I looked round to where Dobrynya sat on his thin and weary horse. He lifted his sabre and saluted me. The little prince, of course, was already trotting triumphantly round the village square, demanding that Farolf be brought to him.

Farolf was already dead and Gyrth's long-axe was so buried in his chest that both Finnlaith and Glum Skulasson were hard put to get it out. Finn was nearby, kneeling by the side of Harelip, who had taken two arrows in the back from the tower before the archers could be felled.

'Farolf? Dead is he?' shrilled Vladimir, irritated. 'Well, he shall be staked anyway.'

Gyrth grunted, a coughing sound like a poked bear.

'He is mine. I killed him. He will lie at the feet of Runolf Harelip here.'

Finn, as if coming out of sleep, stirred and blinked, then nodded at Gyrth and extended his wrist for the Boulder Brother to haul him to his feet. They both stared, cold-faced, at the little prince.

Vladimir frowned angrily, then he saw Finn's look and was clever enough to see the mood – for which all the gods had to be thanked, I thought. Still, he was a prince and had been since four, so he was not so easily cowed.

'You fought well,' he agreed, then added imperiously. 'I shall consent.'

'Now there's good of him,' muttered Gyrth. Finn sagged a little then, suddenly seeming old and stiff. He dusted the snow off his knees and turned to me, eyes glassed with misery, one loose-held axe rimed with freezing blood.

'Harelip,' he said to me, almost pleading. 'Harelip, Orm. I sailed everywhere with Runolf Harelip.'

I had no answer for him. There were fewer original Oathsworn left than could crew a decent faering these days. Seven seasons ago, when a boy I no longer recognized scrambled up the strakes of Einar the Black's *Fjord Elk,* there had been a full crew, sixty or more.

'Aye,' grunted Onund Hnufa, shoving Vladimir's horse aside with the lack of ceremony a man from Iceland always showed to men and kings both. 'It is a hard life at sea, right enough. Now – where is that dog?'

THIRTEEN

They had not known what we were, these Slavs of the Novgorod *druzhina*. A Norse band of sometime outlaws, ragged-arsed brigands at best and not to be compared to fighting men, who spent all their time training for war.

They had swallowed the tales of the were-wyrms of Malkyiv, but they had never actually seen us fight. Now they had. The village had been taken in less time than it took to eat the dog in a stew and those defenders left alive were shaking with it yet, for they really were no more than hired knife-wavers.

The villagers liked us, too, for we had not run mad as they had feared, killing and raping and looting and they were grateful for that and thought us decent. The gods would need to help them if other northers ever arrived at their door, who were not so cold that a short fight stole their strength and who could be turned from skirt-lifting by the first piece of chewable bread.

Little Vladimir was stunned enough by what we had done to become polite. Sigurd, the only one who had suspected what we were capable of, was lip to ear with Dobrynya for days afterwards, while Vladimir's uncle had a calculating look when he glanced over at me.

The rest of the company, Slavs and thralls and those of Klerkon's men who remained alive, walked soft round the Oathsworn and the fear rose from them like stink on a hot day. There were mutterings of 'Jomsvikings' – which was close to the truth, for those Wends of Wolin have stolen half our tales, puffed like pigeon chests by the saga-poets.

However, the heroes of Joms had, the tales revealed, strange rules on women which Finn was quick to refute for the Oathsworn. The Oathsworn did not ban women from their hall, for any man who did not hump was a limp-dicked Christ-priest and a not a fighting man at all.

Folk laughed, though uneasily, for fame is like that, even when you know it to be mostly a lie. Skalds will tell you the sea is a desert if they think it will get them a free meal, but the trick is to make it sing with poetry; that will get you a good armring as well. Such matters taught me that fame is the fault of rulers with fat rings to spare and who know the worth of a skald's praises spread far and wide. Rulers such as Vladimir.

'We did not properly discuss your share in this mountain of silver,' the little prince piped up, after summoning me to his royal presence in the best of the mean huts available. Beside him, as ever, was Olaf and, looming at his back, was Dobrynya, stroking his iron grey beard. Sigurd was in the shadows beyond the light, where only his nose was visible as a faint gleam.

'I do not think you should risk your life so readily, Orm Bear Slayer,' added Dobrynya with a warm smile that never quite crept to his eyes. 'After all, you are the one who knows the way to the hoard.'

I looked back at the boy prince, his face made paler still by the violet rings round his eyes and the red chafe of his nose. We had not discussed any such thing as my share because, at the time, there was nothing to discuss – I had traded knowledge for life and nothing more. I wondered if he suspected the hilt-runes on that sabre were useless until we reached Sarkel. I hoped he did not suspect, as I did, that even then they might not be enough for me to find my way to Atil's howe.

What had changed, of course, was that Dobrynya – and so also Vladimir – could not be sure their *druzhina* was strong enough to handle the Oathsworn. So the little prince, as advised by Uncle Dobrynya, smiled and acknowledged how marvellous we were at taking fortified places and lavished silver he did not yet have on all our heads.

We sat round leather cups of good ale, speculating on what had happened to Morut the tracker, as if we were really friends, while I felt the sick dull ache of knowing that Cod-Biter fought for his life nearby and that Short Eldgrim might already be dead.

Then, of course, Olaf put us all right on the matter of princes and friendships.

'There was once a prince,' he said into the awkward silence.

'Let us not call him Vladimir,' interrupted Dobrynya smoothly, 'unless he is a good prince.'

Olaf looked levelly back at the Dobrynya, then to where his silver-nosed uncle stood in the darkness, as pointed a gesture as to make Dobrynya stiffen. I doubted if Sigurd was as solid a protection as Olaf believed; if he lived to be older he would find that blood-ties are not enough to be relied on. Only hard god-oaths are to be trusted.

'There was once a prince,' Olaf repeated, 'whose name does not matter, in a land, do not ask me where.

'There was a girl who was so splendid everyone called her Silver Bell. Her eyes were like wild black cherries, her brows curved like Bifrost. Into her braids she plaited coloured glass beads from distant lands and on her hat there was a silver bell, bright as moonlight, which gave her her name.

'One day the father of Silver Bell fell ill and her mother said to her: "Get up on the bay horse and hurry to the *detinets* of the prince. Ask him to come here and to cure your father, for it is well known that true princes can heal the sick with a touch."'

'Well that is right enough,' beamed Sigurd, trying to show the tale was headed in the proper direction. Olaf smiled, sharp as a weasel on mouse-scent.

'The girl leaped up on the bay horse with the white star on his forehead,' he went on. 'She took in her right hand the leather reins with silver rings and in her left the lash with a finely carved bone handle. The bay horse galloped fast, the reins shook up and down, the harness tinkled merrily.

'The prince was in the courtyard of his fortress, playing with his hawks. He heard the clattering of hooves and saw the girl on the bay horse. She sat proudly in the high saddle; the bell fluttered in the wind, the silver in it ringing where it struck the gems sewn in her hat. The beads sang in her thick braids and the hawk flew, forgotten, from the prince's hand. "Great prince," said the girl. "My father is sick, come help us."

'The prince looked back at her and said: "I will cure your father if you will marry me." Silver Bell loved another, a fine, strong hunter of wolves – frightened, she pulled the reins and galloped off. "At dawn tomorrow I will come to you," the prince called after her.'

'This does not sound like any prince I know,' growled Dobrynya meaningfully.

'Really, uncle?' said Vladimir with a delighted chuckle. 'I know two brothers just like this.'

Olaf smiled quietly and went on, soft and level and compelling. 'The stars had barely melted in the sky, the meat in the kettles had not yet been cooked, the fine white rugs were not yet spread, bread had not yet been made, when there was a loud clattering of hooves at Silver Bell's home. The prince had arrived.

'Silently, looking at no-one, he dismounted and, greeting no-one, he went into where the sick man lay. The prince wore magnificent clothes, dripping with silver weighing eighty pounds if it weighed an ounce. All day, from dawn to sunset, the prince sat beside the sick man without lifting his eyelids, without moving, without uttering a word – but it was clear that Silver Bell was not going to come to him and he grew angrier and angrier at her presumption.

'Late at night, the prince stood up and pulled his fine sable hat down to his scowl. Then he said: "Drive out Silver Bell. An evil spirit resides in her. While she is in the house, her father will not get up from his illness. Misfortune will not leave this valley. Little children will fall asleep forever; their fathers and grandfathers will die in torment."'

Dobrynya made a warning growl; even Sigurd shifted uneasily. Vladimir said nothing at all and Olaf did not even appear to notice any of this. Sweat trickled down my back and I felt it freeze there. He would get us all back in the queue for a stake . . .

'The women of the camp fell down upon the ground in fear,' Olaf said. 'The old men pressed their hands over their eyes with grief. The young men looked at Silver Bell; twice they turned red and twice they turned pale.

'The prince smiled to himself. "Put Silver Bell into a wooden barrel," he declared. "Bind the barrel with nine iron hoops. Nail down the bottom with copper nails and throw the barrel into the rushing river."

'This said, he rode off to his hall in the fine, large *borg* and called his thralls round him. "Go to the river," he told them. "The water will bring down a large barrel. Catch it and bring it here, then run into the woods. If you hear weeping, do not turn back. If cries and moans spread through the woods, do not look back. Do not return to my hall in less than three days."

'For nine days and nine nights the people of the encampment could not bring themselves to carry out the prince's orders. For nine days and nine nights they bid the girl farewell.

229

On the tenth day they put Silver Bell into a wooden barrel, bound it with nine iron hoops, nailed down the bottom with copper nails and threw the barrel into the rushing river.'

'This sounds a suitable punishment for one who insults a prince,' noted Dobrynya. Vladimir frowned uneasily and I swallowed the thickness in my mouth.

'It is a tale about Odin,' I declared and saw Sigurd's head come up at this manifest lie.

'Is it?' asked Vladmir, his frown deepening. 'He does not sound godlike to me.'

'A master of deceit,' I acknowledged. 'Always his gifts are suspect. Recall the tale of the nine thralls and the whetstone . . .'

I was babbling and heard myself, so I stopped. Olaf, blank as a cliff, gave me his two-coloured stare and cleared his throat, a high little sound.

'On that day,' he began, 'the day the barrel went in the river, the hunter who loved Silver Bell was examining his traps, saw the barrel, caught it, brought it out of the river, picked up an axe and knocked out the bottom. When he saw Silver Bell, the hand that held the axe dropped and his heart leaped like a grasshopper. At last he asked: "Who put you into the barrel?" She told him.

'The hunter thought for a minute, then went to his traps, where a huge wolf, white as silver glared at him and then got back to gnawing through its own paw. At this point, the hunter would have knocked it on the head; instead, he caught it by the ruff and dropped it in the barrel, nailed down the bottom with copper nails and let the barrel float downstream.

'The prince's thralls pulled out the barrel, brought it to the great hall and put it before the prince, then left as he had ordered. Even before they had closed the door, they heard him knock out the bottom of the barrel and call for help. Faithfully, they did as they had been bidden. They heard shouts, but did not turn back. They heard moaning and cries, but did not look back. For such were their lord's orders.

'Three days later they returned and opened the door. A great, silver-ruffed, three-legged wolf, dead of exhaustion and blood-loss, lay on the floor. Nearby was the prince, more dead than alive – his flesh was torn to shreds, his fine clothes were tattered and torn and, when the thralls crowded round to find out what had happened, all that he could say that made sense was . . . "silver" and "curse". He never spoke sense ever again.'

Into the silence that followed, Sigurd cleared his throat. Olaf, unsmiling and cool as a river stone, hopped down from his bench and silently placed a hand on Vladimir's shoulder. I waited, dry-mouthed, for the flaring of princely rage that would follow.

Instead, Vladimir blinked once or twice, then nodded, as if Olaf had whispered to him.

'When this business is finished,' he said, 'you must stay with me in Lord Novgorod the Great.'

'Of course,' said Olaf with a smile. 'And you will give me ships and men and I will fight on your behalf. Jon Asanes must also come, for he is a clever man. Together we will make your name greater than that of your father.'

The clarity of it shocked me, like the stun of a blow taken on your forearm. Of course – little Vladimir, hag-ridden by his father's memory, wanted only that; to be greater. That was what drove him after Atil's hoard.

I stood up and took my leave while I was in the eye of this storm and – not that I was surprised – little Crowbone caught up with me not long afterwards. Outside, in the dark of the dead day, he trotted at my heels, pulling his cloak round him and trying to keep up with my strides.

'You were right,' I said to him angrily. 'That is an affliction.'

He shook his head, glancing up at me with that two-coloured frown and I was disconcerted, for he looked wise as a greybeard, then grinned like the boy he was.

'That was clever about Odin,' he declared. 'As you say – beware his gifts, as the nine thralls should have done.'

Then he was gone, silent as an owl, leaving me with the vision of those thralls, scrabbling for the whetstone One Eye threw in the air and cutting their own throats with their scythes in their greed. I shook my head over him, and not for the first time. Like his eyes on colour, I could not make up my mind on Olaf Crowbone.

At the hut we had taken over, the original family bobbed and grinned, eager to please and keep their lives while they tried to hide valuables and food. The Oathsworn counted, washed and prepared the dead for burial.

'How many?' I asked and Kvasir looked up, his good eye red and weeping. Thorgunna had warm water and was bathing it.

'Two will lie on either side of Harelip – Snorri and Eyolf.'

Snorri I remembered getting an arrow through the foot. I did not recall seeing Eyolf, whom we called Kraka – Crow – because he was left-handed.

'Aye, Snorri got pinned in the one place and danced round his foot until he ran out of steps,' Kvasir said, waving Thorgunna away irritably. She made a disgusted face at him and went. I saw she had applied more soot-black round his good eye.

'A big Slav cut him down when he could dance no further,' Kvasir finished.

'Eyolf?'

'His sheath killed him.'

I remembered how Eyolf had loved his hand-tooled sheath, leather the colour of old blood, stretched over oak and sheep-lined. I looked at Kvasir and he shrugged.

'He would not take it off and the baldric caught on the timbers on top of the gate. He could not get free and hung there, afraid of being shot with arrows. So he wriggled until the strap broke and he fell – the sheath snapped and the wood of it drove into his liver and lights and he died.'

I remembered the man struggling at the top of the gate while I fought for Cod-Biter's life. I remembered, too, the same man crashing down, the screaming and writhing. An idiot death; no man wears a sheath in a battle, for if it does not tangle in your legs then something stupid like this happens. Stabbed by his own sheath – there was a straw death to make Odin's hall ring with laughter.

'Cod-Biter?'

Kvasir shrugged and pointed to where Bjaelfi was working, Jon Asanes holding up a pitch torch for more light. Bjaelfi's elbow was pumping furiously and I knew what he was doing – trimming Cod-Biter's arm straight, cutting more bone and flesh from him. Cod-Biter was mercifully limp but not dead, otherwise Bjaelfi would not be bothering.

Finn sat nearby, watching and silent and Thordis, between tending to the fire and the food bowls and other business, shot him frequent, worried glances. Then she fetched me a bowl that steamed and a chunk of black bread, hunkering at my knee as she delivered it.

'This looks good,' I said and it was no lie; I was astonished at how savoury the stew was.

'Food is not a problem now, Jarl Orm,' she said. 'It seems these nithings we defeated had stolen most of the supplies from Lambisson. The ones who went on will be hungry by now, I am thinking.'

I would have been pleased, save that Short Eldgrim was one of them. I had the feeling Cod-Biter would not last the night and now Short Eldgrim looked more doomed than ever. What with Runolf Harelip's death, it seemed the old Oathsworn were fated not to get back to Atil's hoard.

Thordis nodded seriously when I said this. She jerked her head in Finn's direction.

'He is getting Klepp Spaki to paint his forehead with the *valknut*,' she said harshly. 'Soon he will come to you and ask for that amulet you have.'

I blinked at that. If it was true, then Finn was dedicating himself to live or die at the whim of Odin and that was as good as hurling himself off a cliff for, in a fight, he would not retreat until he had had some clear sign from One Eye that it was good to do so. I felt like a house whose roof was falling.

I finished the stew, though the joy in it had gone by then. I lay back, feeling the warmth and the full belly, my head full of shrieking gulls; Vladimir and his uncle and what they would do when the howe was reached. Finn. Odin. The silver hoard. The Man-Haters and whether the one who led them was really Hild. The rune sword she had. The one I had.

I tried not to sleep in the hope that I would, but all of that whirled like an ice wind inside my head until it scoured the back of my eyeballs sore. When Finn loomed out of the dark and hunkered beside me, it was almost a relief and I handed him the amulet before he spoke, unlooping it from around my neck.

He did not ask how I knew but took it and looped it round his own neck.

'This is a hard road you take,' I muttered, sick with it. Sailing once in a badly-trimmed *knarr* I had felt like this – every time the wind hit a certain quarter it would heel over and the steerboard would lift clean out of the water, so there was nothing to do but run until the wind died enough to drop the steerboard back in the water – or you hit something.

'Rather this one than another,' he growled, miserable as mirr.

'Which one is that, then?'

He shifted uncomfortably, then looked at me, flat and grind-stone hard. 'The one that ends with me drooling by a fire, with women laughing behind my back at how my *vingull* is limp and my back bowed.'

For all that he was grim with it, I had to swallow a smile, since the word he used – *vingull* – meant the prick of a horse rather than that of a man. So I knew he still had some pride in him yet.

'You listened too long to Martin the monk,' I gave him back. 'Too afraid to live? Too old? Is this Finn Bardisson from Skane?'

'Who knows? Who will know? Who will remember Pai? Or Harelip? When all of us are dead, Bear Slayer, only Pinleg and Skapti and others will be remembered, locked in that stone we raised in Aldeigjuborg. They are the ones with fame-luck.'

'We will have a stone . . .'

'Too late, Trader. It seems to me unlikely we will make it back to where Klepp Spaki can carve it. And if we do – what then? Back to that steading with the chickens and all the silver we can carry? What then, the point of raiding? So we squat and wait for the Norns to snip off the last threads of our life.'

'So all that is left to do is find a good death, Finn Bardisson?'

He grunted and said: 'I made a vow in the pit prison. To One Eye. He kept his side of the bargain.'

Then he straightened and forced a grin. 'In the end, as Pai knew, there is only one thing.' Then he intoned:

> 'Cattle die and kinsmen die,
> you, too, soon must die
> but one thing never will die,
> the fair fame of one who has earned it.'

'There is that, right enough,' I said, bitter as lees at him for finding it so easy to follow this path. Then I gave him back a verse of the Sayings of the High One, the one everybody forgets.

> 'The lame can ride a horse, the handless drive cattle,
> the deaf one can fight and prevail,
> happier for the blind than for him on the bale-fire,
> but no man cares for a corpse.'

235

Finn might have had a reply to it, but Cod-Biter woke up and moaned then. He did that for most of the night and then died, his screams shaving the hairs off our arms, just as the dawn came up.

There was too much food in the end and men came down with the squits and belly gripes, so that Bjaelfi had to feed them a cure made from the newest root of a bramble which had both ends in the earth, boiled up with mugwort and everlasting and the milk of a mare, a goat and a cow.

'Does it work?' demanded Skula, a raw-boned youth who had started skinny and was now yellow and wasting. Thorgunna, who was feeding him with it, assured him it was infallible, but from the face he made swallowing it down I was glad I did not have the squits.

'He will get more out of the other part of Bjaelfi's cure,' Thorgunna muttered as she passed me. 'The bit that has him rest in the soft and warm.'

Too many were dead, or dying, or sick. In the end, I had to gather the Oathsworn together and ask for people to stay with those too sick to travel, partly to make sure the villagers remembered their manners, partly to try and make sure they lived.

I had expected a torrent of volunteers, but was surprised; only two said they would stay, making out that is was for the good reason of tending their sick comrades but really because they were too weak themselves and knew they could go no further. The others were determined to go on and, in the end, I had to tell two more they would stay and listen to them grumble.

One was Skula and, though he curled his lip at my decision, looked more relieved than annoyed; he was weak enough to die if he left the village and knew it.

The other was Tjorvir, whose boils were now beyond Bjaelfi's powers to prevent and Thorgunna and Thordis' lancing prowess with a needle and wool. They erupted where clothing chafed, so that his neck and wrists were a mass of sores and pus – but he was frowning at my leaving him behind.

'This is not a good thing,' he declared, shaking his head, so I pointed out that he could barely walk, use a sword or wear a helm but it made no difference. In the end, Finnlaith clapped him on the back – from Tjorvir's wince, he had found a new boil – and said: 'Don't worry – I will serve the weregild and make sure you get your share.'

It was Jon Asanes who explained it to me, which did not make me feel any better about being put on the straight path by a stripling and one who had been weeping-sad since his friend, Pai, had died.

'The ones who came with Thorkel feel bad for what he did and do not wish you to think badly of them,' he told me. 'They will follow you to the door of Helheim – as will the others and not because of the oath they made in the eye of Odin.

'They don't call you Bear Slayer, they call you Trader,' he added with a quiet grin, 'because everyone knows that, if you fare with Orm, you get a good deal. They know you are All-Father's favourite and think that will bring most of them home, too.'

We spoke quietly, under four eyes only, about Olaf's plan to keep Jon in Novgorod. I knew enough about Crowbone not to find it strange that a mere boy of nine should be deciding the future of one I had known since he was a child himself.

Jon did not smile. He looked uncomfortable and scrubbed at what I saw was the beginnings of a passable beard, dark against the pale olive of his skin. The gesture made my heart skip, for it was so like old Rurik, the man I'd thought my father, as to have been a copy. Then I realized he had picked the gesture up from me.

'Little Crowbone dreams his dreams,' Jon said wryly, 'and

depends on the actions of birds to make them come true – one more to a flock here, a flutter to the left there. He will fail in the end, for no true god guides his hand in that.'

'You can say that?' I countered. 'Even after all you have witnessed with us?'

'Always the hand of the White Christ – the *Hvitkristr* – is in it,' Jon answered levelly. 'That has ever been a barrier between us.'

Not on my account, nor would it and I said as much, so that he flashed those white, straight teeth at me, big as rune-stones now in a face made too thin from hunger.

'You call him *hvitkristr* for a reason,' he answered. 'Perhaps you have used it for so long that you no longer hear it as I do.'

'Which way is that?' I asked, though I already knew it.

'The way that *hvit* means not just "white" but cowardly,' he replied, then dropped his eyes from mine. 'That and worse. So I am tarred with the same. I cannot fight well, nor can I take the Odin-oath. I am neither fish nor fowl in this company.'

It was true enough, though I did not see how a godlet who let himself be nailed passively to a lump of wood could be anything but white-livered, as we Northmen say. I did not say that, all the same, out of deference to Jon Asanes' beliefs.

I had not known – or not thought – of any of this and it came as a shock of cold water to hear him speak as though we were strangers. I looked at him and remembered him as the skinny Greek boy on Cyprus. It rose up in me and barred the door of my mouth, so that the words I should have spoken were blocked.

He grinned, shamefaced, his too-large eyes bright. 'I know bribage and port dues and lading weights,' he said. 'I know the worth of a dozen coins and how they relate to each other and how to tell bad amber from good. I speak Greek and Latin and write in both and my runes are passable. I will be a good trader myself one day. But I am not a northman and I am not a pagan and I am not Oathsworn and never will be so.'

238

'All true,' I managed to reply, but the wormwood of the moment made my tongue bitter. 'Perhaps you should also remain here, being so valuable.'

He shook his head sadly, which shamed me to silence. Then, he lowered his eyes to stare at the floor.

'When you first arrived in Novgorod I was . . . ashamed. Finn stank and Kvasir was not much better. Even you, Trader.'

I shrugged. He had been too long away from honest Northmen, that was all. And we had left him when he was but a boy. I said as much and he nodded, still ashamed.

'You looked like all the tales the priests told – hard men, who smell bad and spend your days killing men and humping unwilling women.'

'Not unwilling, some of them,' I managed and that trembled a grin on him but it vanished just as quickly.

'I am a Greek who is no longer a Greek, fighting with a *varjazi* and yet not a Northman. Crowbone imagines he is favouring me; the prince also – but I have my own ideas on what my life will be.'

It was true enough and the ache of knowing it, having it said and so made real, was keen and swirled in me like molten metal until it finally forged itself into anger. We had been good to Jon Asanes and I said so. Whatever his life would be, he owed it to us.

He looked at me and there was dark fire in those olive eyes.

'You came to Cyprus and what you did there killed my brother and forced me to go with you into the scorching Serkland. I was shot by an arrow and almost died, then finally carried far from the world I knew to the far north, a bitter cold place of unwashed folk who wear skins.'

That made me blink with the harsh of it, but he had more of the same.

'I have had no say until recently and had plans of my own – until you returned to my life. As soon as you did I faced the stake and am now here, in this frozen waste, where I may die.'

He stopped and smiled sadly. 'That is your goodness to me? I would hate to have you be bad to me, Trader.'

The anger went from me; sadness and loss surged in to fill the space. Whatever the future held, it seemed the Goat Boy was gone from us.

As Gunnar, my real father, had often said – everything you need should be in a sea-chest; everything else can be left behind. Like all simple solutions, it was flawed, relied on making no attachments to people. In the end, of course, even he realized that for he could not leave me behind.

'It would be nice all the same,' Jon Asanes added wistfully, 'if I could have a cut of those runes on your stone, just like all the others.'

I nodded, unable to speak. Runes on a stone, or a fine-kenned verse. That is why no-one wanted to be left behind, huddled in a bed in a village – those left standing get the most honour from skalds, unless their death was particular.

Finn, it seemed, had decided on a particular death.

As the dawn struggled up, we stood and watched him stand in the cold – no Northman kneels, even to the gods – bare-headed and facing north, sprinkling the best white emperor salt in a cup of meltwater, which he then dedicated to Odin with all of All Father's names. Finally, he rammed The Godi into the earth, bowed his head, clasped the hilt and made his chilling vow, as promised to the god in the pit prison of Novgorod.

I was filled with a distant, dull pain, a swill of memories of myself at the same age as Jon Asanes, hunting out thrall women in Skirringsaal in the first long winter with the Oathsworn, while Einar plotted and watched. Had Einar felt this same ache? He had been as separate and alone, I remembered.

I was a couple of summers past twenty but I felt there

were stones under that frozen, dun earth that were younger than me.

Two days later, we crawled out on to that snow-scattered waste and headed away from the village, leaving the boat-marked ground that was the last home of Harelip and Cod-Biter.

FOURTEEN

A brass sun seeped through the dull lead of the sky and the stands of birch, no higher than a man on a horse and clumped like a bad beard on the face of the world. They were grim, clawed affairs, these trees, as black as if they had sucked their own shadows back up. Snow lay clotted on a brown heave of land and the air was still and raw.

The carts lurched and rumbled to a halt, ponies standing splay-legged, heads bowed. We had fitted the wheels since there was more earth than snow, but that had been a mistake – the ground was hard frozen and the carts banged and slapped in every iron-forged rut, so that even the tired and sick got out and trudged with everyone else rather than suffer the lurch and bruise of it.

Gizur and I stood at the stirrup of Vladimir's big black, all rib and bone hips, while he looked at the trees. We all looked at the trees and the opaque ribbon they fringed – the Don.

'See,' said Gizur, his breath freezing in his beard as he spoke. 'The middle is darker, where the water is only just starting to form hard.'

'A thaw is coming,' Dobrynya declared, but Gizur knew the ways of water and shook his head, hard enough to rattle the ice points of his moustache.

'No. The ice was broken recently. Less than an hour – look, you can see where the grue of it reformed from a time before that, too.'

'There is traffic on the river,' Sigurd grunted, wiping the icicles from the bottom of his silver nose, where they clogged the hole that let him breath.

'Just so,' Gizur beamed. 'Boats are breaking their way up and down to Sarkel and regularly enough to stop the centre channel freezing hard.'

We all knew that we were on the Don, where it turned east into a great curve that went south, then slithered west to the Maeotian Lake, which the Khazars call Azov, meaning 'low' for it is so shallow. Following that great curve would bring us to Sarkel and take weeks.

Gizur was beaming, because he had navigated us from a point four days east of Kiev to here as if we had been the ocean – give or take a tack here and there, as Avraham declared later, sullen and mournful over the loss of Morut. Yet now we had to choose, either the short way, a plunge straight across the Great White, or follow the Don's long, cold curl to Sarkel.

'A long way still,' Dobrynya said 'with no respite at Biela Viezha.'

No-one had to ask why; the Prince of Novgorod, arriving with a tattered band like us, miles from his own domain and firmly at the far frontiers of his brother's lands, would excite more than a little attention. If his brother's name still held sway at Sarkel – called Biela Viezha, the White Castle, by the Slavs – now that Sviatoslav was gone.

All eyes were on me. Somewhere in that bleak ice waste was what we sought and I had to steer them all to richness with the hilt runes on my sabre. The smile I gave them back was, I hoped, as bright and sure as sunrise.

We turned back to the line of carts and people, where only a few of the *druzhina* were now horsed and everyone else so

243

swathed in shapeless bundles that it was hard to tell man from woman, or warrior from thrall. They huddled into their clothes and stamped feet made fat in braided straw overshoes, which the horses kept trying to eat.

'What now, Trader?' demanded Kvasir, wiping the weep from his good eye. Thorgunna made to help and he slapped her hand away, irritated. She scowled in return.

'It needs proper attention.'

'I am doing so. Go and weave something.'

Thorgunna fixed him with her sheep-dropping eyes. 'It is time I died,' she declared firmly. 'Time I was dropped in my grave, for I have nothing left, it seems, to offer this life or the man I have in it.'

'You may live or die as you see fit,' growled Kvasir, sullenly, 'providing you decide without poking my eye. Whatever your decision, we will all have to live with the consequences.'

Finn, hunched up like a seal in clothes and swaddled cloak, offered up a cracked bell of a laugh as Thorgunna threw up one hand in annoyance and left Kvasir and his eye.

'We should cut across the Great White, south to Sarkel,' Finn added. Avraham, hearing this, gave a short, sharp bark of laughter, while Gizur frowned and crushed the ice out of his beard, for the Great White was one sea he could not navigate.

'Did you bleat?' Finn asked, sour-faced.

'What has been crossed so far is as nothing compared to what lies out there,' Avraham said, waving a hand in the general direction of the east. 'That is a howling wilderness, which offers nothing to men, summer or winter.'

'You have been there?' Gyrth interrupted and Avraham cocked a haughty eyebrow.

'I am Khazar. I have been everywhere.'

'But there especially?'

Avraham shifted a little. 'No,' he admitted, then thrust his chin out belligerently. 'What sane man would go where there is often no water for flocks in summer, nor reason to be there in the depths of winter? Anyway, it is . . . cursed.'

He looked half-ashamed, half-defiant, but it was clear he believed it and it came to me then that where Atil's tomb lay would be thought a cursed place, even if no-one knew it was there. So many deaths to build it, stock it, carry him to it; the steppe here was crowded with moaning fetches every time the wind blew.

'So,' said Jon Asanes sadly, 'you cannot guide us then, if we choose that route.'

Avraham bristled. 'I am Khazar and this is my land – I can guide you anywhere. For a reasonable price.'

'Ha!' growled Finn. 'This is not your land now, though, you prick-cut thief. The Rus rule here.'

'What price?' I asked, seeing Avraham's face darken. He remained staring into Finn's glare for a moment longer – which was brave of him, I had to admit – then quoted the cost of a small farm.

Finn roared before I could even speak. 'You can have the rust off my balls, you arse.'

Avraham smeared a sneer on his face.

'Balls of poor iron – that explains the clinking I heard, for I knew a man such as yourself could not have a purse so rich.'

'My balls were smelted in northern forges, little man,' Finn replied with a broad grin, 'in such a heat where the likes of you would smoulder like an eider duck's tail. They were quenched in cold that makes this seem like a balmy day.'

'I suspect we are speaking in the singular,' Avraham answered. 'I had heard the Norse had to share a pair between two.'

'You heard wrong. Gulls use my prick as a perch, thinking it a mast. When I shit over the side of a racing *drakkar*, my turds choke whales. I piss fire and fart thunder. And that which you call a howling wilderness is just another little sea to me.'

Others were gathering, hugely enjoying this. It drove away the cold and misery and I was grateful for that. Better still, the chances of them coming to serious blows had slipped away.

'You spout a deal of empty nothing like a whale does, that much I have seen,' Avraham replied and those nearest gave approving noises that made Finn scowl.

'That which we have called the Great White,' Avraham went on, 'is merely those who know being kind to you. The real Great White is a few wheel turns from here, directly south. You will see it from a long way off, because it is a dazzle of ice. After that, if you should survive, you will just have time to make peace with your heathen gods before your famous perch freezes and snaps like a twig. If you ever find this silver hoard it will be because some wolf, tired of gnawing your arse-bone, drops it nearby.'

Finn made a dismissive gesture into admiring 'heyas' of those who thought this a good flyting.

'You are like all who have not had the benefit of being born in Skane, when faced with open space, whether sea or land,' he declared expansively. 'You fear to lose sight of safety. No open space frightens us from Skane and a horizon is an invitation, not a limit. Odin and Vili and Ve fixed the stars for us to find our way and, with them, I know where I am in this world to the length of a sparrow's fart.'

He cocked his head and closed one eye reflectively, blowing out his ice-hung moustaches.

'Anyway,' he added, 'you have never seen a blowing whale, you land-fastened nithing.'

There were appreciative hooms and nods at this, though everyone knew Finn could not find his arse with both hands when it came to navigating a ship and had never seen any live whales himself.

'The steppe respects no-one,' Avraham declared haughtily and I thought this had gone on long enough and said so.

'If the steppe respects no-one, then a guide such as yourself would be useless,' I added and everyone cheered at that – even Finn. Avraham acknowledged defeat with a rueful smile, which he lost when I asked if he could, in fact, guide us.

He looked from me to Finn's challenging grin, to Gyrth and Jon Asanes and then back to me. Then he shook his head and would not meet anyone's eye.

Gizur shifted a little and thumbed snot out of his nose.

'Well,' he declared challengingly, 'I admit it with now shame – the Great White is not known to me and none of my skills will take you safe across it. Best we follow the river.'

'Ah – who needs this Khazar,' Kvasir bellowed. 'Cross the Great White. It will not be a hard trail to find, I am thinking, Just follow the ruin of Lambisson.'

That thought threw ice into all our veins, though none admitted it as we set off across the Great White. In the end, Avraham came with us, since he had the choice of doing that or staying by the river to die, but it could not be said he guided us anywhere after that.

The Great White swallowed us. The snow drove down in small, slanted flakes, persistent as gnats, piling high round camping places and kept at bay only by the heat of fires and our own bodies. We woke every morning, moving carefully within tents and shelters so as not to shake down the frost which had formed on the inside. We chipped the horse tethers out of the frozen earth, made fires, cooked porridge and, after three hours, were usually ready to move off.

The cold rot turned more noses and toes black; Bjaelfi, Thorgunna and Thordis kept little knives sharp for paring off the spoiled flesh and, at first, we seemed aimless as ants on a sheepskin. Then, as Kvasir had said, matters grew simple; we followed the ruin of Lambisson, while the snow sifted out of the pewter sky, trailed along the land like smoke, stung like thrown gravel in our faces.

It was a trail of tears a blind man could track, from

splintered wagon to dead horse to blue-white corpses, little knots of tragedy in an ice-rope that most thought would hang us all. At each one, sick with apprehension, I searched for the familiar face of Short-Eldgrim.

Then, on a day where the sky was the colour of Odin's one bright eye, I was moving carefully to a private spot – but not out of sight – to risk a shit and saw little Olaf standing wrapped in his once-white cloak like a pillar of dirty snow on the dark earth, watching black birds wheel.

They were waiting for us to quit the latest wolf-chewed remains, followed us, hungry and hopeful as gulls on a fishing boat and, like them, a handful of wary men trailed little Crowbone, seeking scraps of wisdom.

'So – you are saying that if one more bird joins them from the west something terrible will happen?'

Red Njal's voice was suspicious, but the thickness of disbelief in it was like the ice on the Don – broken and uncertain.

'Mind your words, too, boy,' he added, 'for there is naught so vile as a fickle tongue, as my granny used to say.'

Olaf said nothing at all, merely nodded, watching intently.

'Freyja's arse,' growled Klepp Spaki, his voice muffled. No more than his eyes could be seen in the swaddle of hood and *wadmal* round his head. 'What makes that happen? How do you know? What runes do you use?'

'The birds are their own runes,' answered Olaf.

'How?' demanded Onund Hnufa, lumbering up and towering over Crowbone, who did not even glance up at the terrible hunch-shouldered effigy hanging over him like a mountain. 'By what rules? What signs?'

'Here,' said Olaf and touched his head, then his heart. He hunched himself back in the cloak as Red Njal grunted scornfully.

'Thor's red balls, boy – I was the same when I was your age. Running about making black dwarves and trolls appear and fighting them with a wooden sword.'

248

We all chuckled, for all of us had done the same. Olaf broke his gaze from the birds to turn his odd eyes on Red Njal's cold-roughed face. The *seidr*, it seemed to me rolled off him like heat haze, so that I had to blink to steady my eyes.

'No offence,' muttered Red Njal hastily. 'Be never the first to break the bonds of friendship, as my granny used to say.'

A bird fluttered in and landed. 'Aha,' said Crowbone. 'Today, something bad will happen.'

'This is all shite. A boy's will is the will of the wind, my granny said,' declared Red Njal when Olaf had trudged out of earshot. He turned and looked at me, his eyes like small animals in the ice-crusted hair of his face.

'Is it not shite, Trader?'

'I saw and was silent, pondered and listened to the speech of men,' I offered, remembering the old saying; his frown chewed that until I thought his forehead would crack.

'Shite,' I clarified and he cracked the ice of his face with a smile, then left me to my own awkward business.

An hour later, at the lip of a great scar of *balka*, the axle pin on a cart snapped and the wheel came off. Ref Steinsson took an axe and the handle of another and fashioned a new pin with delicate, skilled strokes, while men heaved and strained to unload the cart then lift it and put the wheel on again.

Red Njal, crimson with effort, looked up at me, then to where Olaf stood, a quiet smile on his face.

'Shite,' said Red Njal, bitterly accusing and I shrugged. If this was as bad as it got . . .

'Heya, Trader – look at that.'

Hauk Fast-Sailor, arms full of bundle from the unloaded cart, nodded across the steppe with his chin.

'The *djinn*, Trader – remember them?'

I remembered them, and the little Bedu tribesman Aliabu telling us of the invisible demons who could never touch the

249

earth, whose passing was marked by the swirl of dust and sand. For a moment, the memory of Serkland heat was glorious.

The snow swirled up in an ice crystal dance. Those who had never fared farther from home than this – most of these new Oathsworn, it came to me – gawped both at the dance of it and at Hauk and me, realizing now just how far-travelled we were, to have seen *djinn* in the Serkland desert

'I did not know the *djinn* were here, too,' Hauk said, grunting with the effort of moving the bundles. 'Lots of them, it seems.'

I did not like it and did not know why. Snow curled in little eddies and rose in the air, dragging my eyes up to a pewter sky and the figure flogging a staggering horse towards us and yelling something we could not hear.

Work stopped; the wheel was on, but the pin still had to be hammered in and all eyes turned on the horse and rider, the frantic fever of them soaking unease into us.

It was Morut the tracker, shouting as he came up, his voice suddenly whipped towards us by the wind.

'The *buran* is here!'

We had just enough time to find shelter. Just enough before it pounced on us, hard as the lash of a whip, a scour of ice that shrieked like frustrated Valkyries.

We unhitched the ponies and dragged and pushed them down the V-shaped *balka*, taller than three men and so steep that most of us went down it on our arses. Those too slow were moaning in agony at the barbs of flying ice; horses screamed, flanks bloodied by it. We huddled, people and beasts together, while the world screamed in white fury.

Light danced like laughter on the water, the sea creamed round the skerries and a drakkar bustled with life on the edge of a curve of beach. I watched the boy stand in the lee of the ship, up to his calves in cold water, clutching a

bundle and his uncertainty tight to himself, his shoes round his neck.

Someone leaned from the boat, yelled angrily at him. Someone else thrust out a helping hand and he took it, was pulled aboard. The drakkar oars came out, dipped and sparkled; the dragon walked down the fjord.

Me. It was me, leaving Bjornshafen with Einar the Black and the Oathsworn on board the Fjord Elk. I was young . . .

'Fifteen,' said the one-eyed man. He was tall and under the blue, night-dark cloak he exuded a strength that spoke of challenges mastered. Little of his body showed, other than a hand, gloved and clutching a staff.

His single eye, peering like a rat from the smoked curl of hair framing his face, shaded by the brim of the broad hat he wore, was blue as a cloudless sky and piercing. I knew him.

'All Father,' I said and he chuckled. One Eye, Greybeard, the Destroyer, The Furious One. Frenzy.

Odin.

'Part of him and all of that,' he answered. He nodded at the scene, which wavered and swirled as if the sudden wind ruffled it, like the reflection in a pool.

'The White Christ priest with Gudleif,' he said and I saw the head on a pole, a head which had once been Gudleif, the man who had raised me as a fostri. Caomh, the Irisher thrall who had once been a priest – always a priest, he used to say – stood beside the horror Einar had created and watched us row away.

'Bjornshafen was woven together after Gudleif's sons died and the White Christ priest did it, so that they are all followers of the One God now.'

He said it bitterly, this Father of the Aesir. Why did he permit this White Christ, this Jesus from the soft south? He was Odin, after all . . . ?

'We wear what the Norns weave, even gods,' he answered. 'The old Sisters grow weary, want to lay down their loom, perhaps, and can only do that when the line of the Yngling kings is ended.'

It was a long line. Crowbone, great-grandson for Harald Fairhair, was part of it. Did the Norns seek to kill him, too?

One-Eye said nothing, which annoyed me. You would think a god would know something about such matters, about such a rival as the Christ.

He grunted with annoyance. 'I know enough to know that enough is not yet enough. I know enough to know what I may not do and that is true wisdom.'

Something rumbled, thunder deep and a grey wedge pushed forward from shadows. Amber in stone, the eyes looked me over and the steam from its grey muzzle flickered as the wolf licked the god's gloved hand.

'See, Freki,' said One Eye, 'she is coming back.'

In the wind, a shredded blackness fought forward, descending in starts and jumps until it thumped on his shoulder. The black, unwinking eye regarded me briefly, then it bent and nibbled One Eye's ear, while he nodded.

Munin, who flies the world and remembers everything inside that tiny feathered skull, returning to the ear of All Father Odin with a beak like a carving of ebony, whispering of slights and wrongs and warriors for Valholl still unslain. I felt no fear, which was strange enough to make me realize this was the dreamworld of the Other.

'So it is,' answered One Eye, as if I had spoken. 'And you want to know what will happen. That, of course, is in the hands of the Norns.'

'Silver,' I said and, though there was a whole babble of words, of questions that should have come from me, that seemed to be enough and he nodded.

'Silver,' he replied. 'They can weave even that, the Sisters,

252

but they weave blind and in the dark, which helps me. The silver has to be cursed, of course, otherwise it will not work for this weaving.'

I understood nothing.

'Ask this, Orm Gunnarsson – what is silver worth?' rumbled the voice.

Farms and ships, warriors and women . . . everything.

'More,' agreed One Eye. 'And that Volsung hoard, the one they gave to Atil is a king's gift. A cursed gift. My gift.'

And what does the god want in return? What could a god possibly want that did not already have? Warriors for the final battle? If so, all he had to do was kill us.

One Eye chuckled. 'There are more wars than you know and the battles in them last a long time. This one I have been fighting since before the days of Hild's mother's grandmother's grandmother, back to the first one of that line. Remember this, when all seems darkest, Orm Trader – the gift I give is the one I get. What you are, I am also.'

I did not understand that and did not need to say so – but he had spoken of Hild. The one eye glittered as he looked at me, amused and knowing.

'The first of her line was the spear thrown over the head of the White Christ priests to tell them a fight was on,' he said and left me none the wiser. He chuckled, a turning millwheel in his throat, and added: 'You have to hang nine nights on the World Tree for wisdom, boy.'

The raven, Munin, spread tattered wings and launched itself into the air. We watched it go, then One Eye grunted, as if his back bothered him, or he needed his supper.

'He goes to find his white brother and bring him home – Fimbulwinter is not on us yet and he has shaken enough pinfeathers.'

The blue eye turned to the amber of a wolf even as I watched it and I felt no fear at it, only curiosity to see All Father shapechange, for that was his nature, to be

neither one thing nor the other and never to be trusted
fully because of it.

'That is one knowing you take from this place back to
the world,' he rumbled, his voice deepening. 'The second
is that One Eye will force a sacrifice from you and it will
be something you hold dear.'

The wind shrieked and the snow drove in like white
oblivion, stinging my eyes and driving me to my knees.

But I was not afraid, for this was not Fimbulwinter . . .

'That's a fucking comfort right enough, Trader,' said the voice
in my ear, 'but not to those still buried to their oxters in
snow.'

Hands hauled me upright, shook me until my eyes rattled
and opened. Light streamed in. Light and the sear of cold air,
as if I had stopped breathing entirely. Onund Hnufa, a great
lumbering walrus, peered into my face from his iced-over
tangle of moustache and gave a satisfied grunt.

'Good. You will live – now help the others and stop babbling
about Fimbulwinter.'

We kicked and dug them out. Snow mounds shifted and
broke apart; people growled and gasped their way back into
the living light of day.

Fifteen were dead, ten of them thralls, among them Hekja.
Thorgunna and Thordis, pinch-faced and blue, clung to
each other and made sure the tears did not freeze their eyes
shut.

Three of the *druzhina* were also dead and two of Klerkon's
men, which left one alive, the large snub-nosed Smallander
Kveldulf, Night Wolf, dark and feral under a dusting of ice.
He and Crowbone glared at each other and I saw, in that
moment, that Kveldulf was more afraid than the boy.

'That was a harsh wind,' noted Hauk Fast-Sailor.

'If it had not been for the timely warning, it would have
been harsher still,' growled Gyrth, slogging heavily up through

the snow which lay hock-deep in the V of the *balka*. His tattered furs trailed behind him like tails.

'Worth an armring,' I said, turning to Morut, who was grinning into the tangle of lines his journey had ploughed into his face. 'Which I promise when I can get it off my arm in the warm.'

He acknowledged it with a bow and then turned his grin on the scowling Avraham.

'See? I have returned, as I said I would,' he declared. 'The steppe cannot kill me and I hear you have been seeking a way across the Great White, you who could not find your prick with both hands.'

Avraham, eyes ringed in violet in a face blue-white, had not the strength to answer, nor hide his relief that Morut was back.

Led by the little tracker, we hauled the horses down the *balka* to where it shallowed and opened out into a great expanse of opaque ice, tufted with rimed grass and across which the new snow of the *buran* drifted in a hissing wind. This let us backtrack to where the carts were, but so many horses were dead that a score of carts were abandoned and anything that could be was left with them.

No horses remained for the *druzhina* and even little Vladimir was on foot now. Cleverest of us all were Thorgunna and Thordis, who had the frozen horse carcasses chopped up and loaded on to a cart, with the smashed-up wood from several others. Now we had food and wood to cook it with, even if Finn said he was hard put to decide which of the two items would be more tasty.

'I thought you could make anything tasty,' Thorgunna chided, her wind-scoured cheeks like apples as she smiled and Finn humphed with mock annoyance, staring with a rheumy eye at one stiff, hacked off pony haunch.

'You boil it in a good cauldron with one of its own horse-shoes,' he growled. 'It will be tasty when the shoe is soft.'

The rest of the carts we burned that night, making camp there and hauling out the large cooking kettles to boil more meat in, as much as we could. Horseshoe or not, we had heat and full bellies that night, enough to stitch us together again. We, who seemed set to die this day or the next, even started to talk about what lay ahead.

'Another storm like that will end us,' growled Red Njal and little Prince Vladimir scowled at his elbow, for we were all one sorry band now, leaching the same heat from the same fire.

'We will succeed,' he piped and no-one spoke until Morut fell to telling us of his journey.

He had tracked the Man-Haters a long way, down a *balka* filled with ice to a big frozen lake with an island. All the way, he had come upon ruined carts, dead horses and dead men; those of Lambisson. He had seen no women, though – but the brass-coloured horse, he said, was dead of cold and hunger, as were others that were clearly steppe ponies. Avraham groaned at the loss of the heavenly horse.

That, I offered up, was a good sign, for surely now it meant all the Man-Haters had died. Save one, I thought to myself, for you cannot kill the fetch who owned that sheened horse, or swung the twin of my sabre. I had not planned to say anything, but reached up one hand to touch the rag-wrapped bundle of the sabre on my back and caught Finn's knowing eye across the fire.

He growled and would have spat his disgust, save that he was nestling Thordis in the crook of his arm and thought better of it.

'There's no Hild-fetch, Trader,' he said. 'That bitch-tick is long dead.'

He knew I did not believe him and I looked for Kvasir to take my shieldless side in this argument, but he was wrapped in the arms of Thorgunna and asleep.

'Well, at least I know it isn't Fimbulwinter,' I offered them.

Then I told them of my dream. A few, Gyrth among them, simply shrugged; they wanted to say that it was only a dream brought on by a dunt on the head, but kept their chapped lips together out of politeness to me. Others, though, were stronger in their belief.

'A witching form often brings the wise,' Red Njal declared, 'as my granny used to say. It seems to me that Trader Orm has just made a good deal with Odin.'

He beamed, but Finn had the look of man more concerned that his jarl talked with gods in his dreams, while Klepp Spaki was interested in the riddle, but added that thinking it out was like trying to row into a headwind.

'A sea-farer at last, are we?' growled Hauk, though he grinned when he said it. Klepp, who had discovered he had no legs or stomach for the sea, acknowledged his lack with a rueful smile.

Finn eventually growled that there was nothing much about my visit with All-Father and I did not know whether to be relieved or angry at that.

'After all,' he went on, 'it has told nothing more than we know already — even that part about a sacrifice of something held dear. Odin always wants something expensive draining lifeblood on an altar. It might even be me, since I took the *valknut* sign after the vow I made in the pit prison in Novgorod.'

'In return for what?' asked Sigurd, his silver nose gleaming in the firelight. Finn shifted uncomfortably, looking at little Prince Vladimir; what he had wished for was the death of that little prince and thought he had got it, too, when we heard the bells ring out.

Of course, it was the boy's father who had died and Finn simply put that difference down to not being specific with a shapechanger such as Odin — but we had still been got out of the prison. The memory let me save Finn's face.

'To be free of the prison,' I offered up, smooth as new silk. Finn nodded eagerly and thanked me with his eyes. Vladimir frowned, considering the answer; he had an unhealthy interest in comparing the advantages of different gods.

'I am thinking,' piped up a voice, 'that the reason men give offerings to Thor is because he is less likely to betray them than All-Father Odin.'

All heads swung to Crowbone, sitting hunched in his cloak and blooded by firelight.

'What do you know of the betrayal of gods?' asked Gyrth curiously and those who knew Crowbone's early life stirred and wished he had never voiced the question.

Little Olaf favoured Gyrth with his lopsided look and cleared his throat.

'I know the treachery of gods and men both,' he said and brought one hand out of his cloak to take a twig and poke the fire so that sparks flew and the flames licked up. Few men wanted to back away from it, all the same, even though their hair was scorching, for we all knew we would be a long time cold after this.

'There once was a shepherd,' he said and there was a whisper like sparks round the fire, the relish and apprehension of a tale from Olaf.

'It was at the end of a deep and dark winter, almost as bad as this one. He brought his sheep into the field to find some grazing and sat down under a tree to rest. Suddenly a wolf came out of the woods. A lord of wolves, it was, with a ruff as white as emperor salt and a winter-hunger that had his chops dripping.'

'I know that hunger well,' interrupted a voice and was shushed to silence.

'The shepherd picked up his spear and jumped up,' Crowbone went on. 'The wolf was just about to spring at the man when he saw the spear and thought better of it, for it had a fine, silver head and he did not like the idea of a shepherd with so clever a weapon. They stared at each other and neither dared to make the first move.

258

'At that moment, a fox came running by. He saw that the wolf and the shepherd were afraid of each other and decided to turn the situation to his own advantage. He ran up to the wolf and said: "Cousin, there is no reason to be afraid of a man. Jump on him, get him down and have a good meal."

'The wolf eyed him with an amber stare and said: "You are cunning, right enough, but you have no brains. Look at him – he has a silver spear, which is surely magical. He will stab me and that will be the end of me. Be off with your stupid advice."

'The fox thought for a moment, then said: "Well, if that is the way of it, I will go and ask him not to stab you. What will you give me if I save you?"

'The wolf told him he could have anything he asked for, so the fox ran to the shepherd and said: "Uncle shepherd, why are you standing here? The wolf wants to make a meal of you. I just persuaded him to wait a while. What will you give me if I save you?"

'And the shepherd promised: "Anything you ask." The fox ran to the wolf and said: "Cousin, you will have a long life and sire many cubs – I have persuaded the shepherd not to stab you. Hurry up and run now before he changes his mind. I will see you later."

'The wolf turned and leaped away as fast as he could – which, in truth, he could have done at any time but for his fear. The fox came back to the shepherd, saying: "Uncle shepherd, you did not forget your promise?"

'The shepherd said the fox was no nephew to him but asked him what he desired and the fox answered: "Not much, only a bite out of your leg. That will be enough for me."'

'Ha – even that seems tasty to me,' shouted a black-browed Slav and those of us who had known oarmates to have done such a thing once shifted uncomfortably and said nothing at all.

'The shepherd stretched out his leg,' Olaf went on. 'Just as the fox was about to sink his teeth into it, the shepherd barked. The fox jumped back, asking: "Who made that noise?" The shepherd shrugged: "What do you care? Take your bite and be done with it." The fox cocked his head cunningly. "Oh, no. I will not come near you before you tell me who made that noise."

'The shepherd sighed. "In that case, I will tell you. This winter in the village we had nothing to eat. And then my sheepdog had two puppies. Well . . . I was so hungry, I ate them. Now the pups have grown up in my stomach. I am thinking they smell you and want to get at you, so they are barking."

'The fox got even more frightened but he would not show it. He said with dignity: "I would have no trouble handling your pups. But I must run and see the wolf on some urgent business. Hold back your sheepdogs for a while. When I come back, I will teach them such a lesson that they will never attack foxes again."

'The shepherd smiled. "Be quick," he said.

'And the fox went streaking off into the woods, happy to get away with his life. After he caught his breath, he set out to look for the wolf and said to him: "Well, cousin – I saved your life when you were frightened of the shepherd and you made a promise."

'The wolf howled, a long howl. "What promise?" he growled. "I am no cousin to you. I am the jarl-king of these woods. Who dares to say that I was frightened?" He raised his paw to strike the fox down – who ran off before such a thing could happen, thinking to himself: "There is no gratitude in this world."

'Then the fox slunk into his hole to teach his children to stay away from men and wolves both.'

'Aye, true enough,' Red Njal agreed. 'The cod who swims with sharks is swiftly eaten, as my granny said.'

'Heya,' muttered Gizur, 'I hope you are friendly enough

with men and wolves to get away with that insulting saga, little Prince Olaf.'

'And gods,' added Onund Hnufa meaningfully.

'With shepherds only,' answered Crowbone and some laughed, though it was forced. They still did not know how to read the runes of this boy.

Into the gentle warmth of this stepped a large, dark figure – Kveldulf, his bearded jaw thrust out challengingly and a scowl between his brows.

'I am the last of Klerkon's men,' he declared, glancing at little Crowbone. 'I am known as Kveldulf and noted as a shapechanging berserker. It comes to me that you are short-handed and could use a good man.'

This was right enough, but I did not like or trust Kveldulf and did not want him in the Oathsworn. Crowbone's face was stiff and not all of it was cold; his eyes glittered, one ice, the other dark fire. I remembered that Kveldulf had been Klerkon's man and wondered what had passed between them when Crowbone was a thrall there.

'True enough,' I said, 'but we are the Oathsworn. You may have heard of us and the oath we take. Can you take it and keep it?'

'I am known all over Smalland as a man of my word,' he replied, angry at the hard sneer from me.

Crowbone cleared the choke from his throat, which turned all heads.

'Just so,' he said, in a voice thin as an axe edge. 'You promised me I would never see my mother again, the second time I ran off. True enough, I never have.'

The wind hissed into the silence that followed that, until I forced myself to speak.

'What skills have you that we might need?' I asked Kveldulf.

He blinked at that. 'I have said. I am known as a shapechanger and berserker. A killer am I. A serious jarl would welcome me.'

That was insulting and I felt the burn of anger. It was a surprise, that feeling, for it made me realize how much the cold had seeped in to the centre of me and numbed a great deal.

'Not known to me,' I said careless of insulting this man's fame, which was a dangerous business. 'Nor have I seen you bite a shield, for all the fighting we have done so far.'

'I was not well during the fight at the village,' he admitted, at which Finn gave a snort of laughter. Kveldulf curled a lip at him.

'I am well enough now to show those with no respect some manners. I have heard that the way into the Oathsworn is to fight one already in it.'

I felt Finn bristle and wanted none of this – wanted none of Kveldulf.

'Times are harsh and we are fewer,' I said. 'I have chosen a new way.'

Men leaned forward, curious now and not having heard of this. It would have been hard, since I had just thought of it and I blame the cold and the weight of events for making me savagely reckless.

I held up my left hand, swathed in a leather glove, which was still stiffened with rime. If I had not been at the fire there would have been a mitten over it.

'How many fingers do you see?'

He blinked, then grinned, clearly thinking this was a formality and no more.

'Five, of course.'

I bent the stiff, empty sockets of the glove and those who knew I only had two fingers and a thumb on that hand chuckled. Kveldulf's scowl returned, more thunderous than ever.

Kvasir laughed, loud and hard.

'There are stones with more clever in them,' he said. 'Jarl Orm should get one of them to swear to the Oathsworn.'

'Heya,' rumbled Gyrth, smiling. I felt only the hot rush of

shame, for it had not been right to smack Kveldulf so hard with words, him who blinked with the effort of understanding.

Kveldulf, trembling like water on the brink of spilling, finally spun round and lumbered into the dark, Finn's savage chuckles goading him. Slowly, conversation resumed but I sat silent, aware of disapproval across the fire.

Eventually, Thorgunna gave a snort. 'The hasty tongue sings its own mishap if it be not bridled in,' she intoned.

'You sound like Red Njal's granny,' I answered, trying to make light of it. 'Or my foster-mother.'

'You never had same, it seems to me,' she replied tartly, 'for she would surely have taught you to be kinder.'

Which was a tongue-cut too deep and Kvasir put a hand on her elbow to still her.

'Look where we all are, Jarl Orm,' Thordis interrupted, leaning forward so that the fire glittered her eyes. 'Here, in this place. Following you to an uncertain doom. If your wyrd is upon you, it is right we should speak. There are more lives at risk here than you know.'

That smacked up memories of Einar, too harsh for me to take easily and the hackles rose on me.

'Do you want Kveldulf? Take him and welcome – but I do not want him at my back . . .'

Then it struck me, what she had said and I stopped, gaping. I looked from her to Finn and back. Finn looked stricken and Thordis chuckled at his dismay.

'Not me, Horsehead . . . not yet.'

Thorgunna, swaddled in a cloak, raised her head. 'I am not alone.'

It was the way we announced it in the north and Kvasir had clearly known of his wife's condition for some time, since he did not even stir at this. I did, more than a few times. Jon Asanes laughed; Red Njal and others swapped the news, which sprang from head to head like a spark whirling from a fire.

'Are you sure?'

It was a question a rock would have asked and her sheep-dropping eyes raked me with silent scorn.

'Even with the cold and the lack of food I can tell when life quickens in me, Jarl Orm,' she snapped. 'Anyway, I slept with an egg and lopped off the far end next morning. By the yolk, it will be a boy.'

I sat back a little, looking from her to Kvasir, feeling that, somehow, they had conspired against me. One of the big Slavs – the same who had sworn he could eat someone's leg – growled, 'An egg,' in a tone that wanted to know where she had got such a prize.

'So you see, Trader,' Thordis went on, ignoring all this, 'why we are concerned.'

I did and felt twice as ashamed as before, had to shake my head to clear it.

'The words were hasty,' I admitted, 'the reason was sound. What's done is done. The unwise man is awake all night and ponders everything over; when morning comes he is weary in mind and all is a burden as ever.'

'As your foster-mother used to say,' added Red Njal. 'She knew my granny, I am thinking.'

This last was greeted with chuckles; talk resumed, low and soft round the fire. But I could not take my eyes from Thorgunna, kept flicking back to her, wondering about the life there, marvelling at it happening at all in this place, fearing it at the same time.

I had women and youths enough to crush me with the worrying. Now the unborn were weighing my shoulders, even before they sucked in their first breath.

FIFTEEN

I stood on the back of a dun-coloured whale breaching a frozen sea and stared into the maw of its blowhole, listening to Finn and Kvasir and the others scoffing at me for having failed to recognize the place when I had seen it from the edge of the frozen lake.

We came to it down a slick of cold tragedy, each rimed droplet a huddle of stiff, jutting limbs and fleeing scavengers.

Little Morut led the way, waiting patiently for us now and then, stopping to feed his rib-thin horse on chopped straw mixed with animal fat. I admired the little Khazar, in the same way I had admired the Bedu who tracked so easily over the Serkland deserts and for the same reasons. Even Finn offered a nod to the little man while Avraham, that noble Khazar Jew, had scorn and relief chasing each other across his face like fox and chicken.

It was Morut who pointed out the splendid golden horse, no longer glowing, its limbs stuck out like a wooden carving and that glorious coat now sheened with ice. Wolves slunk from it when we came up, red-muzzled and thin, though they did not go far. They dropped to their bellies on the frozen, stiff-grassed steppe and waited, paws crossed, for us to go away. Patient as stones, Odin's hounds, for they had put in a lot of work on the beasts and men littering the area; there were no soft parts to start gnawing on an ice-bound corpse.

'A waste,' mourned Avraham and those coming staggering and shuffling up in time to hear his words, nodded and grunted agreement – except that the Khazar was not talking of the dead men, but of the golden horse.

Morut merely grunted scornfully, which gained him a withering look from Avraham. Curious, little Vladimir asked the tracker what he meant by it.

The tracker indicated the once-splendid horse and then looked as his own rag-maned, shaggy mount. 'They are the same,' he said with a grin. 'Turkmen horses. But the Blood-Sweating Horse is too fine for this place, while my little one is trained for it.'

'Can you train a horse for this?' asked Thorgunna, who was eyeing the rimed litter with a look I knew well. She and Thordis could teach wolves about scavenging.

Morut nodded as men moved among the bodies, though they gave up trying to plunder them when it became clear they were were frozen to the steppe, or each other.

'It will kill two out of five who undergo it,' he admitted and, horsebreeder that I was, I reckoned at once this was only possible with the possession of an unlimited number of animals costing next to nothing to keep.

'Pick out a likely one, rising seven or eight,' Morut said, feeding another handful of fat and chopped straw to his mount. 'Before that age no horse should be selected for such training, which is for war and raiding, after all.

'You load a saddle with a sack of earth or sand, at first only the weight of a rider but gradually increased for eight days, until the horse carries the weight of two steppe riders – about one of you big northers with your mail and all your weapons to hand. As the weight grows, the horse's ration of food and water is lessened. He is trotted and walked six or seven miles daily.

'After the first eight days you gradually make him lighter over another eight days – still, however, decreasing the food. When the load has gone completely, you give him two or three days of absolutely nothing at all, simply tightening the girth at intervals.'

'By which time,' growled Avraham, poking a foot under a corpse and trying to wrench it from the ice, 'you have killed him.'

'One like that Heavenly Horse, yes,' agreed Morut. 'And those you rode for the great Bek's army. But not this one.'

'What do you call your marvellous horse?' asked Crowbone in a thin piping query from the crowd – then held up one hand and waved the answers away before the scorn crashed on him. You did not give a name to something you might have to eat.

'I should be grateful, then,' he muttered, 'that I have a name.'

Morut, still grinning, went on talking while we moved among the litter of gear and wreckage and dead, his voice like soothing balm on that bruise of horror.

'About the twentieth day you work him until he sweats, unsaddle him and pour buckets of ice-cold water all over him, from head to tail. Stake him, all wet, to a peg on the open steppe, allow him to graze, giving him, every day, a little more rope for seven or eight days, after which you turn him loose to run with the herd as usual.

'A horse that has undergone this discipline is a valuable animal and a fortune to a man, being able to travel almost continuously for four or five days together, with only a handful of fodder once in every half-day and a drink of water once in a long day.'

He stroked the whiskered muzzle of the unassuming beast. I vowed then to have Morut and his horse-skills back in Hestreng.

'Perhaps these men should have undergone something of

the same,' growled Hlenni Brimill, jutting his chin at the dead as he stamped his feet against the cold.

'No dead Man-Haters here,' noted Ref. 'Either they suffered no loss, or carried their dead away.'

'No plunder taken, either,' growled Gyrth and we all stared at the men, still in their helms and their mail, all white with ice.

'Perhaps these *amazonia* did not have the stomach for it, being only women,' Jon Asanes noted and Kveldulf's hawk and spit answer to that made the boy flush with anger. No-one spoke up for him, all the same, for Kveldulf had the right of it; it wasn't stomach the women lacked, but strength to waste. For the same reason, we left those dead untouched and unburied, but not because we were squeamish about breaking limbs to straighten them for burial – what was that to the dead?

It was the strength we grudged. As Onund pointed out to Jon as we shuffled away, a man can make himself a shelter and sleep out a three-day blizzard provided he has not exhausted himself beforehand. It is exhaustion that turns such a snow-wrapped, snug sleep into death. What would be the point of struggling to gain plunder we could not carry, or waste energy digging a shallow grave that the wolves would scratch out an hour after we had vanished over the milk-white horizon?

So we kept our strength to stumble down the frozen scree of a slope to the great bowl in the earth which held a frozen lake and an island in the middle. An island so shaped that it looked like the back of a whale breaching a sea. An island with a huddle of six carts and a hole on it.

It took me a while to work it out, as we staggered down to where the survivors of Lambisson's party had chipped out the lip of the iced lake's bank down to a level where they could struggle carts over it to the island.

Here was where Finn and Short Eldgrim had hauled me

out of the brown, roiling water that first time. Down there, locked somewhere in the ice, lay the bones of Wryneck, Long Eldgrim, Sighvat and the others. This was the place, right enough – we had just come up on it from another direction, in another season, and seven years difference. It came to me then that I had no need of the runed sabre.

The weight of that was crushing; we had slid and staggered across half Serkland in pursuit of this sabre. Men had died and gone mad to hunt down this weapon and the only reason for it was the secret I had marked on it. Yet, now, it seemed, I could have spun myself in a circle nine times nine out on the Great White and still walked to this place with my eyes closed, dragged by Odin, or the fetch of Hild. Or both.

I looked at Finn and he looked back at me, grinning from his cold-split lips. If he thought of the uselessness of the sabre on my back, he did not show or say it, merely wiped the blood from his cracked mouth and said:

'Here we are again, then, young Orm.'

I shuffled across the stippled, snow-drifted ice, the others following me, then stepped on to iron-iced land, up to where the hole lay.

For, of course, this was no island.

It was the roof of Attila's tomb.

We found Hrolf Ericsson, called Fiskr lying in one of the carts and the last of Lambisson's men left alive on the island. He was called Fiskr – Fish – because he had once swum ashore in a storm with a line in his teeth and fastened his ship to the land, so saving everyone in the crew. Many of us knew him well and were happy enough to find him alive, even if he was on the wrong side.

'I should have stayed on the land,' he moaned to Bjaelfi, as the healer rooted among the salves and balms he had secreted all about him. 'Getting back on a boat only took me to Birka and trouble.'

'You should have kept off the land,' Bjaelfi offered grimly, 'that way, you would not be looking at losing most of your toes and a bit of your nose from the cold rot.'

'At least you have a rich bed,' Sigurd noted. 'And a nose is nothing much to mourn over.'

Hrolf Fiskr laughed, for he lay wrapped in ragged wool cloaks and furs on a huddle of silver, looted from the tomb. Three carts were loaded with the stuff and the men whooped and scrabbled, plucking age-blackened ewers and bashed bowls and litters of coins until Sigurd and Dobrynya had to roar and bellow at them to leave it alone.

Lambisson, said Hrolf Fiskr, was down in the tomb and had been, perhaps for days – it was hard to know for sure, since Fiskr admitted he had been sleeping for a time, until the fever he had broke. There had been others with Lambisson down in the howe, loading silver in a bucket and hauling it up through the hole, but that had stopped three days ago and nothing had been heard since. Everyone had come up but Lambisson.

'What of Short Eldgrim?' I asked, as Bjaelfi waited, sharpening his little knife. Hrolf eyed it nervously and licked his chapped lips.

'The little man? Aye, he was one of yours, right enough.'

He paused, shook his head and tried to work up spit, but his mouth was too dry. 'That Christ monk did him harm, trying to get his mind to work. Burned him bad to make him remember.'

He broke off and looked at me steadily. 'I did not like that, nor thought it right.'

'Did nothing, all the same,' I told him and took pleasure in watching him squirm. 'Where is the little man now?'

'Gone,' came the answer. 'He was here when I closed my eyes and gone when I opened them again.'

'Not below, then?'

He waggled one hand. 'Maybes yes, maybes no. Brondolf

Lambisson is still below, so said the men who came up and left him,' he growled, then found enough spit to use it.

'Then they ran off, the nithings,' he added. 'Said Lambisson had lost his wits and that it was the little man's curse on him for what had happened. Left me because I could not walk. A dozen of them, big Slavs and none prepared to carry me, the turds. They were too afraid of those mad women, who kept coming back and shooting arrows . . . look, I am after telling you all I know. There is no need for a knife.'

'This is to help you, oaf,' snarled Bjaelfi. 'Of course, I could leave the black rot alone and let it eat your face and feet . . .'

I knelt by the hole, which was a wide, rough circle, dug down through a layer of earth – but not silt, I noticed. It was clear that, even flooded, the water in the lake did not cover the roof of Atil's tomb and someone had known that. Large slabs of roof-stone had been removed, a finger-joint thick and hefty and I saw they were laid over a cunning trellis made of great split logs. In a treeless place like this, that was riches as much as the silver it covered and these had been brought a long way. Even five centuries had not rotted them – but there was no sign of the ones removed. Burned, probably.

Now there was a black hole and, a foot down from it was part of one of the great stone arches, a hand-span thick and three wide, which curved into the centre and supported the entire yurt-shaped howe of Attila.

There were two thick ropes tied round it – a knotted one for climbing down, the other attached to a leather bucket which was empty when Onund hauled it up. The cold seemed to drift out of that dark hole like smoke.

'No tools,' growled Dobrynya, coming up to peer down into it. Behind me, Hrolf yelped as Bjaelfi cut too deep into his nose and drew blood. 'A fortune in silver, some bits and pieces of gear, a little flour and dried meat, but no tools.'

No tools in the carts, which meant that Lambisson had not made this hole. I did not like to think who had.

'We lost our tools,' admitted Fish when I went back to him. Thorgunna dabbed the blood from his fresh-carved nose, but Fish felt little pain, since the black parts were dead flesh. He was happy we had arrived, enemies or not, since his friends had left him to die here, crippled and alone.

'We counted it great good luck to find this hole,' he went on, 'but now I think these madwomen did it, like a baited hook to catch a fish.' He beamed at the clever play on his own name.

I glanced at the hole. Short Eldgrim could be down there and, if so, he was either dead or wandering like a madman, wondering where he was. Only a few of the Oathsworn cared for that above what else could be down there. Even Finn, I saw, when he swayed up, tossing something in his hand and grinning. He turned it over in his fingers and then held it up.

'Familiar, Bear Slayer?' he asked.

It was a coin and I had the twin of it round my neck under my serk, punched through and looped with a leather thong. It had once been around the neck of Hild, the woman who had somehow known the secret of how to find this place, with neither chart nor rune scratches on the hilt of a sword; now I knew how that had been managed.

I looked at the baleful wink of that coin, Volsung silver, part of the hoard of the dragon Fafnir, the one Sigurd had killed and the cursed gift Odin had promised us. I felt Hild's presence then, as if cold, invisible fingers stretched out of that hole, seeking me, the sword, the coins . . .

I did not much care for the memory; she was down that hole, I could feel her and remembered her, black against the dark, stalking us with that light-curve of sword, the twin of my own. It was no surprise to me that Lambisson had not been heard of for some time and I would happily have left him there – but for Eldgrim.

No, not even him, if the truth of it was being laid out. I liked the little man well enough, but it was not him alone that would take me back into the black maw of Atil's hov. It was bone, blood and steel, a fear greater than the one I had for finding mad Hild waiting at the bottom, all white-eyed and armed with the twin of my sabre.

It was fear of breaking the Oath and what One Eye inflicted on all those who did.

'Put that back.'

The sandpiper voice snapped me round, to where a furious Vladimir glowered at Finn, little fists on his hips. 'No-one is to loot my silver. No-one.'

Finn's grin faded. He looked at me, then back to the pinch-faced little prince and saw which quarter the wind blew from. He shrugged and flicked his thumb, never taking his scowl off the prince's face, and the coin arced back into the cart it had come from.

Vladimir, his scowl merely turned to a boyish, petulant pout, glared pointedly at me – then Dobrynya moved in, smooth as oil, suggesting we all manhandle the silver-laden carts across the ice and off the island. He followed his prince at a respectful two paces.

'We should kill them all now,' Finn growled at their disappearing backs and my look answered him – there were too few of us for that and we could not count on any but ourselves.

'Besides,' I finished, 'even the gods of Asgard would be hard put to help us if we cut down a prince of Novgorod, a son of Sviatoslav. Those two brothers of his might be rivals – but they will not embrace us for such a killing.'

Finn thought, then shrugged and went off without another word, picking his teeth with a filthy, horny fingernail; the swagger of him told me he had seen the sense of what I said, yet it was of no account. When the time came . . .

Silver smoothed matters. The Slavs and my Oathsworn fell to moving it cheerfully enough – it was their loot, they had all decided – while Thorgunna and Thordis made sure a camp was made in the lee of all the carts. As fires flowered and the day sank into leaden cold night, I saw that Avraham and Morut were gone.

We had meat and bread, a measure of warmth and shelter – so, of course, the proper divisions slid back to us. The *druzhina* sat apart from the Oathsworn, rowdy round their own blaze, while the prince and his two pillars sat apart from us all, heads together – but Crowbone sat with us, almost buried in a once-white fur cloak and that warmed me a little.

But the fret of Short Eldgrim was on me and drove out all else – I wanted to be down that hole and yet, to my shame, used the excuse Finn brought up, about food and warmth first, to avoid sliding down into the tomb.

I looked at Finn while Thorgunna and Thordis stirred and served and the Oathsworn horn-spooned horsemeat into the spaces in their beards, chaffering and grinning and growling like pleasured cats. We were in a waste that still froze the nose off your face, with only *wadmal* for shelter and stringy horse and water to eat, yet compared to before, we were all grunting-content with life.

Well, not all.

'Those cowholes are being sleekit,' Finn growled, none too quietly. Jon Asanes glanced across at the prince's fire, then frowned back at Finn.

'He is a prince,' he said. 'An eagle among sparrows. You do him injustice calling him sleekit.'

Finn worked grease into his beard and cheeks, good proofing against the cold and looked Jon up and down, shaking his head.

'You learned a lot in Holmgard, right enough,' he declared. 'How to yabber in a dozen tongues and count in most of them. But you missed much, young Goat Boy. Like how eagles are not above stealing another bird's kill, for a start.'

Jon flared, bright as the fire with temper. He rose and I

274

thought, for a heart-stopping moment, that he would fling himself at Finn, an act so beyond belief that being struck by Thor's hammer seemed more likely.

Instead he quivered on the cusp of it, red and raging.

'The eagle is a noble bird. That is why you will never be a prince, Finn Horsehead,' he said in a trembling high voice. 'You do not have enough eagle in you.'

He stormed off and Finn watched him, then shook his head and pulled a bone needle from behind his remaining ear. 'I preferred him when he bounced like a goat and wanted to know everything,' he growled, picking his teeth. 'Now he knows it all and tears around like a high wind through trees.'

'Whim rules the child as weather the field, as my granny once remarked,' Red Njal growled.

'She knew the Goat Boy well,' Finn muttered sourly.

'Heya – what do you know?' Red Njal answered, chuckling. 'You do not have enough eagle in you.'

The needle broke and Finn sighed into the laughter and shook his head sadly.

'True enough – but I am beginning to think our little Greek has had some Rus eagle in him,' he leered moodily and pitched the broken needle away.

There was silence at that, while everyone turned over in their head what they believed they knew about the unnatural passions of Greeks. I was blinking with the stun of it when Thorgunna whirlwinded in, harsh and anger-bright as embers.

'That is unworthy, of you, of Jon Asanes and of the young prince. If I were a man, Finn Horsehead, I would smack you to the floor and make it so that you could only eat meat someone else had chewed, for lack of teeth of your own.'

Finn, knowing he had sailed too far on this course even to back water, simply hunched into Thorgunna's rage and stayed shamefacedly silent, scratching the red cold sores on his knuckles until they bled. Everyone else, however, sat and chewed horse-gristle and tried not to think too deeply on Jon, his love verse, his closeness with Pai and how it was well-known that Greeks were boy-lovers and Slavs lascivious.

Thordis plucked Finn's empty bowl from his knees and handed him one of her own bone needles. 'Here,' she said flatly. 'Pick your teeth. Not only will it make what you say sweeter, it will keep you from speaking at all for some time.'

'A woman, a dog and an old oak tree,' muttered Finn, taking the needle. Everyone silently finished the old saw for him – the more you beat them, the better they be. No-one said it aloud, all the same, not even Red Njal's granny

Thorgunna snorted, clattering bowls and heaping snow in a cauldron to melt. 'Little Olaf, if you have a story now is a good time to hoik it out.'

It was a pointed remark, since folk had grown so used to the boy's presence they had all but forgotten him – but now heads turned to where the boy perched, friend to prince and Goat Boy alike and he smiled into Finn's scowl, though it never reached either of his different-coloured eyes.

'There was an eagle,' he began and I held up a warning hand to him, for his stories bit like a dog on the hand that feeds it and there had been enough discord. I said as much and he shrugged his bony shoulders under the dirty white cloak.

'I will hear it,' growled a voice and we all turned to where Kvasir huddled, a cloth across both eyes, for his good one ached, he said, in the bright of the fire. He asked for the tale for Thorgunna's sake, I knew and I cursed him for it. Silently.

'There was an eagle,' Crowbone began, once I had nodded agreement. 'Young and in the first of his strength. Long ago it was – do not ask me when – and in a place far from here – do not ask me where – in the time wyrm were still seen above ground and not curled in the secret earth on a bed of gold.'

'If there is gold in it, this sounds like a tale I will like,' Finnlaith interrupted cheerfully, but Ospak nudged him silent.

'There was such a wyrm,' Crowbone went on, 'and the

eagle and the wyrm were friends, or so the wyrm believed, for he took pleasure in the eagle's company and was lavish with his generosity in his cosy hov, so that the eagle returned again and again.'

'Heya,' agreed Hauk, grinning. 'I also have tasted the wyrm's generosity.' And he hoisted up his wooden cup to me, as if it was a mead-full horn and we were all in such a cosy hov.

Others chuckled, echoing the sentiment; so the allusion to my name was well made and quickly, too. Nor was it hard to work out who the eagle was and I felt despair creep in and curl up in my belly. This would be his worst tale yet, for sure.

'Each time the eagle flew away,' Crowbone went on in his wind-thin little voice, 'he laughed, because he could enjoy the hospitality of the wyrm in his hov on the ground, but the wyrm could never reach the eagle's eyrie, which was so far above the wyrm's place.'

'Not enough eagle in you, either, Orm,' chuckled Red Njal.

'The eagle's frequent visits, his selfishness and ingratitude became the talk of the other beasts and one thought it best to tell the wyrm of it,' Crowbone continued, ignoring the interruption.

'The eagle and the frog were never on speaking terms, for the eagle was accustomed to swooping down to carry a frog home for supper, so the frog called on the wyrm and told him. The wyrm did not believe him, so the frog said, "Next time the eagle calls, ask him to give you a lidded cauldron, so that you can also send food to the rest of the eaglets in their eyrie."

'So he did and the eagle brought a huge lidded cauldron, enjoyed a feast and, as he left he called out, "I will be back for the present for my eyrie." Then he flew away laughing to himself as usual. The frog said, "Now, wyrm, get into the cauldron. I will cover you over with fresh food, then the lid and the eagle will carry you to his hov in the high crags."'

'I do not care for this frog much,' Finn grumbled. 'Sleekit.'

'You are not yet done picking all your teeth,' Thordis told him and he shrugged, but fell silent.

'Presently,' Crowbone went on, 'the eagle returned and flew away with the cauldron, little suspecting that the wyrm was inside, listening to every word the eagle said as it flew. They were as harsh as the frog had described, so that the wyrm was smouldering by the time the cauldron was emptied out into the eyrie.

'The wyrm crawled from it and said, "Friend eagle, you have so often visited my home that I thought it would be nice to enjoy the hospitality of yours."

'The eagle was furious. "I will peck the flesh from your bones," he said – but he only hurt his beak against the wyrm's scales.

'The wyrm, saddened, said, "I see what sort of friendship you offer me. Take me home, for our pact is at an end." The furious eagle sank his talons into the wyrm's scales, which did not hurt the serpent one bit, and lifted him into the air. "I will fling you to the ground and you will be smashed to bits in your fall," shrieked the eagle. The wyrm closed its own fangs on the eagle's leg.'

'He should just have breathed on him,' shouted Onund. 'Smouldered him to smoke.'

It was so unexpected an outburst from him that it brought gusts of laughter and the hunchback, unaccustomed to the attention, dropped his neck down and his hump up and went quiet again.

'He would have singed the eagle's feathers, right enough,' offered Finn pointedly. 'Fried him up, there and then. Why did he not do that in this tale, little Crowbone, eh?'

'And been stuck, unable to get home?' retorted Crowbone. 'The wyrm has much more clever in him than you, Finn Horsehead.'

'That is why he is jarl,' added Gyrth pointedly to Finn, 'and you are not.'

That brought more chuckles and cat-calls at Finn's expense, which made him grin and scowl in equal measure. Then Kvasir slapped his thigh with one hand, sharp and loud and silencing.

'I asked for this tale – now let us hear how it ends.'

Crowbone acknowledged his marshalling with a slight bow, then cleared his throat.

'The eagle groaned and moaned,' he continued. 'He demanded to be let go. He turned three times red and three times white, he threatened and then he begged to be released. "I will gladly do so when you set me down at my own home," said the wyrm.'

Here, Crowbone muffled it out like someone talking and biting at the same time. It was so like Finn with his Roman nail in his mouth that thighs were slapped and appreciative roars went up.

'The eagle flew high,' Crowbone went on. 'Then he flew low. He darted down with the speed of an arrow. He shook his leg. He turned and twirled, but it was to no purpose. He could not rid himself of the wyrm until he set him down safely in front of the door of his own hov.

'As the eagle flew away the wyrm called after him, "Friendship requires the contribution of two parties. I welcome you and you welcome me. Since, however, you have chosen to make a mockery of it, you need not call again."

'And so it is that wyrms took to the dark places of the earth, for they did not trust in eagles, or anyone else, not to steal from them.'

'Share your wealth, or men will wish you ill in every limb,' Red Njal added, but did not have time to speak of his granny, for Dobrynya had stepped into the last lines of Crowbone's tale. He did not acknowledge that he had heard any of it, nor show that he knew what had been meant by it, only nodded to me and made a little movement of his fire-bloody beard to draw me apart.

I went to him, while the mutter and growls and low laughs

started behind me and my men, who had not missed the point of Crowbone's tale, fell to arguing over it.

'The prince has decided that we must go to Biela Viezha,' Dobrynya said softly, giving Sarkel its Rus name. 'We will take all the horses we have and use them to haul out the carts of silver we have here and one with supplies. We will then get more supplies and carts and horses from Biela Viezha and return. I have sent Avraham and Morut ahead, to see how matters are in the fortress.'

A clever move, to see if the garrison at Biela Viezha was willing. Now that Sviatoslav was dead there was no guarantee that this frontier fortress, so recently Khazar, would stay loyal. If it did, then it would be loyal to Jaropolk, prince of Kiev, not Vladimir, prince of far-away Novgorod.

Dobrynya nodded blandly when I pointed all this out.

'They will be loyal to profit,' he answered smoothly. 'Novgorod's prince is still a son of Sviatoslav. We will get supplies and horses, enough to use as a pack train. We will come back, take what we can from this place and organize boats to take us downriver to the Dark Sea, for it is clear that the ice has been broken that far.'

Out and away, fast as raiders, that was what Dobrynya had persuaded his nephew was best. He was not wrong; we could not plunder the whole wealth of Atil's tomb, but even what we had now was a fortune. After a visit to Biela Viezha, though, the place would be no secret; scavengers would arrive in droves and the fighting would begin over who owned it.

I nodded agreement, adding: 'As soon as I have seen to Short Eldgrim.'

Dobrynya blinked a bit and I saw he was hoping to go at first light and that my hunting around in Atil's howe for someone he clearly thought dead was a waste of crucial time. To be honest, I thought this also and did not much care about Brondolf Lambisson, huddled in the dark with his cold silver. That and the fear of what Hild-fetch lurked there made me want to agree with Dobrynya – but Short Eldgrim and the Oath drove me into the dark.

His pause was brief, then he nodded and smiled. We clasped wrists on it and he went back to his little eagle, sitting at the fire and laughing with silver-nosed Sigurd. Crowbone was now there, sitting with his uncle – and Kveldulf, which I did not like.

And Jon Asanes, which I liked even less.

SIXTEEN

It was the heart of ice, that dread tomb. So cold it froze flame, as Finn had once promised and even he now saw the raw, gleaming power of it as he slid down the knotted rope with his nail in his teeth and one hand clutching a guttering torch.

I held its twin, clutched the rune sword in my other hand – I would not have gone down into the maw of that hole without that blade – and waited for him. The flicker of torch-light turned the rime-slathered place into a bounce of sparkles, like the sun on moving sea, as we turned, half-crouched and prepared for anything.

I had been in this place once before, but Finn never had and I saw his jaw slacken so that the slavered Roman nail fell from it, hitting the frosted floor. It should have clattered out echoes, but that place sucked sound in and he only noticed it was gone from his mouth when he breathed, ragged and gasping.

The rope trembled when he let it go, a thin hope that led back to the patch of pale light and the world of the living. Here, though, there was only death, grinning from the huge, silver throne, leprous with cold; I could hardly bring myself to look at it.

When I did, I saw the faded brocade of once rich robes, laid neatly on the throne as a cushion for bones, including the skull that smiled welcome. Atil's skull.

'Einar?' Finn managed at last from lips that trembled and not from the cold of the place.

I shook my head. There was a scatter of bones in front of that great ice-slathered throne and some of them belonged to Ildico, the princess who had killed Atilla – one forlorn wrist and forearm, five centuries yellowed, hung still from the shackles that had fastened her forever to Atil's last seat.

The others belonged mostly to Einar; I saw a skull, still with long straggles of black wisping it, all that remained of his crow-wing hair, and pointed to it it. Swallowing, Finn made a warding sign and fumbled to pick up his Roman nail.

'Heya, old jarl,' he whispered, as if afraid to speak aloud. 'We have come back, as you see. Treat us kindly.'

I did not think he would, much. I had left Einar sitting on that throne, skewered by me but dying even as I finished him. Atil's remains, swaddled in those rich robes, had been torn from the seat by Hild in her frantic eagerness to seize one of his two rune swords.

Yet now they were back, neatly placed and Einar had been scattered like a dead dog at Atil's feet. I peered and poked warily, found and rolled other skulls into the light of the torch – Ketil-Crow, Sigtrygg, Illugi, who had all died here.

I said their names, the sound of my voice falling like snow off a roof, dull and soft.

'And her, Bear Slayer?' Finn asked, tucking the nail down one boot, recovering a measure of his old swagger. 'This one looks a little small to be any head I remember. Perhaps this is Hild.'

Ildico, I was thinking, as he held up the yellow grin and empty sockets of her, whose arm was still fastened to the throne. I did not think we would find Hild, for I did not think she was dead. Someone had restored Atil to his throne and made a clear gesture with the bones of intruders. I did not think Lambisson had done it and said so.

That made Finn frown and think and not like what he came up with. He held the torch up higher, shifting the light on the dark paths between tall cliffs of bulked blackness. I saw his face the moment the truth hit him, knew that he was about to ask where all the silver was hidden, when he saw it.

He gasped aloud and sank to his knees with the sheer scale of it. All that bulked blackness WAS the silver, age-dark and heaped up like old lumber. Bowls, ewers, wine pitchers, statues, plates, cups, most of them decorated with embedded gems, half buried in seas of coins and armrings, fastened together by age and ice.

There were shields, too, spearheads, blades, even bits of armour, crushed together with great platters fixed with mother-of-pearl, silver statues of animals with gold fangs, dancing girls poised on alabaster bases, gleaming, cold-frozen birds with amber eyes and ivory wings.

Under our feet was a massive auroch horn, banded in silver and jasper, a necklace of silver with porphyry stones, a great two-handed silver cup studded with deep-green serpentine, the mask from an ancient helmet, fixed with staring amethyst eyes.

Finn lifted each one, letting them fall from fingers numb with wonder and cold, then unearthed a half-bent silver plate, big as a wheel, crowded and leaping with ornamental life – palm leaves and lilies and grapes, silvered birds clinging and fluttering among branches, all twined together into an endless network of gleaming buds and plumes. Coins spilled from it like water, a ringing chime of riches.

He knelt, this man who never bowed the knee and his head and his shoulders shook as he wept at the sheer immensity, at the fact that, after everything that had happened and all who had died, the wild hunt of the Oathsworn ended here, now.

I was not sure whether he wept for those who had died,

or what we had found, or that we had found it at all after all our trouble. Nor did he. It was a sky-cracking moment, seeing Finn shed tears.

Eventually, he laid the great wheel of silver plate reverently down and fumbled The Godi out its sheath, stood it point down on the silver-litter and clasped his hands on the hilt, head bowed.

'All Father, one of your own gives thanks this night,' he said. 'Warrior he, faithful he, with companions you know and who walk with you already and who died here. To them I say: "Not now, but soon." To you, I give our thanks and your names.'

Then he started to recite them, grim and cold names, one by one. As godi, I should have been more reverent, but I had experienced One Eye before and did not think he deserved all this for bringing us here – we had already paid dearly and were not finished, I was sure of that. Distracted, I looked round and saw, from the corner of my eye, a balk of wood and moved to it across an ice-slither of floor.

It was the collapsed mouth of our old tunnel, the one we had dug into the side of the howe when first we had arrived here with Einar leading us. I remembered Illugi, slamming the butt of his staff into the ground a step away from here, calling on the gods – who were deaf to him by then – to aid us all against the black fetch that was Hild. It had splashed, I remembered, for the howe was flooding . . .

It had not flooded, all the same. The timber sticking from the wall was from the cart-planks we had used to shore up the tunnel and I remembered floundering in the sucking mud, felt the crushing panic of it while Hild sliced through the supports with the scything rune sword she wielded in her desperate, savage, snarling desire to get to me. The water had been flooding in then, pouring down the *balka* as it always did when it rained on the steppe, making a lake here, save in the drought of really high summer.

I laid a palm on the cold, slick freeze of that timber. In there, she was. Her efforts had brought the tunnel down, sealed the howe and left only a slick of water inside it in the end. If she had died, she lay only a few feet away, perhaps only inches, still grasping the other sword; I touched the wall, but it was iced as tempered steel, too hard to dig out the truth of it.

'Vafud, Hropta-Tyr, Gaut, Veratyr,' intoned Finn, then finished, unclasping his hands from The Godi's hilt and climbing to his feet like an old man.

'By the Hammer, Orm boy,' he kept saying, shaking his head. 'Just look at it.'

I blew on my numbed fingers and laid the other hand, lamb-gentle, on one shoulder; he blinked once or twice, then took up his torch and sword and puffed out his cheeks.

'Well, I have stood here and seen it for myself,' he said and his eyes were bright when I met them. 'All the silver of the world. Now I know. Now I know, boy.'

We moved down between the frowning *balkas* of riches, guttering torchlight throwing eldritch shadows and bouncing diamond-sharp darts back from the hanging icicles that made a silver hall for a warlord's hoard.

From his mouldering brocade cushion, Atil grinned and watched us go with his dark, dead eyes.

We found Lambisson a little way down one of the rat-nest passages – or, rather, he found us, for he was crouched in the dark and we came up in the red glare of torches. He was sitting on a pile of scraped-together spoil, all the lighter stuff such as coins and neckrings, little items you could put in a bucket. He looked like a mad frog on a stone.

'Brondolf,' I said to him, companionably and stopped well short of him, beyond blade reach, for he was just a shadow against the dark to me and I did not know what he had in his hands, or where Short Eldgrim was.

'You must be Orm Bear Slayer,' came the voice, a whisper

of a thing, faint as a Norn thread in that place. Finn moved closer, held up the torch and we saw him more clearly.

Lambisson was all but gone. The white raven had made a wasteland of his dreams, turned his mind to silver-white while tearing his face to a raw sore and he was so thin his fine tunic hung on him like a drying net on a beach. Hunger and sickness had leached his life away and he no longer resembled the Brondolf Lambisson I had seen, seal-sleek and confident in his fancy mail and helm on a hillside long before. That man was dead; this one surely would be soon enough.

Yet he had a steel handful that gleamed sharp in the twilight between us and could still summon up a laugh, like moth wings, as he shifted his eyes away from the glare of Finn's light.

'I do not remember your face and we scarcely met,' he sighed out to me. 'I remember Einar, but not you. Yet the Norns wove us together more fixed than brothers. Is that not strange, Orm Bear Slayer? I know you better than any woman I ever had.'

The laugh fluttered out again and was lost in the dark. Finn moved sideways and I squatted.

'Not so strange,' I answered. 'The Norns weave and we can only wear what they make.'

'This is a poisoned serk, right enough,' he whispered back – then flung some iron into his voice. 'It would be better, I am thinking, if your companion stayed still.'

Finn stopped at once, waved an acknowledging hand and squatted, as if by a friendly fire.

'I am Finn Bardisson from Skane,' he said easily. 'I can kill you if I want to, Brondolf Lambisson, whether you have blade or not. It is better you know this from the start.'

'I want Short Eldgrim,' I added. 'There need be no killing here. Frey witness it, there has been enough of that. All I want is Eldgrim.'

He stirred and I saw the head droop, but the steel-holding hand was steady enough.

'You speak as a friend,' he hissed. 'We can never be that.'

'No, but we need not be enemies.'

There was silence for a heart-beat or two, then he said: 'Do you like my new fortress, Bear Slayer? Fine, is it not. Rich.'

The chuckle that came with it was the hiss of a corpse's last breath. 'Rich enough to save Birka, I had thought – but that place is dead.'

'Keep it,' I replied flatly. 'I want Eldgrim. Then you can fill your boots and go away with no fighting at all.'

He leaned forward, that ice-sore face even bloodier in the light of my torch, patched by the black of cold rot eating his cheeks. He shook his head, his eyes glittering like rime; blood oozed from the cracked remains of his blackened lips.

'I did not think so,' I sighed. 'Well, here is my last offer. Finn and I will go back to the hole in the roof and climb out. You send out Short Eldgrim. Then you can stay or go, as you please.'

'And you will walk away, leaving all this?'

'All what?' I countered. 'You can eat none of it, Brondolf, nor suck warmth from it. You are cold, sick and starving to death down here. I do not . . .'

He moved, so fast that I only realized how tricked I had been when he flowed like darkness itself across the space between us, his blade already hissing. Not as sick as he had made it seem.

I had a flash, like a moment seen in lightning, of Ketil-Crow, stumbling over heaps of tinkling silver with the blue coil of his entrails tangling his ankles, with the same flowing darkness after him. Only then it had been Hild and her rune sword.

That memory almost did for me, for I hesitated with the vision of it. He had strength enough for this one mad rush and the sword hissed round, so that I lurched backwards and my own rune blade, laid handily across my knees, reared up – and blocked the cut.

It sounded like a hammer on an anvil. I heard a cracked-bell sound, knew it to be his sword breaking on mine and then he hit me, raving and slavering, following the ruin of his sword, half-turning as he smashed into me like a mad bull with just a hilt and a jagged nub end in his hand.

We went over in a rush of panting breath and crushing bone and whirling stars. There was a grunt and a scream and a moment of mad thrashing, which ended with a wet smack of sound.

A hand grabbed my forearm and I came up into Finn's embrace, wet with Brondolf's blood and brains. He lay face down, a diamond-shaped hole in the back of his head and blood spreading thickly under him.

'All we wanted was Short Eldgrim,' panted Finn, as The Godi dripped gleet and blood. 'He did not have to take the hard way to it.'

He did, all the same, for he had no Short Eldgrim to trade. We skulked and slithered around and over the gleam and the dark of that place and found no trace of him. Then we came back to where Lambisson lay and turned him over into the grue of his own blood, for it was said the truth lay fixed in a dead man's eyes.

His raw sore of a face was sucked in with hunger and collapsed and already blue-white, his dead eyes glittering with reflected ice, sharp and bright as silver. So the truth was there, right enough. Just not what we needed.

Finn looked round, at the great piles of silver and the shimmering walls, then peeled off the *valknut* amulet and looped it round the stiffening, dead fingers. I was astonished; the amulet was mine, for a start and I would not give the skin off my shit for Lambisson. I said as much and Finn nodded as if he understood.

289

'It is not for him,' he rasped. 'This is the end of it, Orm, and that cursed little monk had it right – all the struggle to get to it and for what? We would have to live here to make sure of keeping it all and fight everyone and his mother every day. I would give twice the amount to have Pinleg and Harelip and Skapti and all the others waiting at the top of that rope. Aye, even Einar, though you would not agree, I am sure.'

He shook his head and climbed to his feet, while his words crashed on me like a fall of snow. He had the right of it, for sure – we could fill our boots and carts and make sacks out of our tunics and cloaks and still would hardly dent the treasure heap of this place. After us would come a ravening horde of others, friends of Morut and Avraham and friends of their friends and brothers and the relations of every man in the *druzhina* and Oathsworn, all ripping the heart out of Atil's last resting place. There was no secret now.

Odin's gift. It had not been worth it, as I suspected all along and I said so. Finn agreed with a nod and then made a gesture so surprising I almost dropped my sword. He laid a hand on my forearm and said, straight into my face and serious as a fall of rock: 'You had the right of it, not wanting to return here. We should have listened to you.'

Then I felt the hot wash of shame. Oh, aye, I had railed against it, scorned it, dug in my feet like the point man in a heaving boar snout – but who was it had scratched those runes on the hilt of the sword, knowing full well he would need them, sooner or later, knowing he could not resist coming back?

We were climbing stiffly to our feet when the voice drifted like cold mist down through the dark heaps and round the rat passages. A high, thin, voice. Female. Calling my name, so that it wrapped chill round my heart.

Hild.

I looked at Finn and he at me and, for once, I saw no scorning scowl, only the flick of his tongue on dry lips.

'O-o-orm.'

'By Odin's eye, boy,' said Finn in a hoarse whisper.

'F-i-nnn.'

'Did you hear that?' I asked and had back a suitable curl of lip.

'Even with my one ear, I can hear that,' he growled, then hefted The Godi in one hand and the torch in the other and rolled his neck muscles. 'Well, if it is that dead bitch, I am coming for her.'

Finn was noted for being afraid of nothing at all, but the fear was an unseen force that I had to push against, step by step round one gully of age-dark riches, half-way round another, to where a torch flickered and the pale light spilled from the hole in the roof. No more than a score of steps, it was the longest walk I ever took.

A figure stood there, dark and menacing, holding the torch high and peering like some hound from Hel.

'Here I am, bitch!' yelled Finn and even if his voice cracked a little at the end, I admired him, for my throat had so much dry spear rammed in it I could make no sound at all.

'Is that you there, Finn Bardisson? Step to where I can see you – and, if it is you, stop calling me names.'

We blinked, looked at each other and then Finn grunted as if he had been slapped. 'Thordis. It is Thordis, by Odin's hairy arse.'

If she wondered about us charging out and all but raining kisses on the upturned petal of her sweet face, she was too agitated and fearing to comment on it.

'Get off! Get off me,' she panted, cuffing us like dogs.

'Aye, but you are a sight, right enough,' chuckled Finn, trying to grab her again. The Godi whirled round her ears and she winced back, so that he fell to apologizing and trying to grab her and sheath it at the same time.

'Why are you here?' I asked, feeling a coiled tendril of new chill unfold in my bowels.

'Right enough,' huffed Thordis, tugging her linen kerchief back over her hair, one braid unfastened and dropped almost to her belt. She blew a stray wisp off her chapped cheeks and wriggled herself together. 'I would have said before, but for this . . . this . . .'

'Tell it now.'

She told it and set us frantic, scrabbling to the knotted rope and calling up for help.

Vladimir and his company had taken the silver and gone. Our men had grumbled about it, but I had told Kvasir not to do anything rash, so he kept them from the *druzhina's* throats and the Oathsworn let themselves be herded on to the island and disarmed under the bows of the big Slav warriors. Their weapons were left a little way off and, as soon as the treacherous little rat prince was beyond bowshot range, the Oathsworn lumbered out and got them back.

Then Kvasir went after them, on foot, for we had no horses. Gizur was left in charge and – I cursed him to the nine worlds and back for it – Thorgunna had stayed behind when everyone trekked back to the tomb with their weapons. Then she had set off after Kvasir. Once back at Atil's tomb, Gizur sent Thordis down to find us – and the fact that he had sent a woman into that place should have told me all that was needful, but I was too red-raged to see it.

'What possessed Kvasir?' roared Finn, levering himself out of the hole.

Below, Thordis yelled back: 'Jon Asanes is missing – Kvasir went after the boy.'

'And Thorgunna?' I demanded, putting both hands on her backside and shoving her up the rope.

'She went after Kvasir' she answered, panting with the effort of climbing. 'And watch your hands, Jarl Orm, otherwise we will have to wed me for the liberties.'

'Sorry,' I muttered and followed her up.

At the top, Gizur waited and we were ringed with backs

292

as all the Oathsworn formed a shielded circle round the hole, facing outwards. Nearby sat Fish, with Hauk Fast-Sailor's bow and his last six arrows.

'What made her go after Kvasir?' I wanted to know, raging, half-turning to Gizur. 'And why did you fall in with her plan, you gowk?'

'He is her man,' Thordis answered. 'The sight is going in his remaining eye and he can barely see at all and soon will be blind entire – for all that, he has clearer vision than yourself, Jarl Orm, for that has been staring you in the face for months.'

I gawped; Finn scrubbed his beard with embarrassment and it was clear he had known. Gizur, too. Everyone, I suddenly realized, but me. Yet the truth of it was there now and I saw it, in every axe stroke Kvasir had missed, in that bird-cock of his head to focus better, the ragged linen strip against the light.

The despair stripped away the anger – briefly. Gizur cleared his throat and I sprang on him, fresh prey for my abuse.

'You should have stopped her,' I yelled. 'Stopped him, too, you cow hole. Have you sent men after them?'

He staggered under the wind of it a little, righted himself and came about, grim and quiet.

'Kvasir commanded, so what he said I did,' he replied evenly. 'Allowing Thorgunna to go after him was the best I could do under the circumstances, Jarl Orm.'

'What fucking circumstances?' I bawled, red-lit with anger now.

He pointed, out beyond the shoulders of the Oathsworn – all of them weaponed and mailed and with their shields up – at the snow-whirled steppe.

The anger hissed from me like the last breath of a dead man. In a ring, on both sides of the steep-banked frozen lake, the woman warriors sat on their little steppe ponies, silent as trees. Hundreds of them – three hundred, at least I saw, with that part of my mind that still worked – waiting like wolves in a circle round the tiny wall of shields on the island of Atil's tomb.

There were twenty of us, no more than that, the last Oathsworn in the world, each one worn as a whetstone, a dark snarl of beard where ice glistened like tears, cheeks sunk, eyes rimmed red, noses dripping. The men who called me jarl hunched under rust-spotted helmets, knees no more than lumps of bone above ragged garters or shredded boots, feet two lumps of frozen flesh and knuckles purpled with sores that itched and bled.

Yet they had shields up and spears greased and blades that gleamed with edge, reflecting in the eyes that watched the ring of horsed women. They parted those frozen beards and grinned the same old fanged grin, of men with cliffs before them and wolves behind and not one of them with the thought to run or throw down their weapons – not even Fish, who was not oathed.

I loved them then, none more so than Finn, who put out a voice for them all, blowing out his cheeks and grinning until his lips bled.

'Odin luck for us, then,' he beamed, 'that we got our weapons back in time. Now we have these Man-Haters where we want them – they will not get away from us this time.'

The others roared at that and banged on their shields. The riders stirred and then threw back their heads and started up a shrilling, that yipping-dog sound that so chilled us every time we heard it; from three hundred throats it swamped our bellows.

Fish, hirpling painfully on the wrapped ruins of his feet, forced his way to where he could shoot, drew back and let fly. Whether he meant it or not, the shaft zipped true and the arrow he had picked had a making-flaw in the head, a small hole that fluted the wind. It shrieked, loud and shrill, all the way into the trembling throat of one rider, cutting her dead in mid-yip and tumbling her backwards off her pony.

As if he had shot them all in the throat, they stopped. There was such a silence after it that we could hear the stricken rider choking, drowning in her own blood while her horse snorted at the iron-stink of it.

'Fuck,' said Hauk Fast-Sailor admiringly. 'I never got a shot like that out of that old bow.'

'First time I saw a Fish hook a catch,' added Gyrth and there were chuckles. Men banged on their shields again and grinned at one another, as if they had won a battle.

'I think,' groaned Klepp Spaki, 'you have annoyed them just a little.'

They were nocking arrows and my mouth went dry at that. We had barely enough men to form a tight circle as it was and none to spare for a rank to make a roof of shields; three hundred arcing arrows, from every direction, would nail us all to the frozen ground.

I saw riders moving, heard angry shouts. Finn thumbed snot from his nose and squinted at them.

'Women,' he sneered. 'Argue about everything, even the way to kill us.'

The whack on his helmet was loud and some heads turned. Thordis, flat of the blade she held up and ready for another attack on Finn's dented helm, scowled blackly and men chuckled. Finn, though, grinned admiringly at her.

'Here they come,' bawled Fish and stepped back to allow the two mailed shoulders on either side of him to clash together like a wall.

It was just one rider, edging out on to the ice, her pony stepping uneasily, sliding and slithering. I had a salmon-leap of hope, then, that they would be madwomen to the end and try and charge us across the lake ice. In the chaos of that we had, perhaps, the sliver of a chance.

She came on, black cloak billowing, hair snaking in dark

braids around her sloped brow. I swallowed; she held up an arm and in it was a scythe of light – the rune sword. Hild's sword.

The voice floated across, slathering my bowels with ice.

'Orm, who is called Bear Slayer.'

It was in good Greek, but even those who did not know the tongue could recognize the name – even Finn, who knew just enough Greek to get his face slapped – and he looked at me as I stood, stricken. He knew what I was thinking . . . Hild.

'Your girl wants you,' he said into the air around us, tense as creaking bowstrings, but the chuckles were forced.

'Let him speak soft words and offer wealth, who longs for a woman's love,' Red Njal intoned as I shouldered to the front, my legs trembling. I could not feel my feet, but tested the sharp of my tongue on him.

'One day, Red Njal, you must tell me how this marvellous annoying relative of yours lived so long in the close company of other folk,' I snarled.

He grinned at me with chapped lips. 'True, my da's ma was given a place of her own and rarely visited – but there was wisdom in her, all the same.'

Then he nodded out to the ring of horse.

'Do not keep her fretting there, Bear Slayer,' he said wryly.

I saw the woman nudge her pony on and all the bows dropped a little, though the arrows stayed nocked. I moved forward; she moved forward, off the ice and on to the lip of the island, where the pony had more purchase. She swung a leg over its neck – no small feat in her lamellar coat and thigh-greaves – and dropped lightly, the cloak floating down like hair.

It was not Hild. I thought she wore a Serkland veil until I stepped closer and saw it was a whirl of skin-marks covering her chin, nose and cheeks, a blue-black knot of some steppe magic marred by the deep scores of old scars, three on each

296

cheek. Her head sloped backwards, too, in that long, eldritch way – but I did not care what she looked like, for it was not Hild.

She lifted the sabre, the twin of the one I held, wary and watching – then she slammed it into the earth and moved to one side, an arm's length from the hilt and squatted.

Dry-mouthed, I moved forward, careful to stay beyond sword reach of her, out of politeness. Then I did the same as she had done and took a knee, Norse-style.

We faced each other, the width of a man apart, no more, and studied each other in silence, while the wind sighed, lifting little *djinn* of snow over the stippled ice of the lake.

She was nail-thin and wasted, but had all her finery on, from golden beads in her braids to necklets of silver animals and fine bangles. Her armour was polished bone leaves pared from the hooves of horses and she wore baggy breeks worked with gold threads. But what glittered most brightly on her were her polished jet eyes.

The silence stretched until I could stand it no longer, so I nodded politely at her and said: '*Skjaldmeyjar.*'

She cocked her head like a quizzical bird and, in good Greek, answered me with a smile. 'I hope that is friendly in your tongue.'

I told her what it meant – shieldmaiden – though she seemed more like someone who could be called *valmeyjar*, which most ignorant people who are not from the fjords translate as shield-maiden, or battle-maiden. Really, that word means corpse-maiden, chooser of the slain and is a name to hand out to a woman who looks like a wolf's grandmother two weeks dead. I did not tell her this.

'You know my name,' I added and left that hanging like a waiting hawk.

'*Amacyn*, they call me,' she answered. 'Which is the name given to me as leader of the *tupate* and the name given to all such leaders, who then forsake all other family ties. It means

Mother of the People, but the foolish Greeks once thought it stood as name for us all and so called us *amazonoi*.'

'Who are the *tupate*?' I asked, my mind whirling already. She spread her hands to encompass all the riders. 'We are. In Greek it would be *tabiti*. It is hard to translate correctly, but the nearest would be – oathsworn.'

I sat back on one heel at that. Oathsworn. Like us. I said so and she made a little head gesture, as if to say perhaps yes, perhaps no.

'You have a sword,' I said in Greek. 'Like mine. Hild had it last.'

She smiled, covering her face with her hand, which was custom, I learned. 'Hild. Is that the name you gave her, then? The one in the tomb of the Master of the World?'

'That is the name she gave herself,' I answered, breathing heavily, for I felt on the edge of a cliff with a mad desire to fly. 'How did you come by the sword?'

'Hild,' she repeated, then laughed, a surprising sound of lightness. 'Ildico. Yes, that would be part of her penance. Or a twisted joke.'

I did not understand any of this and she saw it, nodded seriously and adjusted her squat more comfortably, so that her knees came up round her chin, long, thin hands clasped in front of her.

'Long ago,' she said, 'when the Volsungs brought their treasure and a new wife called Ildico to Atil, Master of the World, we were the Chosen Ones, charged with making sure of our Lord's undisturbed afterlife.'

She waved a hand, slim, pale and languid as a dragonfly in summer heat and talked as if she had been there herself, as if it had been yesterday, or the day before.

'This place,' she added. 'We made sure those who laboured on it could not reveal the secret of it, every one, from those who dug, to those who planned, to those who brought the treasure to place in it.'

298

She paused and looked at me with those black eyes, so that my heart clenched. I could almost believe she had been there herself, dealing out the slaughter.

'The steppe ran with blood for days,' she said, 'so that, in the end, only the Chosen Ones and the flies knew where the tomb lay and if the flies passed it on, mother to daughter, generation to generation, I never knew of it. But that is what the Chosen Ones did.'

There was a long, wind-sighing pause while she fiddled with the thongs of her soft boots and gathered her thoughts. Mine were of all the shrieking fetches who drifted in this place and if this woman was one, for she spoke so knowingly of five centuries before. No wonder the rest of the steppe kept clear.

'We did not expect the Master of the World to occupy it for some time, of course,' she went on, 'but the Volsungs came, with their gift of silver and swords and Ildico, the new bride. They did not stay for the wedding – did not dare, of course, since Ildico planned red murder – and when they left, one of us went with them.'

'One of . . . you?' I asked, uncertainly. 'A Chosen One?'

She nodded and shifted. 'Her name, as far as any Volsung knew, was my name – Amacyn. She was then leader of the *tupate* but forgot her oath for love of the smith, the one called Regin. She went back with him to the north and by the time it was discovered, it was too late. The Master of the World wanted her death, to keep the secret of his tomb, but we were told to wait until after his wedding.'

By which time it was too late, for Ildico killed him on the wedding night. I licked dry lips, thinking on all the years between then and now and what that love had cost.

'The oathbreaker was not hunted down, then,' I said, the mosaic of it filling in for me even as I spoke.

The woman shrugged. 'The *tupate* had lost face and the one who favoured us was dead,' she said. 'The sons of the Master of the World did not care for us as much – but we had sworn to guard his tomb and so we did, as best as we were able. The last task of that *tupate* was to carry the Lord of the World to this place – then slay everyone who was not one of us.

'After that, the Chosen Ones went home – but daughters were trained in war, given the secret and served, as best as could be done, down the long years. Faithful to the last task – to keep the secret of the tomb. The oath would not let us do less.'

I knew that oath and how it bound. Who it bound. Hild. The woman nodded.

'The oathbreaking Amacyn could not live with what she had done in the end, so it became known,' she went on softly. 'She birthed a daughter and did what we all do – passed on the secret of the tomb. My mother did so to me, which is how I know that the oathbreaking Amacyn then went into Regin's forge and would not come out, sealed it so that it could never be used again. Regin the smith died and some say his heart snapped because of both his loves were gone, woman and forge. All this was found out, piece by piece, over the years.'

I saw the weft of it then, a harsh-woven cloak of misery visited on the innocent daughters of that forge village. All the ones who came after would not break that chain, waited until a girl was born – or chosen, even – and reached the full of their womanhood, then passed on the secret of Atil's tomb, an echo of what Regin's woman had once been. Then they went into the forge mountain, for the shame of what had been done. Probably those who thought twice about it were forced in; it became a god-ritual for the people who lived by the forge and they would be afraid to break it.

The woman sat quietly and said nothing while I stammered all this out, hammering it straight as I said it.

'Except for Hild,' I said, seeing it clearly, the sad, untangled

300

knot of it. She had been stolen from that little Karelian village because Martin the priest thought he had found a secret and hired a man called Skartsmadr Mikill, Quite The Dandy, to get it. When he could not find it he and his crew of Danes tried to force the knowledge from the villagers by taking what they clearly valued – the young, bewildered Hild, still raw with the whispered secret, still weeping from the loss of her mother, gone into the forge.

In the end, Quite The Dandy found out how much she was valued; the villagers attacked them with such ferocity that those hard Danes had run for it, dragging Hild with them as their only prize. By the time she was delivered to Martin of Hammaburg they had taken out their anger and frustration on her so badly that her mind was cracking.

I laid out the tale of Hild for this latest Amacyn – poor demented Hild, rescued by us, burdened with a secret and a centuries-old sin, burning for revenge on those who had used her and prepared to lead us all to Atil's tomb in return for the death of Skartsmadr Mikill and all his men.

We had done that and Hild had fulfilled her part of the bargain – at the cost of her mind. Had she been made mad by the goddess of the steppe, or the fetch of Ildico, or the guilt of knowing she betrayed the long line of those who had died and kept the secret?

'Perhaps all of them,' agreed Amacyn, uncoiling slowly to her feet. 'It does not matter – the secret was revealed. She broke her oath.'

And all who break such an oath end up dead. That I knew well enough.

'After you quit this place,' Amacyn continued, 'those few of us who survived came here, but war was raging on the steppe and it took some time for us all to assemble, so we missed you.'

I swallowed at that. If they had caught us then, staggering raggedly down to the Azov and the Sea of Darkness . . .

'Afterwards,' she went on, 'the Khazar fist had gone, so the last of us came here in force. We had to dig through the roof to find out what had been done. There we saw a strange dead man on the throne and the Master of the World cast down and other strangers dead, including a woman. She had one of the Lord's swords; we realized then that one of those who had survived had the other.'

My cracked lips were glued, now. Hild was dead; Finn had been right all along. Then I realized what this woman wanted.

'Yes,' she said, though I had not spoken. Then she sighed and rubbed the sores on her hands; I realized, suddenly, that she was in as bad a state as I was – as we all were, out on that frozen waste.

'We are the last of our kind,' she went on, 'It falls to me to be the *Amacyn* in whose time his tomb is no longer a secret. We knew you would be back and listened for word that northmen were moving on the Grass Sea. It cost us much to come out on the steppe and kill them – but we did not expect another band and certainly not a prince from Novgorod. Then we knew it was all finished for us.'

She stopped, stiff as the yellow stalks of frozen-dead grass; her eyes burned.

'We are few and growing fewer,' she said, in a voice like a *djinn* of wind. 'Man-Haters, you call us, but that is not true. We have fathers and brothers and some of those here have men and children that they value. Too many have already died. We have failed to keep the secret and this fight on the steppe has ended us. We are passing from the world. We will go home to men, stop binding the foreheads of our girl children and cutting their cheeks, so that they feel the endurance of wounds before the nourishment of milk. But there is one last service we can perform for the Master of the World.'

The words beat on me like raven wings. Passing from the world. Perhaps all Oathsworn are passing from the world, I was thinking, even as I saw, too, that she had ridden out to find a way to resolve matters other than with blood. I understood that only too well.

Once before, this way had saved the Oathsworn at Atil's tomb and I did not think it would fail us now. I looked at the sabre, then at the woman who wanted it more than the world itself. I knew now how she knew my name and what she thought we would want, but I asked, for form's sake.

'What do you have to trade?'

SEVENTEEN

After I had asked my question, the warrior woman had put two fingers in her mouth and whistled, as if calling up a dog. Riders had come out, one of them leading a stumbling figure on a tether and, as they came closer, my belly flipped at the sight.

Short Eldgrim. I had been right.

He was thin – I had seen more meat on a skelf – and his grin showed that he had lost some teeth. But some of his old wits remained in the summer-blue cage of his head.

'Ho, young Orm. What brings you here?'

The woman called Amacyn looked at me.

'Is this a good trade for you?'

So we took Short Eldgrim into the middle of us and moved away, leaving the warrior women sitting their mounts and watching, their leader now with two swords. Finn came to me then, handed me a wood axe and a grin. 'You will need this until we can find you another good blade, Jarl Orm.'

I shivered, wondering what would happen to me now, for I was sure that rune serpented sword of mine had protecting powers – and now it was gone. Forever. As easily as handing it over, no more than an arm movement; yet this was the blade that had once driven us from the Great City to the forge-heat of Serkland, had goaded us to fight and kill men we had once called oarmates.

I had lingered as the others moved off and had watched what happened, what the women did. When I came back to the Oathsworn, I ignored the questions in their eyes and, since I had given up my runesword for them, they bit their lips and did not ask them aloud.

Later still, when we were far away, we heard cries, faint on the wind, the yip-yowl chorus of all those warrior women. Eyes gleamed with fear then, for they thought the Man Killers were riding after us, but when I did nothing, they calmed down.

No vengeful women came; I knew what had happened and said nothing on it, stayed hunched into myself and against the wolfish bite of wind until we came off the rolling white of the Grass Sea down over a series of shallow cliffs thick with scrubby pine and white-barked birch, skeletal and shivering. The sun hung in the pewter sky like a drop of molten metal.

Ahead, hidden in the ice glare of the marsh that fringed it here, was the mighty body of the river itself, the Tanais, which was once the Scyth name for the Don and came to be the legendary name for travelling the lands we called Gardariki, down among the Mussulmen traders, who gave the name to us that everyone now seemed to use – *Rhus*.

To go down the Tanais was every youngling's dream, an adventure without peer. The reality was always different and harsh and usually inscribed by grieving relatives on a memory stone back home.

I looked to where Klepp Spaki moved, a dark figure trembling with cold; we would not even have a memory stone, for we had taken the greatest rune-carver with us and it was probable he would die here.

I squinted, watery-eyed against the glare. If it affected me this badly, it was no wonder Kvasir's remaining eye had given up on him; I cursed myself one more time for having been blind myself and missing the signs of it.

305

To the south, just above where the Don's black-watered sibling, the Donets, joined it, not far from where both split into a thousand muddy channels, was Biela Viehza, the Khazar Sarkel. Close enough for me to see the feathers of smoke from its fires and, black against their ochre threads, the dark and solitary rider moving steadily in our direction.

'Seems alone,' Finnlaith grunted. 'Shall I shoot him when he gets in range?'

'Get Fish to hook this one, too,' added Onund and there were grim chuckles at that.

'Well, there is no place to hide here,' I said, 'so it seems to me he has seen us as we have seen him. Does he look bothered to you?'

'I can change that,' Finn said, but he made no move. We stood for a moment and then Short Eldgrim said: 'It is cold here.'

'I know,' answered Thordis softly. 'We will be warm by and by.'

I looked at him then, the slow-blinking, washed blue eyes in that white-scarred face, bundled up in cloak and tunics handed over by men eager to see him safe and warm, as if he was a talisman for us all. When we had him safe in the middle of us, Thordis had peeled off his ragged old tunic to give him a fresh and thicker one.

She had stopped and suckled her breath in, then whirled him round, so his naked back was to me. I blenched; it was a mass of blackened, red-raw sores, the half-healed burns of little Christ-crosses, all making up one large one, down his spine and across the shoulderblades. Now I knew how Martin had unlocked the memories in Short Eldgrim's half-addled head.

'If ever we find that monk again,' Thordis said stiffly, 'I will want words with him.'

Now she tried to wrap his head in more wool and he growled at her.

306

'Stop fussing woman,' Short Eldgrim growled, shivering. 'I am warm enough here.'

He stamped his feet against the cold and looked at me.

'I lost Cod-Biter on the way,' he said. Then he stopped and looked puzzled. 'Runes,' he said.

'I found Cod-Biter,' I said and he smiled at that and nodded. Then he said: 'Where are Einar and the others . . . no, wait. They are gone. Orm . . . sorry, I . . .'

He stopped, frowning. 'Lambisson. That fucking little monk . . . he hurt me, the little shit, him and his asking about runes and silver . . .'

He stopped again and a sob wrenched from him, a child's whimper. Thordis wrapped him inside her own cloak and I felt my heart lurch and cold anger settle in my belly.

'What now?' demanded Gizur. 'Are we going back to the tomb? What about the silver?'

We were never going back to the tomb and the silver was gone from us, but I did not say that, or how I knew. I felt as if I had forgotten something important, left it lying back there in the snow – but it was only the tug of that sword, so long a part of me and now gone. I felt the loss, like a missing limb, for a long time after, but never counted it a cost when weighed against the bland, blue smile of Eldgrim's eyes.

'Kvasir and Thorgunna,' I said. Gizur shook his head sorrowfully.

'No sooner do we free one than we lose two,' he said – but the rest of it was in the grim set of his face; our oarmates were there and needing help. There was also silver ahead by the cartload and it belonged to the Oathsworn.

The rider came closer and Finn said, suddenly: 'Morut.'

The Khazar tracker came up to us on his indestructible horse, leading another, a short, stiff-maned, patient little animal. He sat a little way off and waited until we came up to him, moving like wraiths over the windswept snow.

'Heya, wee man,' growled Finn and Morut nodded back,

wary at his reception. Since he had ridden openly up to us, I was prepared to let him speak.

'The little prince is in Sarkel,' he announced. 'Well, not in it exactly. The garrison will not let the prince of Novgorod inside the walls, so they are in the town, down by the river, organizing boats and unloading carts.'

'Is the garrison likely to let Vladimir inside the walls?' I asked. Morut shook his head and pursed chapped lips, rubbed shiny with fat to stop them splitting further.

'Avraham has been sent to persuade them, but I am thinking he has exactly the other idea – there are men from Kiev two days march away, led by Sveinald and his son. They would be here already save that the river has frozen over again between him and Sarkel and they have had to abandon their boats and walk.'

That was news worth the knowing – but I wondered how Morut had discovered it. The little tracker shrugged. 'Tien was with them. They came with only two horses, down the river in those big heavy boats they have. Tien was sent on one horse to Sarkel to find out news and we met, not far beyond the Ditch Bridge.'

Tien. I cursed him, for it was clear he had headed for Kiev to tell all he knew as soon as we had vanished into the Great White.

'Yes,' confirmed Morut, 'but Kiev already knew, for that monk Martin came out of the wilderness, as near death as made little difference. He told all in return for them saving his life – though he lost a foot from the cold.'

Martin. Finn growled and shook his head. 'I wish you had killed him that day in Birka, when you had the chance, Orm,' he said.

That day seemed so long ago as to be no more substantial than breath on polished steel.

'What of Tien?' asked Gyrth, which was clever and which I should have thought to ask. Morut looked blankly from Onund to me, and back again.

'As you know,' he answered slowly, 'we were never friends and once he had told all I wanted to hear I paid him back for the insults. This horse was his.'

No-one said anything to this, though everyone looked at the smooth-faced little tracker with new respect. I was too busy thinking that Sveinald and his son remained in ignorance of events and knew only that their tracker had not yet returned. They were on foot, too and would be slogging through the ice and cold – so we had time yet.

'Avraham is hoping to command the Sarkel garrison to resist everyone,' Morut went on moodily. 'I think he is a great fool, for the garrison is as much Slav as Khazar these days and even they call it Biela Viezha now. Avraham is blinded by dreams of old greatness. In the end, he will tell the garrison of the silver in the carts and that will persuade them.'

Dobrynya and Sigurd would suspect this, I knew. They would want away before either the garrison at Biela Viezha, or Sveinald's Kiev *druzhina* discovered their haul of silver.

'Why are you telling us all this, little man?' Hauk Fast-Sailor wanted to know, a second before I opened my mouth to ask.

Morut thought on the question and frowned.

'Prince Vladimir did not tell me or Avraham that he planned to leave you to face the *Oior Pata* alone and steal your share of the silver,' he answered. 'It was not a princely matter and I said so to Avraham. He did not care, is of the opinion that you are all unbelieving pagans and deserve everything God inflicts on you.'

'I shall let some of the puff out of that bladder,' Finn promised.

'You do not share this view?' I asked and Morut shook his head.

'It was no matter of mine,' he answered, bold-eyed and truthful. 'I thought that a quarrel over such a large hill of riches was a mountain of folly; there was surely enough for everyone.'

'Just so,' I replied. 'And so you are here. Sent by Vladimir, or his uncle?'

'Sent by no-one, save God. Or Allah, for I have not decided where I will go. The prince does not know I am gone, nor anyone else. I came to see if the *Oior Pata* had killed you – but it seems you have tamed the Man-Haters.'

There was admiration in his voice – then he frowned again.

'Truthfully, it was the blind man's killing I did not like. Nor the way they handled his woman.'

Thordis would not stop weeping, even when Finn put his arms awkwardly round her. Eldgrim patted her as if she was a dog or a child, muttering softly, though he had no clear idea why she was breaking her heart out on the cold steppe.

No-one else had much to say; the crushing loss of Kvasir was a burden that made even speaking difficult, so that when Morut had finished the telling of it, there was such a silence that it shrieked.

Kvasir had come up on them, just as the cavalcade of horses, carts and men had reached the bridge over the ditch at Biela Viezha. Here there was nothing more than a rough palisade fence, enough to keep maurauding wolves from the yurts and enclosures, for this was the winter camp of steppe people, who came with their goats and their hairy, two-humped camels from further east and their horses and dogs, sheltering in the lee of the scabbed, white walls of the fortress.

Morut had seen Kvasir arrive, had watched him come up with empty hands held out to his sides and be escorted to just beyond blade reach of Vladimir and Dobrynya and Sigurd.

'It seemed to me,' Morut said, as we squatted in a huddled stand of birch, the wind rattling the stiff branches, 'that he spoke of the boy, Jon, for that one was brought forward and I heard some raised voices between them.'

'He went to bring Jon Asanes back,' I said and Morut shrugged.

'The boy was no prisoner. He came with us smartly enough, smiling with Crowbone and speaking of taking his share of the silver and going to the Great City.'

I had suspected it, but the fullness of it felt like a cold knife in my bowels. Finn growled and shook his head, but I could not tell if it was disbelief at Morut's tale or disgust at Jon's behaviour.

'After that,' Morut said, 'Kveldulf stepped forward and said something. There were words spoken and Dobrynya then told Kvasir to go away. This I heard, for I had moved closer. Jon Asanes also pleaded with Kvasir to go away, before it was worse for him.

'Then Kvasir said to Jon Asanes that he would break Orm's heart in this matter and Kveldulf growled that it would be better if Kvasir stayed, permanently. Then Kvasir hit Kveldulf and a good blow it was, knocking that man clean off his feet, so that even I could hear the ringing in his ears. Then Kvasir told Kveldulf to be quiet, that men were speaking here.'

'Heya,' breathed Finn admiringly. I felt the sickening rise of what I knew would come next.

'Kveldulf came up spitting,' Morut went on, 'and his sword came out and they set too, with Vladimir demanding that they stop and Dobrynya cursing and Sigurd calling for the *druzhina* to move in and stop the fight. But it was clear that Kvasir could not see hardly at all, so Kveldulf had almost no fight of it and felled him with a blow between neck and shoulder.'

Finn gave a long groan at this and everyone else shifted and grunted as if they had taken such a blow themselves.

The cold of his loss numbed us then and I could hardly get the words past my teeth. 'What then?'

312

Morut frowned. 'Well, Kvasir was lying there, with the blood seeping from him and Dobrynya sighed and said that was that, while Sigurd shook his head with a face like a stone cliff and said it would be the worse for all now.'

'He has the right of it there,' Finn managed to squeeze out. His knuckles clenched and unclenched so tightly on the hilt of The Godi that the red sores split and blood welled.

Morut looked uneasily round him, then and I saw he did not want to tell the rest of it. He caught my eye, saw my look and swallowed, nodding.

'Kveldulf knelt down by Kvasir, who was not yet quite dead and said to him: "Stone am I?" which I did not understand. Then he took out his long knife . . .'

The tracker stopped, looking at the stone of my face. There was no reprieve there for what he had to say.

'He dug out the eyes.'

Finn went still, which was not what I expected. Hauk sprang to his feet and cursed; Red Njal pounded the ice until his fist bled and he howled, while Short Eldgrim whimpered, even though it was clear he did not quite know why – but Finn went as cold and still as a snow-crowned stone. When I reached out a hand to his shoulder, I felt the underneath of him trembling like a horse before a fight.

'What of Thorgunna?' I asked and the little tracker nodded miserably.

'They left his body on the steppe,' he said, 'and Kveldulf took the eyes and put them in a pouch on his belt, saying he would add Finn's remaining ear to them in time and that, if Thor permitted, he would perhaps make a whole new person out of pieces of the Oathsworn of Orm Bear Slayer.'

He stopped and considered me carefully, then added: 'He said the final piece of it would be your head.'

'What of Thorgunna?' I persisted, only vaguely aware of the Night Wolf's boasting.

Morut paused, looking round at the glittering eyes feeding

313

on his words, clearly wondering if he was digging his own grave as he spoke.

'We had been at the river bank for no more than a few hours,' he said, 'arranging for boats and had started in to loading them when Thorgunna came up. We knew her at once, of course, and she went straight to Vladimir and knelt before him and asked for her husband's eyes, so it was clear she had found her man and seen what had been done to him. The prince did not look happy and said he was sorry for what had been done, for killing an Oathsworn had not been part of the weft of matters. Thorgunna simply repeated her request and the little prince looked like a dog on the point of being whipped, for he could not deliver the items without commanding Kveldulf – which he did. Kveldulf was not happy at being so commanded, but could do nothing else but hand over the pouch, which he did with ill-grace.'

Morut stopped then and glanced round at all the faces, pale, harsh as moons in the growing twilight.

'Go on,' I ordered.

Morut shook his head sadly. 'Perhaps it would be best if . . .'

'Say it out!' Finn's voice was a face-slap and Morut jerked, then nodded.

'Thorgunna looked at Kveldulf with no fear at all, the pouch in her hand. Then she leaned closer to him and said something I did not catch – but he went wide-eyed with anger and hit her in the face.'

Now there was movement, frantic dashes; Gyrth swung his long-axe and slashed the frozen snow, cursing. But Finn stayed silent and only glanced over once, like a blind man, to where Thordis was weeping.

'She fell to the ground and he kicked her in the belly before Sigurd dragged him off and flung him away. I saw Jon Asanes go to her, to help her up and she said something to him that made him go white and stop dead and shrink, as if he had been lashed. She got to her feet on her own, but then doubled up and fell down again; there was blood and she went limp and did not speak.'

'Is she dead?' demanded Bjaelfi.

Morut shook his head, frowning. 'No. They carried her to shelter on a landed boat. Little Crowbone is sure she has lost her child, all the same. He was crying, for he had seen this before with his mother, he said, and was sure it was the same man who had done it.'

There was silence after that, while the darkness seeped round us and we sat like numbed stones, unable even to think. Morut eventually made a fire and the soft, red flicker of it brought us all blinking back to the Now, as if we had been asleep.

There was no need to ask what we would do next; the cold rage sat on us like some haar from Hel, so that even the fire guttered in the chill. It was Thordis who said what we had all been thinking.

'Odin's gift,' she spat. 'What made us think we could escape the curse of Fafnir's silver?'

'We will kill them all,' howled Hlenni, his face twisted. Red Njal laid a hand along his arm, stilling him.

'You do not have to put out a fire when all is ash,' he said. Then added, softly: 'As my granny used to say.'

All I could think of was my dream, where Odin had told me that One Eye would force a sacrifice from me and it would be something I held dear. Like all that shape-twisting god's promises, it was never what it seemed; the One Eye had not been Odin, but Kvasir and the sacrifice had been himself.

Until that moment, I had not realized how much I hated All-Father Odin. I hated him, cold and harsh, as we stamped out Morut's fire and moved off, hurrying like loping wolves across the mocking steppe, which glittered like riches under the silver-coin moon. I hated him when, led by Morut, we came up to the stiff shape, wrapped tenderly in Thorgunna's blood-frozen cloak.

315

I could not – dared not – look on the eyeless face of my friend; we wrapped and roped him and dragged him after us across the ice and frozen earth like a pack of old furs and no-one complained of the burden, for we would not leave him behind for the wolves.

As the dawn slid up, all haar-mist and pale shimmer, we knelt in a stand of brush and trees at the Ditch Bridge, the black dog of Kvasir's loss at our heels. Beyond the ditch was the dark sprawl of *yurt* and brick-built hovs and enclosures. Little points of light danced here and there, the low growl of noise was split by a barking dog, the plaintive bleat of a goat.

To our right were the great bulked walls of Biela Viezha, red blossoms marking the night fires of the sentries.

I sent Morut in; I needed to know where Thorgunna was and where the boats were.

'You have, no doubt, a cunning plan,' Gizur said. Finn grunted, fishing out his nail from his boot, for he knew the cunning plan and, when I laid it out, Gizur scrubbed the tangled burr of his beard and frowned. After he and a few others had hoiked up their offerings on the matter, it became clear that my plan, cunning or not, was the only one.

So we waited and the dawn struggled, thick as cream, trying to make a new day and foiled by ice mist on the river. There was little talk and that in grunts; men fixed straps and eased mail; everything else they owned had gone with Vladimir, so all they had was what they stood in and held in their hands.

It was all they needed and, when Morut came back, I had everything I needed, too and turned to them, looking for words to say and finding nothing but the choke in my throat. So I looked at the wrapped bundle and the two men who would haul it, so that every eye turned to look at it, then turned to look back at me, bright and fierce as hawks.

'Heya,' Finn growled softly and slipped his nail between his jaws. Then we rose in a pack and wolfed into the crawling haar and across the ditch, silent, fast and vengeful.

It was, as Morut said when he listened to it, not much of a plan – we attack, fast and loose because we would come up through the enclosures and tents, which would give us cover, but prevent any shield wall. We kill everything in front of us, grab Thorgunna and a boat and row like frothing madmen downriver, towards the tangle of channels that led to the Azov.

'Simple, brutal and with no great plan in it at all,' Morut added, shaking his head.

'I like it,' countered Finn truculently.

'Which only makes my point firmer,' replied Morut.

We came up through the buildings, leaping the low fences of withies, scattering horses, hacking out at the odd goat, plootering through the hoof-chewed dark mess of soil and shit.

The fortress of Sarkel, the White Castle, was a pale blur, like some great berg looming out of a dark sea. Around it sprawled yurts and some brick-built hovs, drunken fence enclosures and the framed tents of wintering shipmen. Somewhere by the river Vladimir shivered with his men, waiting for daylight to load boats and be away, before the garrison made up its mind what to do about him.

We were wolves, slithering in a hunting pack, but not down on chickens. We were showing our fangs to the hounds.

I was too busy watching Thordis with Short Eldgrim, making sure she kept him going in the right direction and avoided the fighting, so that I found myself in a herd of skittish horses, shoving them aside to keep Thordis and Short Eldgrim in sight.

Then I was hit by the rump of one swirling, excited pony and slammed into a *yurt*. I heard the trellis bones of it crack and the commotion inside. Light flared as the door-curtain was flung back and someone hammered out shrill, angry words, a dark shadow against the light. I snarled and the woman spat at me; I showed her a fistful of sharp metal and she yelped and vanished back inside, shrieking.

I had lost the others. Blinking, my night vision shattered,

I moved on before any other yurt-dwellers reappeared with weapons. There was a wolf-howl up ahead, a sound I knew well; Finn had found his enemies.

I came up on the nearest fire, where Vladimir's men had been huddled. A dark hump lay in the shadows beyond and I saw, as jog-trotted up, that it was one of the *druzhina*, a luckless sentry, fully-armoured and very dead.

Shadows grunted and struggled; sparks flew, men cursed and slashed. A figure lunged away from the howling pack and ran towards me, though whether he came to attack or was unlucky to find me as he fled I did not know, nor care.

I hit him as he came within arm's reach, a vicious back-hand upswing that took the axe blade into his groin and launched him headlong, screaming. Then I knelt to look at him as he writhed and his heels drummed; no-one I knew, so one of the enemy. I heaved a sigh of relief at that and hacked his throat open, vowing to pay more attention.

I turned back the fight round the fire and heard Ref Steinsson yell: 'Watch out for the big one . . .'

Now I was paying attention and I saw him, a tall, muscular Slav with the face of a young boy scarcely bearded, who came leaping out of the firelight and straight at me, sword up and screaming as loud as he could, exactly as his best mate had probably taught him.

His best mate, I was thinking, was lying at my feet with a second, bloody smile under his chin – but if he had been there to advise, he would have told this giant Slav boy to hold his sword lower and not to swing so wildly.

I stepped out of the way of the downward crash of that fat blade, spun on one foot and hit him with the axe on the lower back, so hard that I heard the crack of his backbone breaking and lost my balance, even as he arched once and went down with a scream. I scrambled up, frantic that someone else was coming up on me, spun round, axe slathering blood into the air in a ribbon of droplets.

'It's me, Finn – watch what you are doing with that wood-chopper, Orm.'

He had a grin like a bear-trap, but his eyes were wary. I straightened from my fighting crouch and acknowledged him with a wave of the axe.

'You are safe enough. Get to the boats.'

'Too late,' growled Finn. 'They have fallen back and are between us and the boats.'

A score of paces further on, the Oathsworn, panting and circling like dogs, waved weapons and taunts in the faces of Vladimir's men, who were shadows and pale blobs of faces in the dark. Behind them was the river and the boats we needed to escape – but we had neither found Thorgunna, or a way of getting to those boats.

'We are finished,' someone said grimly.

'Stow that,' Finn bellowed and spun his iron nail. 'We are not done yet.'

It was not a convincing statement, for it would be moments only before Dobrynya recovered the courage of his men and made them realize there were only a handful facing them. Then they would come at us, Oathsworn fame or not; I saw men plant themselves more firmly, rolling their shoulders and touching amulets, for it was more than likely that they would die here.

Then Gizur came up, huffing, with Gyrth lumbering like a dancing bear behind him.

'We have found Thorgunna,' Gizur yelled and pointed.

On the lip of the long, iced slope that ran down to the river, no more than a long jogtrot from us, a *strug* perched on wooden sledge-runners, staked to the ground for safety. Stacks and bundles showed where the gear waited to be loaded, so that it was light for the final, careful slither down the slope to the water. The crew had wisely made themselves scarce when armed men turned up and Vladimir had thought it a good place to use to shelter the sick wife of Kvasir.

It was as strange as a fish on a horse, that boat stuck on a hill, but we ran for it, stumbling and sliding over the iced snow; beyond were the snow-frozen stacks of rolling logs for ship-hauling between Volga and Don in the summer and, beyond that, the fortress, that brooding ghost shifting noisily awake with light and clanging alarms.

The men swarmed aboard, careless of the creaks and the tremble of the over-straining ropes.

'Thorgunna?' I yelled and a chorus of voices answered me. I leaped up and scrambled aboard the *strug* and Gizur led me to where she lay, wrapped and pale. Her eyes were open and she managed a smile, though one pearled tear fluttered on her eyelash, bright silver in the moonglow. Thordis fell on her knees beside her and both of them shook with grief and happiness in equal measure, it seemed to me.

'We brought him with us,' I said awkwardly into the storm of tears, even as men struggled aboard with the stiff, blood-marked bundle that had been Kvasir. 'We are going home.'

'What about the silver?' demanded Gizur and his stiff beard quivered, so that he looked like a man caught halfway eating a hedgepig.

'We must go back for it, surely, after all this,' thundered Hauk.

'Back for it,' echoed Short Eldgrim, then shook his head. 'Back for what? Who are we fighting now?'

Beyond the humped dead and the fire there were shouts; lights flared and there was the unmistakeable sound of chains and creaking hinges as a heavy gate opened in the fortress wall.

'There is no silver, nor tomb,' I said. 'Only a vengeful boy-prince and a frightened garrison. With luck they will fight each other and let us escape with our lives.'

'We will never manhandle this boat to the river in time,' muttered Gizur, as men sprang to the frozen ropes.

'Time I was gone,' Morut called from below and I sprang off the boat to stand beside him.

'Come with us,' I said, for I liked the little man and his knowledge of horses. He shook his head, grinning. 'What? Spend my life hauling ships across the steppe from river to river? Besides, that great fool Avraham may decide to come up with these folk from the keep and I do not want to have to fight him. If you have to, try not to kill him.'

'Anyway – how can I leave that marvellous horse of mine behind?' he added, 'I must get back to where I tethered him before some Khazar *ben shel elef zona* finds him. You know what these people are like.'

I smiled, then fished out the armring I had taken from Kvasir before we had wrapped him.

'As I promised,' I said, 'in case that son of a thousand whores has indeed stolen your scrubby little pony. I will find a richer mark of favour to bury with Kvasir.'

Morut caught it deftly and touched it briefly to his heart before making it vanish inside his tunic.

'Good journey,' I said and he waved once, then was gone into the shadows. He had barely vanished when the horsemen came on us out of the dark of the fortress.

'Cut the ropes!' yelled Finn and the men trying to knock out iced tether-pegs stopped and then fumbled out blades. 'Cut them, fuck your mothers!'

They hacked and swore; and one of them – I could not see who it was – turned with a shrieking gurgle as an arrow took him in the throat.

At the same moment a horseman surged forward out of the dark, kicking his unwilling mount. Hauk, flailing furiously at the tether with a too-blunt sword, spun round, dipping as he did so, taking the horse in the forelegs, which snapped like twigs. It fell, kicking a blizzard of snow and screaming, the rider's own cries of pain lost in that skin-crawling horse-squeal. Trapped, the rider struggled, wide-eyed, until Hauk's blunt sword crashed on his face and ruined it.

The *strug* lurched and, panicking, men flung themselves

aboard with the job only half-done. There was a crashing sound as Gyrth dropped over the side and ran at us; Hauk turned as another horseman roared out of the dark and I saw they were all round us now.

'Get aboard,' I yelled at Hauk and brandished the axe to show what I intended. He hesitated only briefly, then leaped up for the side of the *strug* and caught it with his one free hand as others pulled him over.

Gyrth looked at me, his yellow teeth bared; he must have known when he flung himself back over the side, that he would never get back aboard – it had taken four men to haul him up the first time. He turned in a whirl of flailing fur and roared himself to the darkness, head back and arms out, the great axe in one fist.

'Orm!' Finn bellowed, but I hacked at the rope and it parted in two strokes; the *strug* lurched again and shifted slightly sideways, swinging on the tether of one remaining rope; I saw the linden bast of it tremble, spitting out little shards of ice.

An arrow hissed like a snake over my boots, skittering through the snow; another plunked at my feet, I felt the wind of a third on my cheek and turned to start hacking at the last rope.

A horse stumbled out of the dark and the noise, wild eyes white, nostrils wide. The rider on him gave a high shriek of triumph and slashed down with a curved sword, but I had already flung myself flat and sideways and hacked out with the axe.

With a dagger scream the horse spun on its hocks, one front leg shattered; the rider spilled from the saddle and landed in a great whoof of driven air and spattering snow. I drove at him, the axe up and coming down, so that it took all I had to twist my wrist at the last, burying the blade so close to the fear-white familiar face that one brow braid was sheared.

'For Morut,' I growled into the cod-mouthed stare of Avraham, then tore the axe blade free, showering him with diamond chips of ice to remind him of how close he had come. Then I whacked him between the eyes with the butt end.

'Orm!'

The bull-bellow from Finn was almost too late; the horsemen were crashing on us and I turned into Gyrth's big, lopsided grin.

'Heya!' he yelled, swung up the long-axe and smashed it down on the rope, which parted in a shower of little ice shards. I was half up on one knee when the *strug* groaned, shifted and started to move, a great bulked beast on its cradle of wooden runners; ice spat and cracked as its own weight started to tear it loose down the slope.

Gyrth's face was suddenly close to mine, close enough to have the rank breath of him on me and the great wild of his eyes staring into mine.

'Jump,' he said and then was gone, rolling forward into the mass of horsemen; an arrow shunked into him, with no more seeming effect than a skelf in his finger. I saw him grab the bridle of one horse, hauling it almost to his knees then, one-handed, slash the axe head into the face of the rider. The horse struggled, trying to tear free and Gyrth slammed his own helmeted head on the blaze of the beast, so that it gave a grunt and sank to its knees, eyes rolling white into its head.

Then more horsemen surged out of the dark, milling around and I heard him bear-roaring his name at them. Steinnbrodir. Steinnbrodir is here.

'Orm, you arse – the rope!'

Finn's roar shook me into the Now of it; the world sped up, the trailing rope whipped away from me and I grabbed it with my left hand. It slithered, iced and slippery, through the few fingers I had, so I dropped the axe and hurled myself at it with the other.

The wrench tore shrieks from my arms, but I held on with both hands, in a whirl of stars and snow, dragged bouncing down the slope as the *strug* bucked and kicked, galloping down the ice, leaping into the air on its wooden runners.

A man, one of Vladimir's long-coated *druzhina* who had run forward to attack us too, was hit as the *strug* lurched forward, gathering speed; he was flung aside with a crunch of bone and a shriek, while the runners were given extra slick with the smear of him.

There was a great bang and objects whirred darkly around me; I clung on, lost in a world of pain and ice, a small, clear part of me seeing the remains of the wooden cradle of runners spinning away behind me in shards. Vladimir's men scattered from the path of that plunging stallion of a boat, their faces white stabs of fear whirling away from me into the dark.

The *strug* lurched and slid, hit the last of the shore, hissing a bow-wave of snow from under it – then ploughed into the black river and the shadows, spouting up a great grue of ice under it as it took us to the slow, cold slide of the crow dark river.

I lost the rope as it whipped me up and there was a marvellous moment of flying, the great wheel of clear stars tilting in a pitch sky – then there was the whooping shock of the water, so cold it burned. I went down and round and spinning into freezing darkness, surfaced once to see the *strug* forging away from me, while men shouted and howled and tried to get it to stop – then I sank again, the world a muffled roar in my ears.

It was Hlenni Brimill and Onund who saved me, the one spotting me, the other leaping in like a bull walrus to grab me and tow me back to the surface.

When I blinked back to the world, it was on the deck, shivering and soaked, bruised and with fingers scorched with rope burns. Hlenni was rubbing me so furiously I shook, but his hands burned feeling back to my limbs. Nearby, Red Njal did the same for Onund, who shivered under a cloak, but managed to grin and wave. I trembled out a nod, acknowledgement of what I owed him.

'Pull, fuck your mothers!' Gizur roared, as the arrows whicked and plunked – but screams and shouts told where Vladimir's men now fought the garrison of Sarkel in the confusion of darkness.

They pulled, fuck their mothers, hard and grunting and too busy hauling oars to think about what had been lost and gained, only that the arrows were fired blindly and we were leaving them all behind.

Later, when the rowers groaned and drooped and tried to stop their lungs burning, Klepp Spaki tallied the loss – Katli Bjornsson and his brother Vigo, both of them gone in that light, leaving, I knew, a mother to weep alone.

And Gyrth. Finn, stone-faced, told how the Boulder had rolled into the horsemen, then vanished from sight. In my head he roared still; Steinnbrodir is here.

'Where is Odin's gift in all this?' Klepp asked bitterly, while I shivered and ached and did not want to tell him how it was a gift, of how One-Eye had held his hand over us. If he had not, we would all be dead.

Thordis found the rest of One-Eye's double-edged gift, when she and Bjaelfi went to attend to Thorgunna. They found her lying, as Fish had been found, on a haphazard tumble of furs – covering roughly-bagged silver coins, armrings, bent plates and twisted jewellery, all the small stuff that had been in at least one of the carts. A fortune, hidden with Thorgunna in a good place and gleaming at me, accusing as a curse; little Vladimir would be furious.

I was still gawping at this, wondering if Vladimir would cut his losses, or stamp his little foot and come after us, when Fish dragged the rest of our wyrd out into the moonlight, while the fit men bent and dug and pulled down the middle of the river.

'Does this belong to anyone?' he asked, limping out from

where he had been scouring the boat for food and warmer clothing. A white-swathed shape hung by the scruff of the neck in one hand.

Hearts stopped; men glanced up and blanched and I groaned. The silver was bad enough, but this would have men rowing in our wake until they threw up, for sure.

'I did not like to leave Thorgunna alone,' Crowbone said, blinking up at me from a tear-stained face. 'She was good to me.'

EIGHTEEN

It took a while for the unease to settle on what was left of the Oathsworn, a haar that dusted everyone with droplets like morning dew. We had silver after all and there was cheering at that – yet we also had Crowbone and that would bring men after us. There was muttering about Fafnir's curse.

Those crew left – nineteen by my count, including the hirpling Fish – had to keep rowing down the fat, sluggish Don to the Maeotian Lake, which the Serkland Turks call the Azov Sea; that hard task did not help matters.

It was a boat made for fifteen oars a side, so we were crew light, as usual. It was made from one tree, an oak the length of nine good men and extended by willow planking, though we had lost some of those in the mad slide. It was two men wide and straked with planks nailed to make the freeboard as high as a standing warrior and fitted to take the oars.

Great bundles of large reeds, each one thick as a barrel, had been laid along the length of those freeboard planks, bound with bands made of lime or cherry. This made the whole thing virtually unsinkable even if swamped – which was useful, for it had no deck to speak of and we had few men to spare for bailing.

It had an ill-worked sail, which proved that it was capable

of going into deeper water, probably along the coast of the Azov and the Sea of Darkness, which suited us all fine. But, as Gizur pointed out, you only wanted the mast and sail up in fair weather; if a blow got up, it was best to row for it.

Finally, the shipwrights had fitted heavy ribs and cross-pieces, slathered pitch where necessary – and sometimes where not – and put a steering oar at each end, since the entire clumsy affair was too long and too heavy to turn on a river, so you simply reversed your rowing and went the other way.

And right there was the problem. It was a light boat made for dragging from river to river with a full crew but, crewed by too few of us and laden with Odin's cursed silver, it was as limber as a quernstone. It would not sink, sure enough, but it would scarcely move either under the oar-muscle we had – and twice we held our breath as the bottom of it tugged and scraped on unseen banks, or balked at crushing a path through the sluggish, half-formed ice.

There would come a time, too, when rowers would have to sit the opposite way from each other and haul until their temples burst to get the beast round the narrower bends.

I remembered, from the last time I had come this way – a lifetime since – that the river split as it reached the Azov. The south fork of it was straight and true and short, while the north twisted and turned and was longer – but that one forked again along its length and so was one more way to lose pursuit. Both were fretted with rills and rivulets, reed and swamp.

The south route was the one I knew and Hauk, Finn, Hlenni Brimill and Red Njal, who had been with me at the time, agreed that way was best, provided we did not find men up our arse before we hit the first fork. Even Short Eldgrim had a moment of clarity and recalled that he had been this way before.

'This is all that remains,' Red Njal said suddenly, looking round from one to the other as we talked, resting our oars

328

and grabbing some tough bread from the stores we had found on board.

No-one spoke, for he was right and it was a hard matter to consider. Seven were all that was left of the original Oathsworn, those who had been with Einar the Black when I joined the crew. Eyes strayed to the wrapped bundles – Kvasir and the Bjornsson brothers, brought aboard and bound for where we could decently bury them. Finn sighed and Thordis, passing on her way to attend to Thorgunna, brushed his tangled hair with one hand.

The mist trailed along the black water of the river and ice nudged the *strug* as we sat, rich as kings and feasting on dry bread and cold river water, each thinking of his share of the silver – and his share of the curse.

Yet we would not dump Odin's gift without a fight.

'We need to haul in and light a fire,' Bjaelfi declared, coming up to attend to a deep cut on Ref Steinsson's arm.

'No,' I said, 'unless you are fancying a fight with those big Slavs Vladimir has.'

'Thorgunna needs to be properly attended to,' added Thordis. 'Which needs hot water and a little time.'

It was a heft of a swell, but I rode it, right through to her black scowl.

'We cannot stop. Let Bjaelfi do what he can.'

'I have done,' the little healer declared sourly, scrabbling in one of the dangling pouches he had. 'But Thordis has the right of it, all the same.'

He broke off, unstoppered a small flask and poured some of the contents into the cut on Ref's arm; the smith went white and bit his lip until blood flowed, while Bjaelfi bound it in a rag marked in charcoal with healing runes.

'The juice of crushed ants,' Bjaelfi said, clapping Ref cheerfully on the shoulder. 'That and runes made by Klepp, who never makes a mistake, will stop the rot.'

Ref managed a moody grunt, for he had lost his sea-chest

and all his tools, some of them made by himself. The possible loss of his arm was almost nothing by comparison.

'She will die,' Thordis declared firmly, glaring at me until her eyes seared through the common-sense and found the heart in me. Finally, I nodded.

'There was once a man,' said a piping little voice and, before it made another sound, there was a sharp whack of sound and Crowbone shot backwards, arse over tip and landed in a knot of rowers, who shoved him off, protesting loudly.

Rubbing his ear, Crowbone scrambled dazedly to his feet, pulling his dignity and his white cloak round him. His eyes filled with tears – more of rage than pain, I was thinking – and Thordis moved to him, glaring seax-sharp looks at Finn.

'Not now, boy,' growled Finn, blowing on his freshly-burst knuckles. Hauk Fast-Sailor chuckled and shook his head at Finn's audacity.

'Hel slap it into you,' noted Onund mildly, 'which is all you deserve if that notable man-boy takes it into his head to work curse-magic on you for that blow. Anyway – I like his stories.'

'Fuck him,' growled Finn. 'I am just after recalling how we got to this place, thanks to him and his little axe. And his stories are always like eating those *limon* fruit from Serkland, which look so sweet and clappit your jaws. Besides – how much more cursed can I be?'

Those who heard this last, despite their admiration for a man who had tasted *limon* from Serkland, groaned and shook their heads, with much clutching of amulets and talisman pouches.

Even I had to shake my head with mock sorrow, though there was less mock in it than I would like. That was not the sort of matter you aired when you suspected any gods were listening – sure enough, we would have an answer to it.

Red Njal's da's ma, as ever, had something to say.

'When you hear the gods whisper,' he offered, savage as a wet cat in a bag, 'hurl your spear into their breath.'

Not long after, we saw smoke as we slid down and round the black, ice-fringed river that had started to wander like a drunk down a street. We steered for those fuzzed grey curls, round one bend which almost had us pulling in opposite directions to turn the *strug*, and came across a swathe of sand and pebble beach with a clot of *yurt* beyond.

People scattered and yelled and I had to balance awkwardly in the prow, my arms upraised to show how my hands held no weapons. Behind me, hidden from view, Fish nocked an arrow and watched.

We came in slowly, not wanting to beach the boat, because Gizur warned that we might not get her off again in a hurry. Finnlaith and Hauk splashed ashore with lines and fastened them securely; slowly, creep by creep, cautious people came closer to us.

They were Khazars, wintering here in their yurts with flocks and herds. When they found the magic glint of silver rather than steel in our fists, all fear was forgotten and we carried Thorgunna off and into a *yurt*, which amazed me with its bright comfort. Almost as amazing as finding I was paying for it with coins stamped with the head of some ruler called Valentian and dedicated to the glory of Old Rome.

We stayed there all that day and the rest of the night, in the cloak-wrap comfort of sights, sounds and smells we had all but forgotten – the hanging braids of garlic and onions, the limp, naked, dangle-necked bodies of duck and hare, the stink of burning hair and singed feathers, the quarrelling snarls of dogs fighting over the same scrap.

That night, Klepp Spaki proudly held up a louse between finger and thumb and declared that, with the return of such vermin, he now knew he was alive.

We spoke no common tongue with these Khazars, for all that we could summon up Greek, Latin, our own Norse, a good smattering of Serkland Arab and even some Krivichian and Chud. The Khazars spoke their own tongue, which some said was the same as the one spoken by Atil's Huns long ago and so no-one among us knew that. They also had the language of the Jews, but all anyone knew of this were the foul swear-words Morut used.

However, trade is a common tongue to all and so we had food and even some green wine – which Finn immediately took charge of – and, above all, news that the ice was melting from the centre of the Azov, for the whole sea had been frozen. It meant that there was now a flow to it and that had broken the ice in the narrowest part, where it entered the Sea of Darkness.

'So there is a way out for us,' beamed Gizur, having labor-iously learned all this. 'We can sail anywhere you want, Jarl Orm.'

Onund cleared his throat meaningfully. 'As long as it does not take us more than a long swim from land. I do not trust this log boat.'

In the morning, I was chivvying them up and loading stores on board. In the night, we had howed up the Bjornsson brothers, re-wrapping them in full view of the Khazars so that they would see the dead had nothing with them worth digging up. That and a gift of hacksilver from the hoard would make sure the Khazars let the brothers sleep peacefully. They had no weapons or armrings, but I had openly promised their shares to their mother, so I thought their fetches would stay happy with what had been done.

Kvasir stayed with us, all the same, though I was not sure where he would finally rest – he would not last all the way back to Ostergotland – but Thorgunna had to have a say in that and she was pale as milk and sleeping when we brought her into the shelter of the boat's prow.

We pushed sweatily away into the middle of the river, while children ran up and down, cheering and pitching sticks at us as their parents looked on and waved, smiling.

Slowly, groaning with the effort of it, we swung the river-boat round the bend and away down the black river, the oars chopping up the thin porridge of ice, while the banks grew thicker with birch and willow. I watched until even the smoke of the Khazar camp had vanished, then turned and almost fell over Crowbone, wrapped in his filthy white cloak and staring over my shoulder with his double-coloured gaze.

'What?' I asked, thinking he still brooded on Finn's blow. 'Do not let Finn's manner bother you; he thinks well enough of you, but tempers are short . . .'

'No,' he said, still looking over my shoulder, 'I am not concerned with Finn – one day, I will claim weregild for that blow, all the same. It is the birds I am watching.'

Then I turned to look, squinting into the low, creeping mist. A skein of ducks arrowed high overhead.

'Good to see birds back,' I agreed, smiling. 'The winter is losing grip.'

'All the ducks are skinny,' remarked Crowbone. 'Like the ones hanging in that village we left. They are feeding furiously now that the ice is broken.'

I frowned, remembering the skinny ducks and not understanding why he was so concerned. Then he turned his flat, two-coloured gaze on me.

'Why, then, are hungry ducks flying off the water?'

It took me several seconds to answer that in my head and when I did, my heart leaped up and threatened to bang through my teeth and out my mouth entirely. Everyone else started with astonishment when I suddenly sprang forward, screaming.

'Row, fuck your mothers – row!'

We were too few and too late. The long black shapes slithered round from where they had set up feeding ducks, seemed to fly up to us, even laden with Vladimir and his mailed *druzhina* warriors.

Two boats; my heart collided with my battered boots. One would have been enough. In the end, I told my crew to ship oars and they did so in a scramble and started sorting out weapons and equipment, even before they had stopped puking and heaving in air.

'Well,' growled Finn, climbing up beside me in the prow that faced them. 'This will be a hard dunt of a day, I am thinking.'

A deadly dunt of a day, I was thinking, as I hefted the only weapon left to me, an adze axe I had found on board. All they had to do was sit back and have those Slavs and their curved bows shoot us down; half of us had no shields and we had one bow and a handful of arrows left.

The boats came closer, one with Dobrynya and the little shape of Vladimir up in the prow, the other with Sigurd Axebitten and a strange half-animal which dragged goose-flesh up on my arms until I realized it was Kveldulf, with a whole wolf pelt draped round his shoulders, the mask up and over his helmet.

'Well, well,' murmured Finn. 'There is the bladder I have to prick.'

'Is he really a Night Wolf?' I heard Ref ask fearfully.

'If he is such a shapechanger,' Onund answered scornfully, 'then he is no danger, for it is broad daylight.'

They came closer, a couple of boat lengths away and backed water, sliding to an ungainly halt. Together, we drifted like leaves, sluggish and turning imperceptibly.

'Give up Prince Olaf and the treasure you stole,' I heard Vladimir shrill. I had half an idea it was not what he wanted; what he wanted was to get close enough to throw his little spear and yell '*Idu na vy*' then slaughter us to a man. What stopped him was . . .

Crowbone. He slithered between Finn and me, clear and vulnerable on the prow and between us and any arrows, making it impossible for them to even try and hit us. I laid a hand on his shoulder: despite the strange *seidr* in him, despite all he had inflicted on us, I liked the boy and did not want to see him hurt.

334

He looked up at me for a moment, then turned his head forward and cupped his hands to his mouth. 'There was once a man,' he shouted, high and shrill, 'let us call him Vladimir.'

'This is not the time for such matters,' Dobrynya interrupted, his voice echoing blackly over the waters.

'Vladimir had to drive his sledge a long way to the wood for fuel,' Crowbone went on, ignoring Dobrynya completely, his voice an arrow aimed at the little prince. 'Then a Bear met him and demanded his horse, or else he would eat all his sheep dead by summer.'

'Prince Olaf,' Dobrynya tried, then fell silent when Vladimir raised one imperious little hand, listening intently. His uncle, face as grim as Perun's wooden statue, fumed silently.

The boats slid closer together, so that Crowbone did not have to shout to be heard.

'The Man was faced with freezing or agreeing to the bargain,' Crowbone continued. 'For no Man likes to see his sheep eaten dead. He promised the Bear he would bring the horse to him tomorrow if he could be allowed to cart home the wood that night. On those terms the Bear agreed and Vladimir rattled homewards, but he was not over-pleased at the bargain you may fancy. Then a Fox met him.'

'Enough of this!' roared a familiar voice, a bellow that startled thrushes from hiding with a whirr of wings.

'Is that yourself, Kveldulf?' Finn shouted back. 'I hear, with my one ear, that there is some part of me you would like to own. It may be that once this boy has finished with his tale I will present you with the gift of a priest.'

'I have heard of that sword,' came the roared answer. 'I shall use it to cut off your other ear . . .'

'The Fox,' trilled Olaf into the end of Kveldulf's scorn, 'asked Vladimir why he was down in the mouth and the Man told him of his bargain with the Bear. "Give me your fattest wether and I will soon set you free, see if I cannot," answered the Fox and the Man swore he would do it.

'The Fox laid out a clever plan, that when Vladimir came with the horse, the Fox would make a noise from hiding and when the Bear asked what it was, the Man was to say it was a bear hunter, armed with a powerful bow.'

When he paused to take a breath, you could hear the water gurgle in the silence.

'Next day, matters worked out exactly as the Fox had said and the Bear grew afraid when he heard of the hunter and his bow. The voice in the wood asked if the Man had seen any bears. "Say no!" pleaded the Bear. And the Man did so. "So, what stands alongside your sledge?" demanded the voice in the wood. "Say it is an old fir-stump," pleaded the Bear. And the Man did so.'

'I have heard this story,' said a delighted Short Eldgrim behind me, but everyone shushed him to silence, for the story held us all, while the sweat trickled coldly down our backs at what might happen when it was done.

'The voice in the woods,' Crowbone continued, 'said that such fir-stumps were worth rolling on a sledge for fuel. Did Vladimir want a hand? "Say you can help yourself and roll me up on the sledge," said the Bear and the Man did so. "Bind it tight or it will fall off," said the voice in the woods. "Do you need help?"

'"Say you can help yourself and bind me fast," demanded the Bear. And the Man did so.

'"You need to drive an axe into that stump," said the voice in the woods, "to help steer it down the steep paths."

'"Pretend to drive your axe into me, do now," pleaded the Bear.'

Even with the tension visible as mist, there were a few who chuckled at what they saw coming.

'Then the man took up his axe,' said Crowbone 'and at one blow split the helpless Bear's head and so the Man and the Fox headed home to Vladimir's farm, where Vladimir said he would bring the promised wether out to him.

'When he came back, he had a sack in which something moved and the Fox started drooling, for it had been a hard winter. "Give me what I am owed," said the Fox and Vladimir untied the sack and two red hounds rushed out.

'The Fox sprang off, too fleet to be caught like that, but his voice was bitter when he said: "Well done is ill paid. The worst foes are those you trust to be honourable."'

The silence that followed crushed all sound save the quiet rill of water on wood.

'You did not behave like a prince,' Crowbone went on, breaking it like a slap. 'I am also a prince and my mother was a princess. She did not teach me such bad behaviour, Prince Vladimir. I counted you as a friend, as did Jarl Orm – is this how you repay friends for their help?'

'I remember your mother, boy,' bellowed Kveldulf and then Sigurd silenced him with a blow on his shoulder.

'I remember you also, Night Wolf,' answered Olaf. 'So does my mother.' His voice, scarcely a whisper, carried across the water, sibilant as the hiss of a snake and like to shave the hair off the nape of your neck.

'Surrender the boy,' Dobrynya persisted.

'Once,' I answered, 'you told me how one day I would be thankful for the friendship of princes.' The cold sweat pooled where my belt cinched my mail tight at the waist. 'There is another side to that coin – a prince may be grateful for the friendship of the Oathsworn.'

'I will stay with Jarl Orm,' piped Crowbone firmly. 'Until he brings me to Lord Novgorod the Great and reclaims his ship there. If any harm comes to him, I will not count it as a princely thing to do.'

He did not say what the consequences would be and, peculiarly, no-one thought to question what such a boy could do – they all had their own ideas on it and only one was not afraid as he bellowed out his anger.

'Fuck this,' roared Kveldulf and there were mutterings

behind him; I saw then that some of the crew in his boat had been Lambisson's men, those who had fled and left Fish behind. That, I was thinking to myself, was a dangerous hiring.

'You will come to me in Novgorod?' demanded Vladimir.

'I will pledge myself to you there,' replied Crowbone. 'Soon, you will need men to fight for you, Prince Vladimir, if you wish to be Grand Prince of Kiev. Between us, we will scatter all our enemies. Here also, Jarl Orm is a better treasure than any silver and, if you fight him here, you lose his strength with you – and I would not be surprised if a careless blade cut my throat.'

It was so close to prophesy that I shivered and I was not alone, judging by the murmurs that leaped from head to head. Kveldulf was open-mouthed with disbelief, so stricken he could not speak at all and I was a little stunned myself; had this nine-year-old ancient just said I would kill him if we were attacked? Had he just pledged me to help Vladimir against his brothers?

There was a brief whispered exchange, then, Dobrynya's iron-grey voice rumbled over the water.

'The prince agrees,' he declared loudly. 'Go in peace and take what you have, Jarl Orm. Bring Prince Olaf to Novgorod by the end of summer next, unharmed. If you fail, the prince will hunt you down and have you and all your men staked along the Volkhov Bridge.'

'By Thor's arse, no!' bawled Kveldulf, turning white and red in turns. 'Did I split my knuckles rowing for this?'

'You were paid,' Dobrynya snapped back at him, 'and will mind your manners. A stake is as easy to find here as in Lord Novgorod the Great.'

I choked Finn's guffaws with an elbow in the gut that left him coughing, for humble silence was best here. Gizur put everyone on the oars and we strained away from the death we were sure had been our lot moments before, rowing hard and hardly able even to believe our luck.

338

Eventually, much later and reined in like bolted horses, sobbing for breath and lashed with sweat and drool, we all realized that it was real. We had escaped. We would live.

Finn, pewter-eyed and so tired he could not even close his mouth properly, turned to where a wet-eyed Thordis wrapped Crowbone in her cloak. He patted the boy as if he was a particularly clever pup.

'Odin's arse, young Olaf,' he growled admiringly. 'If ever I quarrel with your tales again, simply remind me of this day on the river and my mouth is clamped shut.'

Olaf said nothing, simply gazed back along the river, only his eyes and the top of his blond head visible in the swathe of Thordis's cloak. I whirled, suddenly fearful, but there was nothing; when I turned back, Crowbone forced his chin out from under the cloak folds and smiled thinly.

'The ducks still fly. They fear the wolf.'

By night we had grown dizzy swinging round the narrowing bends of the river, unable to see much on either side through the thick, skeletal white branches of the trees. We did find an ox-bow curve of shingle where we crunched through the thinning ice and unloaded ourselves.

Crowbone's wolf comments had reached all ears by then, but the Oathsworn were defiant now and lit good cooking fires, daring the Night Wolf to come and find us. All the same, as Finn stirred what herbs and spices he had left into the two upturned helmets filled with a savoury stew, I had Toke and Snorri take first watch.

It cheered us all when Thorgunna hirpled, leaning heavily on the arm of Thordis, into the firelight and, wincing, took a cloak-cushioned seat by the fire. She smiled wanly at the smiles around her and accepted a wooden bowl of stew and even managed a few mouthfuls from her own horn spoon.

After a while, as everyone ate and talked quietly, about everything and anything other than where we were, where we were headed and what we would do with all the wealth when we got there, Thorgunna laid down her bowl and turned to me.

'Thank you for bringing Kvasir,' she said. 'Tomorrow, I will surrender my man to the water, to Ran, who surely lives as much in rivers as in the sea. I do not trust those hereabouts to leave him in peace on land and now that I have his eyes back and he is whole for Valholl, I am content.'

When I looked in her dark eyes I saw the opposite of that – saw, too, that it was not for Kvasir but for the almost-bairn kicked out of her.

That night, I raked through the silver hoard while Finn held a torch up and finally found a hinged torc that even Finn whistled at. Twelve ounces if it was any weight at all, solid and carved in little S-curves connected by rosettes, which were fitted with red stones, most them still there. It ended in an intricate lock and Finnlaith swore that it was Irish and he might have had the right of it.

In the morning, with the mist still in tendrils, I placed the torc inside Kvasir's corpse-wrappings and had a fond smile from Thorgunna for it. She took his stiffened fingers and gently trimmed his nails with her little scissors, for it is well-known that Naglfar, the boat captained by Loki and which carries the giants of Jotunheim against Asgard at the start of Ragnarok, is made from dead men's fingernails. It is right to delay the building of it.

Then she pulled out the bloody little pouch I knew contained his shrivelled eyes and tied it round one wrist, so they would not be lost. We weighted him with stones from the shingle beach and slid him over the side with scarcely a ripple and he sank quickly, while I commended him to the gods and tried not to choke on the loss.

Then, almost before we had shaken ourselves from the dark of it, like dogs losing water from a swim, Crowbone raised his head and pointed one arm.

'The Night Wolf is here.'

He came on loping swift, hoping to take us by surprise –
but everyone, in honour of Kvasir, had been armed and mailed,
so all I had to do was go to the prow nearest to the black
ship that held Kveldulf and, as I had suspected, Lambisson's
old crew.

Kveldulf was in the prow roaring them on, his wolf-pelt
draped on him, a snarling mask on his head and shoulders
while the oars dipped and sprayed. He had too few men to
both row and fight and I knew that he would back water
soon and let the forward motion of the riverboat carry him
crashing into us while his men got their weapons ready. It is
what I would have done.

Finn leaped on to the prow alongside me. Fish leaned out
from the side, took aim and shot; there was a sharp cry and
a rower pitched forward on to the man in front, driven by
the smack of the arrow in the back of his head. The oars on
that side faltered, the boat slewed sideways and Kveldulf
whirled, bellowing with anger and frustration.

'Another good hooking, Fish,' roared Finnlaith, but Fish
scowled.

'That cost me dear – that was Milka and he owed me
money,' he grumbled.

Kveldulf's ship sorted itself out and Fish fired four of his
last five arrows, three of which found targets. He yelled out
with each man who fell. 'Leave me behind, would you? Leave
me behind . . .'

I knew then that Kveldulf had no archers with him and
told Fish to stop firing and keep an arrow nocked and in
view, so they would not realize we only had one left.

'Good,' growled Finn, bringing his iron nail out of his boot.
'Now it comes to blade edge and arm strength – and we are
the Oathsworn.'

This last he roared out and everyone behind clattered their
weapons on the bulwarks or on what shields we had. I hefted

my axe and turned, putting my back carelessly to where Kveldulf bellowed and roared his men back to setting his boat prow on to us. It was a spear-throw away, no more.

They looked up at me, even Thorgunna, tucked under my feet which I did not think such a safe place and said so, before turning to those savage grins and reminding them what we were and who we were. Then, just in case any were still afraid of the reputation of the Night Wolf, I reminded them that we had never seen any exploits of his.

'Anyway,' I finished. 'I am Orm, slayer of the White Bear, so a wolf is nothing to me.'

They roared long and loud at that and, when I turned, I saw Kveldulf's men look uneasily, one to the other. Kveldulf, on the other hand, was in the prow, waving a sword and the sight of it made Finn growl, low and hackle-raising.

'Kvasir's sword.'

Once, we had found three north-forged weapons in an Arab pirate hoard. I had kept one and given Finn and Kvasir similar swords, perfect blades, with the story of their making written just below the surface of the metal. *Vaegir*, they were called – wave swords. Finn had called his The Godi and had it still. I had lost mine long before. Kvasir had died with his in his hand and now we knew who had taken it.

'Take it back,' said a voice and Thorgunna started to scramble weakly out of her shelter under the prow planks.

'Move to the other end,' I ordered her, but then Crowbone shoved between us, as he had once before, and distracted both me and Finn.

'No tales this time, little prince,' Finn declared grimly. 'I do not think the Night Wolf is in the mood to listen.'

Crowbone nodded, but pointed, out into the black ribbon of river and the trails of milk-mist. 'My uncle is coming,' he said.

It was true and everyone saw it. A second black shape creamed round the bend behind Kveldulf, the slap-bang of oars like the feet of a running man. Up in the prow, silver nose flaring bright in the sudden early dawn sun, Sigurd was bawling curses on Kveldulf.

The Night Wolf's men turned and twisted, half-rising from their seats. I remembered Klerkon in the market square of Novgorod, as I came up on one side and Finn on the other. *A fronte praeciptium, a tergo lupi* he had said – cliffs in front, wolves behind. The wolf himself was now trapped.

Our prows were closer now, a man and a half apart, no more. Finn clenched his nail between his teeth and howled triumphantly and, like the wolf he claimed to be, Kveldulf bristled.

He was brave and strong and skilful was Kveldulf. He would have been a fine man to have fight with you if it were not for the fact that you could not trust him at your back. Yet he showed us the wolf-worth he had claimed that day.

He launched himself, in full mail and with his pelt flying, off his own prow and towards us, stretched out so that the snarling head came alive on his helmet and he seemed to be, just then, a real wolf pouncing on sheep.

He flew up to the thin pole of our prow, grabbed it with his one free hand and let himself whirl round it on to the little half-deck. One booted foot hit an astonished Finn on the beltline and he flew backwards with a sound like a grass-blown cow being pricked open, scattering men like so many tafl pieces.

I dropped into a half-crouch, but Crowbone was in the way; then Kveldulf's swordhand was round and I barely managed to get the axe in its path, so that his hilt alone smashed into the side of my helmet. I staggered back, slipped off the planking of the half-deck and crashed down along-side Finn, struggling like a black beetle with all its legs kicking.

Kveldulf, grinning his savage grin, grabbed Crowbone by the collar and threw back his head to howl out his own

343

triumph. In one smooth, astonishing moment, he had defeated us and his men answered the howl with cries of their own, bending to the task of stroking their ship up to where they could board us before Sigurd got up to them and put a stop to it all.

I sat up, my head ringing and my mouth full of blood. Beside me, a frantic Finn was scrabbling to recover The Godi; Fish was screaming with fury, for Finn had crashed into him and had smashed his bow.

Kveldulf leered down at us, Crowbone held in one paw, Kvasir's sword in the other.

'Stone am I?' he thundered. 'Well, you have seen how I fight now, Finn Horsearse. And you Oathsworn fools – pitch this pair over the side and join me, for I have surrounded the kingpiece in this tafl game.'

He was right and we were finished, but I would go down with a blade in my hand and not sinking under black river water, bound and helpless . . .

A hand snaked up and Crowbone looked down and saw it. A pale spider it was, white-gripped round a small pair of scissors that you used to trim hair, or the frayed cuff of a tunic – or the fingernails off your dead husband.

Thorgunna, with what strength she had left, brought it down, savage as a snarl, driving it deep into the foot that had kicked the new life out of her.

Kveldulf shrieked and tried to jerk away, but she had rammed it through boot and foot-bones and into the planks, so that he stumbled and had to let go of Crowbone. Thorgunna fell back weakly to the deck and Crowbone fell into a crouching huddle as Kveldulf, blind with rage and pain, wrenched himself free and brought Kvasir's sword up in a whirling arc, to bring it down on Thorgunna's sprawled and helpless body.

It came as a shock to the Night Wolf, then, when Crowbone popped back up, his face a shrieking, vengeful mask of hate,

344

leaping salmon-high as he had done once before in the market square of Kiev.

'For my mother,' he said, just loud enough for those around him to hear.

It would have sounded like thunder to Kveldulf. Like Klerkon, he suddenly found his worst nightmare staring him in the face, a brief eyeblink of a moment in which the sharp of my adze-axe, plucked by Crowbone from where I had dropped it, must have seemed as big as the edge of the world. Then it split Kveldulf's two faces, wolf and man both, straight across the forehead, side to side.

For a moment the Night Wolf hung there like a strange, one-horned beast, a look of astonishment freezing in the last moments of his eyes; the sword slipped from his fingers and clattered at my feet and the inside of his head leaked down his face in a wash of yellow-white gleet and black blood. He toppled backwards, hit the water with a splash and vanished.

After that was chaos; Kveldulf's crew, close enough to leap aboard, saw their leader fall overboard, dead as old mutton. The Oathsworn surged to the freeboard planks, tipping the whole *strug* dangerously sideways, but bringing it down to a level where spears and edges could cut and stab across the freeboard. All of this quailed Kveldulf's men; they scrambled for the oars and backed water.

Sigurd came up, his archers opened fire with a hiss like rain on the river and men died in that sleet. Some leaped overboard, tried to swim for the bank, but the arrow storm cut them down and, finally, none remained who could make a sound.

When the screams were done, Sigurd stood in the prow and saluted me with his sword, while his men closed with Kveldulf's stolen boat and clambered aboard to recover it, killing any who still showed signs of life

'No work of the prince, this,' Sigurd growled. 'He sticks

to his oath and sent me to keep your sky from falling, as you did his.'

'I see you, Sigurd Axebitten,' I answered and he nodded, then hesitated.

'Take care of my sister's son. It took a deal of time to find him in the first place.'

'Since I found him in the first place, I am unlikely to put him in harm's way,' I reminded him. I laid a hand on Crowbone's shoulder, as he trembled in the aftermath of what he had done. Less than before, I noted; killing got easier each time you did it and I had no doubt that, one day, little Crowbone would not tremble at all after a day's slaughter.

'An adventure in a strange place, some sweet things to eat and then home,' said another voice and I knew who it was before I saw him, remembered the same words, spoken by Short Eldgrim to soothe a boy wounded by an arrow on the shores of Cyprus and near death. Jon Asanes had the white scar of that on his ribs still, but now he was wrapped tight in a blue cloak, standing behind Sigurd.

'Heya, Goat Boy,' yelled Short Eldgrim, as Jon Asanes came up to stand alongside Sigurd. 'You are on the wrong boat.'

'Am I?' asked Jon, but it was Thorgunna who answered, climbing unsteadily to her feet and held there by Thordis. She said nothing, simply spat in the water; Jon's pale face bowed between them and his cry of anguish was sharp.

'No mercy?' asked Finn softly.

Thorgunna's black eyes raked him. 'Mercy is between him and his White Christ,' she answered hoarsely. 'My only obligation to Jon Asanes is to arrange the meeting.' She handed me the hilt of Kvasir's sword with a hard, black-eyed look.

That was bleak enough to stop all conversation and Finn was hurting in his ribs too much to argue, while my head pounded and sickness welled in me.

I stood watching, all the same, Kvasir's sword dangling limp and accusing from one hand, the other on Crowbone's shoulder as we rowed away from his uncle and Jon Asanes, while Thordis led Finn away to strip off his mail and look at his ribs.

Left to herself, below us, Thorgunna held on to the prow planking to keep upright and stared at the swirling black water where we had loosed Kvasir to Ran's mercies.

'At least he has the best of offerings,' I said to her, 'for the enemy who killed him is now at his feet.'

She looked up, smiling radiantly, but I knew she could not see me through so many tears.

'There will always be a place for you at Hestreng,' I added, thinking to comfort her and she knuckled her eyes clear with a swift gesture.

'Ingrid has her feet so far under the high bench that I will never get my keys back, I suspect,' she answered, with a flash of the old fire that made me smile.

'We could be married. Then you would be mistress and no gainsay.'

I said it lightly, as a wry jest, but the words tumbled out of my heart and the rightness, the answer to what I would do now, fell in to replace them. I was so stunned by it that I was left blinking as stupidly as she.

Her mouth opened and closed, then she snorted. 'You can say that, after carrying on with that Aoife like you did?'

'That was then – besides, she is only a thrall.'

'Ah, so you had to hold up her bottom with both hands?'

'No – well, not entirely . . .'

My tongue stumbled to a dry halt and I was not as sure of matters as I had been a moment ago.

'Rams rut quieter than you,' she declared softly.

I stifled a groan. My stomach churned. 'Such matters are expected of a jarl,' I managed.

'Such honour and duty from a raiding man, even one of account. Anyhow – my mother warned me. Never marry a raiding man, for his heart is in the wind.'

'Was she a sister to Red Njal's da's ma, I am wondering? Besides – the one time she was right and you did not listen and married Kvasir anyway.'

'So now you mire the good name of my mother? I should get Thordis and both of us will thrash you.'

'Is that the same Thordis who let Kvasir sneak in and away again in the morning?'

She smiled at the memory; we both did. I felt better – then those sheep-dropping eyes hardened and her chin came up.

'Do not you try and throw mud on my good name,' she growled. 'I never let him stay the night until we were proper wed. And I never will you, either.'

'As I recall, your sister and Ingrid begged Kvasir and me both, on bended knee to take you off their hands.'

'They did no such thing!'

'Pickleface, they called you. Thor-fist, too.'

'Lies. They would not dare slander me . . .'

'Did you really trap Ingrid in the privy? And left a dead rat in Thordis's bed-space once?'

'I will kill them both . . .'

She stopped, caught my eye. The wind blew her hair away from her red-cheeked face, streaming it back and flattening the thick cloak against her prow-built shape. She saw me look her up and down and flushed.

'Too soon,' she said eventually, staring at the slow-shifting wake in the black water where Kvasir slowly turned and sank. 'But I thank you for the offer.'

I smiled. She smiled. I pulled her to me and she grunted a little, for I was hard in my nervousness – but she did not shove me away, all the same.

'Was Odin's gift worth it all, then?' she asked. I had no answer to that.

We left the crow-black river for the Dark Sea and Odin's gift became perfectly clear on the evening, weeks later, when we slid into an island bay to make camp for the night. Our minds were glass, where the breath of home misted clear thoughts and we all but missed the three ships arrowing out the dim. It was Onund, his great shoulder-hump made bigger where he hung from the prow, who yelled a warning.

They came sidling up, wary and circling like winter-thin wolves on a fat wether.

'Heya,' Hauk called out, while bows were unshipped and arrows nocked – we were well armed now. 'Who are you there?'

'Men from Thrond,' came the reply, floated faintly across the water. 'With three ships to your one and hard men packed in all of them.'

Thrond was far enough away in the north of Norway for me to realize that these were raiding for preference, though they would claim to be traders if challenged by stronger men. Now they thought they had a fat prize and I could not deny they were right. For all that, I sat with my chin in my hand and tried not to look concerned, which is hard when your knees are knocking.

'We are the Oathsworn of Orm Bear Slayer,' Hauk called out. 'We want no trouble, but will give it if we get it.'

There was a long pause and one boat started backing water at once. On the other two, it was clear that arguments had broken out. Eventually, a voice called out – more polite in tone, this time, I was thinking – that they would come closer to see if what we said was true.

'Come as close as you dare,' bawled Finn, annoyed, 'but Finn Horsehead warns you to keep beyond the length of my blade.'

They turned then, all three of them, and rowed furiously out of the bay, chased by our laughter. Later, I met one of those who had been on the main boat, a good man who came to Hestreng on a trade *knarr* selling leather and bone craft. He told me that they knew they had met their worst nightmare when they saw Orm Bear Slayer sitting, unconcerned by them and calm as a windless day, chin in hand and waiting patiently for the Oathsworn to serve supper.

I did not tell him I was sitting, stunned, for I had just realized Odin's gift.

Fame.

The one he gave to himself, for our fame was All-Father's fame. Men gave up their White Christ thoughts when they heard of us and what Odin had given us. As long as the Oathsworn stayed in memories, Odin could keep the White Christ at bay in one small part of the north, no matter that the blind-weaving Norns warped the line of Yngling kings to an end and brought in the new god of the Christ.

We were a weapon in One-Eye's hand and had been, as Hild had been and Einar and all the others; the silver hoard was just the goad that had driven us to fame-greatness, the shine on Odin's name.

Yet the glow of that hoard still smeared the eyes. Later, when we stopped for a brief rising-meal, the insidious glitter slid into men's minds as they laughed about the latest escape they had had and the way the men of Thrond had scattered like starlings off stubble.

It was, I heard Gizur say as he chivvied men back to their benches, a sure sign that Odin's hand was over us still and the treasure we had was nothing at all to do with Fafnir and surely could not be cursed.

'On the other hand,' Ospak said, 'it could mean Odin means us still to have all the treasure remaining in Atil's howe.'

There were groans from some at the thought of doing all this over again – yet nods of agreement from those still silver-hungry enough to consider going back. I thought it time that everyone knew, all the same, and stepped forward in such a way that made them all look round at me.

Then I told them what I had avoided saying out on the steppe, the day we had run, panting, from Atil's tomb and the warrior women who ringed it.

I had stayed behind as the others hurried away, watching the slope-headed man-killers who guarded it and the woman who called herself Amacyn. With a runesword in each hand, she had walked to the hole in the tomb roof and straddled it, while all her oathsworn comrades sat their horses on the bank of that frozen lake and bowed their heads.

I had heard the chopping sounds. If her sabre was like mine, then it could cut an anvil and both together, working on that stone support beam, would slice through it long before her arms started to ache or the edge left those blades. I turned away, then, numb and cold and . . . relieved.

The others were a long way off when I thought I heard the tomb collapse, but it may just have been the blood rushing in my ears, for I hit a crippling pace to catch them up, especially for a man weakened by hunger and cold.

But we had all heard the cat-yowl wail from those female throats, a last salute to their last leader.

I could see it in my head, the collapse of that great yurt of stone and wood and earth. The ice cracking, the swirl and roil of those black melt-waters rushing in to cover silver, dirt, bones – and the falling woman, her last task done, her oath fulfilled, tumbling down to her wyrd at the feet of Attila.

Last of her line, with no daughter and no secret and no longer any need to pass that burden on. I shivered at the passing from the world of these oathsworn, like us and yet stranger than a hound with two heads. I did not like to think that I had, perhaps, seen my own future in the woman's long, slow whirl of arms and legs.

The river flow would wash the silver into the silt, scatter it and everything else for miles down the river. For years people would pick riches out of those waters; some might even brave the fetch of the place and dig for it in those times when the drought came and the lake was emptied. Perhaps, one day, someone might find a rune-serpented sword, or even two and, perhaps, marvel at how they seemed unmarked by time or weather.

But not us. Odin had given the Oathsworn his last gift of silver, I told them.

They were silent after that and eventually Gizur nodded, straightened and scrubbed his hands over his face, as if scouring away sleep and the last of a bad dream.

'Row, fuck your mothers,' he growled. 'It is a long way home.'

HISTORICAL NOTE

A lot of the joy in writing historical fiction comes from the bits that are stranger than fiction. For example – I needed Orm to get in big trouble with Prince Vladimir in the year 972 A.D. in the market square of Novgorod. Enter Crowbone, otherwise known as Olaf Tryggvasson, aged nine and burying his axe in the forehead of his hated captor, Klerkon. You could not make it up.

Unless you were a twelfth-century Benedictine monk called Oddr Snorrason, that is – the story of Olaf Tryggvasson is one of the best-known of the Norse sagas and, even allowing for twelfth-century 'journalistic licence' it sounds plausible. It also fitted in so exactly with what I needed that it raised hackles on my neck.

The saga-story of little Olaf is exactly as I tell it here. The only major change I made to the tale is that it was his Uncle Sigurd who found and rescued him and not Orm – and Klerkon, though a real character, was handed a fictional life.

A couple of other changes were cosmetic – Uncle Sigurd did not have a silver nose, nor did Crowbone have different-coloured eyes as far as I know. I handed out the former on whimsy and the latter because it was a sign of greatness and magic, which described Crowbone perfectly for me.

Nor did Crowbone have a fund of stories, but everything else about Olaf 'Crowbone' Tryggvasson is as the supposed history tells it, including his nickname and the fact that he divined the future through the actions of birds, right up until he converted to Christianity when he became king of Norway in 995 A.D.

To get the necessary cash for it, this viking's Viking invaded Britain in 991 A.D., fought and won a legendary battle at Maldon – according to Saxon accounts – and extorted a deal of Danegeld, that fat payment made by desperate English kings to get Vikings to go away. He extorted even more in subsequent years and, suitably bankrolled, then went off and won the throne of Norway, though he did not hold it long.

All of that, of course, was much later and after he had helped Prince Vladimir of Novgorod defeat his brothers and become sole ruler of the Kievan Rus. The peace between the three Rus princes lasted five years and it was, predictably, Lyut and Sveinald who broke it.

Like Vladimir and his Uncle Dobrynya, Sveinald and his abominable son, Lyut, are also historical characters and much as described – arrogant and domineering. If anyone deserved to be pitched in a fire by Finn, it was Lyut – in 977 A.D., Lyut made the mistake of hunting in Prince Oleg's private domain and then telling the prince to sod off when challenged. The arrogant Lyut then found himself dead and his enraged father Sveinald persuaded Jaropolk to go to war.

Oleg was defeated and killed, Vladimir fled north to seek help from the Swedes and got it; eventually, he returned with an army of Vikings, defeated brother Jaropolk and was finally crowned sole ruler of the Rus in Kiev in 980 A.D. – and young Crowbone was at his elbow, by all accounts. That began the process of turning the loose confederation of Slav states into what would become mighty Mother Russia.

In his three-year exile in the north, Vladimir spent two

of them with Olaf Tryggvasson raiding up and down the Baltic as a Viking. It should be no surprise to anyone that, in the tenth century, noble youths aged eighteen and fifteen respectively should be commanding boatloads of hairy-faced veteran warriors, who never questioned the rightness of it.

Finally, the real-life character of Uncle Dobrynya has since been translated into a Russian myth of Dobrynya Nikitich, the hero who fought a great Worm or dragon – which, of course, is Orm in Old Norse.

In other words, the historical facts – even allowing for medieval embellishment – are as good a set of bones to use to flesh out a tale. In order to weave that tale and create the legend of the Oathsworn, I needed legendary enemies who were all-too real. So enter the Man-Haters.

German archaeologist Renate Rolle found the first evidence of Amazons, at Certomylik in the Ukraine. Other finds, by Elena Fialko at Akimovka, support the idea of women warriors and the work of Jeaninne Davis-Kimball at Pokrovka, on the Russian–Kazhakstan border revealed many fascinating finds, including one girl of no more than fourteen, with bowed leg bones suggesting her short life was spent on horseback. She had dozens of arrowheads in a quiver made of leather and a great boar's tusk at her feet.

There could be no better way of Orm and the Oathsworn gaining legendary fame than following in the footsteps of Hercules and taking on the Amazons – and I just plain liked the idea of Attila's most faithful warriors being women.

The intent of this story was to create the 'fair fame' of the Oathsworn, so great that it stood as a monument to Odin and served as one small check to the tide of Christianity sweeping across the north at this time.

Well, if you want to have a Dark Age northern hero at least as famous as Beowulf, then you need a Dark Age enemy at least as monstrous as Grendel. However, I had always been struck by the saga of Beowulf and Grendel and had difficulty in deciding who was the true monster of the tale – Beowulf, the human who slaughtered both Grendel and his mother, or the monstrously-shaped mum and son, who seemed to have been relegated to the realms of evil demons, yet somehow engender a deal of pity.

Scotland has its own monstrous myths, none more chilling than changelings and elf-shot babies. Many of such tales are now thought to be excuses for child-murder, even as late as the nineteenth century. It is easier to be rid of a strangely-diseased and unwanted baby if you claim it has been swapped for your perfectly good one and is inherently evil.

Tales of fishskinned bairns and scaled changelings take on a new meaning in the light of an affliction which has haunted the ages – and, sadly, is still with us – known as ichthyosis. A genetic condition, it causes the skin to keratinize and scale, like nails, all over the body and the tightening that results sometimes deforms the face. The worst form of it, Harelequin Ichthyosis, is a truly distressing disease and babies who suffer from it rarely survive forty-eight hours. It is exactly as I describe it here and the sight of such a newborn would break your heart.

Of course, people so afflicted are no different from the rest of us, appearances apart, and it seemed right to me that such a nest of seeming monsters would have more family feeling and humanity than the healthy people who sent Orm to kill such feared 'were-dragons'. The legend, as it always does, swallows the shame of such an act.

Finally, there is the runestone, preferred method of leaving your name and deeds to posterity. The range and number of runic inscriptions during the Iron and Viking Ages is impressive, from the Black Sea to Greenland, from Man to Athens. Iceland has few, Denmark has about 500, Norway has around 750 – but Sweden has some 3000 and one-third of them are from the province of Uppland.

Best known is the Rok Stone, a ninth-century memorial block found in Östergötland, Sweden. Carved in granite to commemorate a lost son, it has the longest runic inscription known – 725 runes of legible text which scholars still argue over. It is full of secret formulas, lost allusions, verses of epic character and a poetic vocabulary which showed, to me at any rate, that the composer, Varinn by name, was a Norse Shakespeare.

I thought the Oathsworn deserved no less a memorial.

As ever, this is best told round a fire in the darkness. Any mistakes or omissions are my own and should not spoil the tale.

ACKNOWLEDGEMENTS

Top of the list of people who made this book a reality are the Oathsworn – all the crew of Glasgow Vikings (www.glasgowvikings.co.uk) who are now a seasoned crew and quite proud to be sailing the *Fjord Elk*. Thanks also to the rest of The Vikings re-enactment group (www.vikings-online.org.uk) who continue to strike fear into publicans and provide entertainment and education to an astounded public.

None of which would matter if James Gill, my agent at United Agents, had not spotted the potential in this – full marks to him – and especially to Clare Hey, my editor at HarperCollins, who had the unfortunate horror of getting me as one of her first trials in the role. She made *The White Raven* better than it was, while the Glasgow end of the HarperCollins team, Marie Goldie and her girls, not only make book signings a joy but contrive to make me feel like a celeb while doing it. More power to their archive.

The Oathsworn adventure continues...

The Prow Beast

The Oathsworn have become feared and respected throughout the Viking world. Their name goes before them and men cower in their presence. But fame comes at a price . . .

While the Oathsworn revel in their new-found fame, Randr Sterki, an old enemy with revenge in his heart, attacks their homestead – the Fjord Elk is sunk, old oarmates die and the Oathsworn are forced to flee into the mountains.

Unused to losing, the Oathsworn retreat to lick their wounds. They have been entrusted with the care of Queen Sigrith, pregnant and soon to bear the heir to the crown of the newly-unified Sweden, and much though the urge for revenge is strong, Orm's first duty is to protect the queen. And Orm soon realises that revenge is not the only thing on Randr Sterki's mind; he has joined forces with Styrbjorn, nephew of King Eirik and next in line to the throne of Sweden, if he can only get rid of the current heir.

As the Oathsworn fight to defend themselves and Odin's gift of fame and fortune, they soon realise that the god's favour comes with a harsh price.

Out in March 2010 in hardback.